I0682195

Love, Again…

Love, Again...

Floyd Byars

FM

Fellow Travelers Media

San Francisco

Love, Again is a work of fiction. Names, characters, places and incidents are products of the author's imagination or are used fictitiously, and any resemblance to persons, living or dead, business establishments, events or locales is entirely coincidental.

FM

Fellow Travelers Media

www.fellow-travelers.com

Cover Design and Illustration by Irene Kotnik

www.irenekotnik.com

LCCN: 2011910444

ISBN-13: 978-0615449890

ISBN-10: 0615449891

For everyone who believed in this, you know who you are,
with love and gratitude.

Love, Again…

"Men and women really are different," I told the woman interviewing me. "Her extraordinary azure eyes went dead, blinked out like a failing 40 watt bulb. We were on national TV; she was a famous talk show host, and she just may have heard this expressed before—though the rictus that suddenly sprung across her lips made me know that she was wondering furiously how this fool got past her screener.

"How's that?" She asked.

"Women are infinitely more complicated organisms," I said. "It's a wonder we men even know how to breathe."

A grin slipped out from underneath her basic white smile. Her leg squirmed, a little swing there on the knee joint, and her feet ceased moving around inside her unlaced tennis shoes. These were good signs.

My nervousness decelerated to about 5000 r.p.m.s, just about enough to power a large Mack truck, much too much to keep any part of me still. Hands, feet, eyes, legs, they were moving like a whole shop full of clocks. "We men are an endangered species," I continued. "We still think getting up in the morning is a special present we give to the world."

Another laugh emerged, surprisingly, from the lady, rippling through the air and unnerving me. It was easy to do, for we were underneath a football game's worth of klieg lights, what felt like an entire medium size city's worth of disco spots. This was New York City, the big-time even if it wasn't even close to prime time. And I definitely felt lucky to be there. I'd spent the night before in Charlottesville, Va., a pretty town but nothing like this place. Even the camera here seemed to have more eyes, the Formica furniture was glitzed up for the Big Apple's more discerning taste—a crew three times larger, a producer twice as big, signaling now to my right, clapping his hands about our gender's inutility.

"I have the feeling actually," I shambled on, "that the current courting difficulty, you know the problems men and women are having now are symptomatic of greater dislocations. What I mean is, I think this is a probationary period. Women are testing us, trying to decide if they should phase men out altogether or keep us around for recreational purposes."

Dottie knew what I meant. As most of America knew, she'd long ago phased men out altogether, though word had it that she might occasionally make an exception. Whose word I wasn't exactly sure, but in my delirium I imagined there might be some truth to it, for her smile, her eyes didn't stray from mine. Forgetting that was a tic of too much TV training, I actually was fatuous enough to think I might be one of the fortunate few to win her favors.

It must have been the semi-shaven, uber masculine look still prevalent at the time. How else could I have been so deluded, how else for years could I have considered myself so attractive? For hidden by its scruffy charms, there were two eyes which were, let's face it, much too close together, a nose which drooped toward a thin, barely discernible upper lip, teeth which could have used, way back when, a very good orthodontist. Yet when I peered over the stubble, which ascended up my cheeks, I thought I perceived a woman's interest, the elegant and entertaining Dottie's.

"Men are so delusional," I said, proving the point, "that we're even working today to perfect the technology—frozen sperm, test-tube babies, cloning—which are truly going to make us superfluous…which are going to make us go the way of the snail darter. Imagine that, man is the first being—man, not woman—to invent the technology, the tools to make himself evolutionarily obsolete."

Listen, the TV made me even more addled than usual. Being on TV after so many years of watching was like kneeling down before a real god. A fearsome, disturbing experience, always: first time I was on the thing, at the age of six, I spent the entire five minutes of my abbreviated appearance on the Golden Wishbone Show sucking my thumb. This day, buzzing like a drone on speed, I looked as if I were trying to make up for all the time I hadn't used that once before.

Or maybe that wasn't it at all. It is just possible that my frantic good humor at appearing before the live national audience, the nervousness I imagined as an attraction to the surely disinterested Dottie was instead just my nerves', my body's understanding in advance of what was about to hit my psyche—the synapses' rare five minute advance warning of approaching mental disruptions, cerebral radar.

"Luck for the Lovelorn," Dottie said, as she held up my book and grinned. "'A Man's Guide to a Woman's World.' We've been talking to its author, James Maxwell Adams, and we'll be right back in a moment."

We broke for the compulsory three commercials. I smiled self-importantly, and Dottie sank back into her seat, her eyes closing behind their lids like a bodega slamming down its sliding metal door.

"Am I a little manic? Do I sound all right?" I asked her after a moment of total silence. I didn't get even a mumble in reply, just a small sigh. "Maybe we should talk about you," I tried.

Was that a power nap she was taking? "What are you feeling? I'm not boring you, am I?" I continued asking, to no visible response. Dottie protected her voice like a diva.

Then the cameras starting to whirl again, the other man with the bad teeth and the what must have been a fake smoking said, "five, four, three, two, one, it's yours"—and Dottie lit up like a Christmas tree.

"Tell us, James," she began. "You're a good looking guy, is that what women go for in a man?"

"They're not quite that superficial," I said. "They go for something deeper, you might even say more profound."

"Like what?" Dottie wondered, clearly puzzled herself. "What do women like in a man?"

Since I'd done a number of these interviews, I had an answer for her, even if I'd never quite assumed I'd get all the way to Dottie's show to deliver it. Little Rock, Phoenix, Louisville, I'd been working my way across what you might call America's lower middle belt. It seemed kind of appropriate for the weird titillation my book was offering. I'd wanted to do better, but what can I tell you? Age caught up with me as did time and self-pity and increasing fear of rejection. That and a whole wad of film scripts I couldn't quite get produced (got paid for, earned a living from, but, like Fitzgerald, I told myself, couldn't get made). So what the hell, I thought? I told Dottie the truth, my version of it at the time.

"What does a woman like most?" I recapitulated. She nodded. She had very well toned biceps for a person who spent so much of her time on sets. I loved the way her silk blouse rustled when she shifted in her chair as she did so often. She had a finger under her right ear that pointed like a celebrating athlete's straight up yet was eerily still. Something felt like it was happening. My heart was pumping—the TV, the adrenalin, her scent, a

strange and compelling rosemary aroma I'd never smelled on anyone I'd
dated, all of these and something in the air which I hadn't even imagined,
should have sensed the moment I was booked but hadn't, had been too
thrilled to wonder about, didn't find out about until much too late.

"Need," I said. "A woman likes a man who needs her." Dottie
laughed out loud. "The only people liking strong men these days are other
men. Women know better, know the idea's a contradiction in terms.
Women like a man who needs them, the more the merrier."

Dottie chortled again, and I was deranged enough to think it had
something to do with me. Must have been the thickening stubble.

"I mean show me a self-sufficient man," I ventured on, "and I'll
show you a confirmed bachelor, no way out of it for the guy. Show me a
lover, and I'll show you someone who needs help…needs we're talking
here, someone whose needs are so apparent every woman wants him. Why
do you think Shia Le Boeuf's a star, Adrien Grenier? Look at them. Have
they ever tied their own shoes? They're good looking I grant you, Grenier
anyway, but his every glance cries out to the female world, 'help me! Help!'

"Sam Shepherd, Matt Damon, the thinking women's favorites.
Sam may have played Chuck Yeager in "The Right Stuff," but every
woman, from the gitgo, knows the truth about him. Yeager's a test pilot, but
Sam's afraid to fly…"

I was revved up, zooming along, approaching my own personal
sound barrier, though I didn't know it. I figured I was doing fine. There was
even one more moment when Dottie's pupils seemed to grasp mine, snaring
my flickering attention and hinting of greater, more enduring interest. But
this in fact just pushed me through the last minute of my segment, up until
the producer cut his throat with a finger, and Dottie said, "We've been
talking with James Adams. But we'll be right back with more to come."

When she tucked that professional smile back away, she didn't drift again into three minutes worth of transcendental meditation as she had the time before. Instead her right forefinger bent down from beneath her ear to wrap itself around the uppermost ivory button on her purple blouse. She slipped the button out of its loop, and with what I chose to think was an inviting grin, she turned my way. I smiled back, lasciviously, and said, "Hey, do you think maybe we could go out and have a drink sometime, get to know each other a little better?"

Her carefully composed, cheerful face collapsed into an incredulously and painfully dismissive look. "You're kidding, right?" she said. And before I could tell her that well, yeah, of course, I guess I was, she looked over my shoulder, at her producer and wondered, "So did she make it or not?"

She was inquiring about Angie, the next way more distinguished guest; and though I was disappointed in Dottie's emphatic lack of further interest in me, thoughts of Angie kept my dirigible up in the air. Angie and I—as I had come over to the show from the airport, I'd seen the two of us later, Angie collapsing in my arms, that sensual smile, those lips which promised to envelop, to suck out all your concerns, your worries, your fears, why not mine? I wasn't any less needy than that guy she had most recently taken on as a lover. Was the word "boob" invented for guys like me?

"She couldn't make it," Art, the fat guy with the bright yellow fingers, cruelly said. "You knew it was always a long shot. She went to the United Nations instead." And you could hear the hiss from my deflating inner tube; that much I shared with Dottie, who looked at me remonstratively, her dismay mounting when Art said, "She just didn't want to share time on the spot. She had a whole agenda to roll out here, and Proctor and Gamble weren't happy about it."

6

At least they weren't fooling themselves. If it had just been sharing the time that was a problem, they would have arranged for my plane to make an unscheduled landing and put me back on a bus to Cleveland. Still the producer looked disdainfully, accusingly my way. Where did he get off trying to make me feel guilty?

Before me, I guess, the guy got off a couple of stops before me. For he knew what was happening; I couldn't even guess. Within minutes, I commenced experiencing a singularly different life than the one I imagined I had been living.

After we both swallowed our disappointment, Dottie finally muttered, "So who did you manage to get?" She slipped her button back into the blouse's aperture.

"You've got the info right there," her producer said.

Dottie looked through her cards, past the one color-coded blue that was mine, past the whole raft of yellow cards, which contained data about that near star of this show, Angie the 3 time Oscar winner, before she settled on two pink cards, which she quickly perused. The camera started blinking, and then it shifted into a steady red.

"And now," Dottie began again, the twinkle coming back into those famous eyes as they shifted from the teleprompter to my right to a person behind my back, "we are fortunate enough to have one of New York's brightest acting talents, the co-star of the Public Theater's big new production of Don Juan, Sarah Revson."

The cameras turned right to catch the figure in the wings; the audience clapped politely; the producer with the fake cigarette was now cramming not one, but two sticks of Denicotea into his slightly discolored mouth. He smiled and waved with his free hand. Dottie turned her famous, mauve irises over to the other part of the room where, between the two red curtains, glided a lean woman with magnetic eyes of her own. She bowed gracefully to the audience, looked affably at Dottie, then glanced quickly at me as she walked over to take the seat just on the other side of the famed personality.

This was your Happy Talk kind of show, the set a simulated living room, Dottie in the middle seat of three, we three supposed to be one big family. And we were in a way, a family as dysfunctional as your basic American model, for my heart, on looking over at Sarah, felt as if its personal chambers had been taken over by a swarm of termites. You could almost hear it being eaten away.

"What do you like in men, Sarah?" Dottie asked. "James Adams here has been talking to us about men and women—something I'm trying to learn more about myself. He claims a woman gets most attached to a man's flaws, his neediness. Is that what you're looking for?"

Dottie might have liked me somehow; perhaps she was giving me one extra plug—or maybe she was just tying this show together, neatly segueing from one guest to the next. How was she to know? Or did she already?

"It can get pretty trying," Sarah said, without the trace of a smile. Her beautiful green eyes, looking turquoise right then, peered past Dottie and over my right shoulder. They didn't take in a single color of my variegated Norwegian sweater. "I mean," she continued, "it's kind of charming for a while to be needed so much; but eventually, you find out that the need is never going to diminish. You're always going to have to take care of this guy. The more you nurture, the more that type needs. There's nothing beneath his surface but more insecurity, more than any one woman can ever satisfy."

I think this is where I lost my mind: it just burst, exploding onto my carefully kept three days' shadow, inundating every stray follicle of stubble.

Next to me, Dottie seemed slightly surprised and taken aback by such an unusual amount of honesty for the mid-afternoon. She smiled a more practiced smile than the one Sarah mustered, as the latter continued her discourse. "What you learn," she said sadly, "is you have to move on. Moving on's what you do, what living's about. You just have to make yourself leave." Dottie sighed; as we know, she'd been through some of this herself, publicly. She was braver than me. My central nervous system simply blacked out.

"And Don Juan, what prompted you to do the play?" Dottie asked, trying to change topics. Art at this point had a stick of Denicotea in the web between each two fingers—or so it looked to me. But then my eyes were blurred, fogged over and out of focus. I was seeing things in multiple numbers, five Denicotea, four hands holding them, three Dotties...

And two Sarah Revsons, one only two feet away, just at the end of my reach, the other six years previously, glancing back my way before she turned, as my blood pounded like a lava lamp inside my skull, and walked out of my reach and out of my life.

Sarah Revson was the star of my own little drama, the woman I'd loved most, that one. We'd spent six years together, and I'd probably used her memory against all the women I met thereafter, over the last six years. I was moving toward middle-aged and yet still, the world's oldest adolescent. Here I was, on camera, confronted again with my biggest regret. How was Dottie to know? How did she know?

Maybe by the tears which started streaming down my face. Tears? Tears, yet. I couldn't stop myself.

Somewhere there I caught Dottie's frantic glance (*what is going on here?*). I saw hundreds of hands, like a crowd of pedestrians huddling around an accident victim. I tried to recompose myself; I mean Luck for the Lovelorn, after three and a half decades of trying, this book should have made me seem cool, for five or ten of the requisite fifteen minutes, but what can I tell you? It didn't and I wasn't. I was crying on the air (maybe this was your basic American family—two people pretend to be interested in one another's conversation while a third relation sits next to them, bawling).

The last time Sarah and I had seen each other was six years previously. She was walking out of the apartment we'd once shared, just a couple of miles from the broadcasting room, downtown in Little Italy, as it was still called. She had already left me, six months before, and she'd come back to see me again, but just for an afternoon. I was anxious enough before she got there, but she spun me even further: though we played around a little physically, she'd come to tell me this, that I didn't know what was important any more; she was worried about me; she loved me but she couldn't—wasn't going to—wait for me any longer. As she went out the door, her head with its fine black hair seemed so much larger than it ever had, then much too small as it receded from view, down the street then across Lafayette and into Soho.

Time only improved her, I thought as I looked at her next to Dottie, on TV no less, though thinking is too clear a word for the muddled emotions that washed over me like waves in some kind of final rinse cycle.

"Are you happy with your work now, Sarah?" Dottie seemed to ask, something like that. Sarah glanced my way, then her eyes hastened elsewhere. "I don't know," she responded. "Maybe I'm not in good enough shape to play four parts. When I hear all these voices, it's hard to find my own."

The camera at this point came in closer on Sarah, perhaps because she was so earnest and had something interesting to say, perhaps because someone wanted to make sure I was cut out of the picture. A man crying on television, this hadn't happened since Jack Paar, since one of Pinkie Lee's breakdowns, and both men had left the industry shortly thereafter. But rather than ignoring my humiliation, Sarah ceased responding to Dottie directly; she looked, anxiously, in my direction. Dottie looked my way too, and Art changed his mind. The camera pulled further back to take in all three of us again. Hey this might have been a little grotesque, a guy crying on the tube in the middle of the afternoon, but it played.

I tried to manfully choke back the tears, but the camera kept zooming in and out on me. This was silly, I mean enough already, I kept saying to myself. But my self wasn't listening to me. My self was out to lunch, and Dottie just left me there, out in the open with the camera mercilessly recording my every whimper, the fat producer smiling, moving his hands like a ref calling "traveling," until now he put up his palms. He stretched his arms like a maintenance man bringing in a jet; and Dottie finally terminated the action. "We'll be back after this," said she.

"Great!" Art exclaimed. He reached over, and they bumped fists. Then as if conscious of the slight, he gave me the high sign (as if he'd forgotten—or maybe was confirmed in his distaste for what I'd said before). His thumbs gyrated like hummingbirds on the make. And so did most of me.

For Sarah now stared back at me, and a small grin floated on the edge of her gravid lips, washing over me. But then right behind it, on the moment's very same wave, came a small flotilla of PR personnel and show assistants; and every single one of them seemed to want to know, kindly I'm sure, "are you all right?"

Dottie asked me the same, not all too disdainfully. "Are you okay?" She wondered.

Wrong guy to ask: I felt like I was lying face down at the bottom of someone's plastic wading pool.

"What's going on here? What's happened?" Asked one of Dottie's assistants, the one who most frequently touched up her hair and make-up between breaks. She was truly concerned. My publisher's PR person seemed more embarrassed than moved. She stayed at the far edge of the set. When she smiled over at me, it looked as if all her teeth had been capped, as if they were a little too large for her mouth; they ate up her smile. She was mortified, to put it plainly.

We were all relieved when the break ended, and Dottie could try to finish with Sarah and rush us out in time for the Early Evening News, with Eddie Calvin and Samantha Johnson. But Dottie hadn't foreseen the full extent of her difficulties. "What's this success done to the rest of your life?" Dottie asked, blithely.

"Totally confused it," Sarah said, with that same directness which Dottie and Art were probably deciding was the sign of a mental illness so deep and so pervasive that it even touched their male guest, allergenic as ragweed. "It's funny, isn't it?" She continued, without the trace of a smile, "but so many men can't share in your excitement—it's not the success, which upsets them so much as the disruption of their lives, their routines. You can't concentrate on them as much. Once the excitement isn't coming from them, they seem totally disoriented. Not truly angry, they aren't necessarily even jealous. They're just disturbed, discombobulated; and neither of you can figure out what you're doing with the other. Who's that I'm with again?"

Dottie looked more distressed that these men in Sarah's life, almost as dumbstruck as I was. Dottie wasn't really in the listening business, in spite of her job; but I was. I was listening intently. The tears drying on my cheeks made my skin feel as if it were peeling after a bad burn. My mind seemed singed too. Had Sarah always been this loquacious? Certainly she hadn't had such a clear point of view in my memory, but then, maybe, success was doing for her what my mother had probably done for me: make her take herself too seriously.

"I've got my child, though," Sarah confessed. "I've been in the theater, on stage most of his life. In my Mom's eyes, I probably neglect him terribly. But he's my anchor, the most balanced person I know. I can't fool him. I may be half in character, half out when I come home from the theater. I may not know who I am, but he does; and he seems happy I'm there." Oddly she glanced again my way. Was she contrasting us two?

I didn't care. Her eyes looked as big as conch shells; and I wanted to crawl inside them. (She seemed to me so wise, about five times more intelligent than anyone else I know, by virtue of her wisdom in leaving me).

Art the producer now smiled, of all things; and Dottie switched with a huge sigh to her last commercial break. We sat there like mollusks on a Santa Barbara beach. Yet now Dottie looked my way with more concern than she'd shown on camera. The insincerity, the daffy cheerfulness, she only cultivated for effect. She knew the difference.

For when she came back on air to wrap the show, she thanked James Adams and Sarah Revson and told the audience that Monday, be sure to be there, because "the world's most glamorous woman, Angie, was going to make a rare afternoon appearance, alone!" Then the red light went off, and she stood up and didn't ignore us. "Do you two know each other?" She asked, smiling broadly, like someone who made her living doing family therapy.

"Kind of," said I.

"About as well as I'm likely to know anyone," Sarah said, in a voice deeper and truer than my own. "We lived together for six years..."

The group around us hummed for a second, like supplicants on a yoga retreat. All of them nodded their heads, even Art who was sadly back to smoking his obviously fake cigarette, his fingernails up against the fag like five small objects flattened on the road. Sarah's attention drifted away from our little entourage to fix finally on me, her eyes gripping mine. "How are you, Jim?" She asked.

"Even further out to lunch than usual," I said, in reply. Others giggled, she didn't. "What do you want me to say?"

Sarah bristled; she was still angry with me; and her body, five feet away, still moved me. There are people you break up with whom you can't imagine touching again. You may still love them, but when you get near them, you can't feel a thing. There's too much scarring on the end of your fingers.

Sarah wasn't one of these, not for me, so I imagined. Yet when I tried to stretch her way as she stood up from her chair, I couldn't quite take her arm.

"I miss you," I said, surprising myself.

She did a double take too. I wasn't sure now if she was going to embrace me or throw her purse at me. Her eyes blazed, then her lips splayed gloriously into a smile. She reached out and took my arm and said, "I can't believe you. Crying on national TV: five years later, you still have to steal the show." She paused again, and then said, "I've missed you too. I can't help myself."

Here are excerpts from the book the author was then hawking. <u>LUCK FOR THE LOVELORN: A Man's Guide to a Woman's World.</u> It gives a good idea of the author's (my) then current thinking.

(Guys are) Guppies

There was a time, you may remember having heard about it, when men were men, when, barely after puberty, men mounted their lives and rode—taking the consequences, children, work, pain. They knew how to fix things, make things work, use their hands, stay out of the house, take life head on.

Those times are gone, though not forgotten.

Of course, even then, you had your indolent elite, a smattering of dukes and rich boys who entered the world gingerly, taking 15 or 20 years to determine that they'd rather react than act, rather think or feel than do. Their numbers were small, but their influence was apparently enormous (is this another of the costs of higher education?). Today the majority of men between 20 and 40/45, the latter number rising with every passing day, see themselves as heirs of these latter, as disenfranchised nobles. Young, upwardly mobile, single (even if 3 times divorced; often, if married, still thinking that way), male more or less, they're a new phenomenon, GUPPIES.

Do we really need to describe their peculiar characteristics? We know they congregate in urban areas, frequent fashionable restaurants, avoid other generations, get increasingly involved in sports betting, cigars, like German cars and Italian suits and overpriced tee shirts, flatter themselves on differentiating among wines. They still haven't learned to close their drawers, pick up a sock, mend a tear; they think sewing on a button is an act of personal liberation (like washing the dishes). They'd prefer not to do either, regardless. They also know they are social misfits. They can talk to you about their marginality. They like wine, women, and song, though not in that order, are more committed to the first and third than to the second, are overly involved in work that exists mostly on screens and monitors, take their pleasures where they can, and have a very limited sense of purchase out the present.

From all current indications, we can safely say that by the time Guppies finally hit manhood, their cholesterol count will rival Orson Welles', their motor skills will resemble Chris Farley's. But their capacity for escape will be twice David Copperfield's. Try to catch them, they're fireflies.

They may, however, be the species' evolutionary answer to our technological prowess. For Guppies, okay let's call them tadpoles, instinctively understand one thing:
Women know more at puberty than we'll ever learn (fortunately the women may not understand this themselves—and it's that illusion which keeps our bodies revving). Watch them. Listen to them. They can change your life—women have their own lottery; they're the ones who do the selecting, and they're the ones who may still decide to keep us around the planet a little longer, for their own weird entertainment, maybe even entertaining purposes. They're the ones who can give luck to all us lovelorn.

And you thought it was the other way around didn't you?

2,300,000 to 1

If guys (guppies) are, as every study indicates, so quantitatively obsessed, here may be why, the troubling equation we're always working out in our heads, the initial illusion, the one which generates all the others—2,300,000 to 1.

That is, putting all squeamishness aside, the number of spermatozoa an average ejaculation unleashes put up against the number of eggs available, on a monthly basis, to be fertilized. If, in a reasonably average couple, coupling occurs twice a week, let's say ten times a month, then 23 million spermatozoa will be out after that one egg.

And most of the time, not a single spermatozoon will manage to reach its destination (men are by definition underachievers). But that's not the point, just a minor corollary.

For what we have here is the relative importance of the two entities, sperm and egg, male and female. Most of the 23 million spermatozoa could be saved, stored, used anywhere, we're getting the technology down; they could reproduce, theoretically, 23 million times, impregnating for better or mostly for worse, 23 million women. But only one person (freakish natural and increasingly unnatural exceptions aside) could come out of each egg. One.

Ponder the fact and understand then its logical result. Men in general, as a whole, as a species, are becoming superfluous. This is the point to remember, that guys, guppies, instinctively understand...go ahead, let yourself admit it. We men are around 2 million times less important to the survival of the species.

Sad, but true.

One drink, she told me, when we left the studio. She had to be at the theater by seven, seven fifteen at the very latest, and it was almost six by the time we made it to the Algonquin. Where else were we to go? We'd loved this place when we'd first come back to the States—it had some of the glamour of the places we'd admired overseas and, more importantly, it offered free appetizers. I'd lived off them for almost six months.

When I walked in again, more than five years later, behind Sarah, a number of waiters smiled my way, remembering me/us perhaps, so I liked to think, though I wasn't thinking much or well. I floated into the room as if it were an antechamber to heaven. So what if my book was a silly trade book, so what if only moments before, I'd been crying on national TV? I was with Sarah again—and I was sure our meeting was what this day was all about. (Actually, it was the first crack, a kind of sundering in my overly developed infantilism—is that too harsh? The first breach in my defenses, the first indication that my world was definitively mutating, though, of course, it would take me some time before I would realize this).

We took two large armchairs, one next to the other, mine feeling just about capacious enough for my emotions. When I remembered our past together, I still felt inordinately attached to the exaggerated faith she'd once had in me. This had been in Paris, where we'd first met. Had we been there still, we'd have been meeting at the Brasserie Balzac, on the rue des Ecoles, near the Sorbonne where she'd studied.

Sarah was half French, half American, her mother French, her dad an embassy attaché, probably a CIA functionary. His assignment back to Paris, toward the end of his career, had sent Sarah to a lycee; and his sickness thereafter had prompted her to finish college in France, near him and her mother—in an apartment on the rue Malebranche, near the Pantheon. She lived in a maid's room, with a mansard roof, my idea of a writer's home. We'd met just as her father was finally dying, after a long illness. We'd supported each other, but our love hadn't quite ridden all the way across the states. Many a time, I'd thought that our love had only lasted as long as it did because she had been so distraught when she met me. It had taken her a while to clearly see the addled, the insecure, the altogether unworthy guy who was on her arm.

Thinking about it, however, at the Algonquin, I managed to keep my self-pity in check (no easy thing for your garden variety retarded adolescent). I was happy she was there and didn't want to discourage her from staying for a while. It's not every day you come face to face, literally, with your regrets.

Not every day when your regret seems shared—she told me she was living in the West Village, in a small loft next to the Cherry Lane Theater, on Commerce Street. She said it reminded her of the rue Malebranche: a tree, much like the huge oak outside our window then, brushed up against the building in the spring. In the summer, the tree outside our *chambre de bonne* had actually extended its branches into the long and narrow apartment. Inches outside our window, birds had sung.

"No finches here, though," she said at the Algonquin. "Just a boy." And her eyes sank some, as her fingers worked around the lemon slice, which she took from her Kir. She put it in her mouth, sucked on it, and grinned. Her green eyes seemed even brighter than they had, in the spring, up against the trees outside our window in Paris.

"Do you have any kids, Jim?" She asked. This intrusion of reality into my nostalgia made me nervous.

"Too busy waiting for you," I said, with my habitually defensive "charm." The statement itself was true, and it was false. I had lived, since we'd separated, with two other women, one for fifteen months, one later for even longer. Both believed I should commit myself to them; and when I knew, really understood they meant this, I had left. That wasn't brave of me, I guess, or admirable; but it had a certain crude honesty to it, however immature. I was seeing another woman at that moment too.

"How's Susan?" Sarah asked. Apparently, though we didn't speak all that often, she had been keeping track; and I guess I liked to hear that.

"We broke up."

"I liked her," Sarah affirmed. "You should have married her."

"You two knew each other? When did that happen? No one told me."

"It's not that big a city; we met."

This thought made me paranoid. I stopped the waiter and asked for a second Bloody Mary. "What'd you talk about?"

"You mostly," said she with an impish grin.

"Okay. Why are you being so tough on me?" I asked in reply. "This has been a difficult day, and I'm a fragile guy."

"So you say," She began, grinning. "But you're getting kind of old for it."

"Ease up, would you?" I stood up and pleaded, a little shrilly perhaps since a "Dorothy Parker" look-a-like, maybe it was Joan Didion, looked up from her chair nearby and smiled nastily enough that Sarah blushed and pulled me down into my seat. Here we were again. "Calm down, Jim, quit acting like a teen-ager, " she said. She seemed embarrassed, but showed a little indulgence.

"How's that?" I wondered, pure and innocent as the driven snow. "What have I done?"

"For starters, you've been staring at my breasts since we walked in here. You really haven't taken your eyes off them."

"Really?" It was news to me, seriously. "Gee, I wasn't all that conscious of it. I…" I looked again, just to check out what I unconsciously had been checking out. I'd been thinking of Paris, our time in Paris, and there was this difference. "They do look uh a lot…"

"Fuller," she said, with a prim and incredulous tone. "Children do that," she continued. "They change you…you don't look exactly the same either."

I wondered what she meant. And she reached over, her hand, her fingers caressing my cheeks. "Feels so much better shaved. You're so much prettier without all this."

"Prettier?"

She nodded. "You look like a roughneck with it."

"You mean like someone from Oklahoma?" Something was wrong here, still.

"More like a male model. I like you better smooth shaven." Was she flirting with me? My heart wondered, leaping, but she started to stand. "I've got to go to the theater."

"I thought you didn't have to be there 'til after 7." My watch read 6:30. "You've got time. We haven't even had a chance to talk."

She hesitated—perhaps my neediness got to her. As she reflected on the thought, a new line, perhaps a blood vessel snaked its way along the edge of her hairline.

I said, "I'm sorry about you and Phillip."

"We're okay. Everything's always a little different than you expect. That's all."

"I'd like to see you act again," I said. In a way, I had once felt responsible for it; with me, she had picked it up again in Paris in a determined, committed way.

"I don't know, Jim," she said and paused, her tone lowering. "I don't want us to hurt each other; maybe this is enough, huh? I don't know if I can handle a lot more tonight. Let me think about it."

Was this true? She sounded so sure.

"Great seeing you, though," she added with that smile which could have brought the dead to life. It didn't help me at that moment, however. She gave me a kiss and left, turning to wave from the revolving door as I sank a good foot into one of the hotel's Persian rugs.

This wasn't possible, wasn't exactly the ending I was hoping for. I felt as if the world had been picked up at its four corners, and I'd been shaken into its center, an earthquake, a mudslide victim. One moment there, the next moment buried.

By the time I figured that this wasn't perhaps ineluctable, I could do something about it--I mean, yes, my legs still did work; they weren't fixed to the ground; my lungs still functioned, my body could get out into the street-- she'd disappeared. But I was persistent. I knew where to find her.

There were admirers outside Sarah's dressing room, in the street, mostly adolescent girls, oddly enough; but nothing there I wasn't prepared for, nothing much different than it had been when we'd gone outside the Theatre des Quatre Sous, on the rue St. Anne in Paris—a couple of guys with bright eyes, a familiar sort, but now they seemed fifteen or twenty years younger. Sarah smiled their way indulgently; so did I, for sot that I was, I supposed that once we slipped past them, we'd slip back into something familiar, a recognizable anonymity. She at least left with me. And she'd seemed unsurprised and surprisingly happy when I went back stage.

We glided into a restaurant, where half the room, 100 strong, seemed to recognize her. She picked this chic spot, half French, half Vietnamese right down the street from the Public on Fourth Avenue. She was something of a regular, I guessed, for the host kissed her on the cheek. I could remember sitting with her at the Café Marseille lo those many years back when the same guy had ignored us at the bar he tended.

But he had a warm eye for me: these Welsh are also compassionate people. He looked as if he remembered me and knew already that she was someone else. Or maybe he saw the desperate need I was suddenly feeling, for happy as I was for Sarah, I felt disoriented, me the ironic proof certain of her insights *chez Dottie*, of a man's dislocation confronting a woman's success.

Ten years before, in Paris, when Sarah and I would enter the Coupole, not a single female eye would fail to peruse her. Slowly they'd turn our way, their lids rising, their glances darting like so many envenomed snakes. Skipping off Sarah finally, they would rest eventually on me. And I didn't mind, I liked the feel even if I understood over time that their attention to me was entirely competitive, coming from their appreciation of my girl friend's style. But here, in the U.S. of A., every regard bore in, gimlet-like, on my friend—and stayed there. (Sadly, I had to admit that they clearly hadn't seen me on TV, much less read my book, that if there was a star of this show, it wasn't I). Here, everyone, male and female alike, seemed to want something from Sarah. There was no delay. The males didn't pick up their cues from their dates, everyone needed and wanted her—and so did I. When I walked through the room behind Sarah, then sat across from her at a prime table (the placement wasn't insignificant to the guy with the 4 day beard), I was excited, aroused, stirred. So much of me was still mixed, so confusedly, with her. Quite a bit more than I knew.

"So what's the problem then with Phillip?" I eventually asked, though of course I don't think I wanted to know the answer: the man's name, thoughts of his relation with Sarah rose to the top of me like a cheap plastic float bobbing up to a wave's surface. I was just making small talk, scared. I'd been thinking of Sarah for so long a time that when I touched my glass, I wondered how I was holding it up. Things seemed to move in spite of me. If I weren't careful, I felt, the table would lose its right angle to the floor—slip to 75, 60 degrees. Were we going to make love?

"There isn't anything wrong with Phillip—he's a wonderful man. What makes you think otherwise?"

"What you were talking about then on the show...about a man and a woman's success?"

Sarah's green eyes suddenly sharpened. "Success brings you the wrong guys. Phillip was there long before." She surveyed the room, somewhat wistfully. And I slipped my right foot out of my black loafer and over and up my former lover's calf.

Was I one more of the wrong guys, this another narcissist's desperate attempt to find some self-respect (in the wrong place)?

That too. But Sarah's left pushed back against my foot. "Jimmie," she said with an enlarging smile, her eyes returning to mine before glazing over...tucked like mine someplace between the two of us, I thought, years back maybe but charged still. "I overestimated you. You haven't grown up at all."

This wasn't un-germane, not to the two of us: it's surely why we had broken up. Sarah had wanted children, kids, issue; and I'd been incapable of imagining any kind of future outside work. I'd barely been able to support myself, once we'd returned to New York; but Sarah didn't think that any kind of reason not to have kids.

"If you want a life together, you find a way," she said one day. "If you want a child, you just have one; you don't get obsessed by the consequences: there are always good reasons not to." Not long thereafter, of course, she had taken her own advice; and, deciding she didn't want a life with me, she had left before I was ready for her disappearance.

She was a decisive woman, as her left foot was making clear, pushing my foot back to my side of the table and holding it there. She wasn't playing footsie with me, however much I might have wanted to imagine it.

"Is this what your foot's searching for?" She asked; and she handed me my black loafer. It wasn't, of course, but I was forced to nod in agreement. She smiled. "I thought so," said she.

I laughed too; and when Sarah looked over at me, her face lifted; her body seemed tilted, on a slightly different plane—one I remembered in the very pit of myself. I got the weird feeling--I couldn't believe it—that in spite of her previous rebuff we were going to make love to each other, just as surely as we'd been going to do when we had first met more than a decade before in Paris. Then she'd seen through the baggy and garish garb I'd worn, the velour pants I'd had tailored in Bombay, the shirt whose color hadn't quite matched—underneath it all, she somehow had discerned the handsome, gallant and disenfranchised prince I always assumed I was. Now again I watched in astonishment, as she seemed to melt a little my way.

"So what would you like to do?" Sarah asked me after we had skimmed over dinner, thought of her touch wiping out the very taste of the food, the scent and texture of my wine. She looked down at her watch. "I only have about an hour, an hour and a half. I want to be back before one. What do you want to do?"

"I think you've got a pretty good idea," I said, more nervous now than when we'd first met. I'd been so much more confident then or just more delusional. Now the thought of making love to her brought new meaning to the term performance anxiety. "I'd like to be with you.'

"Where should we go?" She asked, and a couple of Don Juan's mistresses, half the parts she was playing at the Public looked my way. She knew how to make herself compelling, alluring.

I couldn't think of a thing to say—my tongue hit against its palette like a pneumatic drill on a city street. Then finally, I said, "How about the Grammercy Park?"

She laughed. "You are so hokey, so corny," she said, shaking her head but standing up all the same. "Maybe that's what I miss the most."

We had stayed at the Grammercy Park together before. Panic-stricken and jet-lagged, Sarah and I had checked into the Grammercy the night we returned, definitively, from gay Paris. We'd mistakenly thought it would be calmer there, near the elderly with their park keys, close to the Evangeline Home for Girls. But instead, like most new arrivals in New York, we got the harassment our ingenuousness seemed to beg for. The Grammercy's crack staff shrewdly summed us up as a couple of transients, of undesirable aliens, and they made us pay for our phone calls in advance. When they placed us in a ten by ten room, which looked as if it had been lifted straight from Attica (the Nelson Rockefeller suite), they didn't apologize for the bars over the two airshaft windows or the TV which was less in color than in blue and green nor did they find a way to make the light fixture fully operative.

Yet it was hard not to feel nostalgic about the Grammercy Park. When we'd been there, we'd been two against the world, huddled together in a swaybacked bed watching TV hour after hour, trying to get the nerve to go outside and confront the currency which didn't feel right, the quarters with the greasy notches in them, this city which looked more like Cairo or Bombay than the New York of our memories or frankly, the New York that it's become. We were like the only two members of a vanishing tribe—were we ever that close again?

This time, Sarah watched with a wry smile as I produced a platinum credit card at the front desk (I was American now!), let her hand slip into mine when we were in the elevator. What amazing wrists she still had, like fine cutlery, I thought. They remained as thin as before, even as her body had changed, her face seemed denser, more lived in. My heart's pounding embarrassed me. Was she really there? She had an hour, an hour and a half, she said; what does that sound like to you?

It sounded like a proposition, and the author of <u>Luck for the Lovelorn</u> thought he knew something about listening, was attentive to a woman's words, especially this one's, whose voice he'd often heard in too many intimate moments with too many other women for far too long. In the elevator, I slid my hand off her fingers and held her wrist between my thumb and forefinger like a champagne flute. I felt its delicateness—and I tried to keep my impatience from showing, to keep my cool. I smiled and followed the Eastern European bellhop to the room where I didn't really need him to show me the accoutrements.

"That'll be fine," I said, again and again, and the man paid absolutely no attention. He was from a tribe of his own, the Slow People; and his keen insight into my impatient soul kept me increasing the tip. As I took more ones out of my wallet, he checked out the lights which I would rather have extinguished, the TV set which I had no desire to watch. He made sure the water worked in the bath I didn't immediately need and its color eventually changed from rust to some reasonable approximation of transparent. Had we had any luggage, he surely would have transferred the contents into drawers for us; this was a man from an older school.

"Thank you, thanks very much," I said when he shuffled out of the room with most of my loose bills. And I meant it. Sarah looked up at me with her luminous eyes, which looked more turquoise than the green I remembered. I leaned toward her and gently pulled her full, fuchsia painted lips my way. Her tongue stopped at some point between her lips and mine, just as it once did. Touching mine it threw a couple thousand amps down my legs. Was I so easily involved again, what this what I'd been missing? I started undressing her, but the buttons on her blouse didn't slip out fast enough; the hasp on her bra opened in front. I fumbled around with it, couldn't get it.

"Let me help you there," she said, disengaging the clasp from my stubby, clumsy fingers. She was smiling; that should have made me calm. I'd wanted to be here; I'd imagined touching her while touching too many others; but once up against the reality of it, up against her slightly slacker skin, suddenly my friend Jeannie's face swooped before me like an admonitory vulture, she the girl in California I was seeing. Sarah and I headed for the bed, and I felt as if I had left my body—the ghost stayed and watched as the person, the flesh stumbled on, panicking completely. At the bed and on it, under the covers, I started trembling, here it was, my spirit was trying to crawl back into the flesh and failing at the effort. I was shaking like a dandelion wisp in a strong wind, evanescing.

Yes, the author of that Man's Guide to a Woman's World didn't know what he was doing—and must have looked the part.

"God I can't believe it," Sarah said with a smile. "Years and years later, I still have to take care of you."

And she did. Grinning at me, Jesus, she looked even sexier than I recalled. Maybe it was those larger breasts, with their full, dark nipples; maybe too it was the lines around her eyes which, to this son of an older woman, made her look more womanly, more vulnerable too—aged just enough to make me know she could feel time passing over her, to make me feel wanted again. In a matter of moments, she got me back into my body and my body back into hers. And I felt as if I belonged.

One more time: one moment I was feeling myself smile truly, the smile cracking through pain like dried mud cracking on skin; the next moment, she slipped into my arms, as if I were an alpha male, her eyes looked all the way up the years at me; and suddenly, I was there again for her. When I ran my fingers lightly down her side, over her ribs, all of me moved that way. She gave me a languid look and pulled me inside her; and I felt myself more, felt more of myself than I'd let myself feel for a long while.

I was addled enough (as if I knew that this was just another prelude) I just held on, strapped myself in. There was no way I was letting go soon, and she didn't release me either. We both felt it, and we both, at just about the same time, opened our closed lids and caught the other's eyes, grins sweeping over us, as if we each simultaneously recalled how good it had sometimes been. I wondered then what she wanted, where I was, but thinking wasn't exactly on the agenda; no, I was happy to snuff out each passing thought, to concentrate all y multiple confusions on such a small spot—all of me, years of it smelted down to push against this touch which seemed, disturbingly, so much a part of me but oddly, just a little different. I had a leg outside Sarah's, a hand cupped underneath her, her larger breast filling my other fingers; and I slid that hand up to her chin. I turned her to me. I kissed her ears, just as I thought she liked, my tongue feeling what I imagined were memorable grooves. Then she took my lips in hers; she moved her leg back out of mine where she preferred it. She looked as if she thought, if she was really there, really going to do this, she might as well enjoy it. She pushed her body more fiercely against me; she clamped onto her own pleasure and forgot all about me and mine.

31

And it's then, of course, when I felt the least needed, that I felt her desire the most acutely. I sensed her come once, then again as her body stopped for a second before twisting slightly, as she always used to do, holding me tightly to whatever place or memory most sparked her desire.

Her renewed excitement provoked mine, shooting me back out of myself, my whole self just leaving this mortal sphere. Her satisfaction elicited my own, teasing it a millimeter at a time up the tendons in my legs, from the soles of my feet, rushing into the blood, like solid jet fuel, and spilling finally out of the ends of every one of the synapses still sparking in my agitated cerebrum. Was this possible? Was it happening or had it just been an acid flashback?

Maybe it was just stage one of my own little flight, the booster shooting off. There was more. We were going to go further, elsewhere. She lay back and said, "You're so much gentler, Jimmy," which rather puzzled me.

"Oh yeah," I said. I felt fifteen miles up, blasted out of myself. "Felt good to me," I continued, to her nod. I exhaled, and I could feel the bristles growing on my barely shaven cheeks. My three day growth and I were getting together again, Mr. Manly returning right when I needed him. "At least we still have that, the two of us," I told her, referring with pride and longing to the pleasure I felt.

"We've got more than that, I think," said she. There was something about her tone.

She looked around, looked serious again, as she had on the Dottie show. I started feeling as if someone were shooting a sheetrock screw into my bones, fastening me back down to the planet. "Uh, what, what's that?"

"Jesse…"

"What?" The author of Luck for the Lovelorn, A Man's Guide to a

<u>Woman's World</u> saw his world spin like a cyclotron, half his protons torn away from the core. "You mean your child?"

She nodded.

"What are you getting at exactly?" I'm not always this obtuse.

"You may be his father." She enunciated the words clearly.

Wham. "Huh? How? Why didn't you tell me before?"

"Because you weren't ready to hear it—and I wasn't going to abort this one."

That felt like a slug in the neck. It's true she had had an abortion about a year before we broke up. And, even as I felt bad about that again, I counted once more the months, seven of them, between that day we'd last made love and Jesse's birth. It wasn't impossible, I supposed, but I wasn't supposing very well at all. I was hurtling through myself, a skydiver at 15,000 feet whose chute hadn't opened, frantically tying to get out of this date with gravity.

Think of what an emotional invalid she must have thought I was. She had never even told me. That was something to cry about but the tears didn't come—my heart beat in my throat, my head felt balanced on a point and then whirled like a top, a yoyo on a trip around myself.

Sometime later, I stopped spinning and found myself on my back. Sarah was peering anxiously down at me. This isn't quite the way I had imagined us here, not quite. She wasn't over me or under me, her eyes closed and her gravelly voice telling me how good I was, how much she missed me: "Oh Jimmie, you're so fine—Jimmie, My Jimmie Max…" something like that.

Instead, she was saying, "Actually there's just one chance in two he's yours. He might be someone else's son."

There was a cheering thought.

"Phillip's?"

"Nope, definitely not Phillip's," she said, shaking her head. "We didn't get really close until after I was pregnant—there are guys like that, you know." She smiled tenderly, at the memory of Phillip back then, I supposed. When she switched her regard, posing her almost iridescent eyes on me, she changed countenance. "I can't believe it. I came here to tell you something important, and I end up mothering you."

Well she should have. I needed help. I felt a fibrillation away from some sort of seizure. "Who's the other guy?" I inquired.

"A director." She reached for her purse and took out a snapshot. "He's pretty large, and he's blonde. There he is." Indeed, a fat blonde guy with towheaded hair grinned fatuously from the photo. Oddly enough, he had a large tussle of hair on the right side of his head, a sort of cowlick, like mine. Beside him was a boy. "That's Jesse," she said, pointing.

He had chubby cheeks, like the director's, high cheekbones like his mom. He didn't look like me, but both these traits, it had to be admitted, exist within my gene pool. And then there were the eyes: periwinkle blues, big, a circle of white around the irises, exactly like my mother's. Sarah had thought of this too. "Hard not to think of your mother, isn't it?"

Indeed. Turned in half profile, his eyes peeking out of his face, he seemed at one cautious and deceptively fierce, just as she often did. My mom.

"You're an asshole, Sarah," I began. "How the fuck could you not tell me?" But my heart just wasn't in either the question or the accusation. My hands out, my palms up, I was waiting for the nails.

She had a few at hand. "You didn't want to hear about it—a guy who wanted to take no for an answer..." She smiled a little tenderly, in spite of herself. "That's why we broke up" (she didn't say "why I left you," anyway). "You weren't ready to be a father, and I wasn't going to lose this one." Back to that. Bang, the one hand firmly affixed to the cross.

"Who says I couldn't have been a father?" I continued, a glutton for abuse. I tried, failed to find a breath, the tadpole coming up on land.

She didn't even address the question directly. She took the other nail out of her mouth and put it up against the other palm.

"I'm so glad I have him," she said. "We love each other. Phillip loves him too; he's a wonderful kid. Don't get me wrong, Jim. I'm not asking you to do anything. I don't want anything from you. Jesse's my responsibility. I know that. Not yours. I just thought you might want to get to know him."

KIDS:

You want them, absolutely, even if you can't abide the sight of them, even if every kid you've ever glimpsed seems a tortured little urchin, a sadistic delinquent, somebody to avoid.

You want them even if, as seems more likely here, you can't help seeing the adolescent—gawky, pimply, and condescending—inside each baby face. You still want them.

I have a friend whose own love life's a disaster—currently she's dating a grad student 15 years younger than she is and unwilling to leave his own self-infatuated model girl friend; previously she had two husbands. She has children from each of the husbands, each so beautiful that they almost make you want to sign up for the possibility of supporting them. They keep her spirits alive. She says, "You'd have to have an unimaginably exciting life not to have kids who'd enrich yours."

Steal her line, whether or not your life's that exciting. Women will appreciate it.

For no woman—certainly few who haven't experienced already the burdens of motherhood (say they've spawned a child star or a divorce lawyer of their own)—imagines that she shouldn't want a child. None thinks she couldn't or shouldn't stand the burden or joy of maternity, even if the life she's chosen complicates the task, even if it almost precludes having that child.

Her guilt is your opportunity. The more dedicated these women are to their work, the more vulnerable they are to your enthusiasm at the prospect of co-parenting—and the less likely that you will ever have to deliver on the actuality of it.

For better for worse, for both of you.

Good way to get laid, though.

THE VULNERABLE YOU...

Try it on for size. Feels better, doesn't it? A little tight in the shoulders, around the neck perhaps (you may be a little more buff than you need to be), but then you never quite fit inside those other jackets—and you're getting a little old for ball jerseys, aren't you? You may have tried for years, may still be trying, someplace deep inside yourself, to fit into a number 7 or a 24, but you've had to face it: the talent, the size, the speed, the genes weren't quite there.

But they're there for the sensitive you. It's only a question of attitude, of recognizing first whom you're trying to please: the driven father you long ago disappointed and are now trying to understand, who's fixed into a totally different idea of manhood, into fighting in a platoon or a company at one time or another, in the company of men. Or might your ambition be to please your Mom , who may already be too pleased with you. Could that be part of your problem.

Or then again you might prefer to please the woman at the end of your own glance. You can't choose more than two, can rarely please more than one at any given time.
But if you go with the species-perpetuating pick, if you let her show you what she likes these days, there's a pretty good chance you'll find yourself fitting comfortably into an angst-ridden, addlepated, somewhat spaced out, imaginative but sometimes even sexy guy—someone more or less, closer to your real self.

For who, after all, is female America's favorite man these days? Not the jocks, whose TV demographics have flatlined for a long time: they appeal to the men of the house. Who's watching when they're performing, unless it's Olympics time and a single mom in the stands or an overcome illness thickens the plot line? Women are swooning over a different type of guy: the handsome doc from ER has made it onto the world stage; with him in their sights, the working woman could find good reasons not to compromise. George Clooney has so engraved himself into the female psyche that macho men are going the way of the Marlboro man. Go for George and a girl knows she's in for separation, long, lonely hours and yes terrible betrayal. She knows for sure that work's her only viable time-filler; he's going to make sure no kids encumber either of them. But what a ride she'll have.

He's not going to be flying fighter planes, our continuing militarism notwithstanding, nor could you find Matt Damon on one, or Brad Pitt either. The women won't let them go. They're way too sexy and way too needy, current prototypes of the 80s favorite guy, Woody Allen. Yes, old as he now is, few women could resist him in his prime, inconceivable as that may not sound. He took all his disadvantages and converted them brilliantly, with feminine help, into sources of pride. He coined sensitivity, has shown us how to get help and comfort in our weakness, strength in our neuroses. He and a few billion made Bill Gates and Steve Jobs sexy. Taking his clue, Robert Downey Jr. rivets, electrifies your energetic woman even without the dinero. She can work—she has to work—but she'll always know that, at any given moment, a man like Robert will be needing her too, needing her as a woman, for without her belief, he'd be creamed in this cruel world; he'd be only too truly like a waif in a maximum security prison, like Tonto in an Indian war, like Don Quixote without a windmill. With her, of course, he's McDreamy himself, the scrim on which every woman's fantasies can freely project, arms open to the whole female world.

Fortunately, you and I, with a little retraining, can get there too, for these are the guys who, aside from their genius and their looks, most resemble you and me, the ones whose clothes we might most easily fit into, whose looks we can approximate and whose style we can learn. Their egregious success in coupling up, in survival at all is proof, irrefutable proof that there's still luck out there available for anyone who knows how to let the lovelorn guy inside of him float up to the surface of his self.

"Are you okay, Jim," a familiar voice asked, faintly, over the Grammercy's awful connection, about two hours later. It sounded as if the call were coming from Antarctica, when in fact it was coming from Oklahoma (which most New Yorkers know perhaps even less about).

"Not real great, Mom," I said. She was clairvoyant, much too bright and energetic to have spent all that time with her children and not be attuned to our every oscillation. Still this was different. "What do you know?" I asked. I needed to see what I was working against.

"Your cousin Virginia called—she said she saw you on some TV show…"

"Sarah was there too, Mom. You remember her?"

She knew. "Your dad always liked her so much," she said. "So how did that make you feel? You okay?"

"I'll make it. I'm a big boy now."

"Do you think so?" She asked. You could hear the grin.

"Okay, I'm a big boy every once in a while, some of the time."

"You wouldn't want to make a habit out of it," said she. "It's so hard to be a man these days." We agreed on a number of things, all I had to do was listen. "Maybe you want to come back home for a little while in the middle of all those shows you're doing. Get some rest. I think it'd be a good time for it."

Something else was going on. There was something foreboding about her tone. "Is dad okay?" I asked.

"Every once in a while," she responded, picking up my line, ambiguously. She seemed to be waiting for me, asking, wanting a confession, which sat, like a muscle tic, on the edge of my skin.

"Look, mom. I can't leave in the middle of a book tour. I'm kind of getting lucky with it. Who knows if I'll get another chance?"

"Lucky? Didn't sound exactly that way to me." My mother, as noted, had cornflower blue eyes, long grey eyelashes, which almost never blinked. "Sarah is a smart girl. She's got a real will of her own, Jimmie," she continued, with a pause. No misstatement there, I thought, drifting toward a familiar nostalgia but being pulled up just a little short. "I like her, don't misunderstand me. But I'm not sure she was ever right for you."

It didn't quite seem like the time to tell her about the kid, whom I was supposed to discuss, in just about an hour, with Sarah and her friend Phillip.

"I hope she wasn't the reason you were crying," my mother now asserted.

She liked the double negative, but did I truly know the answer? I tried to pull back into myself, though I didn't quite get there. I was like an opened oyster hit by a splash of lemon. I had no place to go; so I squirmed.

"You don't have to tell me," my mom said, sensing my discomfort. "I'm sorry for asking—it's just I feel so anxious these days."

"Me too, Mom," I said. This was as honest as I was going to get.

"Well, then, stay in better touch, would you, Jim? Don't run too far away, okay?"

All things considered, Phillip Arnstein—that's the theater director and aspiring filmmaker and somewhat more importantly, Sarah's long time companion—was a prince. Think about it. You meet someone when she's four months pregnant, fall in love with her, stay the distance and then for the long haul, for the next four or five years. You embrace her kid and treat him, not exactly as if he were yours unequivocally to cherish, but at the least as if he were yours to guard and protect; and suddenly you're presented with the physical evidence of your own tangentiality—the presumptive seed carrier.

On second thought, that may not have been as difficult as I suppose—given the man who came to dinner, me. This black-haired, green-eyed guy couldn't keep his hands from feeling a subcutaneous sebaceous cyst which may or may not have grown on the back of his neck in reaction to this very evening. Listening, he had hands like gnats, independent operators on the make.

Whether not really a prince but just a duke, a viscount, Phillip was considerably calmer than I was. The proud possessor of his own better-maintained three-day growth of stubble, he wore aviator glasses, which were affixed to him by a black rubber coil that looked like a telephone cord. That kind of guy—his hips were pretty large too. Here's what he said when the three of us ate together three nights after Sarah and I met on national TV: "Just don't ask me to participate in this. Of course they should get together, but uh just not around me, okay? I don't want to be there to watch the happy reunion."

"It doesn't mean Jesse's going to feel any different about you, Phillip," Sarah said. We were eating sautéed vegetables, brown rice, and yoghurt. Phil was a vegetarian. The meal sadly didn't offset any of the conversation's difficulties.

"I know that. I know he loves me," Phil said very reasonably.

"Anyway we don't even know if Jim's the real father," my former love added, so sagaciously.

"I'll get the blood test," I said, not having thought this out all that clearly. Fatherhood—why had I not been let in on this before?

"If you want," Phillip said. He could barely look in my direction; and when he did, his lips seemed to disappear into the corners of his mouth. I think he thought this was smiling.

"Would you really?" Sarah asked me. "My doctor says it's easier and a whole lot cheaper than messing around with DNA."

"There probably no point in taking either one," Phillip continued, to Sarah. "I've always told you that. Look at their chins-- that curve up the cheek. Richard's is rounder; and his nose doesn't have the same crook— that kind of Saracen look."

As she scrutinized my decidedly bent nose and angular cheeks, Sarah lofted a hand onto Phillip's shoulder. You have to encourage these men, comfort them all the time. "And the eyes too—I guess they really are similar," she said, as if she doubted her own judgment, was ready to defer to Phillip's greater discernment.

"They don't mean all that much—yours are the same color."

"Actually," I said, "hers are green."

"Blue green, like Jesse's," Phillip retorted.

Why was I going to get into an argument about it? I hadn't even seen the kid yet.

"I guess you're right," said Sarah and pushed her full plate to the side. "Maybe he should have that test."
"I think I should have had it some time ago," I said—Bogart watching as Ingrid's plane taxied down the runway and out of his life. I was lucky to keep an eye dry.

"Maybe not," she said coyly. "We've been fine. I don't know if I want to know."

"No need," said Phillip, the final word on it here. "I tell you—it's in the chins alone, there's no doubt about it. The chins…"

It was in the eyes, the thick, tousled hair front and back. It was in the shape of the jaw and the chin too, yes. But most of all it was in the nose and the lips. It was one generation removed from Phillip's sight, and he couldn't have known. Sarah had seen it first.

When, two days after my meeting with Phillip, I first looked at the kid trundling along to the park, on the arm of his Guadalupan au-pair, I saw a chubby faced five year old with a deep forehead and those coruscating eyes. They were my mother's, just as Sarah had concluded, my mother's at 5 as she looked out at the world from the sepia photo in our hall back home. Though mom was decked out sweetly in the photo, in a white Easter dress and a nifty bonnet, it was her face that sprang right out of the center of this kid's large, dark-haired head. My lungs batted their wings, all of me spinning at the sight of him.

I had agreed, however, not to speak to him; not to "confuse" him (Phil's word) before we knew for sure who is father was. I was only supposed to watch, to look at him, this time at least. But the kid, as he walked past, seemed to stare at me, to sense some consanguinity—or was I imagining it? His glance rapidly spurned mine for the less puzzling confines of the sandbox, the jungle gym, which he rapidly began to scale, leaving his nanny in the lurch.

She let him crawl, smiling, her teeth resplendent in her exquisitely teak colored face. She told him, in French, to take care of himself. "*Attention*," she said, but he didn't bother to listen; he was already half way up the gym before she managed to find herself a seat and take up her book, Camus, *La Chute*. She winked at me over the page, a kind and complicitous recognition of my increasing anxiety. I felt like a helicopter twisting over Lower Manhattan.

The kid peered out from his metallic tower, an introspective frown on his face; and he didn't look like anything I'd ever seen. He looked heavy, flaccid and maybe wiser than anything my family had produced. This didn't stop my helicopter's whirling, though—if anything, it made me feel more disoriented.

We were on Greenwich Ave., near Chambers; there may be some use in knowing that, at the base of Independence Plaza—a huge apartment complex built long ago for the rich, which, a total bust initially, had been transformed into middle class housing before going upscale once again. It has Tribeca's only park larger than a putting green. The area's most verdant spot, it is now filled with the young and solidly comfortable, the procreating children of the already rich.

To join them, I'd canceled my next TV interview—this wasn't so difficult, for it had been scheduled for New Haven, a place where its only potential readers would be preoccupied deconstructing other texts and vaguely condescending toward my humble work if they noticed it at all (though they were guppies, both straight and gay). I couldn't wait, even had they been interested, as they'd claimed to be later than day in Hartford. I wanted to look at this child.

Was he really mine? Or wasn't this Sarah's most perverse dig, the thought ripping into me when, financially more or less comfortable for a moment, for a change, I had begun to think of the possibility of a family.

I hadn't been planning to start with a five year old…with another father, who looked like he loved him….with a succession of nannies, a doting mother, a developing life—58 months of which I had already missed, every one of them.

Still there he was, off the jungle gym and out of the sandbox, now kicking a soccer ball with a bullet headed brute about half again as tall. "My" kid—or the one that might have been "mine"—looked my way as the other kid bounced him off the ball with his hip. He looked as if he could use some help; and I rose with his imagined plea. I inhaled, tried to tuck in my stomach, couldn't keep it in for long. Maybe dads were just always pot-bellied, part of the deal, like dyspepsia and self-pity. It makes the species look more protective.

Most men have months, years to prepare for this. I had only had two days. How was I supposed to look convincingly paternal? I'd worn corduroys, a couple of sweaters, and no overcoat. I might have been a wimp as a guy, but as a dad, I wanted to show bulk and strength. I had a smile worked out, though, spontaneous and tender. I felt affection toward the guy whether he was mine or not and gentle toward this boy's mother.

When the larger kid, the hulk, punched the ball through the improvised goal, Jesse rose from his abortive dive and looked back my way, so I thought. I beamed; he was doing fine; I shook my fist in encouragement. The kid looked brave, engaged, his body fearlessly up against the other kid's. He tried to counter with an immediate shot at the other goal, but when the brute responded by knocking Jesse down, flat on his face, Jesse got up howling with anger and fear. I rose too, looked around, saw the nanny's enraged reaction, and did what I wasn't supposed to do. When after all had I heeded instructions before? I went toward the two kids, but before I could reach them, Jesse had jumped up, dribbled the ball, and been bounced back down a second time. He got up again, shedding not a single tear, and went at the colossus a third time. It wasn't hard to predict what was going to happen.

When this had happened to me, at about the same time, my father had taken me to the blue, red and yellow rag rug in the GI bill house which was my family's first, and he'd shown me a hammer lock and a scissors hold, how to defend myself. It was one of the few gifts from him I never ceased to appreciate, still felt nostalgic about.

But when I yelled "hey," the two kids seemed more annoyed than intimidated; and Jesse used the break in the action to hustle away. He raced past me and leapt into the arms of his nanny, who comforted him, as I would have wanted to do. Within seconds, in her arms, he was smiling and giggling, gurgling in her affectionate kisses. This seemed a better balm for the occasional slight, the best kind. And he was wise enough to know it. Radiant, he knew there were few better places than inside a woman's arms. Maybe, thought I, we did have something in common.

So I went to the second part of this many sectioned paternity (or yes, pop) quiz, to NYU and the offices of a med school professor where I immediately felt impugned. Shame would come next. First off, after I entered the marbled office and spoke to the receptionist from Queens, they needed to know--besides the predictable name, birth date, social security number and address—"name of Lawyer."

On the line below was the supplementary question, "Is this matter currently under litigation? If yes, please explain." Underneath that was three quarters of a page, left blank.

It took me a little time to fill out the page and even more to each the supervising doctor himself, Dr. Maurice Spirman. It was days before I understood that the man's nickname was obviously "Mo." Dr. Spirman, much to my surprise, was anything but the glassy-eyed, greed-filled technocrat we've come to know and loathe in the medical profession. (That role in this medical family was filled by his son Dr. Larry, the guy in the polo shirt I saw entering as I left, with the Ralph Lauren look about him). Dr. Spirman Sr. was kind, tenderhearted and befuddled. He had dedicated his life to propagation and just couldn't fathom why it had taken me four years, ten months, to attempt to discover if I were the parent of this "marvelous youngster."

I tried to explain how Sarah hadn't made me privy to my own

possible co-responsibility. But the good doctor, though he knew Sarah and must have known something about her willfulness, just couldn't, didn't get it. "But why wouldn't she tell you?" He kept wondering.

"Maybe she didn't want me to know," I said, honestly. There was a nurse around, make that two. These offices were in a brownstone on Washington Square Park; and the paint was peeling around the molding. His son Larry's office, I'm sure, had gleaming gold door knobs, walls you could eat off. The nurses bustled near me; for they wanted my blood.

"Why wouldn't a woman want her boy to know his father? Particularly one as sophisticated and beautiful as Sarah. I don't get it." Were all these guys in love with her? "Did you mistreat her in some way?" He asked, following up, a stern eye on me.

"Only morally, I guess, doc." I ventured.

"I mean, if not for you, at least for the child's sake, don't you think she'd want him to know?" The good doc wouldn't let go of this.

I was a deflating tire, being spun slowly on my rim.

"You know I'm sending this out; but hematology is a very inexact science; they can't always give us an answer. DNA can, but of course it's expensive. How many others did she say there were, Ruth?"

"Just one other," the nurse, Ruth, said.

"It's a pity you had to wait this long," Dr. Spirman continued. "You know there are certain things you can pick up from as early as 20, 23 weeks—you just don't find later on." The Doc searched for the right needle, took one out which looked like the nose cone on a supersonic jet, about a foot long. "Sometimes I think you can tell more just by looking at the kid."

"How much blood do you need?" I asked. The syringe looked like a bottle of Bordeaux; he was going to fill that thing up?

"Not all that much, really," he said and his eye hardened

narrowed, looked as sharp as the needle which he held over my disappearing veins. His nurse patted by arm with alcohol, I breathed deeply. I mean come on, this wasn't going to hurt, I told myself.

But my self didn't listen.

"The only unpleasant part is it lasts awhile, kind of like a tetanus shot," the doc said as the needle pricked my arm, missing my vein. "Just relax okay, tighten your fist. Ruth, come give us some help, would you?"

Ruth, whom I hadn't really noticed, was built like a female weight lifter—her biceps way more ripped than mine. She squeezed my upper arm like snake swallowing a rat. An artery popped up, and the good doctor hit it like a cobra, like a mako on chub.

Blood came spurting out of the blue, blue vein and into the syringe, up a tube and into a bottle. "The odd part about this," Dr. Spirman continued, "is we can't always do much more than eliminate people this way... as possible parents, that is, not as people." He thought that was droll; but then he wasn't looking at my face.

Ruth, however, turned from writing something in her ledger, glanced my way and let out a cry of concern. The doctor turned back and his face just spread over my windshield.

J.M. Adams, that lucky/lovelorn guy, the manly man behind the three or four day growth, the twinkling green eyes and the slightly splayed nose finished off this day filled with real concerns—fatherhood, kids, procreation—by disappearing altogether: I blacked out.

So what did I do thereafter, feeling groggy, disoriented, certain that
I was more uncertain than I'd been since puberty hit?

I didn't immediately take Dr. Spirman's advice after I opened my
eyes to see Ruth and felt her holding up my head and smelled the salts they
still use on neurasthenics like myself. The good doctor suggested "more of
your iron vegetables. You should try to pick up a taste for beets, spinach,
cut down on your salt intake." He had a finger on my pulse. "But don't
worry," he continued. "It happens all the time, to more men that you'd think
really" (was he going to use the dreaded word 'metrosexual' next I
wondered?). "Just eat differently. You'll feel better too."

Though I did indeed exit his premises and head for the friendly
confines of a diner, I skipped the legumes. I called instead my agent.
There's mental dislocation for you—as if my agent were part of any real
world I inhabited. The man was so virtual to me I was astonished when he
actually got on the line within seconds. This wasn't his habitual practice.
Normally, I was deflected by the gatekeeper, his assistant, whom I liked to
think of as my agent Irv's own agent, Irv's Irv (though his name was Eric).
He usually gave me a time some time in the following two or three days
when he might be able to slot me in with "the big guy," as Irv2 liked to call
him, though of course Irv was about five foot three. Irv's Irv liked to let me
know thereby that Irv was a much bigger agent than I was a client—kind

enough to work with me but well aware, as were his co-workers at the agency, of my lower place in the larger entertainment pecking order.

Imagine then how puzzled I felt when Eric excitedly said, "he's been waiting to hear from you. Where've you been? I'll put you right through."

"Jimmie," Irv, the real Irv said in a voice which bespoke of a personal intimacy I'd never known us to have. "How are you, buddy? Where have you been? My God, we've been calling everywhere."

"Who? Huh? Irv, this is James Adams. I'm sorry to bother you, Irv…"

"Of course it is. Who'd you think I thought I was talking to? You're my only James…"

In fact, I figured he had about twenty of us. He never showed me his list, didn't have to in order to get me to sign on. The hypermanic tone of his voice, though, rather scared me. "What happened, Irv?" I ventured, thinking maybe my publisher had folded again, like the last one.

"Nothing, just your book sales have gone through the roof."

"Say what? How's that?"

"The Dottie show thing. What a genius idea."

"What?"

"The crying. Your bawling, bud. It moved them. Can't you hear it in my voice? They're moving your way."

"Who? Who's moving my way?"

"Why women, of course, man. Who do you think buys the books in this country? I mean your kind of book anyway. 96 % of your purchasers, women! The publisher just told me. Who knows, the other 4 per cent are probably transsexuals. But do we care? What a stroke of brilliance. I didn't know you had it in you."

"But, Irv, I didn't do that on purpose. You see, Sarah, Sarah Revson, she…"

"Of course you didn't…tell him I'll call him back within 2, Eric….Of course you didn't. You're too sincere a person. I know you. We've been together a long time."

He had been good to me, yes, even if he couldn't always get my name right.

"You're going to be in the top ten trades, Jimbo. Figure number five or six…I think this is your chance, really. I'm getting a publicist for you, 3 grand a month, but she'll get you on everything."

"3,000 dollars? A month?"

"I know, she's giving you a special rate, just for me. But you'll get it back in spades."

"But…"

"Stop arguing with me. Eric, tell her it's done."

There were, I suppose, clients who dictated to their agents, but I wasn't one of them. I was too happy to have an agent whose name people might actually know. "She's a good friend of the Today show, they all love her there. Andrea, Hymie, the fat guy, they all love her. They're crying for people like you. You're going to own this town…you can't buy sincerity. You have to have it. Don't go looking for it. Okay, I'll take that right now," and he cut away, leaving me with his own Irv, who sounded more or less like his mentor, only he'd learned to modulate, to deepen his voice slightly.

"Here she is. We've got her for you, James. Linda meet James Adams."

"Love your performance. The Dottie thing. Isn't she great? I couldn't have invented anything better. Perfect for the book. The modern guy, sensitive, tears. Does it smell of money, or what?"

"But I didn't do it on purpose."

"You will next time, I hope, right?" Linda opined. "Give me a moment. I just need a couple of facts. They help with the work."

I am not all that sure about that. They were a little grim. I'd wanted to be on National Book Award lists by this time, wasn't quite close. I'd written three serious novels, which, as Irv said once in a less than kind moment, I hadn't been able to sell to my immediate family. "Try something frivolous, James," he'd said. (No sobriquets then, no terms of endearment, just "James" then). "Do it for me and we'll get the others back in print for you one day." Thus <u>Sea of Fertility</u>. My personal favorite, speculative fiction, futuristic in part—a novelist's present dream and his future work, all intermeshed with the egg, the sperm and the egg. Who was going to control the test tube, control birth once the ovum left, once and for all, women's bodies. After Irv read it (did he?), he suggested Hollywood. "It'll be good for you," he said. "You need to stop stepping on your own cock. So many others out there will do it for you."

He was right about that. There were thousands ready and willing out there. But, surprisingly, the place inspired me. L.A. made me envious at first (look at all the money they are making, talents as modest as mine, said I), then anxious, and then finally when all else wouldn't work, very productive. I just started working all the time, exactly like my dad. I abandoned the screenplay of Sea of Fertility and instead did two rewrites and two more screenplays, including Good Hands. Maybe you heard about that one—it's the one the Pieta decided not to do when she became instead a lawfully wedded woman. I almost expired; the producer's wife left him; he sued the Pieta herself and her husband Sam. But all the publicity that generated put me on the map and got me some work. The tale was amusing enough in its details that producers liked to have me sit in when they needed one more person at more important tables; and some of them, so rarely meeting writers that weren't terminally embittered, actually hired me. I got dizzy at times, thinking how hard I was toiling.

But none of that, nor Saturn's Children, the novel I was now trying to hawk (with no clear success as yet), nor my three day weekend with Amber Stiletto featured in a Them magazine spread (maybe it's because they spelled Adams, my last name, with two "d"s or because I only appeared shortened in the corner of pictures, the legs soaring above Amber in the sand) had ever prompted Irv to get on the phone immediately when I called. For better or worse.

One of the many of my life's little transmutations: all thanks to Dottie. Imagine if she had been interested, in the least, in my overtures. No forget about that. Let's go back to the park, which I did a mere day after I talked to Linda. Someone else lurked there, though I didn't notice him at first, was too immersed in studying Jesse, scrutinizing the lines, the shape of his bone structure. He didn't look like my mother all that often. He didn't have her radiant personality either, though his wild mood swings may have resembled, somewhat, her son's, mine. He was in the sandbox when I arrived, constructing what looked like the Chrysler Building. He employed a small twig to etch on the ascending tower the scalelike lines that ran up the building's face. It was, really, a remarkable likeness.

I went over to tell him so. (I'd been failing at "follows simple instructions" since I was his age). "Hey, Jesse, that building's beautiful," I said.

He didn't even glance my way. "You again?" He grimly asked. "What are you doing here?"

His formerly chubby face looked drawn, almost gaunt. There was, in truth, something ferret-like about the boy. Must have been the other guy's. "I'm a friend of your mom's," I declaimed.

"So's Phil," the kid precociously concluded. "But he's not here every time I come to play."

Did I deserve this? I might have claimed him way back when if I'd been given the chance. Who knows? The kid seemed to think he did. When he grimaced, I walked the three or four feet to the jungle gym and sat on the bottom metal rung beside him. His face looked up at me, a disdainful rictus distorting his otherwise handsome features. "You're not going to cry again, are you?" He wondered. One had the feeling that this was a subject he'd heard discussed at home.

I didn't immediately reply, in fact did my best to avoid a response. As I looked away and around the playground, I saw a photographer, didn't get it, though I felt my eyelids twitch. "You like playing on the jungle gym?" I blithely inquired. "I used to love it."

He looked toward his governess, who glanced tenderly but remonstratively my way. I wasn't supposed to be doing this, talking to him; that's what, I supposed, her reproachful look was designed to make me understand.

Her displeasure, however kindly it was expressed, was probably justified, I thought. There was a wistfulness about her, however, which I found mildly inspiring (had she seen me on the tube? Was I still capable of eliciting more than a maternal response?). I smiled back at her, while Jesse climbed up a level on the bars, from which he couldn't quite pull himself to the next rung. So I helped. I could do this standing, and he let me boost him. Rather distrustfully at first, as if he'd just seen a PSI film on "stranger danger," he didn't resist my good intentions. When he succeeded in putting all his body along the fourth row up, he turned around and surveyed the entire park, before darting a quick look my way.

Though this time I couldn't discern any clear indication that they might derive from my gene pool, I saw his mother's eyes distinctly. They somersaulted me into a deep and gratifying melancholy. Frank and fierce one moment, terrifyingly ingenuous and earnest the next (made you wonder, every time Sarah went to the store, if she'd make it back all right), his mother had eyes which made you understand this: when she was little more than Jesse's age, she'd made three new friends at school. They introduced her to a game, which tested how long during recess each could lie on a wall. Sarah lasted halfway into the next class, when an assistant principal pulled her off the wall and called her parents. The other girls, playing her, had left stealthily after a minute or two.

It was this extraordinarily pure spirit which moved me from the first time I saw her—in the *Jeu du Parme*, in Paris, in the subterranean room where Monet's water lilies float, where every breath, including mine right then, seemed to echo for all to hear. Immediately, I felt like protecting her; but of course, as time went by, if anyone had done the protecting, it had been she sheltering me. I instinctively wanted to do something similar for the short dark kid with the big head, who swung before me on the jungle gym, his eyes firmly if nervously fixed on mine.

Was he mine or not? Did it matter?

Before I could even begin to ruminate further on the matter, the nanny collected her things, her nearly finished version of the Plague, in French, her big carryall with the Galeries Lafayette logo, her two or three wraps. She called to Jesse, and he leapt down from the jungle gym's upper reaches, apparently breaking nothing in the process, to grasp her hand. When he walked past me, he looked at the ground. Nicole the nanny smiled obliquely my way, maybe it's she who was responsible, for five steps past my bench, he shook loose from her hand and came back my way. Nicole stood there smiling proudly when he reached up and offered me his hand. "Au revoir, monsieur," said he, with a shy look as I daintily took his tiny hand in mine.

"Take care, Jesse," I said, a muscle tightening in my throat.

I watched the kid's back as he left; I looked above him at the girl still in her teens with the huge retro Afro; and behind the two of them, I saw Sarah getting out of a taxi on Greenwich street to greet them. Following an old and clearly unforgotten tug, I went her way. Nicole and Jesse were climbing past her into the cab when I reached it.

"Hey," I said.

"Hey," said she, taking me a little to the side, kissing me on both cheeks. "How did it go?"

"I think I survived it," I said, while I noted Jesse peering, somewhat worriedly my way. "I'm not sure about him."

"Oh he's fine, I guarantee it. He's stronger than you are." At least she grinned when she said that.

"I hope so. I went to your doctor's today."

"So I hear," she said. "You are some kind of mess."

"Thanks, I appreciate the encouragement."

"Mama, *viens*," Jesse said from the peanut gallery in the cab. "We've got to go."

"Bye, Jimmie," Sarah said, and before she disappeared into the cab, she reached over and brushed some hairs off the cardigan I was wearing. "I don't mean to be rude. But we're in a hurry."

"We can see each other some other time, perhaps," I ventured. "The other night was…"

"An exception," she said, as she fingered my sweater, buttoning up a button. "The other night was probably a mistake. I knew I shouldn't have." She shook her head and slipped into the cab to sit next to her kid, her eyes all the while continuing to look my way. Was that a wistful look? Or a reproachful glare? Somehow I preferred the former thought. When they waved to me from the cab, I saluted them back, feeling as I did when I was a kid and my parents went off someplace without me: hurt, guilty, abandoned, relieved and surprisingly exhilarated.

"Lucky Guy Still Lovelorn," the caption the next day said, under the pathetic washed out photo. That's right, it took Linda the publicist less than 48 hours to come through for me, if that's what one calls getting me a photo on page 31 of The Star. It was underneath the more important, issue oriented article, "Human Head Kept Alive Six Days—Decapitated Accident Victim Blinked Eyes to Communicate." But there I was, looking as befuddled as George Bush on the White House lawn, Alfred E. Newman. The caption went on to explain my tear-spattered performance on the Dottie Show, but the photo was me, a couple of seconds after Sarah and Jesse's cab evacuated the area.

"How sensitive can you get?" The headline wondered.

"Pretty doggone *sensible*," my friend Jeannie said when we next spoke, going French on me, knowing my proclivity, but not fully realizing perhaps what engendered it. "For a narcissist."

"Great to have you around, just in case there might be a moment there when I was feeling, say, self-satisfied. Just a moment, mind you. Where'd you hear about this?"

"The Sta-ar, where do you think?" Jeannie was the only person I'd ever met with a subscription to the tabloid, to all the tabloids. She had developed three movies whose premises had derived from very close readings of the Star's fantastic offerings. It was the secret to her reputation in Hollywood as an "idea person," a "creative whiz." (You never see truths like this in the Times' discussions of the State of American Film, do you?). "Do you think you could get a publicist to wedge something in there which slipped by me?" She already knew I had a publicist. She was the working definition of savvy, which may have been our problem.

"Not even close."

"That why didn't you call? Out of sight, out of mind, huh?"

"Embarrassment will do that to you."

"Well, it looks to me like you could use a few friends. First you're crying on Dottie. Next, you're mentally disturbed at some park..."

"Jeez, how do you know about that *already*?"

"We've only been going out a year, you remember—people tell me things. Women are like that. Reality checkers."

"Sounds like something you'd find on Fox."

"More like Bravo."

"Has it really been a year?" I wondered, to a sudden silence on the other end of the line.

Let me say a few things in my defense. Even then I wasn't this much of an asshole. Jeannie and I only dated once, at most twice a week. She was too busy cultivating industry "friends" and taking meetings and reading scripts to see me more than that, even if I had wanted to do so, which I did, sometimes. That's the first thing. The second is she was still pining for Jerry, the man she claims she should have married. Jerry, an entertainment lawyer, her lawyer was dating someone off Crossroads, the high school reality show—he claims it's a teacher. Rumor says otherwise. I don't care; but Jeannie still talked to him every day. She only let me forget that when it was convenient, like when I was pulling away.

This time, if I was, I had a good excuse anyway: I'd gone off on my thrilling national book-signing tour. Jeannie and I hadn't spoken since the night before I left L.A., when we had a strained date. I hadn't heard from her since I arrived in NYC either until now, until she'd seen my picture in the tabloid and heard about me from "friends." It's conceivable my desirability was actually enhanced in her eyes, though the prospect's too depressing to contemplate for long. But she did exist on a reality plane occupied frequently by agents, say, my agent.

"What's going on? You okay?" She asked.

I didn't answer swiftly enough. Maybe I deserved this:

"You know, Jim," she continued, "whatever you want to say about The Star, whether you want to sue them for it or decide to just go with the publicity like any sensible person, you know what?"

"What?"

"That photograph of you confused, just not getting it…

"Yeah," I said, encouraging her.

"That's you in a nutshell."

I raced down the street from my hotel, to find the nearest news kiosk with its friendly (and astute) Indian at the helm, and I procured the aforementioned tabloid. The Indian asked me to sign a copy for him, but I was too busy checking out the quality of the picture, the ink (poor, smudgy, bleeding onto my hand before the page was turned) and my appearance (pole-axed, slightly cross-eyed, utterly dismayed). Then too the guy with the 3.5 day beard was disturbed, let's be honest, not just by the photo but by its venue. The Star: couldn't a publicist have done better than that?

"Forget about it," Eric, my agent Irv's Irv, exclaimed when I voiced my concerns to him over the phone. "I've got two new words for you—who would have thought I'd hear them connected to you? CHUCK ALPHABET." His voice jumped up octaves, sounding and more like Irv's. "They want you."

"Chuck Alphabet?" I asked back, incredulous, my voice higher than his. This was a eunuchs' duet, a boys' choir. Chuck was actually someone I watched; locusts swarmed through my chest; they should have been a warning system, I guess, but I just thought the two of us, each equally sardonic and a little smarmy, maybe, would get along famously.

"Yeah, Chuck," Eric said again, knowledgeably. "One of his writers was watching Dottie for some reason when you were on…one of the 3 percent males in her demographic…and he thought you were great, a scream. You don't even have to pre-interview." Hey, that was true celebrity status, wasn't it?

I felt very queasy. You might call it modesty, false modesty; but this was a little ridiculous. A trade book? Me nobody special ("Sure you are, you are special," Eric tried to reinsure me, sounding like an elementary school teacher teaching "self-esteem"). I don't know. Something's funny here."

"What?" Eric screamed.

Clicks popped on the line as if I were Martin Luther King, Dennis Kucinich, anybody opposing whichever war we're now waging. But it was only Eric's mentor, my main man Irv. "Chuck Alphabet, Jimmy," Irv began paternally, in a voice which would come to sound ever more like George Steinbrenner's at his most psychotic. "So he pokes a little fun at you. You're a mensch, you can take it."

"Since when?" I asked him. "You do know who you're talking to, right?"

"Right. A client, a favorite client, one of them, who's smart enough to know we're NOT TALKING AFTERNOON SHOWS FOR WOMEN ONLY. We're talking the major leagues of late night. You're too old to hold out, to get squeamish, you know what I fucking mean?"

I did. I understood. You do a "trade book"—"something frivolous, just for once," as Irv had insisted, and they own you for life. It's the literary equivalent of doing your borrowing from a loan shark. No way you can ever pay them back. They own you.

And then deep down (okay, not all that deep down), I was too vain to ask any questions. Maybe that's why Irv had suffered with me all those years. My 11th grade History teacher had warned me about it, in my high school yearbook. "Listen to your inner self," she'd written. "Beware the yapping of the pack."

But, unfortunately, my self was so atwitter that it sounded like an entire platoon firing. Irv told me, "Not to worry. I'll take care of it"— whatever the "it" was. And so, I said, yes, of course. I'm down with it (down where?).

Chuck Alphabet: I bought myself a new pair of blue jeans, suitably faded, to go under my suit top, an overpriced tee to accentuate my difference from the host with his goofy ties. I can barely remember what happened the rest of the early afternoon; I think I ate, though being famished may explain my behavior better. And at 2:30 in the afternoon, I found myself about to go on Night Time with Chuck Alphabet.

As you know, Chuck first sticks you into his "green room" which, he likes to note, is a soiled white. Generally, a guest squirms back there until it's his or her time; (s)he eats the bad food and gets revved up by an agent, a publicist's flattery until the music calls and (s)he's tossed out like chub to Chuck. Though I was told it would work that way this day/night, it didn't exactly.

On the monitor Chuck, after his lengthy monologue and his two or three standard shticks, said, "As you know here on the Alphabet show, we pick a letter every once in a while and we do something with it. Tonight, we're up to 'S' and we're getting tired of doing 'Sardonic' and 'Sick' and 'Sadistic', all those 'S's you know and love us for. So we thought we'd do something different."

He picked up a hand mike and exited the set, followed by his cameras. "Tonight, we're going to go back into the bowels of our networks, and bowels is the right word when you consider the shows they've been putting out this year…and we're going to take a visit to Chuck's Temple of Truth and Tears."

The man was hurtling down the corridors, until the door to the green room opened and he entered with a manic smile. "Tonight it's S for Sensitive!" He chuckled dementedly.

The guy, in fact, was pretty frightening looking. The color of his "toupee," a kind of sophisticated copper didn't match the bright red of the real hair which trickled around it; and his teeth were twice the size of most mortal's. Looking at him was like looking a pit bull in the mouth: you knew, even I knew, immediately that there was no way to get out of there without being eaten, without having a big bite taken out of whatever self-respect you had spent a lifetime mustering.

"James, I want you to know we men are real darn proud of you," Chuck said, his famously insincere grin making him look like an albino Barney hitting middle age. He was speaking quickly, almost unintelligibly, about fifteen or twenty rpms over your norm, sounded like he was going 90 rpms on a 45 turn table. Dogs could hear him. "We're in your camp, on your team, buddy. We know you're going to out emote that Ursula Anne Platinum."

"What? Ursula Anne Platinum?" The woman had sold about 150 million books, all predicated on man's callous inhumanity to women. She was sponsored by a company fabricating drops for Red Eyes, Visine or something. My own metabolism raced upwards, as if I'd ingested half a pound of pure sea salt, as I realized that Chuck's eruption into the green room wasn't spontaneous. This was why I wasn't pre-interviewed.

"Ursula's the other contestant here in our sensitivity battle," Chuck explained, ever so graciously. His eyes didn't pause a minute on mine. Give him some credit for embarrassment, I suppose. "We're calling it the 'Great

Tear-off.' I know it's a tough challenge, but all of America's men, or at least those that don't know how to ride a real horse, all our urban armies of maladjusted males are counting on you to shed that first tear..."

"Tear? Uh tear-what?" I repeated, dumbly.

"Tear-off," he explained. "Now just to show you folks out there that we run an honest outfit—this entire contest will be conducted under the eagle eye of our referee Julius 'Julie' Guardino. He'll be making sure there's no cheating here, no special substances, no thumbing of the eyes— as he does, regularly, refereeing fights in Atlantic City, Julie..."

Out came a pug with oversized glasses and skin the color of Kaopectate. "Thank you, Chuck," Julie said. "Yes, my years as a drug abuse counselor and ring side second to various losers of championship belts have given me the training to see who's tearing up and who's just scared s-less— what's a real tear and what's mere flimflam."

"We're sure of that, Julie," Chuck said condescendingly. "But though you are the ref here, I'm going to help the guy out. He's one of us or he would be any way with a little more Viagra. And fixing these fights is something real men know how to do, right Julie? So, Jim, just to give you a head start, I want you to ponder this..." He raised his cue card and looked at the monitor rather than me. He was sweating profusely, as of course I was too. No wonder Chuck always looks like a stroke victim to come, no wonder he keeps the temperature in the place at around 45 degrees.

He gave me a card with a yellow dog on it, and the cameras focused in on the pooch. "It's Old Yeller himself, recognize him? Every boy's favorite canine friend, pictured just seconds before he bought it. Brings tears to my eyes just remembering. Close your eyes, Jim, and think what a tragedy Old Yeller's death was to all of us in this great country of ours. Now if that won't bring a tear to the eye, you have to be as heartless as

Sister Teresa…maybe that makes no sense, okay, but while James is working on his emoting, we'll take time off and go over to talk to our other contestant on 'Sensitivity' Day, Ursula Anne Platinum. This is really darn exciting. Who's going to give us the first tears here in Chuck's Temple of Truth and Tears? The big moment is almost upon us."

He left, a plethora of technicians trailing him out like mangy bread crumbs—I knew he would be back. To my right, I saw a monitor on which Chuck was now interviewing someone purporting to be Ursula Platinum. He was holding up one of her dozens of mega-selling romance novels; and then one of his minions was dispatched to bring a copy to me.

This was the deal, as Chuck explained to Ursula. "What we thought we'd do, just to make this interesting, we're giving Ursula a copy of *Luck for the Lovelorn*, a man's guide to something or other; and we're giving our friend James a copy of Ursula's best selling *Love Potions.* You see the two contestants here on split screens. Now we're going to let them go ahead and just read and the first full-blown tears we get—now we're not talking misty eyes, we're talking honest to Goodness pathetically sniveling drops—whoever gives them to us first is going to win a very handsome prize. Okay, on your mark, let's go."

Everything shut down except for one camera and some mood music left over from a morning game show. Julie wandered in and out of my room, "refereeing," checking for "illegal substances." Fifteen or twenty staff faces peered snottily at me. I was a gibbon in Chuck's little zoo. I was offended, but the weird thing is, you have to understand me, some part of me wanted to cry not because I felt ridiculous and absurdly sorry for myself, no, but because this was a contest—and that's what was required to win. That's right. I'm a competitive guy; every competition punches my sick buttons.

Only simultaneously there was this other instinct, an anti-authoritarian bent *chez moi*, which didn't want to please, which absolutely wanted to frustrate anyone who insisted I do anything. My old man gave me both, the need, the obsession to win and the ambivalence, the longing to lose. My old man, was he watching? My face heated up at the thought; I could feel tears there of anger and shame boiling up to my surface.

A method actor, I looked down now at Ursula's book, seeking to place my great sadness on the page. Only I couldn't read a word; not one would stay on the page. They just slid off like rocks over water. I guessed Ursula was experiencing the same ambivalence. Wasn't that the American paradox? Hadn't she too probably been frequently trotted out before dinner to entertain her father's boss with panegyrics to the "American Free Enterprise System" before enough Scotch made the exercise a matter of supreme indifference, absolutely moot? Had she, obedient pre-pubescent, delivered the discourse, watched the affectionate and pleased response of the boss' wife, a weird twinkle in her eye, saying "wow, this is one brilliant kid you've produced here, where'd you learn all that?"--only to chime in with "I didn't learn it at all. I don't have a clue. Dad made me memorize the whole thing"?

The answer was a resounding, "No, half-wit!"

Ursula Anne Platinum had surely repeated the discourse twice, backwards and forwards, smiled shyly and demurely, then retired sweetly to her room where she put a new gold trinket on her charm bracelet just as Ursula right then was handing me my lunch in the "Tear-off."

Yes, while I was feeling foolish, wondering how I could have debased my potentially National Book Award winning self, Ursula was shedding shot glass after shot glass worth of tears. Finally a bell went off; my make-up girl flipped me her towel; the red light flashed once more in the camera in front of me, and then disappeared forever. The assorted technicians and ever-snide writing staff all rushed Ursula's way, while Chuck hastened back to join them.

"There it is, folks," Chuck said, "the definitive test. Science shows once again that this sensitive male stuff is just so much public relations nonsense. When it comes to feelings, there's nothing like a female, right?" The audience booed, but Chuck continued on. "It's not my opinion. You saw it here…now Ursula that was just an amazing performance. Could you come out front with us…you can? Great!"

The weird thing about embarrassing yourself in public is that a substantial part of the public you know doesn't notice, doesn't think you're making a fool of yourself at all. Like me, most of my friends seemed so dazzled by my appearance on the tube that they altogether missed out on the content of the stunt. They stubbornly saw me, the friend, up there, not the dingbat trying hard to cry—and failing at that.

There were a few discerning eyes, however. Jeannie called to say she was happy to see me confronting, for a change, my "competitiveness." This woman had me down pat, though she may not quite have approved of what she found there—one of the many reasons why, probably, she kept me at arm's length, though here I heard her surprisingly say this, "I think I'm going to be in New York soon."

"Oh, good."

"Does it scare you that much? I've got work to do, agents to talk to…though the fact is you do need some help."

She was right, but I preferred keeping the conversation brief; we did better when we kept our grievances sheathed. "I'll be happy to see you," I said. "You can stay here if you want."

"Luckily I don't need to," she said and laughed. "The studio is sending me. They can afford a hotel of their own."

I laughed too, happy at the thought of seeing her. Jeannie was feisty, and I was confused. The two were for me a strongly erotic combination.

Then too, as I've previously noted, she preferred her friend the lawyer, Jerry, and that kind of distancing was exciting to an insecure guy like me. It explained my inconsistency with her, like hers to me, allowing me to move toward her then drift back, slightly rebuffed, into a hollow spot inside myself, a certain melancholy that I didn't often name but would have called, if pushed, Sarah. (Jeannie, however, never pushed). The girl, you may remember, who walked away from me down Lafayette Street, many years before.

Sarah called right after Jeannie and I hung up, as if she'd overheard our exchange. I felt guilty, just out of habit, though she quickly gave me better reasons for my chagrin. She didn't like the Chuck Alphabet performance. "How could you let them talk you into that?" She asked, irritated and angry for me. "All of it—the book, the shows, the Alphabet debacle, how could you, Jimmy?"

"I took my agent's advice, okay. I wasn't supposed to be on any 'tear-off'—just the biggest gig of this east coast swing. Keeping me here to do more of these, that was the point which, given everything, I thought you might understand--this is something I need to do right now."

I heard nothing from her end of the wire—the dead space between two heartbeats.

"You know," she said, "the thing that worries me is the book's pretty good for what it is. I think it's making it not because of your crying on the shows, not because of any of the PR; it's making it because, for its kind, it's a very good book. Actually is about something maybe more important than you think. And, just as you always used to say, it's just as difficult writing a best seller as writing serious literature. The people who succeed at it aren't simple sell-outs; they are people with different ambitions. They are very good at writing pulp fiction, summer reading, what have you. That's their talent. Maybe writing this kind of book is yours…"

Thanks, Sarah. And Brad Pitt is really Laurence Olivier reincarnated. I thought of Jeannie and her large round burgundy nipples, the kind I'd liked looking at in magazines when I was a kid. Were my mom's like that?

"It's just show business, Sarah," I articulated as clearly as I could. If my mind had come on hinges, I would have unscrewed it and put the cerebrum over to the side.

"Who would have thought you'd get so involved in it?" She responded.

Jeannie had a stomach, which seemed the exact definition of "tummy," a tight protrusion, just a little round. Now I seemed to miss it. Isn't pain the beginning of delusion, of denial?

"Why are you saying this to me now, Sarah?" I asked, when my mind stumbled back her way. "Couldn't this wait?"

"I've been worried about you."

"Gee thanks. Just find out if the kid's mine."

"I don't know if I want to know," she said after a minute's pause.

I put the telephone receiver down on the floor—then spun it. The trees outside looked particularly lifeless—no leaves there, nothing green sticking into this room.

"Me either, actually."

73

This took her aback for an instant. "I can't be honest any more with you?" She asked, in a little voice. The tinny sounds vied with the room's phthisic radiator for my attention.

Honesty was never all that good an idea really in our family—it was always an excuse for a paternal reproof. I preferred, almost always, illusion to any hard truths.

She'd forgotten. "I hope I can be frank...because when you can't confide in someone, it's really all over," she opined. She took a deep breath. Sarah was distraught, I finally understood. Was it my fault, really? I didn't think so, but it didn't matter. Her intent, her mood, her voice on the phone suddenly came in very sharply, audibly, loud and clear. "Are you all right, Sarah?" I asked, finally starting to glean that there was more going on than a commentary on my "performance."

"No, not really. Things just don't work out. Nothing happens like you plan...oh, I'm such a baby. I should be happy now. I'm so lucky. I have no right to be crying like this."

In the glass the cold morning outside formed for me I saw nothing but our distorted reflections, both of us fresh, her face as pure as a fawn's. When I'd first met her, her dad had been dying, right at his end. She'd come to my zero starred hotel to visit me after guiding twenty tourists around gay Paris, then spending the rest of the day in St. Cloud, at her father's side in the American hospital. I imagined that I was giving her strength and support, that I was taking care of her. I thought I knew then what I was feeling again this day—how easily Sarah could be hurt, how much I wanted to protect her from any other pain, from the long agony of her dad's death.

A dad's death. "I'm sorry, Jimmie, this is embarrassing," she said. She was angry with herself, but her distress pushed all of my buttons. "What's the matter?" I inquired. "Are you and Phillip..."

"Yes. We're not getting along. He's trying, but in reality, he can't stand this, that I'm doing something independent of him, of our work together...and I can't seem to make him feel better about it. I don't even know if I want to..."

I heard a call waiting click on Sarah's end of the line. "You won't get mad at me if I take this, will you?" She wondered nervously. I hesitated. "You won't feel too sorry for yourself if I leave you for a second?"

"No...well, of course I will. But I like the feeling. I'll try to forgive you."

She giggled. "Promise?" The voice was already slightly different, sweet still but more composed. When she returned to the line, she had another tone entirely. "It's my agent. She says she has a lot to tell me. I thought she'd forgotten I was a client. You don't mind?"

As if I could argue with that. But she hadn't quite finished with me anyway. "Thanks, Jimmie—you're still my ticket"(my tee-kay, as the French say, about hot tickets, Lottery tickets, good luck, loves). Once, three months after we'd known each other and a month and a half after we'd moved in together, we'd put more money than we could afford on a rash of lottery tickets—a drunken idea at 3:45 a.m. coming out of a bar and seeing the lights of a café tabac and we'd won 10,000 francs, *une brique,* months worth of our then frugal living. How I missed that time. Does love ever get so sweet again?

"Did you hear me?" Sarah inquired.

"Actually I was thinking of the lottery ticket we won...is that what you were talking about?" I had faintly heard her continue speaking, just missed the words themselves.

"Uh, no."

"Oh sorry, what were you saying then?"

"Nothing much. Phillip and I are going to break up." Did I hear that right? Many volts of electricity shot up my right arm, down my side, and buried themselves in my stomach. Her voice was so anguished, though.

"I've got to go," she said. "Don't worry. It's okay, Jimmie. Jessie is fine too." Then she paused before continuing. "I'm going to take him in to the doc's. You know, I'm just afraid he's not yours. That's my only fear."

"Huh," I managed. "What was that? Would you repeat that?" But she had hung up, history to me (again). I looked around the empty room, the dead phone in my hand. Eventually that annoying warning blast appeared, but I didn't recognize it at first. I felt elsewhere, tripping again, a flashback with me and my friend CJ in the tower room at college at midnight; CJ was playing the organ, his foot down on the stops, letting it up slowly when, suddenly, amazingly, the sound changed. Every one of the school's hundred bells, just a couple of feet above us, started ringing out Brahms. I felt as if a real sea had just roared through my shell.

These things come in waves, like troops invading beaches, brain cells blowing out like bodies in front of machine gun nests. No sooner had I put the phone down into its white plastic cradle than it rang again. I wasn't very certain that I wanted to answer, but the phone kept ringing.

I finally picked it up, to hear my mom and thereafter her husband, my dad. They too had seen the show, and they had slightly different reactions. My mom—this was the Official Mom, my father's wife—had liked it: "just your cousins and aunts and uncles alone must have doubled Dottie's ratings in Texas (and Lord knows she needs help there)," she said. She'd called them all, only to see her son participate in a "tear-off." "Pretty funny," she said, "but you know, I'm not sure that Alphabet boy, Chuck Alphabet, likes women all that much."

"You think he liked me more?"

"Well, he seemed to *sympathize* with you anyway. I expect he's known for being something of a smart aleck (though he's always pretty nice to dogs)," she observed. "But with Miss Platinum, he was really odious. It's hard to see how someone that insecure about himself is doing interviews for a living."

"Actually he's a comic."

There was another click on the line; and E.V.D. Adams (Eugene V. Debs Adams, his first names unused, unknown since his high school days, after which time, an ambitious guy in a conservative state, he'd dropped everything but the initials—to everyone but his wife who called him Gene and one army friend who called him "Debs" anyway, just to annoy him) entered into the conversation with a clearing of his throat. "Didn't seem very damn funny to me," my old man said.

This wasn't surprising. Little, at this point in his life, amused Dad; his days were often focused on the dwindling amount of oxygen circulating through his lungs. After a lifetime of continuous, obsessive work, he was resentful of this physical debility, this somaticizing—if I might say so—of his inability to relax.

"I don't know," I said. "Chuck's pretty funny sometimes, like the snidest guy in your sophomore class." I think I thought I had been that guy in my class.

"I don't mean Mr. Alphabet,' my dad said. "I mean the whole show...I didn't find it very funny."

The man had come out of the womb bristling. What made me think I could appease him, in any way?

"Oh, Gene," my mom said. "It was just a TV Talk Show; they're not supposed to be serious." Did I hear the tinkle of ice cubes in my mom's hand? Where'd the bravery come from otherwise?

I leaned back against one of the two sofas in the living area. It was blue velvet and camel backed. Across from me was a mirrored wall—and in it, I saw a head a little bit too big for its frame, mine, in the middle of which, toward the left part of the forehead, there was a large blue blood vessel coiled like a snake, which kept pulsating ominously throughout the conversation.

"I know that, Eve," my father said. "I was happy he got the 'exposure.' I'm not totally naïve about the way these things work..." ("Not totally" was true: since I'd gotten into show business, he'd never missed an Entertainment Tonight, even if it was background music to his toiling over a drilling contract). "I just always figured writing was a more dignified profession that that."

"Tell your son how much you love him," my mom said. "I'll get off here so you can do it in private. It won't embarrass you that way." I wanted to join her in another drink, to let the old man, as was his wont anyway, hold both ends of the conversation. "You were fine, Jimmie," she concluded conciliatorily, sensing her husband's difficulties restraining himself for a couple of seconds more. I thought I could hear him breathing back there, trying to take another breath, maybe finding it and holding it— he'd taught himself a new and different way to breathe since he'd contracted emphysema). "Wonderful—it was too silly a contest to win anyway…" And there she went, hanging up.

"I don't know about that," my dad said. "What's the point of entering if you're not going to win?"

"I didn't 'enter,' Dad. I was hoodwinked into it."

"Tell yourself whatever you want to, but it was the winner who got the interview afterwards. That was the point of going on there in the first place, wasn't it?"

He coughed and so did I, most of my available air knocked out of me. But, relentlessly, he continued, "Why didn't you go ahead and cry? You'd think it was hard for you."

When I was eight years old and batting second for the Blue Sox (a name I'd found in a John Tunis book), I struck out exactly twice during the season. I don't remember the first time, but I still recall the second. We were playing the Wright Flyers, and I whiffed in the clutch, stranding a runner on third. Thereafter things got blurred as, crestfallen, I meandered down the third base found line and, yes, began to cry.

Afterward, in the car going home, my old man, who'd been dramatically silent even since I'd fanned, finally interrupted my mother's encouragement of my friend Greg's game, just as we eased up to his house (but before Greg actually left the car). "Men," my dad opined, "men don't cry, Jim. Not in public...I've never been so damn ashamed. Crying over a strike-out! Jesus, son." His eyes faced the real world outside, a grim place to which, he'd frequently assured me, I was going to have trouble adapting. He shook his head with irritation. My mom gave him a look of dismay.

Greg, paralyzed for a moment, hurriedly made his exit in that instant of quiet. Before the door slammed, however, my dad continued his cogitations. "I don't know how many times I've told you, though. I don't even know why I bother...but if you would just keep your eye on the ball, you'd never strike under the thing. Your shoulders weren't squared up either..."

"But, Gene," my mother interrupted. "Jimmie got three other hits."

"And cried about the strike-out. If he'd just square up the ball with his right hand, he wouldn't embarrass himself or us!"

Did I bawl then? Did I scream?

Probably not, anymore than I was doing now, when the old man, after he told me how silly I looked on the show, decided to explore, Lee Strasberg-like, the motivations I could have given myself to prick more than an extra tear or two. "You could have thought of your grandfather—I thought his death might have meant something to you." My mind was like an egg after a quarter hour of boiling, the shell fissuring right and left. "You could have thought of your own pop too, you know I don't have enough breath left in me to blow out a candle." He coughed again.

My mouth was open, but no word got through the line, over to my dad. Thoughts inflated like gum bubbles, then popped. I couldn't figure out a response, any approach to the multiple layers of accusation, the load of warheads launched my way. The silence didn't bother my dad: "I hope that the damn thing was good for you anyway—that Platinum woman certainly doesn't need the extra money. What did your buddy Chuck Alphabet say, she's sold how many million books—fifteen, twenty?"

"Hey, Dad, basta. Enough, okay?" I said.

Did he hear me? "Of course," he continued. "She only writes trash; your mother has a couple—nothing as serious as you used to attempt."

I was out for the count, but he was still punching. "Hey, this is your son over here. Let up a little." Why I thought he would, after all that time, still surprises me.

"Huh?" He said, a momentary halt in the castigations to come. He wasn't going to wind up rapidly; but, fortunately, his watch alarm rang. This seemed to deflect him from more analysis of my books, about which he'd once delivered the unforgettable, "I've always figured you were 'getting some,' Jim, but do I really have to learn all the details?"

I'd responded, "it's fiction, Dad, fiction. I invent this stuff." And he had retorted, "I'm sure of it. I can't believe a girl like Sarah would indulge in any of that."

His watch alarm rang a second time. You could hear a wheeze. "Are you okay?" I wondered, feeling guilty about depriving him of more air; I couldn't help myself.

"It's been a long time since I've been okay," he said, his voice turning suddenly lugubrious, heavy as a cock's wattle, wagging. Self-pity ran in the family, I had to note. "It's for my pills," he continued. "I've got to take them every 22 minutes now." 22, exactly: "I get this thing to ring off

90 seconds before…gives me the time to get the water." There was my dad, the organizer, the line producer.

"Eve," he went on, "Do you want to say anything else?" He continued, when she didn't answer immediately, having forgotten she'd left the phone many minutes before. "I'm going to go now," he said, before confiding, "but, you know, we were glad to hear you got to see Sarah again." The very mention of her name made his voice leap.

And he left the line, leaving me to feel like a diving board just leapt off, vibrating up and down with an audible hum.

After a second's thought, I decided I'd communicated enough for one day. I unplugged the phone.

My dad and Sarah were saying more or less the same thing. Maybe they were right, I concluded after I'd given myself the time to think about it. Both of them intimated that I might be well advised to cogitate on a few more serious matters than my six minutes of relative notoriety. The wheel, mine, was turning, even if I decided to stay in one place, New York City, a little longer.

I called our old landlord in Nolita/Little Italy, guessing correctly that he still had the pied a terre that he rented, illegally, by the week or the month in his rent-stabilized complex. He made more in a month from this one bedroom tenement with the floors slanting up at 30 plus degree angles than he made in a year off most of the other apartments. At least the view was fine and verdant, of the church across the street and its flourishing courtyard.

On the way to Joe's, I called Irv, didn't get him, got Irv's Irv, Eric, and told him I wanted to take some time off the hype circuit; I was feeling like a hamster. Eric wasn't sympathetic. Here's how he responded to that in his smooth, preternaturally calm, quasi-psychotic voice: "I think that's not a very good idea, James. Irv's in conference now; but I, well, I'm not even going to tell him about this when he gets out."

"Eric, it's my career, man."

"You think so, really?" He replied, with a deep and knowing sigh--
that as much an Irvism as the following: "you're not going to flake out on
us, are you?"

"Only temporarily," said I, and after fighting and losing the battle
to keep my privacy—the guy started screaming and didn't stop until I gave
him my new address, this the secret of his future negotiating success—I
took refuge across from the church in that apartment whose crooked rooms
seemed appropriate to my own current sensibility.

Less than 24 hours later, the metal door which, triple-bolted,
protected me from the outside world, was pummeled again and again. I was
in Little Italy, you recall, not exactly the place where you remain calm when
someone's pounding on your door. My adrenalin level was high enough to
cause individual muscles I didn't know I had—a spot on the forehead,
another in the inside right thigh—to sound off like boot camp recruits.

"Who's there?" I called through the door.

"America, Max, crying out for you."

Relieved, I grinned, unlocked the door and opened it to CJ, one of
my oldest friends. Unfortunately, C wasn't alone. He led an altogether too
large cross-section of our great country into my sublet living room.

"Actually, it's US magazine," C said with a shame-faced grin as
six guys and two woman, all business, lugged a studio's worth of
photographic paraphernalia past me and began to unplug the lamps, move
the furniture, set up tripods and lights. "Meet Linda, your publicist. She's
the one who set this up for us."

"Us?" I inquired, as a slightly horsy, very blonde woman with too
many teeth and an absolutely lascivious smile extended her hand. How
could I refuse it?

"Yep, you and your former college chum C.J. 'Clement' Jones," he
said with a guilty look, though it's not clear that guilt had ever entered any
of C.J.'s emotional equations. "Linda called—and I figured, sure, for Max,
I'll do anything. Even come back to the city." He was the only person in the
world who called me Max—"such a goy for a Max," he liked to say.

"We're looking to get a feeling for you, James," the other woman,
Helen explained. "You at home, with your friends…the other parts of your
life, what makes you as sensitive as you are." She was short and dark and
looked rather like a very attractive chow. While she talked, she began taking
down the pictures in the room, she and Linda putting up posters of Javier
Bardem, Ingmar Bergman, Ingrid Bergman.

"Your over-all ambience," said she, by way of explanation.

"I think there's a communication problem," I began.

"Yes, sirree Bob. US was difficult to get," Linda explained, "but I
managed to convince them they had to do something on you."

"Women love you there too," Helen said.

"Oh yeah, why don't they show it more often?" I said, only mildly
fighting the flattery now.

A man identified as " Mel," small, grimacing like a neglected Shar
Pei, one of those guys who make New York the great place it is, held a light
up to C, then momentarily blinded me with it.

"Women," Linda explained to me, "like a man who can cry." The
idea, while appealing, wasn't altogether convincing: Linda herself, for
instance, had eyes only for my friend CJ, though this wasn't unusual. Girls
used to call CJ at school when we were freshmen, just off his yearbook
picture. Tall, lean, ridiculously handsome, CJ had blue eyes which gleamed
out of a face which was always tan, seemingly fabricated from some new,
better brand of skin.

This day, however, those iridescent eyes kept darting away from my frequent, questioning glances. "C, what is this?" I finally had to ask. "I told them I was retiring from this. I don't care if the book sells or not."

"Don't give me that, Max," he said, and his large hand pulled me to the side by the elbow. "Look, Menshkevic's finally forgiving me...he may be giving me my chance. I need this, guy."

There were a couple of things involved here: first, C had the totally delusional sense that his failure to make it as a TV actor, his inability even to get a pilot picked up, was related to Jeff Menshkevic, the president of NBC's not getting tapped into a secret society that C had been a member of. It's more likely, though, that Menshkevic had viewed C's work. A jinx was not working on him. He'd been in five pilots, every one of which was, as he liked to say, "no worse than all the rest of the crap on the tube"; and it's true, his good looks and slightly lopsided grin made him the perfect cop. All five had expired with their pilots; and the only series he glommed onto for a minute ended with him. His character may have been personally responsible for its demise. Maybe you saw it, The White City Roughnecks; C was the goalie who came out of the hospital for the Roughnecks championship game against some Canadian team. He played two whole periods attached to a colostomy bag. When the inevitable collision came with a deranged Ukrainian penalty killer and stick man, the resulting explosion sent millions upon millions of American hands reaching for their remotes. You could hear that clicking of channels turning far, far away.

It wasn't C's fault, though. He hadn't written the show. I think. "Give it up, C," I said again, referring to his faint hopes of getting on the great American money machine. "You and I'll produce something when I get back."

An assistant to Mel put a light meter up against my skin. When I turned and tried to brush him away, I noticed that C had also turned, professionally offering the man his cheek—was that make-up on it I saw?

"We're giving you four, six pages, we think, if they come out right," Helen explained to me, as Linda lovingly arranged C's shirt collar. I got the feeling they were prior acquaintances. She looked on as a make-up person touched up his tan.

"It's me or Bob Reflex," C said, as the flashbulbs began to pop around us (mostly him). "He had his chance and opted for politics until he… lost badly. Got drilled in the primary by 15 points. Tried to be be a Democrat in Kentucky. Gotta be my turn now."

"Hold that. Fine. I like that, Clem," Mel yelled, and his camera whirred wildly like a helicopter over Baghdad. "Go over to him now, Jim, would you? And give him a book."

Linda put something into my hand. It wasn't even my book. It was something called, "How to Make Love to a Man." They hadn't even bothered to buy a copy of my opus.

"This isn't what we're here for," I ventured. "I don't know about this."

"Of course not. You never do, Max," C said with a grin.

"Nobody ever looks that closely at these pictures," Linda offered. She turned the book over.

So hey, thought I, fuck it. Why fight it? Maybe, probably I just didn't like being shot next to my handsome and well-burnished friend. It was tough on guys like me to be juxtaposed to someone like CJ. However charming we could sometimes be imagined in the abstract—even pretty good looking really, we might think—it was different standing there "reading to his good friend CJ 'Clement' Jones," as US said later. All eyes unequivocally went his way, bringing more humility into the day than any author, even one of a trade book, could easily accommodate.

And then it got worse: the doorbell rang; someone opened the door; and another visitor was announced--a woman who found the situation pretty amusing. She looked at the book in my hand and laughed heartily. My friend Jeannie smirked at me from across the room.

"Fuck you," I mouthed back, and the camera went off, recording my obscene remark and my lopsided smile. CJ, though, looked like a million, got 1543 cards off it from teen-age girls in Texas alone.

"Were you two on the same plane, tell me?" I asked when an assistant began to reload Mel's camera. "Jeannie, you were in on this, right? I'm sure Helen's happy you're here."

C smiled. "Yeah, as a matter of fact, we did travel together—though she was in business."

"I'm passing on the photo, though," Jeannie said. "But thanks for the opportunity."

"What are you doing here then?" I asked. I wasn't thinking very clearly.

"I came on business. We spoke two days ago about it, or don't you remember?" She seemed genuinely curious. I was puzzled. "Jim, you're getting flakier by the minute."

Here, everyone nodded; and Mel's automatic motor caught my dumbfounded look once again, right before it whirled to a stop. That was it. "Thanks, everybody," Helen said. "We'll meet you at the park in let's see...35 minutes, at exactly 3:15."

"Nice to see you," I said to Jeannie, a couple of minutes later, after she and CJ had embraced one another, a little too fondly for the paranoid eye. "I just hadn't figured you'd be here so soon." Her truce with CJ was even less easy than Jeannie's and mine—he was too handsome; it made her nervous, which was fine, really, right in sync with the general mood. I was paranoid as a ferret on speed, myself. Something was happening here, and I didn't know what it was, did I? Maybe just CJ's presence made me feel as if I were tripping once again, college having been the place where, in C's memorable words, "we'd competed to see who could burn out he most brain cells—a San Francisco Fire of the Mind."

"I get the feeling you wish I'd called first before coming," Jeannie said.

I nodded. I was that obvious, that easily read. "Well, we're a little busy," I tried. "I mean, I'm happy to have you here to snicker at me, to revel in my foolishness…"

"Oh, let's not exaggerate the uniqueness of the opportunity."

"Right," I said. "It's pretty much a daily occurrence."

She warmed up at this particular truth. "I tried to call, to be honest," said she. "But your phone was unplugged. So I called Irv—he said I could find you here."

"Irv? You got right through?"

"Why not?"

"Well, it's taken me 3 years to do the same, and I'm his client."

"I've known him since I was 16. He's a third or fourth cousin of my dad. They used to go to the track together when they were young."

Hard to believe, but of course, the entertainment business being the cradle—and the charnel house—of nepotism, the last great repository after politics, she and Irv would have known each other. And even if they hadn't shared a relative, she worked for the studio; I was merely talent; all the power and permanence resided with the former. Any sane person would have understood their deeper connection, but I wasn't a sane person. I was thinking like a prisoner of war. "C, did Irv set this up? Is that what you're doing here?"

We were walking down five flights of stairs. C was in high spirits, Linda too. She had her large, fine, bejeweled fingers around his right arm. "Can we save this for later, Max?" My buddy replied. "You're doing fine so far. Let's just wait 'til after the park to deconstruct the fun."

"The park? What park?" I was so far behind the eight ball it looked like a granite wall.

"We want to get a picture of you in all your different venues, your contexts," explained Linda, somewhat disinterestedly, as we got into a car and headed west.

"But I don't go to the park," I said, referring to Central Park, of course, one of New York's greater wonders, a green treasure in this steel grey city.

There was a pause, our silver Volvo with the tinted windows turned left on Varick, turned south toward Canal, and I began to get the bigger picture. Central Park's nowhere near where we were headed. We passed Grand, passed Canal, and overtook a couple of mounted policemen venturing from their North Moore Street stables. We glided by the Odeon, still extant after all these years; then we took a right on Chambers. We weren't going to Battery Park, as I might have hoped, for a view of the water or the Manhattan picture postcard Wall Street skyline in the background. We weren't going to Brooklyn Heights either.

"How the fuck could you do this to me, C?" I shrieked. C had made, like most actors, a final choice between career and friendship. Amity hadn't made the cut. "Jesus, man, what were you thinking?"

"I didn't know Jeannie would be here," C said, as if that were the issue. He couldn't suppress a shit-faced grin, as if he'd just swallowed most of Linda's breast. "I thought this would be good for us, all of us."

"All?" Jeannie asked.

"All? What do you mean? Who else are you talking about exactly?" Pressure increased dramatically behind my corneas. My optic nerve felt like a golf ball, just as it begins to slice.

Right in front of our sleek vehicle was Independence Plaza, the Tribeca park where I'd recently spent many of my afternoons spying on a chubby kid who may or may not have been my son. Needless to say, Jeannie hadn't heard anything about the little guy, my possible little guy. Somehow I'd forgotten to talk to her about him when we spoke.

Didn't mention either that Sarah told me she and Phil were a dissolving couple. Didn't tell Sarah about Jeannie either.

Then there we were, sure enough, rolling past the newest new age food emporium, to the neat little park floating on landfill. People piled out of the cars, Linda, C, Jeannie, a couple of assistants. You could see them outside through the tinted glass. It looked cold out there. I wasn't moving.

C's face was the first back inside. "Leave the kid out of this," I whispered gruffly. "How could you, man? Who knows whose he is?"

91

C put a hand reassuringly on my arm, as Jeannie looked perplexedly my way, through the dirty windshield.

"I can't even sign the release for him," I tried. "You'll have to get that from Sarah—and good luck!" This was a last ditch effort, the mind still twitching when the head had already been cut off.

C and Sarah had also known each other for a long time. He'd been our first houseguest when we lived on the rue Malebranche. After 24 hours, Sarah became convinced that he was the original man who came to dinner. Maybe she too found him overly attractive: she found him a nearby hotel before that first meal was finished. They do those things in France; they know how to handle trouble—very discreetly. But C hadn't been pleased. Maybe this was a late payback for my lack of support. Here's how he expressed it: "We actors are sluts, Max, tramps. We'll do anything for..."

"...The exposure," I said snidely.

"You were great on Chuckie Alphabet," he responded, with too wise a smile. "I've already told you...now you just have to follow through on the opportunity."

His overly bright eyes gleamed and flickered over my shoulder. With that sickening feeling in the viscera which almost always accompanies unwelcome knowledge, I turned my head, sensing what he was seeing. Just inside the elaborate black fencing, nattily attired in a black and white print blouse over threadbare jeans with stylish silver studs holding the denim together was the co-star of The Public Theater's latest production, you guessed it too, make-up in place, her short hair now spiked, just out for a simple stroll with her Guadalupan nanny and her handsome young son.

Five, ten faces now looked in at me—Mel and his myriad assistants joined my "friends and comrades-at-arms," as US would later phrase it. I saw myself reflected off ten reflective sunglass lenses. Ten different shots of my outraged, yet still dumbfounded mug. In each and every one, my face had that kind of hydrocephalic look irritated babies get, the forehead about a foot long, only slightly smaller than the length of the rest of the torso. "How could you do this to me, C?" I was still inquiring.

"There are no secrets left in America, Max. They already knew."

"This is what all of America's loving in you," Linda said, next to him. "What moves you moves us—we're a sentimental people."

"Oh, shut up," I said. For one thing, Jeannie may not have known, wasn't sentimental at all.

The sunglasses separated--pushing his way through them was the pudgy kid with the round, blue-eyed face of my mother at five. "Come on. My mom says we're in a hurry, we've got a lot to do today." The urchin announced.

Before I could respond, another lock popped up, the door swung open, and there she was, one more time, the (former) love of my life. "Lezz get this thing over with," she said. "I don't have all that much time." Then she added, conspiratorially, "I'm only doing this for you, Jimmie. I wouldn't do it for anyone else in the world."

"Oh, well, if that's the case…" I began. I got up and out instinctively. But I must have sounded insufficiently convinced when I added, "if you're only doing this for me!"

She responded, "Wait a second. You don't think I want to do this, do you?" Her snub nose turned away from me, then turned back again.

The thought, admittedly, had occurred to me; but she, uh, dispelled it. "Your agent called me twice; CJ's spoken with me five times. Everyone says you need this; I can't imagine why—but this Linda said they wouldn't shoot this without me, and she couldn't get you on I don't remember what all, the Today show, the Night show, you name it, without a magazine spread. I risked tainting my whole career…so don't look so condescendingly at me. I know you well enough to think you might like to see your picture there, anywhere."

My head must have been pivoting like a swivel chair. Here was Sarah. Where was Jeannie?

Not far away, actually, looking extremely interested, a little hurt, she glanced at me in the mirror of Sarah and saw what?

"She's telling the truth, Max," CJ chimed in, as if I were interested in the truth right then. "Ask Linda. We, uh, they wouldn't give this to us if the two of you weren't in it together, like on the Dottie thing—that's their deal."

Here was Helen of US chiming in too. "We think you'll photograph so well, all of you together. The kid's so cute."

Sarah took my arm and pulled me a little to the side. Her eyes, when they glanced my way, looked like the double-hinged mirrors clothing stores feature, getting me from every angle. "Let's cut out of here," she said.

How long had I been waiting to hear this? Was I hearing it right? I looked for Jeannie out there—saw her much too close by, looking even more disturbed. What was I going to tell her? "I, uh, I don't know, Sarah. I uh…"

"See, just what I thought," she responded, with a cruel smile. "You want the pictures, you want them to take the pictures—that's why I finally came."

"It's not that, Sarah," I tried. "I…"

"Yes it is—you're maybe the vainest guy I know. You're happy to be in that ridiculous magazine."

Didn't sound all that much like "love" to me, but US magazine differed, when the article came out: "'I've never lost a friend I've ever loved,' says James," the magazine wrote under that photo of Sarah and her son and me and CJ. "'Getting together with Max,' says his oldest friend, the frequent TV star Clement 'Clem' Jones, 'is like checking back into America's oldest running party.'"

Who invents this stuff? That particular writer must have been on our most powerful mood elevator, disconnected from any known reality. What a party I was: I was about as lively as a pet rock.

CJ and Sarah looked good, however, particularly together. When we sailed into the park's west end, where we viewed the sun kissing New Jersey good-bye through its chemical veil, Mel captured these two silhouetted to my right. They looked like the lovers in mattress ads, so handsome I'd have been paranoid if I hadn't already been millimeters this side of dementia—and if I hadn't seen them jockeying over page space, two egos on the loose. Somehow Sarah got right into the thing, sacrificing herself valiantly for me.

But not that valiantly: on our way down the yellow brick (cobbled rock) road, I noticed Jeannie noticing me, talking every now and then to someone, but essentially scrutinizing the lovely couple Sarah and I had once been.

I was confused and puzzled, but eventually I got the idea too. She was wondering how the kid, the nanny, the mammy and me all fit together. So was I. When Mel posed me next to her, I finally asked her, "Is he or isn't he?" My voice was shaking.

"He might be," she said, without losing her pose. She looked off toward Battery Park, the ever-expanding city. Her steady grin for the camera didn't even flicker.

"What do you mean? You took him in for a blood test, too, didn't you?

"Come on, James, smile, let's get this thing over with," Mel said. He had to get back home to his rabid dogs.

I smiled.

"Of course I took him in. You know I did," she said.

"Is that what C's doing here? Kind of a belated godfather?" Chills went up my arms.

"I think he's here for the pictures." She sounded less excited.

"So what do you mean he 'might be'?"

"Well, you're not *not* his father…"

"What in the fuck does that mean?" Out there in the distance, I saw Jeannie talked to Jesse's nanny. I didn't figure anything good was going to come of it.

"Just one roll more, okay, James," Mel said, rather kindly. "And we'll wrap. Try to look romantic."

More chills, these on my neck, the left side. Sarah was on my right. She patted my arm. "I'm sorry, Max. I guess you've never been through this before…"

"What do you mean? I've been on half the South's most remote stations, I'm up to my ears in phony publicity, I…"

"I mean, forced to contemplate some form of adulthood."

She grinned, probably for the cameras. And actually, I liked the way she touched my arm then, even patted it. In Paris, when we'd walked together in the street, Sarah had always looped her arm through mine, her fingers resting in the crook of my arm—and I'd been not simply proud but giddy, marveling at my good fortune, Sarah's radiant beauty and her peculiar, almost inexplicable attraction to me.

"Not *not* his father, what does that mean?" I was still troubled.

"You know it feels good being here with you..." She changed the subject.

"It's that much of a surprise?" I asked her, tenderly, not sharply. I wanted to know.

"Sort of," said she. "It's been a long time." Her voice seemed to catch—was it the actress in her? I might have wondered at some other time. Instead I was trying to keep my eyes wide open, as large as I could, for I knew if they closed, blinking, I'd probably be crying again, pathetic as it sounds. She squeezed my arm.

"So?" I asked.

"We don't know. They can't do positive identifications, only negative ones...and Richard (*the other contender*) hasn't gone in yet."

"Thus, I'm not *not*..."

"You got it. You could get a DNA test, if you want; but they're a little pricey, and I'm a little short on cash now."

She looked over at me and turned on her most charming smile. We were alone at this point; Mel's camera had long since ceased running. There was, however, a small crowd, I now noticed, to our left. C, Linda, the assistants, they were waiting for us to finish our talk.

When we turned back toward them, C smiled. "Still a beautiful couple," he said. I felt like retching, my connection to that "couple" about as tenuous as a chromosomal strand. You'd think maybe she'd want to know more, need to know more.

"The shots are going to be great, look at that sun," Linda said. And effectively, it was glorious, though I couldn't quite focus on it. When I glanced at C, at Linda, at the small crowd, what I now saw, over their shoulders, were the angular shoulders, the sharp features, the black spiked hair with that bleached streak, the distressed eyes of Jeannie, huddled up against the fence, looking forlornly my way. She turned; my stomach sank, and she went down Greenwich, away from us. She didn't wave back when I waved her way.

"Who's your friend, Jim?" Sarah asked.

"Who? What friend?" I didn't want to get into that too. I'm a chicken shit.

She just shook her head.

"A friend from California, Jeannie. I've been, uh, seeing her on and off. I uh didn't know uh…"

Sarah's head kept shaking, nodding, and the lights in her eyes gleamed like kliegs, then flickered toward off.

So I couldn't help myself. I mean, maybe I didn't do it at all, maybe it was just done by the four day stubble on his cheek pulling down my lips. "Do you think, what would you say to dinner, Sarah?"

She laughed. That was her response. "I think you should catch up with your friend there…" She clapped her hands, smiling radiantly for her son—and he came running to her and bounced into her arms.

As she embraced him, the two were rapidly enveloped by his nanny, the make-up personnel (evidently she had brought her own stylist), some guy who was probably her manager, and the rest of the US magazine crew. "That's it, then?" She asked Linda and Helen and walked back their way.

"Just a couple more questions, I promise, no more," Helen said, turning to Sarah confidentially, putting an arm on the latter's shoulders. After they conversed for a very few minutes, Sarah turned once again and said to her son, "Come on, Jesse. It's time for us to go."

She did turn at the car, as she entered, and seemed to look in my direction. She didn't wave, however, though her son did.

Sure made me feel better. "So how do you feel, Max?" CJ asked me when we made it down Reade and turned up West Broadway.

"Like a trailer park, a government issued RV just hit by a hurricane. How the fuck could you have done this to me?"

He paid no attention to me, got a nostalgic look in his baby blue eyes. "Seeing Sarah again...we're getting older, middle-aged, Max," he said. "I never thought you two would get back together—I mean, even in the same room. How'd you do it?"

C's a sly operator, as the name "Clem" would suggest ("never trust a man with a name like Clem," I heard myself thinking. It was my friend— my former friend perhaps—Jeannie's line. "It's one of the first rules, like never eating at a place called Mom's.) He managed to have me still talking to him, even after he'd hustled me through this wondrous, "career-enhancing," self-imploding photo op.

"I didn't, remember? It was an accident, the Dottie show had us both on. Now, she probably won't talk to me either."

"Is that a problem, really, kid? There are so many more women just aching to take care of you."

"Clarify this for me, would you, C? What are you getting at?" This sounded suspicious. "I can't take much more today."

"Sure you can, Max. The human being is a marvelously resilient organism. Take my word for it."

Ten minutes later, after we'd passed through Soho and told at least fifteen overly solicitous folks we didn't want any loose joints, Oxycontin or other artificial opiates in friendly Washington Square Park (what was I thinking? I should have taken them by the handful), we stood in front of C. Trainers Book store, C. Trainers for Christ's sake.

"Quit whining," C said. "You're going to like it in there. Irv and Linda guarantee it." C had a big smile. "They're sorry they can't make it."

"Who they? Linda? Irv?" I squeaked. In a previous life, I'd been a squirrel who disseminated rabies.

This didn't faze CJ. "That's right. I told Irv I'd get you here: that was our deal, and we don't want to disappoint him."

"Deal?"

"You got it," he confirmed. "He guaranteed the..."

"Exposure," I said.

He nodded. "He's a powerful guy. He can make things happen; that's why I assured him you'd make the rounds...you've been getting even flakier than usual, Max; everybody's worried. These things don't come around twice, you know." He took my arm and walked me into this swanky bookstore, through the metal detectors, the shoplifting devices, and the security personnel that make this such a delightful, neighborhood place. "But CJ, CJ," said the coy, fading violet I was.

"CJ, CJ," he mimicked me in a high falsetto. "You've been looking for this all your adult life. This is your 15, no 12 minutes of celebrity, Max—it's no time to get proud."

Indeed, he knew me too well. The bristles on my four-day stubble perked up at the sight of a small crowd. Now you understand, don't you? I'd been to quite a number of book signings, done them in large conglomerations like L.A. and Denver, and in smaller ones like Sioux City and Tucson. But in all this time, whether working the illustrious Book Soup or the odd K-Mart, I'd never seen more than six people at any one time lined up for a signature of mine. Of these, half might know my name; another third (i.e. two people) would place blank sheets of paper inside the book's front cover so they could get my "autograph" without wasting any money on the actual book. A tough, peculiar group of people, (some just wanting the air-conditioning)—but never before, unfortunately, a crowd.

Well, we got to Book Stew's, and there were perhaps a hundred people present, the largest number of people I'd seen around me since Brad Pitt showed up at a friend's birthday party (his sister was Brad's hair and make-up person). There was this too in common with that other evening— ninety percent of the crowd seemed to be female.

Am I sounding anywhere as overwhelmed as I felt? This was like something out of the movie "The Knack"—or as close to it as I was ever going to get—with this twist, particularly salient for a guy selling luck for the lovelorn: I'd been abandoned only minutes before by both Jeannie and Sarah, the only two women—one real, one largely fictive—in my life.

Perhaps all these other women smiling seductively my way were actually lured in by the scent of my intense (even perpetual) need.

The first two who came to me, books in hand, wore furs, one fox, one animal I couldn't recognize. The fox was dyed purple. The woman had plucked eyebrows, what looked like real jewels (I couldn't tell the difference) on her fingers and arms and ears. This is the kind of woman one imagined clustered around better, more celebrated authors.

"What are you doing here?" I asked her, as my heart skipped, pollen scattered in my respiratory system.

"I like to see men cry," she said in reply. And she laughed.

When I signed her book (no blank page inserted here), "To Olivia, lachrymosely"—I couldn't think of anything better—she started to leave. "If you'll stay awhile," I said. "I'll try to satisfy your hopes." Weirdly, she stayed.

"Could you sign this, 'To Kate, who taught me how good it could be'?" asked Kate, next in line. She was frail, freckled, small—she looked shy and dear. Of course I'd sign anything she wanted. I guess that should have been the first sign.

Olivia in the fox fur looked on. I looked back at her. No wonder Jeannie had left the park so quickly.

I signed two more books, "Here's looking at you," and Kate stayed put, Olivia over there, Kate next to me.

"Leave your phone number, would you?" Kate asked, rather more forcefully than one would have expected.

I smiled stiffly and looked at the next woman coming up. But Kate pushed her book in front of me again. "I'm thinking of leaving Jack, and I'd like to know how to reach you, just in case."

This was a little embarrassing. "I can't do that," I said.

And she began to cry. "Why can't I communicate with men?" Other people thrust their books my way, and this one stood, her thumb between the book's first two pages, crying. She said, "And I thought you were different! I had hope for you."

Always a mistake. Olivia's attention drifted toward a book rack; her head turned and there she went while I continued my Sisyphean task. One, two, three "To Mary or Jane or Kim, you'll never be lovelorn for long," I wrote, kind of depressed now, the boulder rolling my way.

"It's the men who don't know how to communicate, not you," I tried, to Kate.

"What difference does it make who's to blame?" She replied, keenly.

People are so much smarter than you imagine. I was sweating, the line of the women, the occasional befuddled guy coming my way; it wasn't going to end soon. I took the beleaguered Kate's book and wrote in C.J.'s phone number. He had the rising starlet's version of the personal license plate—the personal phone number. His spelled C-L-E-M-E-N-T in his area code, maybe all metropolitan area codes for all I knew.

Kate thanked me sweetly and continued to stand there beside me, as if she were my date. This didn't bother me, but it seemed to upset one of the store's least distinguished officials, a bulky bullet head in uniform. He looked like the ushers/security personnel you find at rock concerts, guys who think they're in Paris Island, Marine Boot Camp. He started to take Kate away.

"I'm sorry, Miss," he said. "But you're holding up the signing. We've got a lot of other customers who want to talk to this guy."

He tried to veer her to the right. Another store salesperson arrived and suggested that "it might be more comfortable over this way." He turned her in the opposite direction; she turned her confused face back to me; and I turned hero.

"Leave her alone, would you?" I said. "She's not bothering anyone."

The store security man looked back at me, his arm on poor Kate's sleeve, and couldn't believe what he'd heard. "This is my job, you do yours…just sign the books and move them along."

Here Olivia, of all people, made another appearance, pumping air into my dirigible. "Hey, Sarge, I don't think so," I said, puffing up in importance, the gallant. "Let's see what the store management has to say about that."

Olivia smiled, and Kate looked puzzled as I reached over to free her arm. The man smiled broadly and stiff-armed me, pushing me about three feet further back. The store's PR person attempted to intervene. "Easy there now Lewis, be careful," he said gently, before explaining to me, "He tends to get carried away. Likes to do his job right."

Deluded, the putative star of this show, I didn't listen well. I charged straight back at Lewis and fortunately wasn't maimed permanently. I just got a palm shot in the jaw. My lower lip immediately began swelling, ballooning up so emphatically I had trouble passing my tongue over it.

"Still having problems with authority, Jimmie?" A familiar ironic voice asked gently. I looked to my right to find my greatest college summer vacation sweetheart, Heather Anne Sedgwick, grinning my way. Next to her, brought into the joke, were three girls with almost identical faces— freckled, blue-eyed strawberry blondes, each one smiling and each smile hovering, like their Mom's, above a half inch of exposed gum.

"Just like you said he'd be, Mom" said the shortest of the three, as her oldest sister glanced disapprovingly at her.

"She's a very clever person, right most of the time," I said and kissed their mother. "What are you doing here?"

"Getting remarried. We're trying an editor this time, aren't we girls?"

They answered breathlessly yes. From my calculations this was numero three. The last I'd heard she'd left her first husband for a California Dionysus, and the two had set up the first wind-surf shop in Zihautenejo. Though I'd imagined her brown and lean, her hair a pale white from the wind and sun, Wick looked great, even a little pudgy and pale like me. The girls blew so much life into her.

"I've been taking some photographs," she said.

"She is having a show at the Center for Photography," one girl began.

"Capa's place," a second daughter explained.

"You know the Life photographer, the guy who did the war picture stuff," the third clarified further for me. She was tiny, eight years old at the most. And all three, with their sharp, glittering eyes manifested indications of their mom's great intelligence—and her singular elegance. I particularly like the eldest, with the silver streak in her hair. When I pointed out its attractiveness, she told me the gray was real, not dyed: "this is what you get when your parents keep divorcing," she said. Her mom kept smiling.

"Mr. Adams," the PR man said. "We've got a crowd here, and it's just not moving. You've got to keep signing."

Wicki shrugged her shoulders. I looked angry, and she laughed, showing all of her molars. She looked 25. How those eyes gleamed! "Let's go, girls," she said, "before Jim gets himself into trouble."

The three girls giggled together. Then all three pressed my flesh, with comely smiles and precociously grave looks. The world was a serious place, needing all their attention and considerable intelligence to get through gracefully—as Wicki indeed knew.

Was she nineteen, twenty? So beautiful still. Or wasn't I nineteen, emotionally anyway (what an awful age to inflict upon yourself), she moving on and ahead, her little train of daughters putting her in tune with the time while I stayed on, flummoxed to the end?

Ah, I felt deliciously sorry for myself, even as I signed some more Janes and Robertas and one Edwina, with the imperious and marginally solicitous store PR person looking on critically and suspiciously. Hey he could have his store back, thought I, until wasn't that....yes it was...Olivia peeked through the line again. Suddenly my eternal youth returned, reinvigorated. I smiled her way; she smiled mine.

And a woman suddenly asked, "How could you have said that, James?"

This was a woman more or less my age, trying to look like Madonna. Same nose, same bleached out hair and air, same probable facial "sculpture." Though she had less grace, she did have, I could feel, a first hand sense of me. This was old home week. I wanted Wicki back.

"Said what? What did I say?" I asked, with an eye on Olivia.

"Don't play the innocent; you never were," the woman said imperiously. "When did you, of all people, ever know anything about women?"

I looked more closely. "Ailene?" I asked. "Ailene Mazlak?" We'd tried, never quite hit it off, something like that. I smiled Olivia's way, suavely, unconvincingly.

"Yes, of course. I had another name but I got rid of it," said Ailene with a sneer. Next to her now, with a truculent and menacing glare of her own was a friend of hers, then a second. Both sneered at me.

Stanley, the store PR person, sensed a potential problem. "Are these people bothering you, Mr. Adams?" Stanley was coming to my rescue. "Why don't you just leave Mr. Adams alone?"

"Because he's a complete fraud," Ailene asseverated.

"Ailene," I began. "Why pick on me? I haven't even thought about you for 15 years, what's…" Olivia looked interested.

Ailene's front lip trembled menacingly, "Why would you? You don't give a shit about women. Imagine you writing about them! Jesus, you're the worst lover I ever had."

"The worst?" I said. "Isn't that a bit of an exaggeration? Maybe bottom five, but the worst?"

"The worst! We date on and off and finally I let you make love to me, and you didn't know what to do. Imagine that?" She asked the assembled women. "He didn't have a clue what a woman likes, what we need, how to satisfy us! How dare you write a book about women?"

Steam dripped out of the pores on my forehead. Was this true? Probably was, yes it was; the truth is I'd been afraid of Ailene, and that hadn't changed a bit.

"Why, you hit on me for nine months, every time we saw each other…you were all over me until I said 'yes'…god it ruined my relationships with men for years, years!"

"You're giving me too much credit. We barely knew each other." This was becoming disturbing. New veins were dancing on my forehead. My body temperature was around 108, and Olivia over there looked like she was laughing. Was she?

"You knew me enough!" She was yelling now.

"I uh didn't know, I guess I disappointed you, I…"

"Disappointed, you asshole? You crushed me. I'd have given you a second chance, a third; but you weren't just an awful lover. You ran away, my God you didn't even leave a note…"

"Did I really do that?" I did, I guess, but I couldn't recall the details at that moment. I couldn't remember my name either.

"You hurt her so much," Ailene's friend now pitched in bitterly. My breath was leaving the building, disappearing entirely.

"You don't remember! Oh that makes things so much better. You are such a liar, James!" Ailene screamed.

"You're a misogynist," her friend yelled out. "You hate women! Hate, hate, hate them, you miserable little shit."

"And why shouldn't he?" Asked Stanley, returning to the rescue. "Look at you two."

Oh this was great, a singular twist—just the support I was looking for. Stanley pushed one of the women aside and stood between the angry horde and me. He shook a finger their way.

Then another male voice entered the fray. "Max, how can you do this to me?" Declaiming his grief now was my friend CJ. He'd smelled the commotion, I guessed, at least the weird locomotion of my ideas, memories, instincts, all chugging off in contradictory directions. Was that Olivia's back, yes it was—her fur or fake fur receded into the distance. No way.

"What?" I finally managed in response to CJ.

C held up a book. "How could you give her my phone number?"

"I forget," I said.

"You don't remember a thing, do you? You never listen." I think that was Ailene who screamed. "I kept telling you 'let's just be friends,' but no, you had to fuck things up. You had to fuck me! You couldn't leave well enough alone."

Indeed that seemed still a specialty of mine. I wasn't registering well or even well enough. This was completely out of my control now; even my own hands were out of my hands. Too many different accusations were pinching off my brain's circulation; too many disparate guilts were vying for my mental time.

So what did I do?

"Chill! Move it along," Stanley's overly buffed assistant ordered—and I followed directions, for a change. I ran. Instinctively and immediately tried to flee the premises.

It wasn't easy, for I felt just as queasy, just as guilty about leaving as staying. But this, at least, was a culpability I was familiar with, I'd been living with for years, ever since I could remember—ever since, anyway, this much I'm sure about, I had to tell my mom, my large and imposing and hurt mother that I still loved her just as much, but I just needed to spend more time on my own. We were in a car, on the way to school. I can still remember how coolly the light seemed to penetrate the trees in our very suburban city, the briskness of the morning. She responded, "But why, Jimmie? So you need some time to yourself, that doesn't mean you have to be so cold and withdrawn, especially to the people who love you the most."

Mom was right; but I couldn't understand that then or later either. Fears are always on the surface of us hysterics; our giving seems just as unilateral, as unequivocal as our anxieties. We don't feel the line between the world and us. Right at that time, as tears welled in my mom's beautiful periwinkle blue eyes, I ceased to feel much at all; my brain, my emotions took the ultimate powder: they fled the car's confines and raced away almost as fast as my body took my mind out of Book Stew's.

I didn't escape unscathed. Following, a voice or voices screamed,

"Just where do you think you're going?" This or these must have belonged to Ailene and her friend.

"Get back here, right now!" Stanley order, his voice echoing off that of his bullet-headed heavy.

"Ma—ax!" CJ yelled. "Don't do it, Max. Not that."

"No, no, no!" Various other voices chimed in. Perhaps they were just passing psychotics—but many feet seemed to thump behind me as I raced toward the door, toward 8th street and (relative) freedom.

The line which had formed for my autograph (this is still difficult to envision; how, why did they care? Was Book Stew's giving us free cocktails with every purchase? Was Irv?) collapsed and fell apart, mimicking me. Still more feet followed me toward the door.

Skilled as I was at flight, I got there first. I ran past the front counter, through one of the four checkout stands. Then I took a sharp left and headed for the exit. After I bowled through the metal stakes framing the doors, the alarm system rang off like the bells in Harkness Towers when I unwittingly tripped them long ago, like the 21 gun salute for a visiting dignitary, like a subway cop going after a scofflaw. Ringgggg...

Lights blinked on and off; the siren continued to sound; and worst of all, by far, the front door of Book Stew's automatically locked. I had three books, all my own, under my arm; and, not having been checked through the checkout counter and passed under the store's demagnetizing devices, the books activated the shoplifting alarm system. Ringgg...the store vibrated and rattled as if the F train were passing through it; and I was locked in and about as happy as a beautiful 5 foot 4 inch kid in a maximum correctional institution. A small brigade of people, all looking right then like a gang of felons, came charging my way. They'd later say they panicked at what they thought was the fire alarm.

"Hold it right there, pal," exclaimed the security chief Mr. Bullethead, as he leapt gleefully my way, over the rail which separated the exit from the (still open) entrance. "I figured we'd have problems with you, my man."

He reached for my wrist, but—this is satisfying anyway, in retrospect—he got crushed by eight or ten other people who leapt toward the exit. Since they all were carrying books too, they also activated the alarm system. Lights flickered; something like a fog horn went off, and I really didn't notice. I was flat on my back, hearing only this from Ailene, "You're such an asshole—don't you dare try to run away from me again!"

"You should be ashamed—say it," said her friend with a screech. "He's not even ashamed! Well fuck you, Mr. Hot Lover."

The glass panes of the door flew toward the street, propelled out by my foot and about ten copies of the unfortunate cause of all this, my obviously mistitled *Luck for the Lovelorn*. Simultaneously a tremendous shocking pain ripped through my right ear, and my hearing screeched like a TV set losing its cable connection. I screamed louder than any of the loons out on the street, loud enough to break my own sound barrier.

I roared so dramatically I found myself, fifteen minutes later, with four police officers in the emergency room of St. Vincent's Hospital. I was simultaneously being booked for disrupting the peace (no mean feat in New York City) and assault (on Ailene and her friend, who were there to press charges) with a deadly weapon (my book). This held up for about five minutes; it was the cops' idea of a joke, something to amuse them, to pass the time while I was being stitched up.

A severe laceration of the right aural membrane is approximate medical parlance for the following calamity. Ailene's friend, pushed from behind by the fleeing book buyers, fell on top of me. Screaming, she had her mouth open; and in the fall, she clamped it shut on my right ear, biting off the top third.

It was stitched together later. I would hear out of it again. But if you listened to Ailene, as we were all forced to do at the hospital, you would have gathered that my ear's health was singularly unimportant. "Why does he need to hear? He of all people!" Ailene screamed at one point. "He's never listened to anybody else. He can't remember a thing!"

THE NEW YORK POST, PAGE 6

SOME GUYS HAVE ALL THE LUCK, OTHERS GET
ALL THE PAIN! *Luck for the Lovelorn* author James
Maxwell Adams got both last night when his book signing
party turned into a brawl. Book Stew's on 8th street, the
stylish and popular village version of the massive chain,
was the site of utter pandemonium yesterday evening,
when Adams was besieged—literally—by tens of new
fans, most of them women. That's the lucky part.
Unfortunately, Adams was so excited by all the attention
that he started giving his books away to startled passersby,
causing a near riot. In the ensuing fracas, Adams had his
left ear bitten in two by one admirer and found himself
thrown out on the street by a second, ending up at St.
Vincent's hospital. Is too much love unlucky after all?
How's he going to "listen now," we wonder…

Twenty-three stitches just in the ear (who would have known there
was enough room for so many in an ear?). But I didn't need that ear to be
hearing perfectly to understand most of the response I received—and not
just because I was vain and narcissistic and self-involved (which I probably
was, having secretly relished appearing on page six, regardless of the
circumstances). I wish I'd cared how superficial my values sounded or that I
was immune to the excitement this whole fiasco generated in my agents and
at US magazine. Sadly, I may have been as air-headed as Ailene had so
kindly implied. I actually relished the hundreds of phone calls I received

from people I didn't always remember, even as I understood most didn't really know why they were calling; they were just operating, in response to the publicity, on automatic pilot.

I did make, however, a call of my own, a sincere call to Jeannie at her stylish hotel Michaels, about 20 blocks uptown from my sublet hovel in Little Italy/Nolita. "I'm sorry," I said.

"I left, Jim. It's okay," she said, too graciously for me.

"What's that mean exactly?" I asked.

"I left," said she nonchalantly. "You didn't ask me to. What's there for you to be sorry for?" A small pause ensued, which she didn't allow to linger long. "Who's the kid?" She wondered.

"What kid?"

"I think you know. You sound like somebody testifying in front of Congress." Her voice clipped my nails for me.

"Oh, you mean that kid?" A second silence followed, until I said, "I don't know."

"How come? How can you not know? She's not telling?" This sounds tough, but her voice was, rather, incredulous. "It's hers, isn't it?"

"Yup," I eloquently admitted. "As far as I know. We didn't do the LeMaze classes together."

"So he's yours, too? Nice of you to get around to telling me."

"As if I knew. Which I don't. She doesn't either."

"You mean she doesn't even know who's the father of her child? I know she's an actress, but how self-centered can you be?"

"Easy for you to say," said I, springing to Sarah's defense. "The kid seemed all right to me. She must be doing something right. At least, a lot better than we are."

Here there was another pause, hers.

"I'm sorry, Jeannie," I said.

"But you don't know what for," she said slowly.

"I didn't mean to imply anything about you and children…"

'That's not the problem, Jim….that girl at the bookstore was right," she said. "You don't remember anything." I wasn't sure what she was getting at. "The problem is that you told me you and Sarah broke up six years ago."

"What did you tell me about you and Jerry, Jeannie?"

This was no argument. "I was there, Jim. I saw you. You don't know where you are with her…"

"No-where. It's a dead end, Jen."

"Maybe. I don't doubt that. But who knows if you really know that? If you've even turned around and started going in another direction." Her voice was calm again.

"Can I buy you dinner?" I wondered.

"When you've figured out if you're a father or not…"

"Oh, Jeannie, come on."

"Okay, when you've figured out if you want to be one…whichever comes first."

Minutes afterward, the doorbell rang, in my downtown sublet, and I opened it to find a tremendous assortment of flowers, a bird of paradise, some irises, daffodils and gladiolas, green and blue, mauve and then that brilliant yellow. A card read, "Are you all right, you sweet fool? S."

This didn't simplify things for me. When, too pleased, I called to thank her, she said, "Well, are you? How's your ear?"

"How are you? How's your son?"

"Doing fine..."

"Really?"

"No, but it doesn't matter. You're the one who's hurt."

"No, I'm not. The ear's okay, me too..."

"Right," she said. "Let's recap: since I saw you again, you cried on TV, fainted at a doctor's office; I read you picked a fight with some security guard, now you've gotten your ear bitten off. Anything else?"

"That's about it, though I did get hit by a soccer ball and kicked by some kid that I just learned may or may not be mine."

"Uh huh," she began a little tartly. "You know, I used to be concerned about you, all the time; but I looked at your friend from California the other day, and I just knew something. You always have a woman around worrying about you. You didn't necessarily need me to." Then she paused before saying something too disturbing for me to absorb.

"And you know? It's got nothing to do with the woman, her qualities, though they tend to be great, I'm sure. What I suddenly saw, really, is that you really think…you really feel that a woman's solicitude is the only way to your father's heart."

What? Say what?

Maybe there was another easier route through my dad's anger and defenses to his tenderness, but I had never found it. As a kid, I'd mostly sensed his love in his anger; as an adult I'd found it in his pain. Between the two of us had always stood my mom, pained by our anger or angered by our pain, puzzled by their constant conjunction. Could that explain my own befuddlement, more complete than partial, at the prospect of a little nuclear family of my own?

I went to check out the constituent(s) of it one more time. I donned "dad's" clothes, replaced the Levis I habitually sported with thick tweed slacks, put on two sweaters—the second thick and Irish—and a windbreaker (did I imagine dads these days were preppies or was it simply that my own dad had always dressed carefully for each part he assumed). Then just in case an errant US magazine stringer might be waiting outside of some starlet's Tribeca loft, I put on a pair of shades, like Greta Garbo, bought a Mongolian rabbit fur cap which covered most of the rest of the recognizable me—the slightly larger than normal ears, the forthright, Irish chin, that "Saracen" like cheek line the every agreeable Philip had so incisively commented upon that one day, way back (was it really only a week since we had first encountered one another?) when he had laid out the rules for my perusal of his ward.

I had four days a week in which I was authorized to see the lad; and this wasn't one of them. When I first hit the park, I thought I saw why: Nicole, with her hair braided now into beaded dreadnoughts, returned my smile with what I took to be a look of deep compassion. I followed her eyes to where her charge was kicking a soccer ball toward an improvised goal— one sculpture of sorts, which must have been left over from the summer's Sculpture by the River program, a beautiful rusted slab that formed one end of the goal with a metal mesh garbage container representing the other. Between the two, complaining vehemently as a ball passed through his spindly legs was Philip. He didn't wear his glasses on a telephone cord this time, looked a little myopic—I liked him more, even if his beard was still, miraculously a five day growth, not a minute more or less (Okay, he was more fastidious than I).

He glanced my way, recognized me, and then, with a pained grimace, turned his attention back to Jesse. The two switched places. Jesse tended the goat, while Phil fed him a series of easy shots to block. Every once in a while, Phil would look back over his shoulder, more or less towards me. It took me a while to get it. I was thinking more of the soccer, wishing I knew more about the game's intricacies. I really didn't notice that when Phil looked back in my direction, he wasn't confirming my existence. He was looking, I soon realized, to my left toward the next bench up and across from me where another guy sat--blonde, chubby, the remnant of a once better body spreading over the green bench, his blonde hair turning just a little white. A cowlick swirled, like mine, around the right side of his head, as he too looked Jesse's way, curious, his eyes never leaving the kid.

Do you hear what I thought I saw? The cowlick—is that what Sarah went for? Phil had one; there it was, in the back of his head. I felt like crawling under the bench, as I'd slipped beyond couches at high school parties. I felt like crawling all the way back into the source.

"Mama! Mom!" A child yelled. "I want my Mama!" The yell seemed to come from the center of me. Was this the primal scream?

No, fool. It was the child of one of you two, lying on the ground next to the base of the sculpture by the sea monument. He'd dived for the ball, missed, and battered himself against the rusted goal post.

The guy across the way stood up. I stood up. I ran to Jesse, so did he. Phil said, "Thanks guys, I think I can handle this. I've been doing it long enough," and he took Jesse into his arms, ran a hand through the kid's thick curls, and walked with him toward the slide.

The other contender, this second cowlicked putative padre, held out a gigantic hand (must have been able to palm the ball in his day). "Hi, you must be Jimmie, Richard Klinger here…"

I guess, everything said, I was definitely a "Jimmie." As if to prove the point, I took umbrage at the nickname. "I go by James these days, Dick," I said, a veritable peacock spreading myself to my full height, up to someplace around Richard's sternum.

"James, right. I remember that from the show—you were great on it, by the way, really very special…that crying, it was a stroke of genius, hilarious."

"Just what my agent said," said I. Does everyone in the entertainment business occupy the same mind? Set someplace in a storage room in North Hollywood, CA.?

Richard's big hand clamped onto my arm. "We know what a great TV interview can do for you…and that, that's going to make your future…really. Have you gotten any spin off it yet?"

I smiled, my grin looking like that of a papier-mâché wolf. Great gobs of paste kept my jaws open.

"I told Rachel Himmelstein about it," Richard continued helpfully. He was speaking of the head of production for Cosmic Studios. "Told her about the whole deal, you know, the Luck for the Lovelorn thing, the crying, this new man stuff and she loved it…most women must, right? I think you've got something there." He paused, his eyes awaiting mine. "Have you developed it into anything yet? I'm reading right now. I'd be happy to take a look at it."

I nodded my head. I think I heard the little crackerjack prize, the pez rattle around in it. Silence makes these guys nervous. I was feeling for the boy.

"Rachel and I'd like to do something together again," he continued. "Besides make out in college, at 'that place.'"

The boy we had, more or less, in common was hanging now on Phil's knees, smiling so tentatively. One would have liked to know how to elicit something cheerful, a laugh, a grin even from his dour mien. His eyes were as grave as his mother's.

"I bet," I said, dumbly. Rachel was a rising star, someone I'd glimpsed from afar, at a luncheon meeting at Cosmic. She was moving with a crowd toward the executive dining area. I remember it took her almost a half hour to cross the room. Passing my table, she stopped for a second and poured water into the glass of the producer with whom I was dining, and left abruptly. A very weird occurrence.

"Is your ear better?" Phil wondered. "You all right? What happened exactly? Page Six never gets anything right." He peered curiously at the bandages, which, enshrouding the right side of my head, made me look like a First World War casualty.

"Fine, yeah. Thanks a lot," I said. "Just got my ear bitten in two. They sew them back on these days. It seems to be working."

He smiled, was no longer paying all that much attention himself. An ear bitten here or there was all in a day's work for this battlefield veteran. "Rachel and I went on to do this TV thing together a few years back."

"A disease?" I asked.

He didn't take offense. "A bubble kid," he nodded. "You know the first of them, the little guy who lives his life out entirely in plastic. No immunity system. What a metaphor."

Mostly for me—my entire life lived in a kind of bubble, though the bubble was finally being pricked, right and left.

"Howdy, handsome," a sharp voice said. "I didn't know you two knew each other." It was Jeannie, and she was holding, shyly, some flowers.

"We don't," I started to say, but Richard said, "we just met." She smiled.

Then Richard leaned over and kissed her on the cheek. "Hi, Jeannie," he said. "What are you doing here?"

She looked shyly my way. And I said, "You two know each other?"

"Sure," she said. "Richard may be directing something for us." This was ridiculous.

"Congratulations, by the way," Richard told her.

"Congratulations on what?" I had to ask. This might have been a large part of our problems, hers and mine.

"Warner's promoted me," she said and held the flowers my way. It was supposed to be the other way around, you'd think, but I'm no chauvinist. I needed help.

When I took the flowers, Richard backed off. "Thanks, Jeannie," I said. The flowers were violets.

"The least I could do. You look like you've been run over by a truck. How's your ear?" She appeared sympathetic, and I thought of what

Sarah had said, of this weird conjunction in me of paternity and pain. I
looked from Richard to Jesse, who was back on his feet and getting a lesson
from Phillip on dribbling the soccer ball.

When I glanced at Richard, he'd changed places, installing himself
on a nearer bench. He smiled our way before returning his gaze to Jesse.
"Guess how I know Richard, guess what he's doing here too?"

She understood immediately. She's quick that way. "Well, she
sure knows how to pick them," Jeannie said, taking my arm. "Poor Jim. No
wonder you look like you've just crawled across the Mojave Desert. I think
you need some comfort food...which I'd cook, if I only cooked. How 'bout
I buy you dinner, instead?"

It was indeed something straight out of my minimal opus, *Luck for
the Lovelorn*, a classic case of seduction through overweening need. And it
was one of the few times, of all the times we'd ended up together, that I was
sure she enjoyed herself, that she wasn't worried about offending Julia
Roberts' manager or cultivating George Clooney's tailor. It was the first
time, too, that I found myself, much later that night, waking up in her arms,
held tightly like a stuffed animal or a favorite pillow.

Jeannie was always clever, but she was particularly prescient that
night—did I telegraph it, merely not know it myself, have it move over me
like a muscle tic, a spasm?

I was dreaming, someplace around 4, when suddenly my father's
face, pinched and wan, filled my little monitor. His eyes were red-veined
and angry, and his mouth was twisted in pain—put a child between his lips
and he would have resembled, uncannily, Goya's Saturn. His lips slid back
from the gums to expose crooked teeth and the bones beneath. Then he

began to scream, though no sound reached me. The rage, which so frequently animated him, left his eyes, and fear filled them. I reached for him, wanting to comfort him, but, grimacing, he turned away from me.

From then until dawn, I couldn't sleep. Every time I closed my eyes, my father's face hovered over me, hooting chillingly, like an owl on the prey of small scared game.

At 7:45, another call came in, and this unleashed new waves of anxiety. I reached for Jeannie, but she wasn't there. She'd told me she had a breakfast meeting—how excited we both were by absence. "Jimmy, Jimmy, hey kid, wake up," a voice cried enthusiastically, as I tried and failed to figure out who it might be. I felt an adrenalin surge; a host of wasps took me over. "This is it, man, it's all coming true, the Dream! The whole program!"

I had no idea what the voice was suggesting, but I felt certain the enthusiasm could only be my agent's, Irv's. Though he hated to admit it, he'd started as a public relations flack for Bob Bailey. "We've got a big meeting, come on uptown. I'll buy your breakfast." (There was a first, as if I were a significant client). "Linda called. I talked to Juanda, she's a client, you know, and Good Morning Caffeine is going to consider you. God you're hot, you're going to get everything reissued."

"Good Morning Caffeine?"

"Yes, Juanda loves the book, Jane too; they say half their husband's friends are fucked up just like you…you're so hot, get out of bed and up here!"

There was more than a hint of irony again—even I, groggy, dazed and California exiled, understood this. "Can we have this breakfast someplace downtown, Irv?"

"My voice is that different, is it?" He asked, with real concern.

"A little, a little different. What do you mean?"

"Good, good," he said, relieved. "I knew it wasn't that different, but it is different…what that means is that I'm proud of you, Jimmy, you're making it. I don't want to hurt your feelings; but, listen, you're not near enough there that I'd actually change parts of town for you. I did call you up. There's that, I grant you; but still, don't take this wrong. I wouldn't even cross an avenue for you yet: it wouldn't be fair to my other clients. You're going to have to come up here to eat breakfast with me."

I couldn't even look at the eggs. I felt as if a herd of migrating geese had taken over my stomach. Then too I was fascinated by Irv and the kid he brought along, my frequent interlocutor, Irv's Irv, Eric. I knew the two sounded alike, but I hadn't really registered previously that Eric might have been a clone of his aging mentor. Though he was certainly twenty-five or thirty years younger than his boss, you couldn't tell it. Eric looked fifty already, had the same balding hair, the same round face, and small eyes, the same manic and dangerous laugh. He buttered his toast with his left hand too, just like Irv. And with a similar suave, soft voice he led me up from the table and toward NBC. "We didn't want to get you nervous," Eric said, "but your pre-interview at Good Morning Caffeine's today."

I was wearing jeans, tennis shoes; you could see my long red underwear underneath my white shirt (if you looked closely enough), could see that pinkish color through the three or four moth holes in my winter sweater. I wished I'd been better prepared. "Don't worry about it. We told her what to expect," Eric said, helpfully.

We left the hotel lobby, where we'd broken our fast, going out onto Sixth Avenue. Snow started falling. Irv took one arm, Eric the other. "New York's so beautiful," Irv said. "Mischa Barnstein called yesterday. We're going to get you that film deal too. He loved the idea we pitched him for *Luck*."

New York looked pristine, virginal. The snow had just started to cling to the trees in Central Park, up ahead.

"It's a kind of 'Looking for Miss Goodbar,'" Eric explained. "Nobody's done it yet. But it's going to happen. I mean women outnumber us four to one in Manhattan." Didn't look like it had done him much good.

"Think of a woman, Jimmie," one of the two began, only God knows which one, "who decides to get her revenge for all the guys who've hosed her...bodies found right and left. *Luck for the Lovelorn* is the story of the cop who has to solve it..."

"Here's the luck for you. Imagine what the cop has to do to solve the case: he's got to sleep with all these women. That's his assignment," Eric said excitedly, taking a stealthy puff on a cigarette now that we were outside.

Irv chortled with equal enthusiasm. These two little round guys with the matching black cashmere coats, plaid scarfs, and sensible, waterproofed shoes were completely out of their minds.

Perhaps, however, they thought they were entertaining me, trying to get me through this morning, to make me concentrate. They did get me to Good Morning Caffeine, fully wired. There I met Anita Lewis the pre-interviewer, preppie, Jewish, a little round and over-dressed. Irv introduced us. And Anita, who was in charge of vetting me, of seeing if I could talk, if I had anything to say that they wanted to hear, had a lot to say and didn't like all she heard. She was mostly curious about aging adolescents, "Peter Pans," as she constantly referred to people presumably like me; she wondered if and when we would ever grow up.

Obviously she was asking the wrong guy.

"When do you guys," she burst out soon after Irv left, "stop looking for the perfect woman? What makes you think there is one?"

"Our mothers," I said.

"But they weren't...most of them didn't even work; they were powerless," Anita proffered. "They couldn't have been perfect."

"They didn't work—but they directed their formidable intelligences our way," I said. "No wonder we expect something similar."

"Total devotion," she said, her face twisting painfully. "God no wonder we're lost. Who wants that? What good does that do?"

"Probably very little—made us all feel guilty, but it sure was satisfying."

I don't think this was what Anita wanted to hear. "When do you get around to accepting a little responsibility? I mean a family, you know..." She asked as if I hadn't just answered.

"Responsibility?" I wondered in honest response to her query. "A family?" There we were, back to that again. I guess it was unavoidable. I thought of my father, of his eighty or ninety hour work weeks, thought of the distance he put between himself and his progeny, even when he was five feet away, at night, after dinner, his anxieties pushing him through another pile of contracts.

Anita grimaced at my stuttered response, as if she'd been through this before. She repeated the question and amplified it somewhat. "Well, who or what is it you're really looking for? Do guys have any ideas any more?"

I shook my head sympathetically, nonplussed.

"What about you?" She asked. "What do you want?"

"A woman who works but needs me too, who's supportive but not dependent upon you," I said. "A woman who doesn't hate you for her own disappointments...or for yours, who lets you go but welcomes you back..."

"The Perfect Woman," she said.

I nodded my head dumbly. (Should I have told her "Mom"?) And Anita's eyes welled; she looked desperate, every bit as distraught as the man in front of her, me (though my desperation, at the time, mostly spilled over in front of the cameras). I put my arm around her shoulders as I started to leave, and she said, almost bawled, "Oh my God, I'm so lost."

"What do I know?" I countered. "Don't take me seriously. I don't have all that much of a clue."

"I know, I know," she said, and a tear or two started to flow down her cheeks. "That's why you're so perfect for the show—you're just as out to lunch as all the other dudes I know. God, I'm going to die old and childless."

"You passed," Irv said gleefully, when I called him up later to find out the results of my encounter. "Passed with flying colors. You're on a roll, I don't know what's happening exactly, but it's your time."

I didn't know about the time, exactly, but something was happening, rumbling underneath my life like the F, B, and D trains roiling under the half criminal underworlds of Nolita, aka Little Italy. You couldn't hear them; you could only sense them—half the time, you simply thought "too much coffee."

When I stepped out of the subway at Prince and Broadway, walked down the street to Lafayette and looked toward the entrance to the apartment building where I was staying, I saw my buddy CJ. My own private albatross, he was standing uncomfortably against the side of the building. He looked less like the film star he wished to be than the purveyor of nickel bags of grass he had been at our over-esteemed and overpriced college. The act was, he liked to say, his idea of a "student work program." When he now covered his chin with his hand, pensively, then stuck it into his back pocket as I walked his way, my stomach felt strafed with little stones.

"Your mom called my machine in L.A.," he began. "Then she called me here. She's been trying to reach you, said no one's answering at your place...is your machine off?"

It may have been but that was no surprise. The surprise was my mother's call—she'd last talked to CJ many, many years ago right before she'd heard he was arrested on misdemeanor possession of illegal drugs (grass). Alcoholism made sense to my mom, as it did to many of the mothers of her generation in the South; drugs were there if the alcohol wouldn't work or if their in-laws were Baptists (and the drugs they got, of course, from their local pharmacies).

But I'm digressing, trying not to recall the pain in my friend's eyes and my own fear when I noted he had trouble looking my way. "What's the deal?" I asked C. But I knew the answer, it had been there for weeks. "It's my dad, huh?"

"I think so, Max," CJ concluded, gently.

I wasn't crazy, just a little slower than I frequently imagined. My dad had called indeed. He'd called for me that morning in the middle of my sleep, and I'd been home for a change.

I phoned home from the street, right there at Prince and Lafayette, in front of a once decaying Mobil station which had been transformed into a slick restaurant. Trucks banged by, stalled cars rocked under the assault of their sound systems, drowning out the dial tones and the rings as I tried to connect to the quiet plains state where my parents didn't answer and their answering devices were full. Instinctively, I started calling hospitals. It's a small state; Tulsa is a small city, and people are gracious. I got the right hospital on the second call, St. Francis. He'd been there, the lady at the switchboard informed me, for two and a half days. She transferred me to him.

Though my old man picked up the phone on the first ring, I could barely understand him. A train may have passed underneath Spring Street; trucks thundered, I'm sure, along Lafayette, but that wasn't the problem. I could hear my father's voice, but I couldn't recognize it.

"Jimmy," he said, sweetly and faintly, "how are you, son?" This was the same man who only four, five days previously, had chastised me both for my foolishness for allowing Chuck Alphabet to coax me into a "tear-off" and for my stupidity in losing it. He hadn't called me "Jimmy" since I'd been caught giving out answers to a girl I liked on a 7th grade history test. "Jim," it had been from there on out, an adult nickname, a shorter one for his diminishing hopes for me.

"How are things going, Jimmy? Do you need anything?" He sounded, my old man, older than I'd ever imagined he could be, bereft of the menace and the momentous weight of his disappointments. In fact, his questions gently traced the fears he'd kept more or less hidden for a long time. Was I going to survive out there? He must have often wondered—and with reason.

"How are you, Pop?"

"Not very well, not well at all." His voice dipped, but he picked everything up, all the fears in my voice.

"But you've been there before, "I said, as encouragingly as I could. He'd been in twice before, with colds, which turned into pneumonia.

"I'm getting tired, so tired, Jimmy. I never would have thought it possible." Nobody would have.

"No, Dad, don't tell me that," I said to this man whose constant effort, at one thing or another, made me seem—in my own eyes and surely in his too—indolent and shiftless, inadequate even in my very minor accomplishments. "You'll pick up…"

My anxiety rose in direct relation to the emptiness I could feel at the other end of the line. My dad, feisty and relentless, wasn't there; and now this other, older man disappeared too—the phone rattled, and someone took the receiver from him. "I'm sorry, but Mr. Adams needs his rest. His medication's starting to take effect."

Leaving me aware, but barely of five young women, five feet away, staring at me. When I clicked off, the planes of my perception seemed to tilt off their right angles, to the East, where a bleached out, jaundiced sun spilled itself toward the city.

I called the hospital switchboard another time and persuaded them to put me through to the nurses' station, where I could talk to someone attending my father. I reached a woman who asked me who I was; and when I identified myself, she said, "Well, your mom's here. She just moved in when your dad arrived...what a wonderful woman she is. I guess you know that. I'll go get her." The entire world loved my mother, no wonder my Oedipal conundrums were endless.

My mom—let me tell you a couple more things about her. She had blonde hair before I was born, and for another two or three years, up until my dad's first major operation. Then her hair turned grey overnight, all except for two swatches of very dirty blonde locks, one on top, one to the right—you could see them still; they make her look like a punk in her late 60s, though she had never had a hard edge about her, has always been patient and gracious, unlike her driven spouse.

You should know this too: she had been an inch and a half taller than my old man when they had met, but with time (and probably his embarrassment), she'd shrunk. With the roundness, which had come once she'd quit smoking (because my father couldn't breathe any more around the fumes), she seemed exactly his size, though in fact she was still a half-inch taller. I'd measured them one Christmas. I'm not sure but she may have kept that half-inch just to spur my old man on.

He hardly needed the incentive. He was a very tenacious guy, my father, enough for the two of them. Most of the time, almost all of the time I can remember, he'd been relentlessly driven, except now, this time. My mother sounded scared.

"What does he have?" I inquired. "A bronchial infection? He doesn't have pneumonia again does he?"

"That too," she said, and air came between her words, slowing them down as it does water in a radiator, hissing off. "And then his kidneys this time—they're infected too."

"How'd it happen?"

"He's 71, Jimmie; and he's exhausted. I'm afraid he doesn't care that much anymore."

My mother is one of the world's braver and more optimistic people. Her smile had lit up all of my seemingly endless youth; but it wasn't there now; and that itself felt so very peculiar. "What are they saying?" I asked.

"They're giving him antibiotics, but he's already gone through so many."

Hospitals make the mind wander when it doesn't rot. Both my parents were drifting inside this large pinkish building I'd often seen looming over the baseball fields and putting greens of my youth. It looked like Stalinist architecture transposed to the more temperate flatlands.

"Is he responding, though? Is he better? Why didn't anyone bother to give me a call?"

"You were so busy; we just didn't want to disturb you."

When she feels pressed, my mom's Southern accent comes back in force, as if she were taking refuge in the large house with the veranda near Dallas, where she'd spent her own sheltered youth. She, my sister and I had that in common. Only my dad had suffered through his childhood, but he was the toughness in our blood, if there was any (and a certain kind of warped sweetness).

"Not that busy, for Christ's sake," I said. She sighed at my taking the Lord's name in vain, and I apologized. She said, "He didn't want me to call. He said you had more important things to do than fret about him."

"Just what might those be?"

"I'll call you when you're needed, Jimmie. I'll want you here."

The last time my dad had been sick with pneumonia, frequently an emphysemic's last pit stop, she hadn't informed me until he walked out of the hospital. Did this demonstrate their worry about my career—or simply their sense of my limited utility?

"I think I'll just come on home," I told her before she could hang up.

"You're better off there," she said. "There's barely enough room for Anne and me here…" My sister, the women, the survivors. They slept on a gurney in his room.

"But Mom…"

"Calm down, don't get so hysterical," she said, with what might have passed for humor, hard to tell, but I think so. She always spoke against the grain, against your assumptions. When she graduated from college, she took a boat from Galveston to Boston, to get her Masters. She too may have wanted to get a long way away. Nobody had understood, they just submitted. I saw her will more clearly these days than I had when I lived under her wing. She anchored us all, all her men and my sister too, to the planet. Or moved the planet to make a place for us, opened up a furrow.

"Call me tomorrow then," I said. "When should I call you if you don't?"

"Three to five, he'll be taking a nap," she said, and then her voice changed one more time. "First time in his life he's been able to…he loves you, Jimmie."

About then, things that were never too clear, let's face it, starting running together. Irv called to say this, "My God, Jim." (We were back to old times, less familiar forms of address) "What happened at Good Day

Caffeine or whatever the hell it's called? You have to flatter those
people…not tell them what they don't want to know." This was a perceptive
point, I think, reflecting on it. All Anita wanted was some inkling, some
hint that during the time when she and other women had picked up their
vocational skills, men had learned something about the way the emotional
world works.

She had come to the wrong comer: had I understood anything
about it, I wouldn't have been browbeaten into leaving town and going to
Philadelphia where Irv had arranged for me "to get back into practice: see it
as your kind of minor league rehabilitation stint." He'd scheduled an
interview there with a guy even more disturbed than me; Philadelphia
produces them in bunches, like disappointing ball teams. Irv said the man
loved my work, but within minutes, seconds of my arrival, I could tell he
hadn't read any of it—out of principle. Preferred golf to women—one of
those guys. Sort of the Michael Chiklis, the deranged enforcer of the
submarine sandwich world. Let's call him Bill, Bill O.

He began by asking me questions, which might have come up
during his last divorce trial. "Have you ever thought," Bill O (though for
reasons of US libel law he's not to be confused with the truculent simpleton
expatiating on "geo-politics" on a cable channel) opined, in one of his first
observations, "that maybe men and women just don't like each other very
much?"

I shook my head no, pussy that I was. "It seems like a bad
operating principle," I said, calmly, patiently.

Post-no-Bill(s) looked to his right, not anyplace even near me. This
was the first weird thing about the interview. Usually on these shows, the
interviewers read off a teleprompter behind your head, maybe your
shoulder. That way, they seem to be looking at their guests even if, when

you're actually a guest, you feel pretty funny, having this man or woman's eyes staring behind you or to your side all the time. You get nervous, paranoid, figure something important is happening back there (a strange psychotic is getting up with a gun—something seemingly particularly likely on the show I was then on, where "going postal" was apparently a term of praise). But this man, who—remember—we're not confusing with Bill O'Reilly, looked at the teleprompter to his left, my right, and it was at a 90degree angle from the line between him and me, from the set. Even on the replay it was clear he was making no contact of nay kind, not even eye contact with me. The subject was apparently so painful he couldn't even pretend to look me in the eye. "Women want it both ways, wouldn't you say?" said he. "They want your respect and your alimony too. They want to eat your heart out on your dime."

I responded, "Not from me. Most of the women I date make as much money as I do, if not more. They may be afraid of giving *me* alimony."

"Really? Then what are they doing with you?"

"I'd like to think they're enjoying themselves, but maybe that's simply self-delusion." He didn't laugh. "Maybe they're looking for some other kind of support," I said a little more truculently. This jerk was succeeding in one thing (maybe that was his job and he was doing it well); he was rousing me, bringing me back to life.

"Just what kind of support would that be?"

"How many times have you been married?" I asked, out of order.

"I ask the questions," said he,."It's my show." And as if to prove it, in the ad break that immediately followed, he lit up a real cigarette and took five or six feverish inhalations. One forty five second break enabled him to consume three and half of the four inches of his cigarette.

"But it's assholes like me who fill it for you," I said between coughs. And he smiled grimly.

The camera's red eye shone once more. "We're with James Adams here, talking about his *Luck for the Lovelorn* deal—kind of a *metrosexual*'s guide to the feminine mind."

"I think it could help even real men like yourself."

"Oh, you do?"

"Yeah." I nodded vigorous, my snide smile matching his.

"Does it work?"

"Work how?"

I'd asked another question and you could see that non-Bill O was relatively peeved at my audacity. "Get you dates, uh women's interest, uh…do they like this stuff? You telling them how unique they are, putting down men and all that?" He nodded as he spoke, figuring it out.

I nodded sympathetically, "You don't think," I wondered again, "that the 'stuff,' what I'm writing, might not just be true?"

Oh, frankly, I don't blame this guy. What a difficult way to earn a living, having to engage with smug punks like me for hours and hours every week. No wonder he couldn't control his temper.

"I'm sure women like to hear the stuff," he said. He was my guest now, and I found his curt answers and general presence a boorish intrusion on good air space.

His producer and director obviously felt differently about this. To my right, where non-Bill's eyes bobbed in front of his teleprompter, a baby-faced generation y-er mouthed, "Stay calm." Was he saying this to me or to non-Bill? I think you know, but it didn't matter. Neither of us was listening; it was a chemical thing, I guess. I looked over at the guy looking away from me; and I thought of the similarly large, baby-Hueyish dad who lived across the street from me when I'd been ten. He'd claimed to be the world's fastest man at 20 (no mean feat for a person weighing in at about 250), the world's pocket billiard champion, the world's downhill racing winner at some European Olympics, you name it. I remembered how my mother grimaced out of sympathy for his wife, every year, when she saw her pregnant again. In front of god knows how many unfortunate telespectators as the French like to call them, while not-Bill O began bloviating about what women really did want (mostly leisure time and leisure goods was his antediluvian attitude), I continued thinking of Mr. Pretties, that was the family name, meandering over to our house to cadge an evening drink off my dad and my father finally tiring of the man's not-Bill-Ovian blather and beginning suddenly to put on his pajamas in front of his startled guest.

In front of the tiny studio audience's lagging attention and underneath—this may be important—tens of thousands of watts of lights, my mind just fried, its sizzle audible even to my hypertensive "host." Together we went back to the olden days when men were men, and I was ten. "How many times have you been married?" Not-Bill asked suddenly.

"Fewer than you, surely," I responded. "You forgot to give me your number...three, four?"

"Three," he said, emphatically.

"Might as well be ten, you know what I mean? You'll be chasing Larry King for that silver cuckold award..." That was more in my father's caustic voice than in my normally conciliatory tone.

Not-Bill's voice heightened responsively. "You think so, Mama's boy?"

"Ladies' Man, I like that better." As I said, I was losing, had already lost "it," whatever the "it" was. Remembering, it's difficult not feeling more than a little idiotic.

"Mama's boy," he repeated. "Mama's boy, always will be. Who do you support, pal?"

Truth is that was a good question, he was right to ask; but clouding my response were other factors: the man was so livid when he turned then to look at me (yes, he actually turned my way, distorting and undermining all of his delicately chosen, long-studied camera angles), I was transported once again, this time even farther back into my endless youth. The man's eyes seemed exopthalmic, huge and bobbing toward me, his nose big and veined and bulbous--he looked Big Bird, like Ronald MacDonald.

I started laughing at the image; and my laughter, twice as shrill as normal, pumped up by the obvious strains, just unhinged Not-Bill—that and the divorce suit, the sexual harassment charges and the already shaky ratings, maybe you read about it, how did this kind of thing always happen to me?

"Mama's boy," he shouted again. "This jerk-off's nothing but a pussy." Kind of a mixed referent, but it surely wasn't what sent the youthful director's hands over his eyes. He didn't want to see this, but I found it so hysterical, I was already laughing; and my hebephrenia just shorted non-Bill out. He jumped toward me and lifted me up in my chair. As I held onto the metal chair arms and laughed like a kid spinning in a Sidewinder ride, not-Bill turned and threw me at the director and the cameraman next to him. "Fuck you, Mama's boy," he screamed at me and all of Philadelphia. "Fuck this crummy town too, all of you."

Flipping out, as they say Pinky Lee did in reality and Howard Beale did on Network, not-Bill gave his 2.1 million spectators the shaft.

Or, as the Weekly News Illustrated said, in a page 37 article squeezed between an ad for surgical implants for an Asian man and a picture of a dog "inheriting 14 million dollars," "poltergeist hits Philadelphia talk show."

"You're losing it," Jeannie said to me when she arrived at my door, in dour downtown Manhattan, the night after my debacle in Philadelphia—and six or seven hours before I was to get up for Good Morning Caffeine. Not even she, the Weekly World News' most avid reader, bought the Poltergeist story. She thought the fault was mine. She had a bag with her, a little larger than an overnight case; and she dropped it a couple of yards inside the living room.

"Ah, you're staying this time," I noted.

"'Til tomorrow anyway," she said. "You need help."

"That's always the case," I suavely responded. "But how'd you hear (about my Philadelphia debacle)."

"We were seen together around town all last year, remember?" Seemed like I'd heard that before; but had I missed the point earlier, she gave me a look which could have pricked even greater bubbles than my own. "People call up and tell me things about you," she concluded..

Jeannie walked around me, looking. She was all angles, razor sharp and holding herself in as tightly as she could. Inspecting the rooms, she was trying to discern, I think, whether they'd been occupied lately by another female. She noted the apartment's spare furnishings (very male-like), the fireplace which may or may not have worked but obviously hadn't been tried, as if she'd hadn't seen any of it before. Perhaps she hadn't. She'd liked me more the first time she came by. "Are you going to go on Good Morning Caffeine?" She asked.

"Tomorrow morning. Why not?"

"Nobody's going to think it's funny if you freak out there...what's happening, Jim?"

I looked over her right shoulder; I looked at her out of my right ear, so it felt. I wasn't articulating very well.

And she responded to my withdrawal, pinching in on me like swollen tissue on a nerve. She looked lost, forlorn; she looked as if she wanted something, and I knew what it was—she wanted what my mother had been offended I couldn't give, the softer self I hugged so tightly to my chest.

I could have told her my dad was in the hospital, which was all I was thinking of. But I didn't fool her, I guess, with this brave and silent act. Jennie reached out over whatever fear of rejection she might have had and touched my cheek kindly, her fingers slipping under my chin and caressing me.

Then the doorbell rang again.

"Are you okay?" Sarah wondered when I opened the door. She was on her way back from the theater (it was only up Lafayette about five blocks), a scarf pulled snugly on her head, much the way it had been when that was the style in Paris and we'd loved each other. "What the matter, what's happening to you, Jimmie?" Jimmie, oh Jimmie Mack, when are you coming back.

Sarah looked past me and saw Jeannie. She started, and then smoothly said, "I'm sorry. I should have called first." Her disturbed look mirrored Jeannie's.

I wanted to evaporate, looked right, saw Sarah's concern, looked left and felt Jeannie's abrasive tenderness (or tender abrasions). My dad was in the hospital but—Oedipally ruled forever—I was the one in pain.

"But are you okay?" Sarah asked me. "Is he?" She asked Jeannie.

Jeannie said, "Do you know? It's always been hard for me to tell."

"Well, actually, he looks awful," Sarah decided. "What is it, Jim?"

"It's my dad—he's in the hospital. I don't think--no one seems to think--he's going to make it."

"Oh, Jimmy," Sarah said with what seemed a real gasp. "I am so sorry." She looked over at me as if I were an abandoned puppy (pretty much the actual case) and three quarters of me surged her way. The rest of me observed Jeannie humming to my right, seeing her moving away from me. My dad lit up around Sarah; in a way, he'd rediscovered some interest in me through her affection. He'd seemed to think well, if she can love him, there must be something there I'm missing. So around her, I'd felt his gaze on me, his attempt to discern what she may have appreciated in his son. And he hadn't been able to understand why, "in God's name," we'd broken up.

Jeannie came up behind me, shortening the distance between the three of us, compressing the triangle by sticking out her hand. She said, "you're Sarah, I take it. I'm Jeannie Kirsch, from California. We didn't get a chance to meet at the park."

As happened only too frequently in this sojourn to New York and the East coast, my mind again took flight. Just left me. Brain death at an early age. Seeing these two together made me think I had to choose (as if the option were mine)—even though one of my visitors hadn't ever shown sustained interest in me and the other had left me years before. Still my flesh felt close to them both, knew them both; and my flesh has always been stronger than my will and far, far stronger than my mind. My mind has abused the flesh frequently enough; but it's the flesh that has held up and brought me this far.

"Should I leave? Do you want me to go?" Jeannie asked me. And I shook my head no. I didn't, though who knows what I actually did want?

As I sat on the sofa, my mind revved up frantically like a tiny twin-engine plane in a storm. I was thinking of my dad, and I was afraid for him while experiencing no little fear for my own sense of the world. I felt somewhat as I had, fifteen years before, when I'd eaten a ball of hash, gotten drunk and awakened the next morning not knowing which drug had left me more incapacitated, all my senses racing beyond my ability to harness them. This time, though, I wasn't able to find a friend's shrink (after being shuttled from one section to the next of Bellevue, New York's psychiatric ward, without ever managing to make a pit stop before a psychiatrist, a nurse, even a pill dispensary) and persuade him, with a mere look, that a dose of Thorazine was in order.

Instead, Sarah reached for me, and we hugged for a long time. There was no sexual tug in her fingers, none in mine either. My dad, I thought, was checking out; he wasn't going to make it. Somehow I could feel it between Sarah and me, inside myself. None of the air there seemed mine.

"Do you want me to stay?" Sarah wondered. "I'm asking you too, Jeannie," she added.

Jeannie smiled. "Why not? I've never really had him all to myself anyway."

Sarah seemed to understand. "He's an awful lot of trouble," she said. "You may just be too smart for that." These two understood each other. They looked my way, to see if I had an inkling, which I certainly didn't. To me, they looked like upcoming lights in a rainy windshield. Sarah's lips came hesitantly, vaguely together, the upper lip like a feather gliding toward the ground. She took off her coat and took my right hand. Jeannie took my left; and, holding me, the two fed me spaghetti, cookies, ice cream. They let me regress about as afar as I could, sitting there looking first at one, then the other.

I have a friend who is a shrink who said she did that for her brother once when he was breaking down—just fed him, let him opt out of all responsibility until finally one day he felt he could cope again, on his own. That's kind of what this night felt like to me, though it's hard to say I was ready to cope at the end of it. Au contraire. Still, between the two of them, I managed to fall into a deep if very agitated sleep—rather like a cow hit (at the friendly butcher's) by a stun gun.

I awoke at 2:45, then again at 3:35, but not because I was
nervously anticipating the Good Morning Caffeine's shot in my morning, its
4 a.m. wake up call. I was roused instead by my father's face writhing again
in my dream, inside something that looked like cellophane. He was trying to
scream; but I not only heard no words, I was forced to watch as his lips
slowed, their movements limp as beached kelp; he put his face up against
the plastic and nothing, no breath fogged its surface. I blew and below from
the cellophane's other side, but only the sack itself expanded--my dad's
face was as glazed and inanimate as a mortician's mask.

When I awoke, sweating and in a panic, I couldn't fully absorb the
fact that Jeannie was there, beside me. Sarah had left, gone home to her
child. But the sight of Jeannie, her long black hair sticking to her temples,
was startling enough, a part of the dream, as was my call to the hospital
immediately thereafter. Nurses were on duty. I needed to know about my
dad. But the switchboard wouldn't put me through. "It's 2:30 in the
morning, sir," a woman with a thick hometown accent said. "We only
process emergencies now."

"Okay, well, I'm not looking to speak to a patient. I just want the
nurses' station."

"We only do that at this hour in intensive care, sir."

"Could you check if my father's there?"

"You don't know?"

"He wasn't yesterday, but could you check to see if he's in the same shape?"

"I can't do that, sir, over the phone. I can't release patient information even if I had it. I'm sure you understand that," said she.

"Well just tell me if he's still in the same room, they haven't moved him. You can tell me that, can't you?"

She did, and he was. "Will you let me know if it changes?" I asked. She hesitated, then relented, though this probably violated every imaginable principle of good hospital management. Yet her kindness didn't work its way into my sleep, didn't give me any more rest.

When I came buzzing into the Good Morning Caffeine show itself, a couple of hours later, the production assistant who greeted me looked at me intently and said, "You look awful." He cajoled a make-up man into giving me a couple of extra layers of beige pancake and hit me with a third operative who, small, bespectacled and ferocious, resembled a dyspeptic Shar Pei. "Do you think you can get through one of these interviews without making a spectacle of yourself?" The Shar Pei wondered.

If only any publicity was good publicity, as some claim, I might have been doing particularly well. Instead, I was feeling as worried as many of my friends on the set looked. Irv and Irv's Irv Rick were there, appearing concerned and unusually garish in Scottish plaid suits. Jesus, they looked anxious, so worried they almost trembled with fear, but they had no reason to be so disturbed. Juana, the fabled hostess who alienated the nation when she replaced Jane, could have handled a rhino. She was gracious and more than a little bemused--I've been told she'd seen way too many versions of me in the cartoons her ex-husband animated.

However, like most women interviewers, she got rapidly to the gist of my little argument. "Do you think these difficulties, men and women are having, are singular, unique to our generation," she asked within seconds of our opening salvos, "or aren't they really problems that have always been there?"

"Sure, they have always been there," I responded. "But I think we are a little different."

"Why? What's so special about us?" She countered.

"We weren't breastfed," I answered. "First generation ever not to be—our mothers just stopped, all of a sudden, here and in parts of Western Europe, like salmon going to spawn. All of them stopped breastfeeding, and we're testament to the consequences, I think. They thought it was unhygienic (forget about what it did to the structure of their breasts), so they brought us up on bottles—we've been suffering from it ever since (particularly us, the males)."

Juana's black eyes, which are always bright, sharpened still further (guess this wasn't in her synopsis of my minimal opus). "So you think our *(read her)* children won't suffer from the same problems, might be able to commit themselves since most of their *(read her)* moms went back to breastfeeding…"

"Yes," I said to her visible relief. "I hope so. They won't be paralyzed, won't have the same kind of overwhelming severance anxiety…won't have to run away all the time just because they're sure the connection is going to be cut off. Or then again, the women just might conclude that the male species is inalterably errant and let us go the way of the snail darter. To the terminus, the End Zone…"

The End Zone, where real men touch down. When I walked off the set, many acquaintances seemed happy for me. Irv and Irv's Irv in particular seemed joyful. Irv's forehead even seemed dry for a change, though Eric had a handkerchief out.

"I think this will do it, James," Irv said. "Got to show them at least once that you don't freak out for the publicity of it all." He looked at his watch.

"6:43," Eric said. "Takes twenty minutes to get to the Dorset from here." He picked up Irv's briefcase for him, had one in each hand—nice leather briefcases tucked beneath pink and grey Tartan plaids.

"20/20 is going for it next. They heard you were a little flaky, but I told them to get a load of this—you were flaky like a fox. That breastfeeding shit today, Jimmy, what a stroke of genius!" He grinned and gave me a nudge. Obviously he hadn't read the book either.

"Tomorrow, Thursday at the latest and you're in, kid. A good performance here on the HyperCaffeinated one and you get a shot on The Jaw. If he takes you, you can coast all the way to the grave. He's simple enough even you can't fuck that up.."

The word "grave" echoed all the way home, the sound reverberating from Irv's capacious larynx way across town to my cell phone's buzzing when I walked in the door. Jeannie was tying a black bow on her white blouse. She was wearing a grey striped executive suit, the skirt cutting right through her knees. As I approached her, her body tilted away from me—but just half way, as if she couldn't decide what she might want to give me, what I might be able to receive.

I had more than one phone message. The first was blurred, befogged. It sounded as if it came from the street; a truck sped by, there was the sound of an exhaust popping, enormous static, then a woman's voice, my mom's. "I'm sorry, this call is…I know you're, this is the day you're on TV again, I guess…I think, could you…"

The second message came from "Nurse Price, I'm at the St. Francis nurses' station, and I'm sorry, Mr. Adams. I was wrong about your father. I didn't know. They've taken him off our floor, the ninth, and moved him to five. That's.. I'm sorry to tell you, but I thought you'd want to know, that's what you were worried about. Five is intensive care. If I can help you in any way, if you'd like to know more, I'll be here until 8 o'clock, Tulsa time."

"I am so sorry," Jeannie said, putting down her briefcase. "Do you want me to stay?"

What would she have been able to do? I appreciated her presence but I was essentially free-floating, my mental and emotional state almost entirely instinctual: a slug inside myself paced the room, trying occasionally, every couple of minutes, to phone home. Nobody answered, and the hospital wouldn't put calls through to people in Intensive Care. They'd only connect you to the waiting room, and that line, of course, was constantly busy.

When my phone finally rang again, it wasn't my mom or my sister, as I hoped it might be. It was Irv's Irv, Eric, "Great performance," he said, making "great" into a polysyllabic word, "Love it, Irv loved it—and what's a little more important here, Maria loved it. We thought, 'why not go for a trifecta,' all the morning shows? They don't like overlapping guests, but when you're this hot, why not? And CBS, hey nobody watches them, maybe 6, 8 million in the morning, but this is the type of stuff they buy, J-Ji-Ji-James…"

He was confused on the name to call me, new at this business, but I didn't mind. I wouldn't have been offended if he'd called me Biff.

"Maria went wild," he continued, "for that breastfeeding line. How'd you come up with it, just like that?" He hadn't read the book either. "Guess you were just hungry."

Where was my mother? That's what I was thinking, missing what I now take to be Rick's weird attempt at humor, feeling it was just like her to have cut me loose, weaned me to listen to goof-balls like this guy in the pastel-hued plaid. My ear was sweating; you know how it is when you just can't absorb any more. I was tired and wired and when I looked out the apartment window, what I noticed at street level was a 20 year old girl in soiled clothes going up to a man at a paper kiosk asking him for money, a hand out. He gave it to her too, then she dunned, unsuccessfully, a middle aged Latina who was set to cross the street. So she went back to the first man and held out her hand again. He hesitated. He had a kind face, some kind of aging glue or stationery manufacturer, maybe a cloth merchant; and he gave again.

"See you, Eric," I said.

It took another fifteen minutes before the call came. The girl begging below never left the intersection's four corners. She went from one base to the next like a utility infielder.

There was static on the connection and an instant or two's hesitation before my mother's voice finally attached itself to the line. She was focused on what she needed to do. "Anne (my sister) told me you were...you made it onto one of the morning shows," she began.

"How's Dad? Are you all right, Mom?"

"She said you were good, Jim. I'm happy for you."

"Doesn't matter, Mom."

"Do you have any more of these to do? All the others... they must want you too. Your dad would probably like that."

"How is he?"

"Well, if he were my daddy," she began. "I'd want to be with him. I wouldn't be going around making a spectacle out of myself on national TV." Mom took a deep and bitter breath, as if she had to bite it out of the air. "If it was my father, I'd be here. I don't think he's going…" She broke off with a small, sharp cry, like a pet, which had just been stepped on. "I don't think I'm going to bring him home this time."

Love, Again…

Part 2

Love, Again…

I had trouble focusing on what was happening; and clearly, my sister Anne who picked me up at the airport had too many conflicting emotions to be able to extract any one from her quiver. Only CJ, odd enough, who dropped me off at Kennedy, had any kind of eye on the big picture, at least on my part and his. He'd come over, packed my bags for me when I couldn't do it, and volunteered to take the rest of my belongings to California ("you won't be back, Max," he' said; "Jimmie Max doesn't come back, remember?"), and ushered me into his rent-a-car. It was a convertible, this winter day, with the heat turned up past 90. At Kennedy, he slowed down to about my speed. "Hey, Max," he said, gently. "I know you had your problems with the guy when we were in school. You had so much bitterness toward the old man; maybe that's what made us so close, me with the manic-depressive who fathered me. But you know, the last three or four years, you've started to make some sort of peace with the guy. I've seen it. And he's got to know it too."

It took about an hour once I arrived home to drive to the huge, pink hospital, which harbored my dad. The trip seemed longer, for I had to fend off the specific remonstrance ("glad you decided to drop in on us") and general grievances of my sister Anne. She hated the Good Morning Caffeine show, commenting that "of course that breast feeding bit was totally ridiculous, but you must know that…"

I didn't at all, but what could I say? She's three years older, three marriages wiser than I—though every marriage added another two inches to her waist and another twist of her embittered screw. When I looked at her in the car, I could barely recall the slightly overprotective big sister and dazzling cheerleader she'd once been. I only seemed to see the middle-aged pill head and lush she appeared in danger of becoming. Still it's a wonder I even saw that much. I deal poorly, defensively with criticism, having had a lifetime of it from my dad before I hit puberty, and I zoned out on hers. But she seemed to sense it sooner rather than later and changed her tone. That defensiveness is something we shared, the only trait that linked us beyond our old man's ferocious will. This day she knew we needed to stay connected and so did I.

My mom, ours, had been with him all night and all day. She was in the lounge sleeping when Anne and I arrived at the hospital. There were dozens of others in the lounge area next to the intensive care unit. Most of these made us feel almost ashamed at our own grief. There was a woman whose baby had fallen from their 4th floor apartment; another whose 14-year-old son had been hit by a truck when he was riding his bike home from school. The baby's functioning had almost completely ceased, except for a heart, which sporadically bobbed, pushing just enough blood through itself to keep the 13 month-old body alive. Her brain was already dead. There were six, maybe eight people around her mother when we arrived, at least that many all the time she was there. They all seemed to carry Bibles, shiny and white with distinct gold embossing; they whispered to her and comforted the woman, whose blue eyes looked, I remember, like kid's night lights, small and dimly glowing at the edges of a great, menacing darkness.

My mom's own peacock blue irises were hidden, while she slept, behind gray and black lashes, ashen lids. You could hear her snore, quietly, when you looked down on her. She breathed with difficulty, like her husband. And so we decided to let her sleep, Anne and I and Anne's latest husband Greg, though we probably wouldn't have had we known she would thus miss her husband's return to intensive care.

We found out by accident, because I walked down the corridor into a restricted area, wanting to learn a little about Dad's illness. When I couldn't find anyone to respond, I stood around awhile and watched the entire parade of the damaged stream past. And there he came among them, though it took me several minutes to comprehend that the slight gray figure on the gurney in front of me, in detention-center garb, bereft of any authority and buried inside memory and pain was my father. He was lying on his stomach; and a small, heavily veined hand lay beside his open mouth.

"You're not supposed to be here, sir," an orderly said to me with a kinder tone than the words convey.

An IV hung beside the old man's left arm. Blood in a plasma bag, plastic and tawdry, like a dour whoopee cushion, drooped down to his right. The man's face turned my way, and I started. "That's my dad," I said. And a nurse responded, "That's why you're not supposed to be here until he's ready to be seen."

A large orderly picked my father up in his arms. When a second offered his help, the orderly said, "Just get the bottles," and he carried my father from the gurney to his new bed. When the accompanying nurses busied themselves with the rest of the room, the orderly pulled down the sheets with his left hand while cradling my father in his right, easily and without strain. Then he eased my dad gently into bed.

Though he was placed on his side, my fathered turned back toward his daughter and me and languidly opened his wan lids. His eyes, though they didn't exactly brighten, focused on me, holding me inside them for a long moment.

"Jimmy," he said clearly, using again, for the second time that day, this nickname of my youth, "good you could come back." He tried to smile, I thought, but his eyes closed again, wiping out his face's complicated expressions like a magician's hands erase the doves, the many handkerchiefs, and the coins between his fingers.

Was I back, as my father maintained? Well there was my sister in the corridor beside me. There was our mom asleep in the lounge, and my small, fading dad fell asleep again nearby, pale as an etiolated stem. Was this back?

We were in a hospital that had at one time occupied the extreme southern edge of town and was now its demographic center. The city itself had stretched 22 miles farther south, a hodgepodge of new subdivisions, of "colonial" houses, and malls and Jiffy Lubes having replaced the forests and farms. The city had in so many ways run away from itself. Just as I had fled the places I once lived, the city had run out from under my memories.

But this much remained: in the lounge there were 30 or 40 people closing in protectively around the woman with the iridescent blue, almost purple eyes and the dying baby. The men wore dark, ill-cut suits, mostly polyester from their shine; and the women wore dark print dresses that covered their knees. They'd come in largely from Missouri, I'd later learn, where most had gone to high school with this desperate woman with the sweet face and the uncomprehending eyes, who was trying and failing to see why God's plan dictated her child's early demise. Helping her understand, her friends all had their white Bibles out, flipping through the red and gold-bordered pages seeking consolation. Though they tried to be discreet, they made the room shake when they prayed. I had to go outside just to hear myself think. Once there, feeling alone and marginalized, I knew I was home.

"Thanks," my mom said to me when she finally awoke. "I sure appreciate your coming." They all did, my dad, my mom; they were happy I'd come home—and hearing them, I realized for once what kind of an asshole they must have thought I was. Thanks for coming—to my father's nearly fatal illness, as if I wouldn't automatically be present, as if there were some doubt. As if this were a shower for a distant and poorly liked liked cousin, a bridge game in need of a fourth.

"She's so happy to have you here, you can't imagine," echoed my mom's best friend Midge as she arrived and gave me a peck on the cheek. And she meant it; they all did; they treated me with that special consideration reserved for the mentally and emotionally disturbed—or maybe just dense, insensitive males.

"I just don't know how much longer I can do everything all by myself," my mom said next.

"Fran is tired to the bone, Jimmy," Midge explained further.

"Anne's here," I responded.

"Oh, Anne," my mom said. "Yes, sure."

"Anne's another deal altogether," Midge clarified, rolling her eyes.

Stay at home and they forget you. Leave and they hope you'll RSVP to your family's critical events. They continue to help you perpetuate this unnatural, delusional sense of yourself—this idea that your presence on the planet, in a place, in somebody else's life is a present you're offering, the gift of yourself the choicest gift of all. I feel for my sister, but maybe she was lucky to have been spared this idiotic sense of self-importance.

"Your dad's going to be thrilled too," Midge said. And my mom looked up and seemed surprised now at her surroundings.

"He kept asking for you last night," my mom said. "Didn't he, Midge?"

"He's going to get a lot better now that you're all here," Midge decided. "That's what happened to Mr. T." Mr. T was her husband, Tom Taylor. Fifteen or twenty years younger than our paterfamilias, he'd already had two heart attacks and was laid up in a wheelchair most of the time. But he was living, getting stronger, Midge said, even if she was drinking more these days. It was not all that far past noon, but there was more than a soupcon of bourbon on her breath. My mom didn't care, of course. Then too she might not have even been too clear on who was around at that point.

"Where did Anne go?" Midge wondered. The least sober of us, she may have had the sharpest eye.

"Who?" I asked.

"Your sister."

"She's probably trying to understand why they brought Dad down here. We couldn't get a straight answer," my mom said.

"To keep him from dying," Anne ultimately concluded, with a brave and wild eye, when she came back into the room.

"They said he was getting a little worse. They just wanted to be cautious." This was Greg, her husband, gently rectifying his wife's hyperbole.

Anne sounded and looked like a frantic diva who had missed a scene cue. "I've been talking to the nurses," she said, while Greg nodded forlornly, like a funeral home director. "They're going to put Dad on a respirator, this afternoon. That's what the nurses say."

"Doctor Walker cares for your dad. He wouldn't do that," Mom replied. "He's the best internist in the state."

As if that mattered. Our father had often said he didn't want his life artificially maintained. He'd said it fifteen, almost twenty years before when I'd been in high school, in a rare aside to his kids at a time when he usually restricted his conversations at home to perorations to the family pets. A bit inebriated, he'd tell them how confused humans' values could get, what kind of wretched torture the species had invented to try to prolong its own end. But, though this may have been a way at the time to distance himself from his two addled kids, he'd spoken of it again to his wife, our mom, just the previous week. "I've talked to Dr. Walker about it twice since," Mom averred. "And that's that. Dr. Walker will respect his wishes. Gene's never going to be hooked up to a respirator. Doesn't want to. Would hate us if we allowed it to happen. The doctor promises me that dad will get what he's asked for." Here her voice began to fade.

"Oh, yeah, sure. He'll respect Dad's wishes until he doesn't," Anne affirmed. "I talked to Walter—that's the male nurse, a very nice guy. And he said we better get ready for it. All the signs point to it."

"You're sure about that, Anne?" Midge asked, watching my mom's face.

"They already gave him a pint of blood today," said my sister.

"I know that," Mom said. "You don't have to go over all that with me." She rose and began to walk toward her husband's new room. Anne and I went to help her. "No thank you," she said angrily. "I'd rather be alone."

She took two more steps before, feeling guilty, she turned sadly around. Her voice changed too. "Thanks for coming, Jimmie," she said. And she embraced me. "I feel so much better with you here; but the doctors are going to do what they want, one way or the other. I'm going to be with your dad. He's the one who needs me."

"What's the real problem with Dad," I asked my sister as she drove us out of the hospital grounds, turning on Yale Avenue and 71st Street, going home. This had been farmland when I'd been in high school. I'd "parked" out here with Susie Benson, and she'd firmly kept my hands away. "Nobody's told me anything about it."

"Nobody's trying to hide anything from you. He's got an ulcer."

"How, how's that?" They'd told me about the kidney infection. I knew about the lungs.

"From the antibiotics—they've given him so many they've caused an ulcer…that's what the internal bleeding's about. Sorry I forgot to tell you."

I'd often thought, after having subjected myself to no small amount of physical and psychic abuse, that the body is so much stronger than we imagine—but my dad's body had taken enough, too much punishment by this time, I guess. Such an indomitable will was housed in such a frail integument.

LaFortune Park, a bowling alley, a burger king and Skelly Drive flashed by on my right. Skelly Drive, named after another oilman subsumed in J. Paul Getty's maw, had to be rebuilt almost immediately upon completion as its surface proved riddled with thousands of potholes. A product of cut-rate building materials, the road's dilapidation wasn't supposed to happen in the Puritanical Southwest, where littering had become a jailable offense. But its occurrence gave me hope when I was 15 that my own flaws might not be so unusual. Everything now in that larger world looked ready to crack open, as if made from the pre-molded plastic Fantastic is designed to clean—frail, flimsily constructed but nonetheless planetarily ineradicable.

Following behind us was my sister's husband Greg. He was driving the family's second car, which was a truck. My sister, as if more than a little embarrassed by her spouse, seemed to be attempting to lose him on the way home. She took her turns sharply, ran yellow lights, which was a ticketable offense, could have lost her license charging through reds. But Greg blithely loped through all of these too, like a gregarious pup.

We'd been silent for a while when my sister said, "I don't know about Greg these days either," after Greg ran a full, bright red light. "I think he's going to get himself killed before I can divorce him."

"You'll do better on the settlement that way," I said, tastelessly.

"Not necessarily," Anne replied. "This is the worst marriage contract I've signed yet. I don't know what I was thinking. I guess I was just Jonesed on love. The settlement depends on whether he's driving a work or a personal vehicle when the accident occurs. Last time I checked, all his work related insurance goes to Jessica."

Jessica was Greg's kid by one of his wives, I think the second. He didn't discuss these things, which was probably smart of him. He knew better. Each marriage seemed to have made the next one more difficult. But each sure helped his career, signaling an upward move. An engineer, he'd worked at that through his first marriage, formed a design/build firm in his second with that wife's father, was a contractor in the third marriage, and was now talking to my dad about oil field construction.

Anne and I finally stopped in front of our family's house, a ranch style American, circa 1955, large and flat with a gravel roof and rather better light than most of the houses built then (that is, with some light, since the house tilted a little South though it was predominantly Eastern in exposure). Very beautifully treed and landscaped, it sat in a handsome neighborhood. We had a nice stand of oaks and pecans, a maple that bled rust red and dark, blood orange, Dad's favorite tree. "So how about you, Anne?" I asked my sister.

"What about me?"

"Kids? How's that coming?" The expert on the subject wondered.

And Anne started crying--one moment laughing, the next crying, my sister. "I'm trying," she began, "but Greg hates the hospital. Going there makes him feel degraded—you know how it works, don't you?"

I'd been told. My sister had damaged ovaries; they wondered about the motility of Greg's sperm. They were trying to conceive in vitro. Greg had to leave his sperm a couple of days a month; she took a raft of shots and drugs, both at the same hospital in which our father was uncomfortably settled.

"He doesn't care bout kids," Anne added. "I thought since he had one...but guys are clever these days. They talk a good game about kids; but they balk before the actual difficulties. You must know something about that, huh, Jimmie?"

Well, uh, yes.

"Where are your kids?" She asked, then paused. "We're awful disappointing offspring, aren't we?"

"Fin du race, the frogs say. End of the line. You want to come inside?"

"I don't think so," said she. "I'm not used to talking this much to you. Let's not push our luck. You know how to get in still?" From under her dash, she removed an electric garage door beeper; and she pointed it at the double doors. Miraculously, they rose. "Dad got this off some late night infomercial. It puts all our doors--his and ours at home--on the same frequency."

"Figures," I said, with an ache in my heart, something dying in the top of my stomach. My old man had gone for every mechanical device America mass-produced. Once he caved in finally on the air-conditioner (after making us sweat out summers at 98 to 109 while our cool friends grinned condescendingly our way), he bought the whole numero, all the rest, from waterpik to electric knife and knife-sharpener to battery powered nose hair clippers. Going into and through the house, I felt acclimated through the objects. But this one set me off, his most recent acquisition: on the stool beside his usual chair, green plaid and tiny like him, on a pile of Oil and Gas journals, there was a six inch golfer leaning on his driver and looking out at a short, dogleg right (Astroturf over a grey metal base). Voice activated, the golfer listened for your call. When he said, as my dad had that Christmas when I'd come home, "Hey, Tiger, let's see that swing of yours," the golfer would bend over an imaginary ball; his arms would rise, and he'd belt the fictive ball 250 yards. "Hole in one," the machine would then say. "Hole in one."

I watched "Tiger" do this four or five times in a row when the phone rang. My father's voice answered before I could, on an old answering machine. "This is the Adams residence, Riverside 23220," he began spryly, as if this were 1970. "We're momentarily unavailable for comment, but if you'll leave your name and your phone number, we'll get back to you as soon as our press agent lets us."

"Eve, are you back there someplace?" A woman asked, taking no note that it was my dad's voice, her friend's sick husband who answered. "This is Norma. I suppose you're over at St. Francis with Gene. I'll try to get you there. We're all praying for you. Bye."

Just above the machine were framed pictures, a couple of which I found myself staring at now. Between a picture of my sister as Tri Theta's Miss Congeniality and another of my mom as Texas State tennis champ 40 plus years before, there was a picture of my dad and his four brothers. This one was sepia, brown and cream, and yellowing with age. Of the four brothers, my dad was the youngest and the smallest. He raised himself to his full height of about 4 feet. He was seven years old—and he and his brothers were carrying boxes out of a small, teetering shack, a general store. There's a Coca-Cola sign, others advertising various pain remedies. This wasn't the family store. My granddad worked for the Santa Fe; my dad and his brothers were earning their keep, buying their own shirts with their pay, six to twelve years old.

Across from this picture, on the other side of the end table, was a photo of me as all-star guard, in uniform at 13. My dad had always preferred it because it had been the last time I'd let myself be seen with the short, cropped hair, the burr cut he'd always liked best. It had been one of the last times we'd agreed about much at all, puberty hitting me late but hitting hard. I looked fit in that photo, cocky and proud of myself, the all-star, a comfortable kid much as my mother had looked, at five or six, in a hand-painted photo on the same wall. She was wearing her Sunday best, a bow in her black hair, a splendid flowing Easter dress, impeccably white and billowing over a petticoat and glistening, back patent leather shoes. A small town banker's daughter, posing in an infrequent idle moment, she grinned slightly at the camera. And she looked, just as I remembered,

almost exactly like Jessie Revson, Sarah's child and possibly mine as well.
Too bad, I was suddenly certain, as tears poised to drop down my cheeks,
too bad he would never know the kid in the other photo, the one with the
hand-me-down clothes, the determined face, the large hopeful eyes and the
future almost entirely behind him now, my dad.

In the hospital lounge the next morning, my sister was one of the
few who knew what she wanted to do. Most of the others, stunned like me,
slept or tried to, turning over from one side to the other, like hot dogs
rotating on a spit. The lady with the dying daughter was over in the corner,
rustling against a clean, white embroidered pillow. She wasn't much over
30, I'd guess, but her blond hair was already streaked with grey. She turned
constantly, trying to escape the light which, though it came from the north,
still seemed to seek her out. There weren't any curtains, only green plastic
vertical shades. In this multi-angled room, the dark corners all felt occupied,
dense.

My sister and I—white, upper middle class in pretensions (if
downwardly mobile these days) and scared by all this—felt entitled to talk
to someone, perhaps a doctor. Anne had discovered that my dad's doctor
had 40 or so clients in the hospital, in different states of distress. He spent a
couple of hours twice a day, from 10 to 12 in the morning and from 4 to 6
p.m. visiting his patients. That would be about three minutes allotted each,
if you didn't consider travel time. He moved fast, obviously; you had to be
quick to catch him.

Trying to find him, we had to change wards, to move through the
double-doored intensive care elevator; through the spare, grey lobby with
the bronzed bust of the oncology wing's major donor, the daughter of a
local oil magnate; to another set of elevators and a different wing of the
hospital, where the less sickly recuperated. Our dad had been under Dr.

Walker's care here, Anne said, the last time he'd come in with pneumonia. I'd been busy that time, hadn't been invited or even informed of the malady until he was well and actually in the car leaving the hospital. When the book I sent him arrived, he was already back home, the book returning to me weeks later in Los Angeles, book rate, dispatched by the hospital staff.

Present this time, I tried to play big brother to my older and larger sister and didn't exactly succeed. "He's not in that bad shape--is he really?" I asked.

"You haven't been watching him the last week," Anne succinctly said. "He can't even comb his hair any more. I've had to learn to do it— Greg and I have."

"But that's not necessarily a sign of anything, that's…"

"Dying, Jim. It's called 'death.' Think what it means to him having me do his hair." She paused operatically and sighed. "He's got a way to do it, you can imagine; and you've got to follow the directions perfectly." The Right Way, it dominated the short list of my dad's concerns: he could show you the best way to the second to reach his office, fold a shirt, floss even your most crooked teeth or arrange the folding money in your wallet. Anne looked my way, and her smile fell into itself as she spoke. "You comb his cowlick to the right three times, then four, five times to the left to soften it up; then you cup your hand around it and comb it straight back. And it will disappear, magically: the cowlick just vanishes."

She gestured toward the large and expansive mane of hair, which rose lion-like on the left side of her head. I had a similar cowlick, too. But I had never noticed my dad's, never thought his hair didn't naturally flow into its gentleman's cut.

"Walter says they're going to hook him up."

"Who's Walker?" I asked.

"The male nurse, you remember very well. They're going to plug Dad in; they're going to wire him up. They don't care how he feels about it."

That's what hospitals do, that's what we do. It was odd how worn the people seemed who worked inside this one, I thought, as we watched a few carts roll by. We were sitting on the lung floor. The people working there looked like fatigued air traffic controllers—and this was the hopeful part of the hospital. Most of these patients would survive and return home.

"Let's go back and talk to Walter," I said.

"You don't believe me?" My sister asked. "What more could Walter tell us. Let's go find Walker, the doc's here some place."

We continued on. Patients seemed cheerier here, in this institutional green, older wing. More light reached them, coming in from the west. They were able to watch the sunsets every night, and you could see that the patients expected to leave. They shared rooms, like fellow passengers on a European train; and the rooms seemed altogether free of the massive and ominous equipment I'd glimpsed, if briefly, in intensive care.

In intensive care, there were more machines than people; and the equipment outlived longer the patients. Every room had a large picture window in its party wall with the main service area, so the staff could always observe the "guests." Most of the time, however, they merely saw the machines operating, registering data or flashing lights signaling high or low levels of some bodily function. Most of the time, the staff took care of the machines.

After some meandering between floors and ells, feeling as if we were jogging and about to hit "the wall," we found our man, Dr. Walker. Tall and unnaturally, absurdly fair, the doc was white and gelatinous as a soft boiled egg, with a receding hairline and bulging pants tied up with a thick leather belt. He looked like he'd recently lost 30 or 40 pounds; and he had a former fat man's cheerless good humor. "Anne," he greeted her, "what are you doing over here?" He continued walking, a pretty good indicator of his level of interest. We fell in with his pace.

"This is my brother, doctor," Anne said.

He turned breathily my way. "I've heard so much about you…"

"And me you. How'd my dad, doctor?" Obviously I thought I was taking charge, all business as I took the man's surprisingly tiny hand in mine. Something about it reminded me of a grub worm, but I don't mean that nastily—that's just what I remember of this time, which has absorbed within itself most of my recollections, like salt absorbing wine spilled on a white cloth.

"Your dad could be better," the doctor said. "I talked to your Mom about his 'progress' this morning."

Odd how doctors always make you feel, even at their most gracious, like disenfranchised, newly impoverished aristocrats—people out of Flannery O'Conner—as if the town, theirs, had passed you by. The doctors of course have more important things to do than talk to you.

"We were worried," I said, "that Dad might be put on a respirator. We'd heard something to that effect, but we were sure that wasn't possible…"

The man gave me an unsparing look. "I'm the doctor here," said Dr. Walker. "He won't go on any respirator unless I so order." He had a precise way of speaking, though he had trouble with his "r"s.

"Because, doctor, I'd just like to make sure we understand each other: it's clear, I hope, that our dad doesn't want to be artificially maintained. I'm sure he's told you that, hasn't he? If he's about to die, he wants to die as naturally as possible." I couldn't be more blunt, finally.

Though my sister, surprisingly, was letting me do most of the talking, her regard, sharper than I'd ever seen it, kept the doctor fidgeting.

"There are a lot of things to consider," the man began, with a quick glimpse at his watch, as if we needed reminding of the importance of his time.

"Not really. Not that many things," I opined.

"He just doesn't want to be wired to a machine," Anne said simply.

Dr. Walker checked his watch again. Not much time had fled from it—perhaps he thought an explanation was going to require more time than he had to give.

So he tried charm. "I know that, Anne. I've talked to Gene about this numerous times. You know Gene's a man with a lot to say on most important matters. And he's always worth listening to."

I don't think I liked him calling my dad "Gene." The doctor was only 40, 45. "Mr. Adams" would have sounded better, and the good doctor may have noticed my disapproving gaze. Then again, he may have thought I was just another annoying smart-aleck (as my dad was wont to call me).

"Still there's this to think about," he continued, rather grim-visaged at that moment for such a suave operator. "Your father is a man I respect immensely. He's had a rich and full life. And I don't want... he doesn't deserve to be tortured here, to have his last days—if that's what they indeed turn out to be—be anything but peaceful. I'm not going to try out any new cures on him."

I nodded vigorously. My sister just kept staring at him.

"But there's another side to this too,' he said. "I also tell myself when I see you two and Eve that he's got so much to live for, so many people he cares about and who care about him. I want to try everything I can to keep him around."

He blinked his thick, nearly circular lids, as if he was batting away unexpected emotions, and he said, "At any rate, before I decide anything, I'll talk to you two. We're not there yet."

He offered his hand to me. When I took it in thanks, phlegm flooded into my throat and my nose. His eyes returned from their disturbed perusal of the perforated white ceiling tiles to settle sharply on me. "My receptionist says you were great on that TV show the other morning. Congratulations." He nudged my arm, and he was off.

"Was he talking about Good Morning Caffeine?" Anne asked incredulously, shaking her head. "What a lying sleaze."

"I don't know," I said.

"You wouldn't, that's for sure," Anne responded, her sharp eyes digging into the departing doctor's fat back. "You're so vain that if anyone takes you half as seriously as you take yourself, you'll believe anything he says."

She was probably right, but I wasn't used to hearing this from another party. I thought I was the only one who saw this.

"Don't be so paranoid," I told my older sister.

"I'm not. The doctor's a liar. He's going to wire Dad up and bleed him dry. I believe Walter." She paused, and her face crinkled up, like a sheet of paper being readied for the wastebasket. "What's a gay black nurse got to gain? Why would he tell a cruel and uningratiating lie?"

Suddenly they wouldn't let us see him. It's true obviously that patients have to be taught to use a respirator. And my dad, a refractory spirit to begin with, was not cooperating at all. So he wouldn't fight against the machine, he had to be sedated, drugged above and beyond the handful of tranquilizers he consumed each day. He hated those too, and he was embarrassed at the way they made him look and feel.

"He says they make him lose his sense of things," my sister said earlier. His "sense of control," she should have said. The doctors were giving him steroids on top of the opiates—and disorientation was a prominent side-effect. He was being spun, my father, like a top, away from himself, his own string, his connection to the world.

And they wouldn't let us do anything for him, though of course there was little we could do. Still we would have liked to be in the room, as I told the nurse in charge.

She understood. "There are times, though," she told us, "when good intentions are harmful. He needs rest—and patience. He needs to work with the machine."

Work he could handle, in prodigious amounts, but patience he'd never had. And he had bequeathed us little too, though that's what we needed then. We could only watch this painful process, standing, my sister and I, with our arms around our mom and looking from outside his room through the large plate glass window at the tiny man who was curled up on his side, connected by a series of yellowish-white tubes to a black and grey machine.

Every few seconds, a light would flash on the machine—and an alarm would sound. Then an accordion-like pleated black rubber lung, at the machine's base, would cease its compression, only to start up again relentlessly the moment the alarm stopped sounding. Yet the alarm would recommence shortly thereafter, for my dad refused to breathe the way the machine required; and a group of nurses, one after the other, would enter the room and remonstrate with him. This was a kind of Chinese water torture, through sound; and it wouldn't go away—you could only fight it, as my dad did, so long. You couldn't beat it, not as long as water flowed through our dams and electricity powered the U.S. of A.

Unlike most of the hospital, the intensive care unit imposed few limits to visiting privileges. They only wanted the patients to themselves between seven and nine in the morning and three and five in the evening, when they could take temperatures, medicate, change clothes and sheets and perform the largest part of their battery of tests. We'd found Dr. Walker right after he'd returned from lunch. Afterwards, we left Dad alone with his nurses, at 2:30, to go and find our own lunches. He looked tired and pale; he was drugged, and he didn't like that. He tried to fight through the sedative's effect, but he didn't succeed—except twice, when he gave us two wan but appreciative smiles, something he found more difficult to do when in good health. I can't recall any similar smiles before—sweet, edgeless, and undemanding.

My mother's presence at the hospital was more familiar. It didn't matter that she was thirty pounds heavier than I saw her in my mind's eye, that all her sharper angles seemed beveled, smoothed down by time like the steps at an old school. Nor did it matter that her hair was now bright white, her face uncovered with make-up, her eyelids swollen. Within this woman there was still the presence, at any give moment, of all the strains upon her, of her multiple sympathies, which pulled her out of herself and pushed her slightly away from us. All of life's competing demands had etched themselves on her soft and doughy face, which was riven with deep and moving lines.

My father's face at 75 was vitreous, smooth as a tart apple's skin, a Granny Smith. Sarah once said, it must have been ten years before, "I like your dad (who loved her) but it's your mom who moves me, who's done the feeling in your family."

I wanted her to go to lunch with Anne and me, but she said she didn't have the strength. "Thank you anyway, Jimmie," she said politely, as always, but this time in a shell-shocked voice. Still though the circles under her eyes were craterous and mauve, her eyes themselves were sharp, white and blue.

When Anne and I came back a little before five, Mom's eyes were tiny, swollen and red. They didn't register much either as she hobbled down the hall to be with her husband at that hour when the hospital promised to give him back to her.

"We almost lost him," my mom managed to say when she saw us.

"And?" I asked, as Anne gasped audibly.

"They decided they had to put him on a respirator," she said.

The phone rang the next morning around seven, minutes after I'd awakened to confront an empty house and unfamiliar morning light. "Jimmie, baby," a man's voice exclaimed, in altogether unconvincing hyperbole. Now we know whose voice this is, don't we? It should be obvious, though it wasn't to me, either because I'd rarely been fortunate enough to get this kind of attention from a male or because I was too shell-shocked to see or hear the obvious.

"I've got great news! Chas loved the Good Morning Caffeine tape. They're just raving about it."

"Chas? Who? Who is this?"

There was a moment of stunned silence, then an umbrageous, "your agent, Jim! Irv, Irving Nettleman. Hel-lo!"

"Wow," I said, as my memory hurtled into another present, like a small asteroid crashing into the planet. "I'm sorry. Irv? I'm just out of it these days. Who's Chas?"

There was a sign of my hebephrenia, prompting a response in that tone of voice that grade school teachers reserve for the chronically underachieving. "Chas Monelli, the governor's son, the morning culture guy on MBS. Wake up and smell your weak green tea, Jim: this is America. You can still be part of it."

This was more irony than I'd heard out of him in the couple of years I'd known him. I didn't even know he used that tone. "Irv," I said, "the timing's not great." I didn't want to disenthuse Chas Monelli, after all.

"No, it's not. He wants you on day after tomorrow. Friday at the latest."

"I don't think I can get there, Irv."

"What?"

"Didn't anybody tell you?"

"What? There was something about a family problem."

"Yeah, sort of. My dad's hooked up to a respirator. Looks like he's dying."

"We all are," said he.

And when I paused, unable to fathom a response, he continued, encouragingly. "I'm sure he'd understand. You know, I talked to him once, he..."

The thing is he probably would have understood, my father.

"And all of America would love you even more. You're on TV with Chas and what a story you'd have to tell."

Who was this asshole? What did I have to do with him? My complete befuddlement and momentary silence seemed to interrupt his reverie. He mumbled, "Jimmy, I'm sorry, really...what was I thinking of..."

And then, as if to answer his own question, "there would of course be another forty, fifty thousand in sales and of course it wouldn't take that long. Uh, you could be back by dinner time..."

"You mean by visiting hours."

"Oh, yeah, yes, of course, you could. Easy." The guy didn't give up.

"But what if my old man doesn't make it that long?"

I heard a sigh. There was a pause and then, quickly, he said, "I'll be praying for you…gotta go now. You need me, anything, I'm here for you. Tell her I'll be right there, Eric." And transported himself off onto somebody else's airwave and "opportunity."

Dr. Walker now disappeared just vanished completely.

So did the slight, saintly spirit I'd seen the day before in my father's room, the frail man with the opalescent skin and the sweet, untroubled regard. I hadn't known what to say to him, had felt helpless before him. He'd been a man I'd never known; and of course he was dying, losing two, almost three pints of blood a day.

That man vanished overnight. When I arrived at seven the next morning at the hospital, I saw my real father again. His face was more obscured than it had been the day before, when a small plastic tube had funneled oxygen to his nostrils. Now his mouth was covered by a think bluish plastic mask, which held in place the respirator tube. A large sack of blood dripped into his left arm. His skin was bruised and almost grey. And for the first time I can remember, his hair was out of place. He hadn't been able to domesticate it. There on the left side of his head was the cowlick my sister and I possess. I'd never actually seen it on my father before.

These differences were superficial, however, grotesque but cosmetic. Above the plastic mask glared my father's outraged eyes, awakened by my entry into the room and sharpening with every step I took toward him—black and burrowing into me as they'd done every time I'd violated one of his many strictures in my oh so errant youth.

"How are you, Pop?" I asked.

He shook his head impatiently. He pointed at the mask, which prevented him from speaking.

"Not feeling so good?" He gestured to me to come closer, his right index finger in the air.

I thought I understood the subject of his anger. "I've been looking for Dr. Walker, but I haven't found him yet," I said.

He replied by shaking his head peremptorily, raising his index finger further before dropping it forcefully down.

"I've been trying. He's a difficult man to…"

Exasperated, my father turned abruptly away from me. And the respirator's alarm went off with a screech. His eyes rose, then closed; his chest heaved and finally the alarm ceased ringing. A nurse arrived at the door and said, "Now Mr. Adams, you have to relax, like I told you. You can't spend all your energy fighting against the machine—it can't help you that way."

His eyes reopened with her departure and focused intently on me again. He lifted his right hand once more and pointed up with his finger. Then he slashed the air, tracing a vertical line and two quick, short horizontal ones.

"What's that, Dad?" I asked him. "What are you trying to say?"

He looked away in pain; the machine heaved, and his eyes slowly came back to me. He appeared dismayed, annoyed at having spawned one of the world's dumbest sons.

"Are you trying to tell me something?" I asked.

He nodded in acquiescence to my obtuse question and gathered his strength again. He'd tried the air. Now he motioned me to come closer to him; and when I did, he touched my chest with the tip of his finger. He made the same downward thrust; at the top of this imaginary line, he made a horizontal line to his right, to my left, across my chest. A little lower, he followed with a smaller horizontal line parallel to the first.

"F," I said. "The letter "F." I was stupid, but I was getting the idea.

He nodded emphatically. His finger shook in front of me, as if from rage; and there, from where the downward stroke of the "F" had begun, next to it, to his right, my left, he made another straight stroke. Depending from its top, he made a half circle to his right, from the top of the straight line to its center, from which he made a downward slash to his right. As he marked the lines on my chest, I watched his finger move—this was an "R."

I said as much; and with a nod, he began a third letter, at the same top point. He made another downward stroke, then returned to the top and made a stroke to his left; and I was sure now this was going to be an "E"; he was spelling "Fred."

Fred had been my father's best friend; they'd worked for the same oil company and gone into the army together. We'd often gone fishing, the two families, and the two men had stayed friends even as my father made it all the way up the company's corporate ladder, and Fred had been content to remain behind. But I knew Fred had been dead for a couple of years—and the thought that my father might not remember this made me grimace and almost cry. "You mean Fred, Pop?" I asked finally.

He shot me a look of total aggravation, his eyes almost leaving their sockets. He vigorously shook his head. This was my father, fully conscious, no senescent old man. He repeated his gestures for his dense son, making the first character again, to the right side of his chest, then the second, then beginning the third.

"I see the 'F' and 'R', Pop; I've got them and the 'E' too."

He shook his head in opposition.

"It's not an 'E'?" I asked.

He lowered his head, took a breath, and closed his eyes. The machine went off, as his lids palpitated with the pupils' furious movement underneath them.

When his eyes came back to me, they were more tired, but still determined. He began high, from the center of my chest. He made an exaggerated diagonal line to his left; after which he went back up to the initial point, from which he made a huge diagonal to his right. Then he connected these two.

"'A'," I said, feeling like an idiot. I thought I understood. "You want Mom, don't you, Dad? Fran…"

And I started to walk away, to go and get my mother; but he rustled in his bed so aggressively that I looked back at him. He had tears, of fury not sadness, in his eyes. I didn't completely understand, though my ribs felt like pickup sticks collapsing into my stomach.

My father lifted himself up with all his tubing; he reached out and made a point on the top right of my chest, a straight line down. Then, going back to the original point, he came down along the first line three-quarters of the way, when he rounded out the line. He made it curve at the bottom and continued the line up the left side of my torso, until it came to a point again.

"F-R-A-U," I said; and he nodded grimly and collected himself as the machine pumped loudly next to us.

He was going to trace another letter on me. But he didn't need to.

"Fraud," I said. "You mean 'fraud,' don't you, Pop?" My head felt as if it had caved into my chest. "Fraud."

He nodded wearily, tired from the exertion, but his eyes were like two flints striking against lesser metal—me.

"You mean the machine, the respirator?" I asked him, his two ferocious eyes eroding my voice and my breath.

He shook his head, a yes and a no, shook it diagonally as if he wanted to indicate more; and the whole world felt like it skipped on itself--tilted on its axis and spun, like a battered yoyo off the ground, like him right now, attached like a damaged puppet to the plastic tubes which fed him, bled him, pumped him with new life and breath while he bobbed from one confused state to the next.

"You mean the whole deal, don't you, Dad?" I understood. "You mean, the hospital, the medication; it's all a fraud, is that it?"

His face clenched around the cheap plastic mask and the tubes going through it; his eyes squinted around their two sharp, wild points; tears welled in them as he nodded his head in vigorous assent. I looked away. I looked back, and he was still nodding, until the respirator exploded with sound right next to me, ringing and ringing.

I had to get out of there. "I'll get Dr. Walker, Dad," I said. "Just wait." I had to see the doctor, had to, didn't know what I could or would do, felt inadequate one more time.

"You've gotten your dad excited now, sir," said the male nurse Walter, our friend, remonstrating me when I passed him at the door. "It just makes things harder for him. Don't you see? When are you people going to get it?"

Finding Dr. Walker became a joke. When I went to his office, I was told he was visiting patients at the hospital. Yet the hospital staff was unaware of his presence on the floor. I contemplated sitting out front of his office, in his parking lot. Might have had I not been sure there was a back exit. Instead, I called one of my better friends from high school, an internist these days, Rich.

Rich took my call right away; and he didn't need to hear anything but my tone of voice to dig right into the subject. We'd run a half mile relay together in high school; we'd been cut from the basketball team at the same time; we'd played three or four years of football, at various less vulnerable positions, like flanker and defensive back (or in his case, punter). Rich seemed to know, right away, why I was calling. He listened to my description of my dad's state, as far as I could understand it.

"I don't want to comment on it, right now," said he, "before I see the charts; but I'll consult with Walker. He's a pretty good guy, Jim. I wouldn't want anyone else for your dad."

"Maybe. I'm sure he is; but he promised us—he said he respected my old man—said he wouldn't put him on a respirator before he talked to us—and wham."

"He probably thought that was the only chance your dad had," Rich said calmly, but gently.

"Then he should have let him go. That's what Dad wanted, and he knew that."

"I don't want to make any judgments about this one way or the other; but I'll tell you, when you have as many patients as he probably does--I imagine he's got forty or fifty over at St. Francis at any one time—you've got to be acting on automatic pilot. You think about the patients more than the families."

This seemed reasonable, but I wasn't thinking very reasonably myself. "Well, we'd like to see him."

"I don't blame you," Rich said. "But you know, doctors aren't all that communicative at the best of times. And they're not all that different from everybody else. We like to talk about our successes, and when things don't look as if they're going that way..."

I didn't say anything. I didn't have a real axe to grind, not yet at any rate.

"I can reach him, though," Rich said, then paused, a familiar wry tone slipping into his kind but professional voice. This was an eerie echo from high school, from his sly take on our coaches, those molders of men who had so much power over us. "Today is Walker's afternoon off. He's a golfer. He'll be out at Southern Hills, one o'clock tee time. He plays with my radiologist. It'd be just the sheerest coincidence if you ran into him, wouldn't it?"

Every small city has its pretensions to elegance, and Tulsa's were largely elaborated from and around Southern Hills, the most socially desirable of a plethora of country clubs and a very great golf course. It seemed appropriate that Dr. Walker would be there for, though we'd once been members for about five minutes, it had been in spite of my dad, against his will. When, toward the end of his career, he'd been made a member of the board of his large oil company, membership in Southern Hills had been thrown in as a perk. My old man tried to refuse it, but his board was reluctant to let him, and his snobbish kids had complained enough that he'd finally let them have what they thought was their due, our place in the blistering Oklahoma sun.

When we left home and he retired, he cut off his association because he didn't want to pay the dues, even though his company, in one of its more gallant moves, had given him a handmade set of clubs along with the watches and silver and gold pins. He, of course, didn't have the breath to swing them.

I found Dr. Walker on 12. He was playing the back nine first, and he didn't look happy to see me. A challenging and narrow dogleg left, it's a hole Mr. Hogan admired, a par four almost 450 yards, with a little water on the right. They often played the US Open here, the PGA; it was a great course. The doc perhaps hadn't played it enough. He sliced his drive into the trees on the right, and he was already mumbling to himself when he headed off the tee into the rough.

I found myself wondering how much money his foursome played for, per hole. Only one golfer in his party really looked serious—a weather beaten man, probably a driller, in grey plaid pants, a pink shirt, and a yellow golf cap with the club's name stitched in green. Dr. Walker was wearing Ralph Lauren Polo exclusively, a pink shirt with matching beige chinos and off-white cream shoes—all displaying that large "discreet" Polo logo. Didn't keep him from slicing, as I said.

"Sorry to bother you out here, Doc," I began when the doctor looked up to see me prowling the tree line, between him and his ball, like a particularly mangy coyote. He started. "But I spent all morning trying to reach you," I continued. "I couldn't seem to catch up with you at the hospital. Your secretary said you were very busy this afternoon too…"

"It's my only exercise," he said. "My only afternoon off—I work Sunday afternoons too most of the time."

I feel guilty much of the time too, but somehow his response didn't move me. "Why'd you put him on the respirator, doctor? I thought you were going to consult with us. Guess you forgot, huh? It'd been all of what an hour and a half before that when you told us you would."

He grimaced and looked around some more for his ball, sweeping through the rough with his five iron. I'd more or less forgotten where the ball was by now. Had the area right, but that was about it. Behind us, one of his foursome was swinging a four wood, just off the center of the fairway.

"Hey, Doc," I said, with what I took to be a Clint Eastwood smile, my three day growth looking very incongruous there at Southern Hills (I'm surprised they let me in). "I'm over here." He still didn't manage to look me in the eye—and I wasn't about to let him find his ball before he engaged me directly.

So he approximated a direct glance, his eyes making my left ear itch, moving every time I tried to hold them in mine. He was a smart man, a guy just doing his job, so he said. "I didn't have time, Jim, to call you folks. It was either that or letting him pass."

Tulsa can get pretty hot, and it felt then about 120 degrees. I felt as if I'd just hit that temperature coming from an air-conditioned 65; felt as if I were hallucinating and my words and thoughts were not connected to my body, were a ventriloquist's trick. "Then maybe you should have let him die. That's what he said he wanted. That's what we'd just been talking about. Dad said he'd rather die than live connected to a machine.'

My voice was rising, like the white ball lofted by a five wood over a patch of green, crashing up ahead into more trees.

"Doc!" One of his foursome yelled. "Need any help there?"

Some time in the 80s, just after playing a round of golf, a tee-totaling entrepreneur—and jai alai fronton owner—was shot to death here, one bullet between the eyes, in the club parking lot. A professional hit, the local police had said: a guy just walked up to the church deacon and snuffed him.

So people were concerned when they saw disturbed looking spirits meandering around the rough. "You okay?" The doctor's playing buddy asked again and came our way. A third man swung a long iron. Nice smooth clicking sound, a big divot following behind in the air.

Dr. Walker nodded and waved. "Just having trouble finding the ball, John," he bravely said.

The doctor looked nervously to his right, half an eye on me. I was totally pumped up and almost embarrassed at the surge of anger I felt, my adrenalin firing up. Dr. Walker probably should have rid himself of me, right there, but people make mistakes. "Let's take Dad off," I said. "You know he doesn't want to be artificially maintained, remember? We went through that in detail. How could you have done it?"

"I asked him, Jim," he said, and here he looked me straight in the eye. "I asked him if he wanted to go on a respirator."

I started to hum, like a dry, rasping engine, like a car without a drop of water in its radiator. I looked out to the fairway, and the guy with the yellow hat and the funny pants, well ahead of us, lofted a six iron toward the hole. It dug into the green. "There it is," Walker said aloud and started to walk forward toward his ball.

"I don't believe you. I just don't fucking believe it," I thought I said, firmly. But I must have been closer to shouting, for Walker stopped in his tracks, and I moved quickly to cut him off, to make him face me directly. The guy in the yellow hat looked back and asked, "You okay Doc?" He started walking our way.

"What did you really say to my dad?"

The doctor looked a little sheepish. He stared forlornly at the man in yellow, who kept directing himself my way. "I asked him—your dad," he began, trying to muster some anger but not exactly succeeding. "He had a photo of your mom at his bedside. The two of them, a wedding photo, you probably have seen it. I asked him if he ever wanted to see her again."

"You what?" I screamed. "That's all you said? Nothing else—you didn't tell him you were going to hook him up?"

Walker shook his head and started walking back away from me. "He's a smart man. You have to figure he understood what I meant."

"Right—while he was bleeding to death. You son of a bitch. How could you have done that, you stupid…" I was walking alongside him, about as lose to being totally out of my mind as I can get; and he brought his golf club up, not to swing, but to ward me off. He held it across his chest, like Little John, as I knocked him back with a shove and started to leap his way when, from behind, somebody grabbed me, somebody else too—the man in the yellow hat and another Polo person pinned my arms behind me.

"Easy there," one yelled. Though they were two or three times stronger than I was, they had some trouble subduing me.

I was still screaming. "You asshole; you're torturing him, you fucking sadist...what do you plan to do about it?" I got away from the two guys and ran toward the doctor; but they grabbed me again before I reached him. "Get him off the thing. How are you going to get him off?"

No answer, no answer at all, which is probably fortunate for me, for if I'd heard the one he could have given, I surely would have gotten myself arrested. I had little enough control as it was.

Walker put his dukes up, which was ludicrous enough. Then when he saw that I was momentarily subdued, he actually made sure there were no rips in his Polo outfit. "I should have you arrested," he continued.

"Fine. Go ahead," I screamed; and I managed to pull the guy behind me about five feet to my right, where I'd spotted Walker's golf ball lying with the doctor's emblem on it. As the foursome looked on angrily, I kicked the man's Titleist into the nearest water hazard.

When Walker came charging over to me, screaming in complaint, I leaned back against the guy holding me and began booting dirt up and all over Dr. Walker's perfectly creased beige pants, soiling them and the logoed shirt, the two-toned shoes, and the tinted lenses of his aviator glasses.

They dragged me to the clubhouse where, though the club assistant didn't know me from Adam, an older member, one of five retirees waiting to tee off, recognized me. He'd seen me, not in my errant youth, but on the Good Morning Caffeine show. This was the kind of town where everyone tunes into early morning TV, at 7:30, switching from Robin back to Nancy between pieces of toast, scrambled eggs, and crisp bacon slices rich in nitrates.

This too was the kind of town where, as I was leaving the clubhouse, I could hear a couple of sunburnt fifty five year old women murmuring sympathy for my mom as they wondered what had happened to me. One was, I'm pretty sure, my friend Phil's mother, whom I'd always liked. She kind of waved my way as I was escorted out in the arms of the club's security personnel, two retired roughnecks and one former Arena League football player.

They threw me rudely into my parents' auxiliary vehicle (the aging white Lincoln Continental which, getting five or six miles per gallon, they couldn't trade in). As I made my way down the club's stately drive, the security personnel followed me in their new Dodge sedans to the exit and waited there, preventing my return.

I didn't look back. I wound through the Midas Muffler shops, the Taco Bells, Starbucks and Ye Olde Innes which now compose this section of my hometown, which filled in all the woods and undulating farmland where I'd made out, those few times I got lucky, when I lived there years, many years now, decades ago.

If you know the "Green Country" area at all, then you know that taking this exit and turning right was taking the wrong way to where I was going. This is the way leading to Oral Roberts University, its "City of Faith," "Prayer Tower," and windowless gold and marble buildings. St. Francis Hospital where my dad waited was, like my family's house, far to the East of here.

For a change, I think I was being self-protective rather than self-absorbed by making my trip to the hospital that much longer. Though I was a couple of steps behind myself, as usual (or as my ninth grade English teacher so crisply expressed it: "Jim is the walking example of the difference between intelligence and wisdom. They aren't at all the same. He's smart, we all know that, but is he wise? I don't think so."), I did know there was a depressing reason behind the doc's muteness, his anger and distance. He'd hooked my father up, but he had no idea how and when he could or would unhitch him from the machine.

Actually, what I learned upon my eventual arrival at the hospital was that Dr. Walker didn't plan to remove Dad at all. "Once they hook them up," said Walter, the gay black nurse with what was becoming ever more apparent was an amphetamine habit, "they don't let them off without a really good reason, like recovery." I think that's what he said. He spoke so rapidly he sounded as if he was talking in a click language. "They can't. A nurse did unhook one in Alabama--man wanted off, his family wanted him off, even his doctor didn't see any hope. They unplugged him and some "Right to Life" girl, a receptionist, turned them in to the D.A. They were arrested for homicide. Dr. Walker's not a brave man; he's got way too good a thing going here to risk his sweet buns for any mere mortal." Walter sounded all too knowledgeable—or maybe, probably, that was just my way of hearing, which was no less twisted, I suppose, than my posture, my self, my face. I didn't know what to do.

There was another nurse nearby, a woman in her twenties with ash blonde hair, pulled slightly back. She had a pursed gentleness, just a little craziness which reminded me of Diane Keaton or Tina Fey. She said to me, "I'm sorry about your dad; he's such a sweet man."

Sweet? My old man? Defenseless, I thought, was more like it-- strapped into this modern Judas Cradle. "Is he losing much blood? Is he getting better?" I asked.

She looked at me gently, glanced away then took a second look as if considering how to phrase her response. She appeared startled at my lack of understanding. "He's up to a little more than two and a half pints now," she said—and her smooth face broke into a bird's nest of strains. Could I huddle there? I wondered.

"When's it going to end?" I asked.

She shrugged, smiled once more a forced grin and went to attend a patient's call. As she left, though I wasn't perceiving much, I did note this: her ass looked inviting, seemed heart-shaped. When in pain, I looked a woman's way. Somehow, I couldn't glance behind me, where my father stirred so uneasily.

I called my friend Rich, reached his secretary, then his nurse; then he interrupted an examination to talk to me. When I thanked him, he said, "it's okay. This guy's just doing some running for me now." He cocked his voice, and it came out a little more sharply. "He needs the exercise, the fat fuck. I've been talking to him about it for years now. You know who it is? Eddie Hankey—he weighs about 240 now."

He cackled with continuing amazement. Eddie Hankey had weighed in at about half that, say 125, our senior year in high school. He had been the best shot on the basketball team, from which Rich and I had been unceremoniously cut. Best shot in town, probably too—but Eddie had preferred getting stoned and trapping pigeons before throwing them off one of our local churches. Very weird guy, he seemed destined to be a serial killer. 245 pounds sounded about right. But I wasn't able to absorb a whole lot of new information right then.

"Tell me, Rich," I said, going back to my original intention. "This nurse at St. Francis says that's it for my old man. Once they put you onto a respirator, they won't take you off."

"That's bull shit," he said. "You must have misunderstood her. People get off them all the time—gives them breathing room, if you will. Lets the body work on what really ails it."

"Yeah, okay, but he said you only get off if you get better—or if you die; they won't unhook you any other way."

"Just keep running, Eddie," he said to the side, as he seemed to reflect on the matter. "Would you like me to consult with Walker?"

"The nurse was telling the truth, is that it? Said there was some Alabama case, it…"

"I'm afraid so. That's true. But I don't want to go into all that until I catch up with Dr. Walker." He was kind here, but firm.

"He may not want to talk much," I said. "I kicked his ball into a water hazard out at Southern Hills. Tried to hit the son of a bitch too, I…"

"Sounds about right. You haven't gotten any saner, have you?" Rich chucked softly.

Imagine getting this kind of help from a doctor in New York City. Imagine even getting a straight answer. But he gave me something of one when I asked him this: "He's in his late 70s, Rich. He's got a kidney infection, an ulcer, double pneumonia, and severe emphysema. Do you think they'll ever let him off that respirator?"

"Miracles happen," he said, to my surprise. Tulsa was a town of believers but Rich wasn't one of them, as far as I knew. "I'm sorry, but it sounds like it'll take one. Still I could be wrong. Let me talk to Walker. I'll get him at home. I'll call you back tonight. You at your folks?"

When I got off the phone with Rich, it was almost five, a couple of minutes before the intensive care people would release their patients to us. I waited outside my dad's room and could see from there, at the edge of intensive care, my mom resting on a chair in the lounge. She was asleep for a change, which is why I didn't rouse her. She looked so drained, her eyes so sunken, her cheeks almost discolored, a tremendously fatigued grey like distressed concrete. She looked like an old woman—and she was, of course, however shocking I might have found that reality.

I couldn't see my dad inside his room since the curtains were up, obscuring the view. But semi-transparent, they gave one a hint of the shapes inside: shadows flickered around a tiny silhouette in the center of the room, in bed, turning this way, then that, nurses maintaining, assuring my father's connection to the mass of machines which kept him functioning.

At a minute or two before five, the nurse with the bleached blonde hair came outside, carrying a bag of something or other, plasma it must have been. "Are you okay?" She wondered of me, kindly, as if my condition mattered much there.

I looked at the yellow plastic bag in her hand and shrugged. "How's he getting along with the machine?"

"Better than you'd think," she said. She reached over toward me and pointed to my bandaged ear. "You should change that bandage…what happened to you?"

I'd forgotten about it."Someone bit me," I let her know. It was going to be five in about a minute. I was learning toward the door. Glum, I didn't know what I was going to say.

"Wait a second," she said. She took my arm and brought me over to a sink, to a mirror. She put her plastic bag down and washed her hands. "Hold still," she commanded; and she carefully unraveled the bandage, though I winced as she dislodged it. The curtains were opening in my dad's room. "Whew," she said with a sigh. "That looks awful. You've got to take care of that right now."

In his room, my father turned over, facing us outside. Huddled on his side, he looked like an old dog with a broken leg. Even from a distance he appeared enfeebled. Yet his will seemed strong; he probably didn't need me right then, at least not for the reasons I'd imagined. What he wanted from me was something else, a little harder.

It seemed appropriate then that I was still outside his room being ministered to by this kind and attentive and predictably attractive nurse. I winced at her touch. "It's stinging," she said, "because it's infected; you're just going to have to hold your horses a minute." She put salve on my ear and covered it with gauze. "Don't wash yourself over here, okay, unless you're going to change the bandage, do you hear?"

I wanted to answer her directly, responding, "Only rarely: I only hear rarely and I debrief myself badly when I do," but all I got out was, "thanks."

Leaving, she said, "I'll get someone to give you an antibiotic in a minute—you're going to need something to fight that infection."

She was so gracious, her eyes as liquid as my body felt. I wanted to stay with her, but surprised myself by departing, my body taking my mind out of there before I knew it. I found myself walking into my dad's room where I began to stare at him from the side of his bed.

He opened his eyes. In a way, suddenly, he looked the least peaked of any of us; his complexion was slightly pink. It took me a moment to realize that this, of course, was largely due to the blood dripping from a three quarters empty sack into his arm. Still he didn't give me any time to feel sorry for him. There was nothing pathetic about his regard. When he looked at me, he looked like an enraged squid—his nose and mouth were covered with a blue grey mask. His cheeks drooped, but his eyes were ferocious and so unforgiving that I could barely return their gaze.

I'm sure he understood, instinctively, why I was so reticent. Mealy mouthed, I said, "I'm sorry, Pop. Are you feeling better?"

He shook his head. His eyes seemed to water. The respirator beside him wheezed—and he closed his lids. He was conserving his energy; and this, I guess, made me hopeful. The machine sighed beside him, and when he took in his oxygen, no alarms went off. He'd bent himself to the machine's force and rhythm. I could barely believe it.

About fifteen minutes later, as I stood awkwardly beside him, he opened his eyes a second time. He looked at the respirator to his right, and his pupils skipped along the surface of his eyes.

He wanted a report, and I didn't want to give it to him. I looked away but felt his will draw me back. I shook my head.

He looked up again, toward me first, then toward the machine--his eyes moving from one to the other, propelled by a tremendous intensity. When I made no move, a tear of anger formed on his right eyelid. His body seemed to rise slightly, as if inflated, and he continued to glare my way, to try and force my eyes, my hands toward the machine.

I wanted to lie to him. I guess my silence was already a form of that. I sounded inside myself, wheezing, like an air conditioner on the fritz, a garbage disposal churning away, a machine burning itself out. I could feel sweat, a couple of beads on my temples.

For a change, it was hard to know what hurt more, the truth or its evasion. Unable to return his stare, I said, "You've got to get better, Pop. It's the only way they'll let you off this thing. I'm sorry."

My vision clouded, but his didn't. "There's some Alabama case," I continued explaining. I was pushing my way through this, absolutely uncertain whether I had a body at all, whether I wasn't just a loud voice in an empty vessel. "A doctor is up for murder because he took someone off the machine, someone who wanted to be unhooked, and the man expired. You need the machine and they're afraid to take you off it. This is Oklahoma. The 'right to lifers' rule."

Most of my mind was in my throat. I wasn't thinking—fat, tepid tears flushed my cheeks. Then my dad opened his eyes again, these bleak semaphores into his tortured self, glancing from me to the machine. And he grinned--he seemed madly, determinedly hebephrenic when I think of it now. But an instant later this wild rictus disappeared into a sweet smile. Nodding his head gently my way, he seemed to dismiss me.

I left trembling, feeling angry for him and inadequate and helpless—and guilty. I was apparently unable to find him any respite from the machines that monitored his heartbeat, pumped his lungs, registered his loss of fluids, and would sound off if nature took over and he began to fail. People on this ward couldn't die of old age or overwhelming illness. They expired instead like medieval prisoners, their bodies stretched on comfortably padded racks. What had happened to mercy?

I went back to the lounge and waited, sitting there, my mind rising a couple more feet out of my body. I'm sure I was looking, already, for the nurse with the bleached out hair, for a woman who could put my mind back inside my body or at least take my pain into hers.

I found my mom. Her bright blue eyes, opening, fixed upon me. "I'm sorry," she said. "I must have passed out." She gathered herself and sat up, slowly. She probably hadn't had more than ten hours of sleep in four or five days. "Is your sister here yet?" She wondered.

Her eyes were sleep-filled and groggy, but she wasn't. "You don't believe he's going to make it, do you?" She suddenly asked, though this wasn't really a question.

"I'd like to believe he will," I said, as if I could lie successfully to my mother, as if I were still holding out in this long battle for a self. Decades into seeming adulthood and still bristling when my mother said, "Your dad needs us, all of us, so much—it's his only chance. You could give him a little more, Jimmy, more of your affection. I know you can. What does it cost you?"

I didn't have an answer. I was still reverberating with the repercussions of the truths I'd just doled out to the man in question. My sister sensed this the moment she walked out of the elevators and looked at the two of us. "So what are you two doing?" She asked us. "Why aren't you with him?" She asked me.

"I'm going in," Mom said. "I'm going in to wash up first. I'll just be a minute."

Once she left us, my sister said, "So?"

"He looks a little better. Like himself. He looks angry."

"Wouldn't you be? They're never going to get him off that thing, you see that, don't you?" I did. "So why aren't you with him? What's keeping you out here?"

She stared at me, then hearing sounds at a decibel level only an animal could perceive, her face snapped around like a door swinging on a loose hinge. "Oh," she said, her voice full of fear. "Oh, no." She ran toward the back, toward the rooms in intensive care.

I followed not far behind her, ambivalent about what I was going to find, not trusting what she clearly knew. How, I don't understand, but she felt it so deeply she pulled away from me, running into our father's room, her bright purple blouse billowing over her black slacks.

She started to scream before I reached the room, and her cry brought interns and nurses running. That wasn't what she wanted, however. "What are you doing?" She shrieked at them. She tried to push them back out into the hall, but they shunted her to the side.

On the bed, curled on his side was our father, his arms grey and his face blue. He had the tubes in his throat still, the mask over his nose. But the machine wasn't working; its lights were dead.

No alarms had sounded. No one had noticed his altered breathing, for somehow, he had reached outside his covers and pulled the respirator's plug from the wall—with both his hands. The cord and its plug lay in front of him, grey in his hands on the bed's white sheets as suddenly a bevy of hospital workers descended on the expiring man, trying to reanimate him and the machines he had been yoked to. They pushed my sister, who was screaming, toward the room's exit.

"How can you be so cruel?" She was yelling. She wasn't angry with them because of their ineptitude, their inattention. "Just leave him alone. Let him be! Respect his wishes, you assholes."

The two of us were thrust back out of the room as an alarm sounded and a "code red" alert began. A whole series of interns and nurses wheeled in new equipment and huddled over my father's blue face. One gave him an injection; another put an oxygen mask over him; a third massaged his heart. With great speed, efficiency and skill, they saved my father from himself. Denying him his wishes, they kept him alive.

Behind us, Midge appeared with Mom. "Is anything the matter?" She asked.

"Why don't you and Mom go back there?" Anne said with a persuasive look, which didn't escape our mother.

"Oh, is this it?" Mom asked, and she moved, blindly, toward the room with all the medical action, Dad's.

A nurse stopped her at the entry. "I'm so sorry, Ma'am, but you have to give us a minute. He's going to be okay, though."

"What happened?" Mom wanted to know, but the nurse steered her back toward us. "He's my husband. What happened?" Mom's swelling face asked her children. "Tell me what happened! I'm his wife!"

"He's going to be fine, Mrs. Adams," the platinum blonde nurse, Ellen, lied with a comforting smile. "It was just a little accident." She took my mother's arm. "He's still in there fighting. Don't get excited now. Don't give up."

My mom looked up at her with relief and trust. And as Dad's room emptied of the rest of the emergency support group, Mom followed the nurse, each step a little less shaky, into her husband's room. His face was extraordinarily pale now, but his eyes opened at her entrance into the room. They gleamed, for one moment, with a proud ferocity before they disappeared a second later behind their lids, his face assuming a kind of scared resignation. Oddly, he'd looked in that first instant younger than I'd seen him in years and more, way more alive.

Walker, Dr. Walker now disappeared, just vanished from my—my dad's, our family's—planet. I tried him at his office. I tried him through his answering service, and I searched for him at the hospital. But he was always in between two places; and he never returned my call. "He's a busy man," his receptionist bluntly told me when I complained once too often. "He's got forty patients in that hospital alone—and they all need him too. He can't be with every one of them at once."

"I understand that," I told her. "I'm not quite that self-centered—or that dumb, for that matter."

"I'm sorry, sir. He'll get in touch with you when he has something to tell you," said she, almost kind in spite of my unusual aggressiveness.

So I gave her my phone number again, and I suggested, "I guess you must have memorized it by now."

"I was wondering," she now said with a changed voice, "Are you the same James Adams who was on Good Morning Caffeine?"

"Well, yeah," I said, using anything she offered. But she just said, reflectively, "You'd think he'd return a celebrity's calls, wouldn't you?"

Some celebrityhood—it couldn't have gotten me past a rope-holder in NYC or LA, even days, hours after my national "exposure." But it did rate me that evening a very strange phone call. "Jimmy Adams," a voice asked in an odd, reverberant tone, two or three octaves below the norm. "This is Dwayne Hinsley."

"Who?" The name was familiar somehow, but it was the voice that tickled my fading memory.

"Dwayne Hinsley—you don't remember?"

"I'm sorry, but I don't really…"

"I taught you 8th grade English."

"Mr. Hinsley!" I said with a squeamish feeling.

"Mr. Hinsley, yes," he repeated. "Who'd ever have thought you would amount to so much?"

I couldn't begrudge him this negative vision of my glorious future. He had caught me cheating with my friend Lee on a grammar test. He rose, all five feet of him, and with that stentorian voice he cast us into the lower cantos of hell and brought his mighty yardstick down on our fingers—a corporal punishment which was in theory forbidden in our school system, but which won the approval of both Lee's father and mine. "I'm hosting the Symposium this year," Mr. Hinsley announced now.

"The Symposium?" Last time I'd seen him he was acting in Little Theater production of The Importance of Being Earnest.

"It's KDET's book show, the old Lewis Meyer thing," he said, with great pride. "I don't usually do trade books, Jim, but we were thinking of making an exception."

"How'd you know I was in town?" I wondered.

"I called your publisher. Your book is in the trade best-sellers."

"They told you I was here?"

"Why not? We reach a big audience in the Green Country region. They want to keep us happy!"

Green Country was a relatively new term for Tulsa and largely inaccurate. One found it all over car dealers' billboards. But the truth is the city is green for only a few weeks per year--after that either the snows hit or the heat and humidity, transmuting yards into a less peppy brown. What was the term doing in Mr. Hinsley's vocabulary?

He was off justifying other literary and publishing misdemeanors. "I really don't do trade books usually, you know..." He repeated.

"I don't blame you," I said.

"They don't need the publicity like worthwhile fiction," he continued his thought--not putting me down so much as clarifying his position. "Still, we were thinking that you're a local boy (over and above your being a former student and all) and even if the book isn't exactly Faulkner...actually it's not even S.E. Hinton, is it? Still..."

"That's okay," I said. "Really. I wanted to be Faulkner but it didn't quite work out." Did it? I had all these pages, thousands of them from unpublished novels scattered on both coasts; but there was this thing about talent and its absence. Hard work wasn't quite enough, pace my pop, whom I couldn't help thinking about right then.

Books for all their importance in my life, particularly as an escape from the man himself, couldn't distract me right then. I was wondering where Dr. Walker was, and I was feeling more disturbed than nostalgic. There was an ashtray nearby, with a lighter attached to it. It was gold-plated and elaborately engraved, reading "To E.V.D. Adams, for 38 years of loyal Service"—a strange keepsake for an emphysemiac. But the old man was tenacious and loyal; he hadn't quit on his one employer, a classic mistake earnings-wise but nonetheless admirable. Had he written, he might have been S.E. Hinton, even.

"Are you all right?" Mr. Hinsley, who was still on the line apparently, called me to order. He'd been saying something about the dates. "If Tuesday the 7th's not okay, we could tape this another day. It's all taped you know."

"My dad's dying, Mr. Hinsley," I said.

"Oh," he responded as if I'd wasted his time. "Why didn't you tell me so in the first place? What's the matter with you?"

After he quickly, abruptly got off the line, I put the receiver down, only to have the phone ring again immediately. I listened to it ring five or six times, tried to feel who it might be, finally picked it back up.

"How's your dad, Jim?" This was Sarah and her voice reverberated inside me like a pebble lofted into a pond. Hadn't I called her?

"Doesn't look good," I said. "But you know all about that." We were again meeting over death. Looking at it from there, just this side of this feeling of loss, I understood. I had a glimpse for a moment of why, how we'd become so close.

"How is he?" She repeated, looking for detail, listening. I could feel her pulse. Her own father had disappeared into semi-consciousness long before he'd died. And she'd been torn apart by it, her family scattered. I wanted to talk to her, felt close to her, but no longer knew how to approach her. I stammered.

"Is he alert? Does he know what's happening?"

"Yep, he's fierce. He pulled the plug on himself this afternoon." I smiled, felt absurd pride, and my eyes welled.

"I'm not surprised...Jesse, stop that. He's climbing all over me, the little monkey. Here do you want to say something to your uncle Jim."

"I don't have an Uncle Jim," a voice said firmly from off the line.

"Go ahead, just say hi." There was a pause; then she came back on. "He's clammed up now that he has his chance…"

"I think what he's looking for is a little more maternal attention. I understand. He's not looking for any word from me." This subject felt more than incongruous than usual. Still I told her, "I've been thinking about him a lot."

"No news there," she said. "You and Richard have similar blood types."

"Is that why you're calling?"

"Not really," said she. "It's confusing though." I was hardly going to disagree. There was a pause; she wasn't there. I felt jealous of the kid. She was whispering, "okay, but say something this time. Tell him we hope his dad gets better…"

Her voice drifted away from the receiver a little more. "Tell him," this was fainter even still, "we miss him. Go ahead."

"We miss you," Jesse's voice sang through the line. "We miss you, Uncle Jim." Sounded as if he was distracted, playing some video game next to his mom. I was envious again. "Bet you don't know who this is," I said.

"Sure I do," said he. 'You're the old guy who's always at the park watching me play."

"But you don't really miss me, do you?

He paused, then finally said with a tinge of embarrassment, a shy laugh, "No…well, a couple of times maybe."

I was hardly surprised when the good Dr. Walker didn't return my call. He probably figured I was lucky he didn't have me arrested. Then too, over and above that and getting down to professional specifics, what was he going to say to me? What did he have to say, period?

As much as I sympathized, I didn't care. I wasn't thinking like a responsible citizen. I was ready to stake out his house. Only Rich refused to give me the address. "What's he going to tell you that's going to help you understand?" Rich wisely asked, when he finally responded to my phone calls.

This was late that night, about ten or so, well after I'd spoken to Dwayne Hinsley and to Sarah and, for the first time, to her son. Rich had returned from a wine tasting. His answering service, like Dr. Walker's, had told me he was busy.

"You don't think wines are important?" he asked when I mentioned this. He sounded looped; I shouldn't have called. He wasn't a callous guy, not even close, which is probably why he was so loose at that moment. "I like those '82 Bordeaux," he admitted. "But I'm going to buy some '81 Petrus." Doctors, despite their whining, are still overpaid.

Rich didn't leave the conversation hanging there. His voice changed, and he said, "I'll reach him tomorrow, Jim. I'm sorry, but he won't dodge me. We've consulted together. He knows me. He'll call back."

I knew the good doctor had done so when, about four the next day, Sunday afternoon, Rich showed up at the house. Dad was with the nurses in Intensive Care; Anne was with her husband and Mom was inside the house cloistered in her bedroom. She'd stayed at the hospital the day and the night before. Anne had spent half that time with her. I'd worried on my own (faint-hearted, a mama's boy as that Philadelphian interviewer had so presciently seen). Every time I walked into my father's room now, I felt as if someone were ripping the flesh off my face. Only Greg, of the four of us, looked fresh at all. But he too had put in more time at the hospital than I had. Twice I'd watched as he'd taken a wet cloth and cooled my father's brow, moistening the skin that the respirator's plastic mask had chafed. I'd begun to appreciate Greg even if he too, as he sat watching Kansas drub BC in the NCAAs, sported a Polo shirt—this one a pastel green that didn't quite match his too new jeans. I'd never liked new jeans, particularly when they were "designer" items, sporting those appalling labels that seemed to occupy the entire back of the seat. These had rhinestones on them--my sister had bought them for him. He'd picked out the chartreuse shirt.

Suffering, mourning resembles psychosis—peculiar elements register on your overcharged imagination, while time passes dimly, elsewhere. Your brain's here, and your body's there—one spilling out of the other, though they don't feel connected at all. At the hospital my mind was memory, anywhere but near my father's shrinking self. Outside the hospital, I saw again and again his ferocious, proud grin at that last moment before the sedatives metamorphosed him into someone less fierce and less recognizable, before pain pulled him back into the hospital routine.

After the parental doorbell rang (to the tune of Smoke Gets in Your Eyes), my sister escorted Rich triumphantly into the room. Doctors are prizes these days, however you get them to your home, even if this one too had a Polo shirt on—an emphatic purple.

"They give those out with the medicines?" I asked him, pointing to the Polo shirt. "One with every case of tetracycline?"

Rich nodded grimly. He looked as if he's spent most of the day recovering from the '82 Bordeaux. Anne pressed anxiously near him; Greg looked up from the TV. The two, when Rich asked them, filled him in on their lives. Anne said it had been great being the first local female cameraperson, for five or six years; but it was like quitting smoking—what do you do next?

Greg said he was in construction. Rich said he was about to build another house, to replace the one he lost in his last divorce. "Guess it must mean," he said, "I'm about to get married again—Sandy hasn't said anything about it to me yet, though." He didn't laugh at the joke, however. He glanced around nervously instead.

"Do you want to take a walk?" I wondered.

"Sounds good," he said and shook hands, looking kindly, calmly on Anne and Greg's drawn faces. This is what he spent his lifetime seeing, I suspected—other people's fears, that tremendous anxiety at the little they knew and the little they could do for those they loved. He'd later tell me how that sense of inadequacy, of not being able to do more, was pushing him away from his practice, toward doing something instead like becoming a forensic medical "expert," delivering opinions instead of verdicts.

We went through the garage—and I pushed the button to raise the electric door to let us out. On a shelf next to the aisle we'd taken was a basketball, which still had some air in it. Rich dribbled it outside, underneath the rising door, and looked up at the white backboard with the rusting metal basket. He spun the ball nervously in his hands, then rolled it back into the garage.

"Has Walker heard about the respirator, about Dad unplugging it?" I asked Rich.

"Sure," he said. "He's not hiding from the staff. He just doesn't want to face any of you."

We began to walk along the sidewalk down this street lined with tall and abundant maple trees. They were just beginning to show some green now, their limbs dappled with traces of spring. Pitch-black branches, pointing like aging fingers, hung over our heads as we walked.

"That's what happens when you're busy as Walker is," Rich said. "You do what you can and then you move on."

"And Dad?"

"I think Walker understands he's done more than he should have— or not enough." Rich's lips were pursed; he wasn't looking my way. He'd always had a sense of vocation, even in high school. He knew, like so few of us, he wanted to be a doctor and was surely, from all accounts, a fine one—but right now he appeared to find the job wearing, looked ten years older than I did (though that might have had more to do with our relative maturities...or lack thereof).

"Does Dad have any kind of chance to get out of there?" I asked. There's a slope up the street from our house, a mild incline in this flat country; and I seem to remember a blue house, the color blue. "He doesn't really, does he?"

"Well you never want to say someone can't recover, but a man his age, with his lungs, his medical history..." He shook his head. "Naw, not really. The problem is the ulcer, the ulcers. They need to operate; he's losing so much blood. But no anesthesiologist will do the operation. You won't find one…"

"And that's all they can do for the ulcers?"

"Oh, they're trying medication, but they probably should have begun with it…you see the ulcers come from the antibiotics. They have to be really potent to make a dent in your Dad's condition. His lungs are immune to most of the milder ones. And the stronger ones eat right through the stomach lining."

"Catch 22?"

"Yep. He needs the antibiotics to fight the pneumonia, but they make him bleed."

"So the anesthesiologist…"

"Is afraid of the consequences of an operation. They should have thought about the medication against the ulcers earlier. It's not all that much stronger than Maalox. It just coats your stomach. Later, though, it won't do any good at all. You have to use it prophylactically. Once the damage is done, it's almost impossible to reverse in a person with your dad's condition."

"So the deal about the respirator giving him more time—it wasn't for any real purpose."

"Oh, it gave him the extra time, but no, most probably, it's not time he can use productively…"

We had known this all along, I guess. Rich and I were walking up toward Pittsburgh Avenue. I'd once dated a girl who lived on the street. We were in about tenth grade, and I think she had been six inches taller than I was then. I had a better jump shot though.

Rich looked up at the dense spring air and saw, I suppose, more clearly through it than I did.

"So how long is this going to go on?" I asked. "Can't you talk to Walker, do something?"

"Doctors don't like to talk much about their mistakes," he said. "But he's tried his best—you have to understand, Jim, that his point of view is he does everything he can to save someone, even if the chances are just about nil. That's the only way he can think. That's why he's so good; he just doesn't factor in anything else into his calculations..."

"Yeah, but my father's the one suffering for it."

"That's right. Walker made a mistake—and he's a little worried about it," Rich said, turning and looking sharply at me, trying to make me understand this.

I didn't—thought I did, but muffed it. I said, "You'll watch over what he's doing now?"

"That's what I plan to do. I'm going to call him again tomorrow morning. We'll be consulting two, three times a day..."

"Is he ever going to let Dad off the machine? What does it take to get him off?"

"I'll be consulting closely with Dr. Walker," Rich repeated. "Two or three times a day." He nodded his head. He was answering my direct question, but I couldn't understand his response. I wonder if that's not frequently, almost always the case. I would see.

Back home, in the driveway, I found the basketball again. Scuffed, still feeling dirty a few decades after purchase but serviceable, it hadn't lost its grip; it seemed to stick to my fingers still after fifteen or twenty thousand previous dribbles. I wet my fingertips and flipped the ball Rich's way. He'd once had a great fade-away jumper, which he shot with both his hands over his head. Now he'd put on forty pounds; his glasses were thicker, and he had the beginning of a nice set of jowls.

He looked wistfully up at the basket, then sadly down at me. "I just embarrass myself these days…I've got to get back to Sandy. Some friends of hers are having a dinner...do something about that ear, seriously, huh? You have to keep changing the bandages. One of the nurses will take care of it for you. Tell them I told them to." Here his tone changed. "I'm sorry, Jim."

He bounce-passed the ball my way, and I took it on the run, dribbling up toward the ride sight of the basket, spinning and shooting the lay-up with my left hand. The ball thudded off the metal backboard and skipped off the far rim of the basket. Wasn't even close, really.

I spent most of the morning in the other wing of the hospital, retracing where I'd been before. I tried both wings in the afternoon, though, of course, I didn't find Dr. Walker—couldn't have, unless I'd been more than lucky. For the doctors rule these roosts; and when they're feeling ambivalent about their work, as Rich might say, they disappear into the bandages, invisible men.

I did manage to cajole the people there into doing something for my old man. If the odds on his recovery were insurmountable, give or take a wildly manic hope, he didn't have to suffer with every compression and every extension of the respirator next to him. Doctor Walker had prescribed valium for him—valium, to make him relax. I talked to Ellen who was on duty; she tried to find Walker too—perhaps she did, I don't know, but by early afternoon, they were giving Dad morphine. When I put in my time with him thereafter, between one and three, his face was as placid and as smooth as the surface, under a clear, swift current, of a stone. Was the morphine for him or for me?

The next morning, when my sister went to see Dad before she went to work, he seemed to turn ceaselessly, she said. His eyes kept opening, then closing with every rustle of his body. She found Walter, the morning nurse; but when he came into administer some more morphine, to still my

father's restlessness, Dad put his hand over his arm, covering the spot
where the morphine had previously dripped into his body.

Walter reached for the other arm, misinterpreting the gesture, but
my sister understood. "I don't think he wants any more," she said, to
Walter's disbelief. "Is that right, Dad?" She had to raise her voice, for
though his hearing was good, he was confused. "You don't want any more
of this stuff, is that it?"

Without opening his eyelids, with them squeezed ever more tightly
together, he nodded his head vigorously, in agreement for a change with
one of his children. He wanted to take his dying like his dentistry: straight
("Men don't use Novocain," he told me when I was about five). Unlike his
son, unlike his daughter too I suppose, he saw what the world gave him
pretty much the way it was. Didn't try to take in too much of the world, not
nearly as much as his wife, for instance; but what he put his attention to he
refused to embellish.

Then too he may have wanted all his strength, not necessarily
because he thought he might stretch himself very far into the future, but
rather because he was preparing himself for this day and the next, taking
them whole. Paying his respects and galvanizing all the rest of us.

He asked Anne for "Fran," spelling the name with a trembling
hand; and when I arrived a couple of hours later, Mom was at his bedside,
her hands posed together on the side of his bed, clasping one of his. When
I'd been more of a kid, 17 or 18 and in my first years of college, I'd often
thought that that my mother's deeply wrinkled face was the product of her
solidity and our conflict, my father's and mine. She would sit between my
father and me while we were fighting over something insignificant,
anything, and we would pull her apart, stretching her in both directions with
our incessant and aggravated demands, both looking to her to arbitrate what

was a conflict rooted in the gene pool. Later, when she and Dad visited Sarah and me on a trip to Italy, I'd thought with surprise how each of them seemed hollowed out of the other, their faces grooved together. Sarah thought that, though she liked my dad, my mom was far more interesting. At his bedside, Fran was his rock; he was smooth, and he hung onto her.

A dandelion wisp in comparison, I was blown off, blown away within minutes every time I entered his room. I couldn't stand to see my father's pain, couldn't watch him wince (hadn't he always in a way, hadn't I often been responsible?). I went to find Dr. Walker, didn't, finally called Rich again.

"I think you'll be hearing from him," Rich said. "I talked to him this morning, a couple of times."

"And what did he say?"

"He didn't have much of a response when I told him he might have anticipated the ulcers. The Maalox stuff I told you about is only effective prior to the appearance of an ulcer. I'd looked at the data. Antibiotics are different for patients with lung problems; they've been through the milder ones. These are particularly potent, you understand, Jim?"

"Kind of," I said, otherwise preoccupied.

He had to explain it more clearly. "Looks to me," he said, "like Dr. Walker may have made a mistake. I asked him about it. Rather, I asked him why he didn't use the medications simultaneously, given the antibiotics' strength. He didn't have a good answer."

"I see," I said, not seeing much at all. My focus was off. I saw the hospital's grey walls and bustling workers, doctors and nurses and gurneys full of wounded and sick there in the terminal wing, as if through a fish eye lens, everything bloated and occupying more space than my vision could absorb.

Rich understood, I think. "Well," he said. "Like I said, I think you'll be getting a visit pretty soon."

Indeed we did, but it wasn't the one Rich expected. Instead one of my dad's best business friends came to pay his respects. The president of a large international oil transporter, he'd diverted his company's jet from a New Orleans to Denver trip to stop and see my father. Odd how these oil company executives, the ones I met, are so radically different from the public's image of them. These corporate executives are oddly austere, fairly simple men, not anywhere near as slick as say their own company's lawyers or their investment bankers. Hard-bitten, country boys, they often are farm kids from modest families who have given their lives to their companies. They wield enormous power but don't seem particularly infatuated with its uses and are almost never self-important outside their companies' domains. So, at any rate, were the men my father liked and brought home to meet his family. So was he. They'd turn off your gas pumps if their companies demanded it; but they wouldn't take any extra ethyl for themselves.

After I greeted Mr. Irwin, I went back to my dad's room where my sister shaved him, washed him, and began working on his hair. She wetted it down, then she combed it as he liked, brushing his cowlick five times— that was the trick, five times, not four or six, he found it worked better with five in each direction, before smoothing it down into a gentleman's cut.

Dad had his eyes closed while Anne worked on him; but right as I readied myself to leave, Dad opened his eyes and looked my way. I could sense their struggle to focus, could feel them rise up to the room's surface. He smiled weakly at me and nodded his head toward the door, for me to let in his friend.

After I found Mr. Irwin again, down the hall in the lounge, and led him toward intensive care, he seemed to become more nervous the farther we walked. He said this to me, though, with a grin of memory, "you know, Jim, your dad's one of the warmest men I've ever met—the only man I've ever known who could hold a conversation and make friends with people crossing on the other side of an escalator. In Houston once, at Sakowitz's, I swear, he got talking to a couple rising on the Up escalator while we were going down to lunch. One of the greatest minds in our business and he's got time for everyone, such a friendly guy."

He shook his head with admiration. I shook mine with dismay. That "friendly" man was one I'd never known. I regretted that I'd missed out on him and envied Mr. Irwin that friendship.

Mr. Irwin spent about fifteen minutes inside with Dad; and when he came out, he looked about five inches shorter than his six foot two or three and thinner. His clear blue eyes seemed opaque. He took my mother's shoulders in his large hands and walked with her for a moment. When they passed me, they stopped. He had a piece of paper in his hand, and he noticed me remarking it. He looked away and then looked back at me. He was embarrassed and proud too, I guess. He decided to show us the note.

On the paper was my father's handwriting, tremulous, shaky, difficultly written but clear: "How you enriched my life! Goodbye, my friend." Mr. Irwin looked away from us, bit his bottom lip; but his facial muscles and his jaw quivered, his whole face defending itself from the tears which welled and jiggled in his eyes but, strong, self-made man that he was, didn't cascade down his face.

"So, how are you?" Rich asked me a couple of hours later when I called him from the Intensive Care lounge, where I was waiting for visiting hours to begin again. The place seemed emptier; the lady with the baby had left alone, without her child who'd finally expired. Lived eight days, the heart pumping after the brain had died.

"I don't have a clue," I responded to Rich. "Dad looked better this morning; you don't think he could actually be getting better, do you?"

"It's the blood," he said. "They gave him over a pint and a half just this morning. That's what you saw, Jim. I'm sorry. He's losing more blood now than he was at the beginning of the week. His infection's spread, and his ulcers aren't going to go away."

"What's happening with Walker then?"

"You mean he hasn't called you yet?"

"Nope. Can't you just take over Dad's care?"

"You'll hear from him," my friend said emphatically. "I can't believe he hasn't gotten the message."

"Which?" I asked, forever dumb.

"We're going to do a little more consulting. He hasn't paid enough attention. He's going to be a lot more helpful soon."

"But I thought he couldn't take Dad off this respirator now..."

"He can't, so forget about it."

"But I thought…"

"I'm sorry, Jim. I keep forgetting…the machine's not all that's keeping him alive now. Ask Dr. Walker when he comes. He'll be there by five."

And he was, looking harried, overworked and anxious—a type A cardiac risk if not for his newly diminished bulk, his baggy trousers and blousy doctor's frock. He looked in every direction but mine even as he walked through the relative's lounge and up to me and asked if we could talk.

The lounge itself must have made him feel uncomfortable, for he took me back into the hall. He was overexposed in the lounge, missed the fluorescent lights and obeisant attentions of various staffers. Still, once in the corridor, he continued to look at the activity surrounding us, never at me.

"We wouldn't have known," he began, "if we hadn't tried."

"Known what?"

"Known that we had done all we could for him." The man sounded like a lawyer whose client he should have plea-bargained, but didn't. He couldn't even glance at me; I couldn't stop staring at him, and I'm sure I saw yellowed fingers. Is that how he'd lost the weight? A lung doctor who smoked…then again, it just may have been my eyes.

"He's a great man," he ventured, "and…

"Yeah, I know. You wouldn't want to see his last days be on the rack. We went through this before, that's why, oddly, you hooked him up without telling us."

"This is what I do, Jim—I save lives. I try to save lives. I can't think of losing them."

"It might be kinder if you did. People die, doctor, why torture them when they're doing it?" Was I shouting? People looked our way as they passed us in the corridor.

"I don't blame you," he said. "I know you're upset. I am too." He still hadn't even cross-eyed my way. There was, of course, a pretty fascinating collapsible steel gurney to our right.

"What do you propose to do, doc? Just keep him here 'til all his organs give out?"

He was surprised by the outburst and stunned I didn't seem to understand. But then Rich had orchestrated this, fortunately for me. He'd tried to make me see what he was doing, but I hadn't come close. My ignorance brought Walker's eyes a couple of yards nearer mine—their gaze rested on my right cheekbone. His body seemed to relax. His fingers even looked pinker.

Here was the deal, as time and eventual clear-headedness (relatively) let me discover. Rich made him think we were contemplating a malpractice suit. Rich's continuing consultations, most especially on the absence of medication to counterbalance the antibiotics' effects, left Doctor Walker feeling vulnerable and brought him back to us now, with a newfound desire to get the case over, to move on with his work. So he found the solution Rich wanted him to discover:

"Your dad's had fifteen points of blood since we put him on the respirator—and none of his signs looks better. His heart's still great, but the infection has spread. He's losing more blood every hour than he was before." I'd heard all this; this was for the doctor himself. On some level, however, I suddenly got he feeling that he may indeed have hated to lose my dad. For he turned his eyes finally on me; then again maybe that was an attempt, in advance, to charm—a prophylactic, as they say, against future litigation. Who knows for sure? I wasn't thinking well here; my memory is more and more like a fried egg.

"At twenty pints," he continued somberly, "if there's no improvement, we'll stop giving him more."

That would mean five more pints of blood. Dad had lost almost three that day, and we were still in the afternoon. They'd begin to give him that fifth extra pint, the twentieth in all, in just a little over a day, at around 6:30—26 hours after Dr. Walker and I talked, after the doctor, seeing my distress at hearing the words pronounced, my dad's death certificate in a way, tucked himself quickly back into hospital routine. A nurse came his way with a question. He shook my hand reassuringly—a well practiced habit—and he followed the nurse down the hall.

.

You'd think that would have been it; but something odder can always occur when you're in your hometown.

As we waited that evening in the hospital, my mom mostly in my dad's room and Anne and I, then Anne, Greg and I in and out of the lounge, we began to be joined by others, friends of mine from high school whom I hadn't seen in years. I'd made the tenth reunion, missed the fifteenth and couldn't remember what happened thereafter—yet here, this evening were three, five, nine people I'd known back then, though only one who'd ever been close to me. Maybe two: I had played baseball in 5th and 6th graces with one of these guys. I'd given a speech for him in 11th grade when he was running for some elective office. I shouldn't have, however, for his election (I was popular then for about five minutes, up until the next grade) assured his admission to the snotty school at which I too matriculated. We'd spent our first year in college changing sides of the freshman dining hall to avoid socializing with one another—who wanted to be seen with a rube from Oklahoma? (Especially one like him who dressed as if he were attending Oxford, who carried his umbrella as if it were a cane...who hadn't discovered the amazing effects of hallucinogens?)

Yet here he was, Will (formerly Billy) Benson, the first face I saw when at about 9 p.m., I came out of my dad's room to take a breather. "I'm so sorry, Jim," he said, and I surely thought he was.

Only in Tulsa, a small but burgeoning city, I concluded. But then I was flabbergasted to see next to him, still 8 inches taller than I, Eileen Williams, 7th grade class secretary, and Eddie Hall, the third baseman on the Stars—his dad, the coach, had died a couple of years previously, my mother had told me. I was having some trouble understanding their arrival, fully absorbing the reasons for this conclave. Was I supposed to be gracious? Who were these other four or five people with them, faces I only very dimly recalled—they introduced themselves; each shook my hand, looking at me deeply and movingly.

Mostly, however, they looked toward Will. The last time we'd seen each other, at our college's annual alumni party one Christmas, Will had been working for a major energy company and feeling some pain at an impending divorce. Today, wearing a spiffy pin striped suit, he looked more like the political aspirant I'd always assumed he would become. Was he consolidating his support group, looking for a contribution from our family? He'd picked up enough democratic ideals at school that he'd surely disqualified himself from my old man's dole. Dad liked Republicans, the more irredentist the better. Even the Bushes were problematical for Dad. And Billy Benson, "Will" or not, had always struck my dad as a goose. My father had known and preferred Billy's grandmother, who'd cleaned offices to put her equally self-absorbed son through school from whence he could eventually rule over all the local public schools and get his kid into the overpriced socialist sympathizing Ivy League school which almost ruined my father's own son, which certainly uprooted him as my dad had feared and took him half a continent or more away for the rest of his life.

Yet here was Will, of all those who might have come—to whom I really was close—trying to give me support, making me feel inhospitable and uncomfortable, like an oyster locked around my grief. We were in the back of the lounge, by the vertical blinds. The seats were made of Naugahyde, a pale sea green. I can recall little else. My mind tried to focus, couldn't, wouldn't. The woman with the dying child had sat back here, she and her group, before they had left us.

"Who's Gene's doc?" Will asked me. How did he get off calling my old man Gene? I think I heard a siren going off, the alarm announcing that my father's lungs weren't working with the machine.

"Walker," I said. "But Rich has been consulting with us."

Will cringed. Eileen smiled—she must have had foot long lips, I thought; that's why she was so much taller than everyone else, had to be that large to give her lips space to grow, to finally tap out.

"Rich Edwards?" Will asked, as if he didn't remember him. Rich had tormented Will for every year of the five or six school years I'd spent with the two of them. Will, though, was larger now, weightier; and his friends anyway listened to him—you could tell Rich Edwards wasn't in favor with any of them.

"What do they say about your dad?" Will was speaking of the medical staff.

"That he doesn't have much time left." I shook my head. "The really sad thing is he worked himself--and smoked himself--to death. Doesn't matter that he quit 15 years ago. His lungs just cooked, and he never got to enjoy his freer years…"

Will nodded understandingly. Eileen did too, and so did all the other, dimly perceived faces. What was this minyan, this conclave for? Still it was touching, I thought—it really was—that they'd come.

"And the two of you?" Will prompted, consolingly. "How is it between you and your dad?"

"We've come to know each other better, I think…you know the funny thing is, he has lived a lot longer than they told us he would when he came down with the emphysema. Most people don't live more than three, four years after they're diagnosed. My dad's going on 20, and he was never immobile." I was saying this to Billy Benson. I could not believe what was happening. I looked outside—you could see LaFortune golf course, the lit baseball field on this side of it. Oral Roberts' teams play there, I thought, Oral Roberts University. You could see its "Prayer Tower" from the hospital's other wing.

"So there were blessings even in his illness," Eileen said. "Blessings" should have clued me in, but I wasn't thinking well. I was thinking how kind of these people to be there, and indeed it was. I was thinking, if I thought at all about it, that "blessings" had evolved beyond being a regional word, that New Agers had incorporated it into their vernacular too.

Yes. "You know, Eileen," I thought I knew, "I think so. I have the feeling sometimes that he simply stayed around this long because he wanted to see Anne, that's my sister, and me settled into life. It took us this long."

A sweet thought, but addled: was it even true, were we settled?

We could support ourselves at least; my book was selling. Irv had called with a report, couldn't help himself, though the idea was to express condolence. Then I did have some kind of a name in L.A., people paid me for scripts even if they didn't produce them. My sister had a new husband, and her job seemed solid. Maybe the marriage was working. Dad had hung on that long.

I explained this to the assembly, just chattering along in the hospital lounge. I'd been waking up at 4, hadn't had a lot more sleep than my mother. Maybe that explains it, why I had a temporary lapse of irony, probably doesn't.

"That's a wonderful testament. Thanks, Jim," someone in the back said. This was a streaked blonde with a pageboy, a print dress. I didn't think I knew her. She looked like a praying mantis.

"My wife Cindy," Eddie Hall explained, with a solemn nod. I saw him at 11 bowling over a catcher at home—and being screamed at by his dad, the coach, when he forgot to touch home plate and was tagged out. Just shook his head under the father's screams, like a duck shedding water as we say in Oklahoma. My dad never embarrassed me in too large a public, anyway. Then, of course, he was never there either.

Eileen Williams looked like she was crying. "That's such a beautiful witnessing," said she. Uh-oh, I did finally think. I was on sitting on the sofa, Will and Eileen in front of me, Eddie next to me, who was that on my right?

"Witnessing."

"Even in our bleakest moments," Eileen continued, letting that tear glide down her cheek, her skin a beautiful rose. "He provides for us. He lets us see."

"He does indeed, Eileen," Will now said sonorously, turning his attention fully on me. I saw myself, weird and distorted in his eyes, as they leaned my way, two feet from mine. Maybe their nodding encouraged my own head to bob on its stem, like a giveaway at a ballpark.

They all smiled with my nod, smiled together; and together they simultaneously reached into pockets and purses and took out eight, nine books, with identical simulated leather covers and gold engraved letters. These were Bibles, likes the ones the friends of the woman with the dying baby had-- New Testaments with pink edged pages.

"Shall we pray?" Will asked, and eight, nine heads bowed, as if they were on hinges, like mechanical rabbits falling off the back of a carny's shooting range. All their eyes closed—and the force of their belief embarrassed me into closing mine.

"Our Heavenly Father, thank you for the healing time you gave this troubled family," Will began in a voice a couple of octaves deeper than it had once been. "Thank you for the courage you gave E.V.D. 'Gene' Adams to wait for his hapless, his prodigal son to return home; to forsake the ways and the means of—let us not be afraid to say it, let us declare it with C.S. Lewis—of the Evil One, to give up the drugs and the debauchery and the philandering he has recently become so notorious for--the lusting after women and the pride, the vanity and the vainglory with which he pursued his solitary path in life—so he could move back now through his father's illness and approaching passing back toward You, our Lord, through us, your humble servants gathered here to aid you in his redemption. In Christ's name, Amen."

"Amen," a woman's voice plangently concurred. I think that must have been Eddie's wife Cindy.

"Praise be," Eddie himself said with great conviction, perhaps because he had once been our high school's most avid and successful skirt chaser.

"Give us your hand, Jim," Will said. "Your hand…" When mine seemed dilatory, it was quickly grasped. Will's grip wasn't relaxed any more than it had been fifteen, twenty years before when his had been the hand which had encircled and personally counted each of the 6800 cans in the canned goods drive he successfully led. That hand wasn't going to let mine go when he as well as He had other plans for me. "Praise be that you've come back to us, Jimmy…"

"Praise be," Eileen echoed. I was thinking of my dad, how he would have appreciated this, how seeing it would have kept him alive a little longer.

"You've been saved. I know that, Jimmy," Will continued. How exactly escaped me. I'd been the last kid, the one holdout in the church of my youth: every Sunday, every eye there seemed to rebuke me as I wouldn't flinch, wouldn't move toward the front of the congregation until the Spirit, much different than this, finally took root in me right around adolescence—and disappeared moments after all my sins were washed away at Baptism. In the full immersion, I thanked the Lord for the fresh start and sinned, when I did, with relief.

"But has he been Reborn?" Eileen wondered.

"That's what we're here to discover," Will answered and turned his beady eyes my way. "We've come to you, Jimmy, so you can rededicate yourself, on your father's death bed, to the principles by which he lived…"

"Now wait a second here," I began, my own voice taking on an evangelical lilt. Was this happening? Or was this hallucinatory, some odd compound of the absence of sleep and full immersion in Oklahoma percolating up through my trembling larynx?

"I know, it can be hard," Will continued, ignoring my outburst, "it can be cruel, but the Lord deserves something better from you than this…" Here he held up a copy of <u>Luck for the Lovelorn.</u>

All heads came up with his hand, magically. Eyes opened. A few "Amens" sounded out there in the peanut gallery.

"What happened to the prayer?" I asked.

"The Lord is listening, always listening to us, whether we bow our heads or not…just like that lady in New York, Sue and Juana and even poor Chuck Alphabet have listened to you, Jimmy…"

I was looking around for help, seeing only white Bibles lifted up like a victorious team's football helmets, descrying only the shining eyes of these high school chums I'd never liked that much (and half of whom I couldn't even recall).

"And you have the opportunity now, Jim, to go back on those television shows—and to tell them, tell all of American that right here…"

"Blessed be," Cindy said. This one, I now noted looked like Karen Anderson. She couldn't have weighed over 80 pounds. She was probably proving her faith daily, living on snake venom. Eddie needed to do something for her.

"Tell them that right here you were Reborn into the world just as your father was leaving it…isn't that miraculous?"

"Praise be!" Eileen said, through somewhat yellowing teeth. What had happened to her? She'd once had the clearest smile in all of Christendom; maybe it was early denture work.

I stood up.

"Hallelujah, Jim," Will declaimed. "Hallelujah, look at him, Lord." Nine white Bibles flashed messages, like ship's flags, my way.

I started walking around them; they moved toward me. I had to walk through them, pushing Eddie aside, pushing aside some other unnamed white guy. This was a Christian gauntlet. And I was heading out the end of it.

"Where are you going?" Cindy screamed. "Oh, you could do so much. Let yourself. Feel the power." She jumped up, flinging both hands in the air, and I realized, my God, this was Cindy Walters. She'd been head cheerleader, girl of the month three times. What had happened to her? What was she doing with Eddie Hall, of all people? Couldn't she have married better? I tried to walk past her, but she took hold of my shirt. Light as a feather, she floated along side me as I walked out of the room. "Feel the power, Jimmy!"

"Come back!" I heard Will command. But I quickened my step.

"He'll be back to Him one way or the other," he reassured his flock. "And we'll be waiting for you, Jim. We'll be here."

But Cindy wasn't. Her eyes distending almost to mine (was it Krone's disease, Graves'?), Cindy raced up next to me. She attached her unpainted, badly bitten nails and spindly fingers to me as I strode down the corridor, hurrying toward Intensive Care. Dangling off me, she started praying. "Lord, help this man feel you, feel the power of the Holy Spirit." We bounced into one gurney, three nurses. One hysterical, aging adolescent interlaced with a prematurely middle-aged hysteric, we burst through the doors to Intensive Care, knocking over an IV before we reached the main area, where fortunately my sister and her husband Greg were just coming out of Dad's room.

"What's this?" Anne asked and peeled Cindy off of me with a whisk of her powerful hand.

"This," Cindy exclaimed. "This is a man going to Eternal Damnation if he doesn't straighten up and fly right."

Anne knew the lingo; I might have expected her to talk that talk too. But instead, she said, "What in God's name is this idiot talking about?"

"He's had his Chance, the Lord may never give him another!" Cindy told her. "Get yourself right with Jesus, Jim...or the Evil One is going to chew you up and spit you out. You're not going to make our next class reunion, Jimmy, if you're in Hell."

"Don't worry," Rich agreed when we spoke the next morning. "You'll get plenty more shots at rebirth, I can assure you of that. The Soldiers of our Savior—SOS, that's what Will's flock call themselves—are always on the attack. Will's been besieging me for 15 months now. Worse than a credit card collection agent, they can't be denied. All you can do is get a court order against them. That's what I got—and they're very hard to obtain."

"Are you kidding? A court order?"

"Yep. I got one. They began stalking me at Sandy's …impossible. I must have found the only agnostic judge in the state."

"My father's dying. I might have to wait a day or two before I get onto that….He is, isn't he? Has he gotten any better?" The hospital was no longer answering questions about my father. Walter, the male nurse, wasn't on duty with Dad, and the other nurses were mute and unavailable.

"They shift the staff," Rich explained. "So they won't get too attached to the patients and their families. Think of how many people die in that place. The nurses have a higher burnout rate than air traffic controllers."

"And my dad?"

"Yeah, well, he's not better. He lost a lot of blood yesterday."

"So what do you think?"

"I think it's time to get over there with your mom."

Though it was 7:15 in the morning, I was dressed and ready to go. Distressed at the prospect, I'd only slept an hour or so. I was speaking to Rich on the phone in my parents' bedroom, fumbling with the wooden cufflink box I'd made for my old man in the Cub Scouts—an oddly competent job for such a proudly white-collar kid. Its green felt lining, though unevenly edged, still had a thick nap to it.

Then too that may have been because, unlike his son, my old man took care of things: there were wing tip shoes in his closet that dated from the '60s. The small gold and diamond stickpin rolling around in my fingers commemorated the 42 years my father had put in with the same company. Going to night school, getting his law degree, he had risen slowly all the way, almost, to the top.

"I wish Dad could see Billy Benson," I said to Rich. "It might keep him alive, just the absurdity of it."

"Yeah, well, I'm sorry, Jim," Rich said, easing me off the phone and toward my dad, "but nothing's going to do that, I'm afraid."

When I reached the hospital, there in the lounge was Eileen
Williams with two of her children—tow headed blondes with green eyes
like their mother's. They stood next to my sister, the kids playing, I now
see, on the major of my sister's many grievances, on her lack of issue. They
bobbed in Anne's eyes like candied apples in a Halloween tank. They
joined Cindy, who sported a chubby Vietnamese kid; and all looked my
way with great (if still puzzling) solicitude.

"Anne," I shouted across the room. "Could you come over here?"

Heads popped up from pillows, there on the lounge chairs, and I
remembered again that ours wasn't by any means the only grief around.
Some, as my mother said, cut so much deeper.

The women didn't follow Anne when she came my way. They
stood looking at her hopefully, eying me reproachfully, these middle-class
women identically dressed in Scottish plaid skirts with big silver safety
pins, their arms crossed over their shiny white Bibles.

"What are you doing over there?" I asked my sister. "I thought you
called her an idiot."

"Listening," she said. "I take belief seriously."

"I thought you'd already been reborn—haven't you?"

"More than once, but maybe theirs will work better."

Was she kidding? "You signing up with them then?"

"Why not? I've tried everything else."

That was the truth. She had been a Buddhist, a Hindu, a Messenger of God; she'd been a Rolfer (during her Northern California sojourn); then she'd been Oklahoma's first Landmark Education convert before checking herself back into the Baptist Church, Pentecostal variant. She liked the singing in tongues. Now she sang at an AME Church—best music of all.

Anne smiled at me, as she looked back at Eileen and her small platoon of the Soldiers of our Savior; and we each reached for the other's arm, though our smiles quickly disappeared, eaten up by our anxiety like metal submerging in acid.

Anne had left Dad's room when they'd begun to give him his twentieth pint of blood. When we went back inside, there were only a few traces of the blood remaining in the transparent plastic bag above his head. Dad's face seemed fresh and animated, pink, the eyes moving there under the surface of his lids. But Mom's face was stiff and rigid, her eyes fixed as if she didn't want to absorb anything more, as if she were trying to keep this away from her. She was standing by the bed, her arms bent out, her elbows flared and her hands clasped. I couldn't see very much; words, when they came, rattled in the room like falling objects.

A nurse held the plastic tubing as the blood finished draining through it, and my father seemed to grimace as she removed the IV from his bruised arm. His tone was good, but the blood, this living hurt him. The machine hummed beside him. He wasn't fighting it any more. He was waiting on his death, just as his father had—and it would be peaceful from now on: Petronius' death, the blood running out of him.

The hospital became again a place of mercy, what it was intended to be. The nurses gradually detached my father from most of the machines around him; and for the first time now they anticipated our concerns. They reached out and cooled my father's brow, adjusted the plastic mask which covered his nose and brought in the oxygen which kept his blood pumping. My mom held his right hand in hers, and he rolled over on his side, facing her, his left hand curling under his chin, its former fresh pink glow transmuted to an ever-grayer pallor.

I took my mom's right arm; my sister had her left, and together we watched the blips move across the green screen by my father's head. These measured his heart's beats; and for an hour or so, I don't have any idea, they seemed very regular; but suddenly over about fifteen minutes, they plunged precipitously. His dove grey face gave way to a kind of cream; the heartbeats slowed; my sister began to weep, noiselessly as did her husband and I too. Only my mother didn't cry; her whole face welled, quivered and finally firmed as the line on the screen straightened and the beats ceased— 46 years they'd been together, she refused to believe he was leaving.

After a minute went by and my mom's eyes still hadn't left my father's face or the green screen, he came back to her: suddenly a blip, then a second skipped across the screen, the line tracing the heart's life rose up for an instant and, like a plane dipping a wing, my father bid his wife (all of us) good-bye.

Love, Again…

.

Part 3

Love, Again...

Losing a parent is like becoming an amputee, losing a leg: you assume everything's there, intact until you proceed as normal, putting some weight on it. Then gravity reaches up and grabs you, pulling you down onto your chin. It hit me within the first hours of my return to sunny Southern California.

CJ picked me up at the airport, this a month after my dad's death. He looked at me, as if I'd had an illness. "The program tonight, Max, is for adventure, looks like you need some." Little did he know. I'd been spending my afternoons playing bridge with my mother's friends, one of the gang. Thinking I was helping her find a rhythm, I'd begun speaking like an Oklahoman again, was operating like a retired housewife (considering a run for take-out food an excursion). I didn't know, though, if I was ready for "adventure."

It was a Friday night, I know by the place we went, a club open all week but suitable to guys like C only on Fridays when the entire "entertainment community" filed through the large barn like structure— might once have been a car dealership, Jeep signs still decorated the outer walls—paying homage to Leonardo Dicaprio or Jack Nicholson, I think. They were allegedly two of the owners. It was a place I would have preferred avoiding, no entertainment here, just the "community" (already an oxymoron, the sense of community out here about as developed as it is in an airport). Good place to perceive if not actually find an agent, better place probably to find female accompaniment if you were, say North African, pretending to be French, wore hundred dollar tees, claimed to be a producer or actually had a couple of bad movies under your belt.

Many "development" people were there, way too many from all the studios, a good quarter of their vice-presidents as well. I should have thought of that, but then, that's what I mean. I hadn't been thinking well for quite some time. I'd had my month away; it was time for another pratfall (like all those I'd taken in anticipation, in the month before I went to Oklahoma); and there was an obvious one to take, too obvious for me to miss.

I was in L.A., ostensibly to find the ending to a script of *Luck for the Lovelorn.* I know it's ridiculous, but Irv had sold it. To Warner's. Jeannie had bought it. We were going to work together on it. I should have wondered why, after 18 months or so of dating, she'd finally decided to do something with me. I knew she liked the story we'd "developed" over the phone while we stayed in touch. An aging (overaged?) adolescent, a Peter Pan who can't commit himself, plays around on this girl we love, comes home one day from a tryst, is hit by a car—and expires. So to atone for his two-timing, our hero, the dead guy, is given the task of coming back down to earth to help the betrayed girl find another man. And when he does, showing her how to act with the confidence she's never had, he falls totally in love with her. There's just this one problem: he's spirit; she's flesh.

It was, in somewhat more prosaic fashion, a dilemma I was familiar with, my personal problem: I was always either the flesh—next to someone and wondering where, how, why my spirit had vanished, or I was the spirit searching for someone else's unobtainable flesh. Jeannie thought I could solve that. I had the feeling she was hoping we could solve it together.

I was still that deluded—but no longer quite as certain of my specific delusions. A newborn chick's head seemed about to pop through the world's shell.

When C.J. and I walked into the club in question, not thirty seconds after he was recognized by the delirious doorperson (C was a member, one of a very select few who actually paid entrance fees to join this "club" with the bad food, the underdressed "executives", the other actors who'd made it enough they were spared the admissions fee), right after we'd walked up the steps and smelled the garlic and tried to wade through the tanned people with the leased Maseratis out front, there she was—not the mother of my putative kid but the woman who was there for me, who backed me up, always supportive Jeannie.

She was dancing to a retro remix of Dock of the Bay, her arms wrapped around a guy who couldn't have been more than 20. They weren't even pretending to fox trot. The guy had an earring, a tattoo on the right side of his neck, and spiked hair. He was wearing a male skirt which in no way stopped him from leaning back, looking at her lustfully, then turning his head, a hand around her neck, and pulling her to him—as she looked directly at me. I got the point. He was a very handsome guy, and Jeannie wasn't embarrassed in the least. She kissed him on the cheek, while he blew into her ear.

And Greg Gravity (or maybe it was Ginny Gravity) grabbed me by the lapels and pulled me down to the ground—started doing push-ups on me, until Jeannie came over and kissed me too.

"You're here early," Jeannie said to me, unapologetically (I presume she meant a couple of weeks early). Charles, her friend, sidled over our way, looking all the time over his shoulder and toward the dance floor. Jeannie glanced nervously his way, and then returned her gaze toward me. "Are you okay?" She asked, with concern.

"Great. Really, I'm feeling great. Who's your child? You forgot to tell me about him," I said, echoing those comments she had made in New York that now felt as if they'd been uttered years before.

"You know," Jeannie said with a tender smile. "You, Jerry (her old boy friend), I finally figured if I'm going to go for a kid, I might as well go for the real thing."

C.J., who was nearby, laughed. There was already a girl on his arm, just minutes, seconds even, after we arrived. He was a magnet, powerfully pulling equine, toothy, toothsome WASPs toward his over buffed arms. This one had a beautiful smile too and an infectious laugh, both of which she directed my way.

"I hear they have their uses, young boys," C's girl—her name turned out to be Zoe—said with an English accent, inviting herself into the conversation.

"Max wouldn't know," CJ said. "He only goes for stronger, more mature women, heavy hitters."

"Who bruise my delicate sensibilities, just beat me up…right," I said. C and Z laughed, but Jeannie, as if to prove my point, missed it. She was distracted, looking around. Charles appeared attached to her now only by the elbow, and she seemed to want to see what he was seeing.

She did turn back my way, not then but many minutes later after I'd tried and failed to make conversation with a number of women looking for another kind of guy, someone who could take care of them, at least career-wise. More than once, Jeannie floated by me, glued to Charles' ample pecs. And people whose parameters were hard to determine at the best of times in Los Angeles, started to lose their shape like amoebae, like squiggles in a light show. It was time for me to pack it in, and Jeannie somehow scented this, appeared on top of a general wave, alone. Behind her, the crowd broke up for a moment to watch four studio executives slam dance with two ample producers (not a pretty sight).

Jeannie took my buzzing head into both her hands, and she rubbed it roughly, as you'd do with a collie, a sheepdog. "I love you too, you knucklehead," she said. "Don't you dare forget it." She kissed me on the forehead, before she turned and folded herself into the crook of the reappearing Charles' arm, slipping back again into the swarming crowd.

Which side of my memory did she inhabit then? The world just keeps changing, too fast for a shut-in though sometimes its permutations intersect with our own imagining. It was 12:30, still early, when C and Z kindly dropped me off home, C in his Prius, Z in her (Datsun) Z. I waved their two cars off; and when I went inside my tiny A-frame house in Laurel Canyon, my hippie pad, as Jeannie liked to call it, I noted that buzzing in my phone that indicated somewhat had been thinking of me. "Hi, my sweet," the voice rang out. Though this particular nostalgia felt as if it was getting old even then, a part of me leapt at the sound of Sarah's voice. "Could you call me tonight—I don't care when—please?"

She pushed my button even all this far away. Though we'd talked while I'd been in Oklahoma, it had all been official statements of regret, which I'd appreciated, and two dozen roses whose blossoming, an ever paler orange, lightened my mood and sense of place.

It was 3:30 her time, but I took her at her word. And she didn't sound asleep, swore she wasn't when I asked.

"How are you, my boy?" She asked over my asking her if really she didn't mind—and she sounded interested in the answer, her question sincere, her voice sonorous and deep, each word articulated--an actress. I tried to tell her about the missing appendage, about falling on your face, how strange the world felt as you learned to negotiate it differently.

"I had you to get me through that," she said, referring to that time we'd first been together, after her father had died.

"But I didn't understand what I was doing," I said.

"I did," said she.

"I wasn't trying to give you any idea of the world really. I was trying to figure it out as I went along."

She laughed, sadly. "Oh, I knew that, but I loved you for it anyway. You were always there for me, even if you were talking mostly to yourself."

"Out loud," I said, a tear in each eye. It was late for California, and I'd drunk too much, more than my normal quotient—as if, of course, I needed an excuse.

"Out loud, uh huh, and when you talked to yourself, your Adam's apple would move up and down, even your lips sometimes, like someone with reading difficulties." She giggled gently again. "But you never let me out of your thoughts—I started living again in them."

Thinking of her dad, this man I never knew, I couldn't help picturing my father, and I welled up, the tears swept down my cheeks, no longer interrupting even my thoughts. I could cry and talk, cry and chew gum and walk: this was part of me in mourning--an odd, Victorian sounding word, isn't it? But apt now in its awkwardness for the state it describes can sweep over you like changes in the elements, coming up like Santa Ana winds and taking you over, taking you by surprise each time.

I didn't know exactly what to make of this particular emotional turbulence, but for a change, it might not have had anything to do with my precarious balance. It wasn't simply my chemicals trying to get themselves back into sync. Sarah's voice was different. There was an uncomfortable quality to it, even to her laughter.

"I'm coming out there Monday," she said, two days away.

"Somebody wants to produce Don Juan? What, as a space epic?"

"No, the Public already tried to sell that in every form imaginable…no, Lifetime's got a couple of betrayed wives they want to talk to me about…" This sounded funny at first, but her voice changed in the middle of it; her voice just fell through the sentence.

"Everything OK, Sarah? Jesse fine?"

"I don't know," she responded enigmatically. And I wanted to ask about Phillip, didn't, figured she would volunteer the information if she wanted to discuss it, figured she'd lie about it probably anyway. The last person you tell the truth to about another man is an old boy friend. I never encouraged that kind of honesty, anyway. I always was hurt by it.

But when she left the line, saying she was eager to see me, I felt as if a hive of bees had settled in my duodenum. I felt them hum; I felt them move out into my bloodstream, up and down my frame. I tried, but I was numb no longer. I couldn't stop the buzzing.

I was still humming a day and a half later, late Sunday afternoon, when Jeannie showed up at my place unexpectedly, a bag of groceries on her arm. She must have sensed, seismographs that we all are, that my psychic waves were flowing out in another direction. Or maybe she was telling the truth when she said she knew I was okay; she just wanted to verify this personally.

"I don't know," I said. "What happened to Charles? Is this exam week?"

"Actually, he had to do the sound engineering for his dad's band— they're cutting a demo…"

"His dad's band?"

"Yeah, the Bad Lads, heard of them?" Pause here, a wry smile as she blew this dart right into my heart. "Some people out there just do it, Jim—they go right into adulthood. You don't have to be middle-aged to breed."

"In fact, it's probably better if you're not, if you're young," I said, knowing so much about the subject.

Jeannie said, "I wouldn't know. I've forgotten to have them too. I'm going to die an old maid."

Who was going to out suffer whom here? Jeannie produced some swordfish steaks; we found the grill underneath the deck where the raccoons often roamed. She'd brought charcoal, starting fluid—she was prepared as always, assuming I wasn't. We lit the fire, washed some asparagus and shelled some peas. All the while she was looking around, as if she hadn't been here before, searching for something. She could sense my absence, part of me, that part which wasn't competing with Charles for her affections. I might not have been exactly the guy she was looking for, but she could miss me anyway. Missing, absence excited her, just instinctively. We were both weaned, in a matter of speaking, too early (she from her dad, who divorced her mom when Jeannie first hit school).

Finally, when the swordfish had grilled, and we'd culled lemons from this amazing tree, which grows in my yard (called a lemon tree, it actually produces bushels of the real thing), she said, "Okay, what's the deal?"

"Deal, what deal? You mean Charles is going into the recording studio all week?"

She leaned across the table and planted, a wet, red kiss, full of lip-gloss, lipstick and saliva on my nose and upper lip. She laughed when I went to wipe it off. "What are you feeling guilty about…it's supposed to be my turn."

"Sarah's coming tomorrow," I told her.

"How was she able to keep herself away so long?"

"What do you mean?"

"I was wondering when she'd be coming."

"To the coast? To see me?"

"No, to get in on the Fred Segal clothing sale."

"I think she's looking for work."

"Do I look stupid, Jim? When did we meet? How many brain cells did you lose in Oklahoma? You were only gone six weeks."

If she would have let me, I'd have been even more obtuse. I was over here, on this side of the line she'd drawn for us—the closer this got to Sarah, the farther away I was going to get from Jeannie and our dinner in the canyon.

At the airport, when I'd left Tulsa, my mom had said, "Thanks for being here. I'm not going to tell you how much I'll miss you because I was so happy you stayed this long."

I'd smiled, my grin like a car fender kissing a hydrant, and walked onto the plane.

In Laurel Canyon, Jeannie was less delicate with my tender sensibilities. "Sarah looked so lonely the last time I saw her."

She was talking about the night the three of us spent together. "I don't know, she got up in the middle of the night and left…"

"Hey, Jim, we're not engaged or even 'pinned' or 'lavaliered,' you know? You don't have to tell me the truth. Just don't insult my intelligence."

"Don't you think, considering Charley and all, this is in a little bad faith, your jealousy?"

"Who said a woman's logical? Who said anyone is…Just 'listen to me,' as your book so incisively put it."

"That's what I'm trying to do, to no avail…"

"Now you know then why your book was out to lunch.'

"I'm not supposed to see Sarah—is that what you're trying to tell me?"

"No way. What I'm saying is if you ask me to take my things out of here tonight—say even my toothbrush—I won't ever speak to you again."

"Be a little more paranoid, okay? Not one of your more attractive qualities…" There wasn't the trace of a tear in her eyes, but her crumpled grin looked so familiar to me. "Who asked you, after all, to pick up your stuff, who mentioned it?"

She didn't have that much there, in fact: a tee shirt with some Rastafarian's picture on it (left over, I suspect, from another better lover— perhaps but not necessarily the guy with his picture on the front), which she liked to wear at night, two scripts which she hadn't liked enough to finish, the bottom of a bathing suit, the book An Anatomy Lesson which she hadn't liked (and I'd made her buy) and a toothbrush, yes, which we had picked up together at a hotel in San Francisco, the Fairmont. It was fabricated out of some kind of pliable plastic, came in two parts, and looked as if it would bend around a well-filled molar. It wasn't a permanent toothbrush, wasn't the kind you kept around if you cared about your dental hygiene.

Jeannie was proud of hers. She was an ambulatory ad for Jennifer Anniston's dentist, whom she used as well. People travel in packs in the film business. Part of my problem, part of her continued resistance to me came from my continued resistance to adult orthodontia—my crooked teeth. She looked on the pain attached to her bridgework with pleasure. She was, at any rate, the kind of woman who surely left a soft bristled toothbrush and a ball of floss at the home of anyone she really cared about. What did that say about me?

Little if anything, really, but this may say more. Already, she'd transmuted my pain into hers, her guilt into mine. She'd felt me fading away, and it touched, mostly, her pride. But her pride was impressive.

And her pain, if that's what it was, her taking umbrage at my putative adolescent infatuation for an old lover, didn't diminish her desire, not at all. It increased it, I think--my moving away moved her. This kind of confusion excited both of us. Up against it, we reached for each other whereas normally, habitually, we didn't fit together with any ease. We rarely cuddled; my stubble scratched her chin, her tongue was too frank and forceful for mine. We didn't even know how to sleep together. She was always over on that side of the bed; I was on the other; and each of us pulled away, over the night, from the other's touch. Yet certain mornings, usually Sundays when she didn't have to read (when she had poured over scripts most of the night) we found a way to comfort one another: she'd huddle on her side, presenting me her back, and I'd put my arms around her. She was fine-boned, considerably more delicate than her eminent position in the movie business might make you assume she'd be, not one of the studio crocodiles people imagine. Yet when my hands overlapped around her, they'd come upon the beginnings of a bulge, which no amount of bicycle riding (in place, in the mornings) or Pilates could erase. Age was doing it to her, and I liked the way this flesh felt in my hands. When I held onto this (very slight) roll of hers too long, she'd move away from me, none too kindly; she's register my affection as condescension, and I wouldn't see her again for a week.

Here, this evening, however, she took my hand in hers and led me directly to bed, as a child might (yet who was the child here? I too was looking down at the ground, on the way out of the room). When we arrived in bed, she turned away from me and wrapped my hands around her. She moved her ass back against my body; and when she felt me harden against her, she put her hand around mine and slid my hand over her stomach, letting me feel her there, letting me take possession of this slightly embarrassing part of her. And she seemed then as aroused as I was, taking off toward her pleasure like a sprinter spurting from her blocks.

This felt like Hollywood to me, like my most paranoid image of Los Angeles—sincere only in its desperation. Here were two isolated egos intersecting for a moment, and then bouncing away, like quarks in a cyclotron.

"F.S.I.F." she said, giving voice to some proof of the insight when our bodies had separated again and only the soles of our feet, her right, my left, now touched, grazing against each other.

"What's that?" I wanted to know.

"Fucking," Jeannie said, with a sad, sharp look in her eye (and surely someone else in her imagination), "Fucking sure is Fine. We used to say that in college, among the girls, when we were all just a little more promiscuous." She paused and looked over at me. "But where's the love, Jim?"

"It's here, Jeannie," I said, moved by her. And I slid over to her side of the bed and put my arms around her. She slipped her hands again through mine, interlacing our fingers.

"Really?" She asked.

"Really."

Sarah called me the next night, at about nine, though she didn't want to see me then. She sounded haggard and said she was jet-lagged; she'd prefer to see me at lunch, which sounded wary and worrisome to me, didn't seem like an auspicious sign at all. We settled on an early dinner in a restaurant in Venice, right off Ocean Avenue where she was slated to have a late appointment that afternoon.

The place was called The Grand Guignol, and though various entertainment moguls reputedly run it, I chose it because of the sculpture, copper with a burnished green patina, which ornaments its bar. Round and tall, it reminded me of the pissoirs in Paris, in the garden of Luxemburg. I thought Sarah might be amused too. But I'm not sure she even noticed (she seemed more infatuated with the pianist of the evening, whom I wasn't even aware of; apparently he might have been Elvis Costowicz). Regardless, when I walked up to her, she took me in her arms and hugged me warmly, even very affectionately. Then she backed away from me, as if to get a better look, and her lustrous eyes welled with tears.

I thought they were for my dad.

And they were and they weren't. Actresses, people sometimes say, turn themselves inside out. Looking at Sarah, I frequently had the feeling that her outside was already the inside of another, of the eye upon her. She seemed to give skin to feeling, to an exterior, which you could wrap around yourself. When she pulled away from me, she looked shy, distressed and hurt, rather the way I was then. But she'd already expressed her condolences. She'd written my mom that she'd considered herself, always and somewhat presumptuously maybe, part of our family—losing my dad echoed losing her own. And I remembered that. The thought pushed me outside my own thoughts, my own cerebral womb--me a newborn innocent out here in the real, cruel world.

Something else, something besides my disturbance, however roiled Sarah. "How's Jesse?" I asked.

"Very lonely, it sounds like to me. I just called him. He misses Phillip."

"What do you mean? Where's Phillip?"

"Not at my place," she said with what resembled a snort, a cruel laugh. "We separated...ages ago, really." She seemed surprised I didn't know. "It's been a long time since we've been anything but roommates," she added derisively. Changing registers, she then intoned, "I'm sorry about your dad."

"Me too. I miss him...how do you feel about separating?"

She took a big breath. "That's only the half of it, though the argument's over between Phillip and me...just like it is when someone dies." She looked away forlornly.

The end of the argument, that was about it. She was right. My dad and I had gotten together, finally, but we never really had gotten along. My dad had risen so far, economically, in his life that there was little chance his swaddled, privileged son could understand or even at time communicate with him, with the person in the tweed cap who, at age 6, had been obliged to buy his own shirts—and at 60 had apparently made friends with people on opposite sides of escalators.

My eyes welled again, when was this going to stop?

Sarah turned her turquoise irises toward the bar; then she looked back at me with a crushed smile, and my tears disappeared. "I'm sorry," she said, trying to compose herself--so it looked. "It's just everything at once. I know you're in no shape yourself to hear this..."

"I want to...really, what's the matter?"

"Are you sure?" Everyone seemed surprised these days that I might not want to be entirely self-absorbed, especially people I loved.

"Do you miss him, Phillip?"

"I don't know. He was so supportive when we first met. I was so grateful, but he's bitter now. Jesse's upset with me too...I'm not giving him the time, the attention he needs. I'm all worried again...how am I going to support us?"

"What do you mean?"

"You think I could afford a nanny? Don Juan's the first full Equity job I've had. Phillip helped with all that."

"Hey, I can help. I've got some money..."

"I still don't know if he's yours. He might be, but I can't promise that you are his father."

"So what does that have to do with anything? I'm not rich, but I can help you out if that's your only problem..."

She looked at me gratefully, but clearly money wasn't her only worry.

"He got so crazy, it got so ugly with Phillip."

"You mean it scared you? Did you leave him?"

"Not really. He felt neglected and unimportant. I couldn't convince him he wasn't. He's been with someone else since rehearsals began. I just refused to see it…in total denial. Maybe that itself is a good reason to leave."

She didn't look too convinced. I put my hands on hers, both of them on both of hers. She looked and felt diaphanous, like a butterfly anchored to the table only by her eyes, her pupil's pins. She looked as if most of her wanted to be somewhere else.

Is it age which did it? I liked the texture of her face, her lines, though maybe, like the rings on a tree's stump, they marked the limits of her endurance. When she'd left me, she'd been so strong and determined. I was startled to see her weak. But then I'd been using that memory for too long against myself; perhaps it no longer had the force it once possessed.

"What would you like to do?" I wondered.

"I'd like to be alone for awhile…" She seemed sheepish, wounded somehow. "There are things I need to deal with by myself."

"Would you like me to take care of Jesse?" I asked instinctively, stunning her as well as myself.

Her eyes widened, sharpened as if the film on their surface dissipated. Her voice was different too. "But you don't know anything about a child…you're totally unprepared."

"I didn't say adopt him. I said take care of him awhile." Saying it I felt vertiginous. "Think about it a minute. I'll be back." I excused myself and headed for the back of the dining room. Don't know how I got there—I must have been on about a 40-degree angle to the ground. The nice looking, beautiful maitre d' there, Francesca, with her winsome smile, her hair back in a pony tail, exchanged looks with me on my way back. I wished for her phone number, almost asked, wanted her body, any body—was anyone home *chez moi*? Was anybody home in my head?

"Change your mind?" Sarah wondered when I sat back down. "Scared?"

I nodded. "Men are babies," I said, repeating something from my book.

"They sure are," she agreed, and her tone wasn't all that amused. She glanced around her with a kind of overpowering composure, a matter-of-factness that transcended resignation. She looked like a pioneer woman, like a French peasant—so this is the way it was, was going to be. No actress here, just the girl with the thick ankles and more of a purchase on the planet than the man in front of her.

"I'll take him," I repeated. "I'd like to."

She paused, and her eyes were clear. You'd think they'd never shed a tear; and in fact this evening was only the third time I'd ever seen her eyes even well.

"Let me think about it," she said. "It'd be hard on you, you know that." I nodded. "I wish I knew more about…his paternity: Richard's out of town working, we could do DNA tests, but he's not inclined and I don't have the time or the energy to get started on them, take Jesse in, organize it with the two of you. And you haven't been all that helpful either." When she took a deep breath then, I felt my innards blown to the side, a small whirlwind picking up twigs and dirt and shifting them around.

"Fuck it," I said. "We'll figure that out later. Bring him on…I just wish I were better prepared."

"Me too," said she, tenderly. "But then that's been the problem all along, hasn't it?"

Sarah was wary for a reason: she knew her man.

I drove her back to her hotel, the Mondrian on Sunset. It had once looked like a Soviet issue hostel with a Swiss' palette cutely checkered on the outside. But it had spiffed itself up not long before, renovating the rooms as well, though I didn't get to see them this day.

Out front, Sarah thanked me and had her hand on the door handle of my shiny mid 70s Buick Riviera convertible. The car expressed my mood at that moment perfectly: "you don't want to offer me a drink?" This may read sleazier than it actually sounded.

Sarah laughed, regarded me as if I were a Venusian, a unicorn. "What do you mean a drink?" She asked, taunting me.

"I thought I'd give you a chance to ask me up to, say, your room?"

"You mean you'd like to make love?"

I nodded my head, demurely. "It sounds like a good idea to me," I said, smiling like a simpleton.

"Uh huh. Well, it's just about the farthest thing from my mind. I haven't even thought about it once."

"Why don't you then?" Always the good listener, I thought I'd give her the option.

Forget the unicorn; she looked as me as if I were a circus geek. "Hey, Jim, it is sweet of you to think about taking Jesse, I won't forget that…even if you want to renege on your offer."

"I don't," I said, a little diffidently.

"But you want to sleep with me because you don't know what to do about him coming if he does. You're upset, huh?"

Women are amazing--all this and they can crunch numbers too.

Sarah looked at me as if I were ten. She stood majestically when I held the car door open for her, and then gave me a tender smile (so sweet there was no trace of her fears, of any reason why she'd need to be alone). "You still can't bear sleeping alone, can you?" She asked me.

I nodded sheepishly, and she grinned infectiously. Jesus, I felt a decade younger—more-- in Paris and in love.

She reached into her black purse and took something out for me, held it in her hand under the hotel's front awning, then produced it like a rabbit, a coin "taken" from an ear. "Here," she said. "I always keep one for Jesse, just in case. He needs something at night too. Take it home. Use it. It'll make you feel better. And…thanks, Jim, just for the offer. I'll call you about it."

She placed the object in the soft and probably sweaty palm of my hand. It was a night-light, turquoise--the color of her eyes.

Weird thing is, when I used it that night, I fell straight to sleep.

Two days later, Sarah called and wondered if I'd changed my mind, if I'd been in my right mind two days earlier. She wondered if I was sick, somatizing my probable distress. All fair questions, but I repeated my offer to take care of her boy. She said she hadn't made up her mind yet, then called the next morning to tell me it was impossible. I knew nothing about child rearing. I was totally unprepared. She was right, I knew and admitted, and maybe this convinced her—that and the limited nature of the engagement for, three days later, I was at the airport freight counter picking up more clothes than I myself owned.

And four days after that, I was once more at LAX, fingering the night-light like a talisman, a fat worry bead as a 747 touched down outside the mammoth bay windows and meandered over to Gate 47. Ten, fifteen minutes passed while the crew negotiated a complicated hook-up to the terminal—and I wondered if a team of Mujahadin were making new demands inside the cockpit. Was I hoping for a reprieve? Wouldn't I have if I'd known what was to come?

Jesse was one of the first off the plane. Striding into the satellite, like Napoleon off to Alba, he looked chubby and proud, undiminished by this exile into a land he didn't know, in the care of a guardian he barely, dimly recalled. Two stewardesses accompanied him, one on each hand, like brighter bimbos surrounding a miniature Hugh Hefner. Their eyes lit up when they spotted someone who might want the child, the blonde one making a quick exit, the brunette with the very short hair doing her duty more conscientiously. She too, however, seemed relieved when I identified myself and offered my hand to the tyke at her side.

He just looked at it, didn't take it, and reached instead toward the brunette, who had plastic surfers dangling from her ears. He grabbed the yellow and white regulation soccer ball, which she carried for him. He cuddled it in both hands, his shoulders slumping under an oversized backpack.

"*C'est vous alors?*" He asked with nearly ineffable disdain. Picked the right language for it, of course—if he were going to be insufferable, French was exactly the tongue to use.

"It's you then?" would be the direct translation of what he said to his volunteer guardian, his "Uncle Jim," but he wasn't doing any translating; he left that up to me. And here's what I made of it: the little fucker, I immediately knew, was going to be no *dimanche a la plage* (unless the beach is overcast, jellyfish ridden and dank; as it is, say, in Trouville, in Normandy, where his mother's mother's family had a summer house). This had a distressingly similar feel to the one time I actually slept with someone out of charity, an old girl friend who'd put on 30 pounds and felt particularly insecure about herself. That eleemosynary exercise gave me a social disease which penicillin eventually managed to treat; I wasn't sure about this one.

"*Vous*," you remember from your high school French is the formal "you"—the word you use with teachers, cops, bankers, all those to whom you're not close, intimate or familiar. In very traditional bourgeois homes— Sarah's grandparents had evidently been this way—parents said "*vous*" to each other, though they chose, each of them, the tender "*tu*" when addressing their kids, as their children always did with them.

But why indeed should the kid have "*tutoyed*" me—as if I were a real relative? He barely knew me, I understood only too well, and felt for him immediately, this international orphan.

"*C'etait bien le vol?*" I asked about his flight.

"*Quoi?*" He asked back, screwing up his entire face in this derisory "what?".

So I asked him again, in French, the language of his choice here, if the flight had been fine and uneventful.

And in response, he said, "What a funny accent you've got." He didn't, of course, say it like that in English. Rather, he said, "*Quel drole d'accent!*" And he looked around the airport, as if checking out the surroundings, like a refugee from a Sergio Leone film.

"*C'etait pas mal,*" he continued, finally responding to my questions concerning his flight. "*La bouffe est meilleure en Air France, mais…*" The food is better on Air France, but of course we already know that, they've been telling us for years.

We went to the baggage claim area, where we picked up the rest of his paraphernalia. He liked the high tech aspects of the new wing he arrived at, the gleaming steel. He told me it wasn't bad, but of course next to Roissy, the place looks like Heathrow. "*Au moins, cest pas aussi moche que Kennedy,*" the world traveler added, ("at least it's not as ugly as Kennedy"). He was apparently an architectural critic too, which isn't bad for a five, nearly six year old.

The day outside, as we left, was overcast, the summer's smog having begun early this year, in mid-April. The daily haze would hang over the city through the morning into the early afternoon. I find it beautiful often, especially when it is dense enough to temper the sun or filter the light at the end of the day.

"*Comme c'est grotesque ici,*" my sweet charge said as we headed up La Cienega, underneath the smog and through the oil fields, the working rigs pumping away in some of the world's most valuable real estate. "*Le temps est tellement bizarre,*" he was speaking about the climate, the weird smog-charged air. He was right, of course, but I was tired of his attitude, the smug superciliousness which may have been inherited, which too many of us hide behind (his temporary guardian, me, included). He had his reasons, no doubt. I understood more or less, but I was inching toward the thought of looking at the DNA now--the other guy's, mine (I was finally ready to test), and his. Sarah was right. I didn't know anything about kids, had a problem with patience.

And, like you I suspect, I had had enough of his French too. "Yeah, right," I said in English, responding to his complaints about the weather, "it is nothing like Paris where it's 45 degrees and raining (a heat wave!); it'll be raining all month, every day when the sun's shining here. You can feel sorry for yourself because you're lying on a beach instead of holed up, sniffling, in a damp apartment."

"*Peut-etre.*" "Maybe," said he—let's continue this in English, though he didn't. He continued forever in French with me, even though he did show some excellent English language skills. He showed he could understand more than most adults. "Maybe," he repeated emphatically, sadly, "but it's still Paris."

He sounded like Maurice Chevalier, singing "*C'est encore Paris,*" though he looked on the other hand like a miniature Charles Aznavour (already a miniature). He looked like somebody's abandoned teddy bear, touching my jaded heart all over again.

"I love Paris too," I tried to tell him in French again, since he seemed to prefer the language. "If it hadn't been for your mother wanting to try the States, I don't think I'd ever have come back." Moved by the thought, I reached over and put my hand on his shoulder.

He scooted to the right, toward the door in the Buick's mammoth front seat. Stranger Danger, I supposed. "*Parle Anglais*," speak English, he said. "I can't understand you."

A familiar problem: the kid sounded like a Parisian taxi driver, a charcuterie owner. At five, five and a half, he seemed to have picked up, wondrously, all the worst attitudes of the world's worst chauvinists, everything that makes many love France and loathe its people. The French think they leave Paris in August to avoid the tourists; but actually it's reversed. Most tourists come then because the French are out of town, on vacation. If I'd felt the same way, of course, there was a fifty-fifty chance the little corporal wouldn't have been born. But no, most French, for strange reasons, perhaps because they were amused by my Oklahoma accent, were way more hospitable to me than most New Yorkers. Few, other than *commercants*, actually would say to me, in their barely comprehensible English, what our little Asterix did: "let's speak English. *Je ne comprends rien de ce que vous dites.*"

Eventually I agreed, and this would be our mode of "communication"—I'd forever speak English, and he'd respond in French. It may sound cute, but it wasn't—when I told him I'd loved Paris when I'd lived there with his mom, he said, "Oh, yeah, what were you doing with my mom?"

We were probably off La Cienega by then—I'm sure we were—driving up Crescent Heights toward Laurel Canyon. I could see the hills both above and below the smog line and was still enraptured by them. A

Plains boy who had previously anchored himself inside big and mostly cold cities, I liked the mystery of the haze, especially when I could convince myself it was fog. I like the green of the hills even though, presumably, the smog would turn the whole city into an etiolated yellow one of these days— bleached out beige, like old straw.

"I loved her, that's what I was doing with your mom," I told him, wishing she'd told him first. "I was in love with your mom."

"So she left you too?"

His lower lip was tucked bravely into his mouth. He held tightly onto his soccer ball. His eyes blinked as both lips started to tremble, and he looked away. A hot tear burned his cheeks and was rapidly rubbed away with the back of his hand. Maybe there was something of me in him after all.

For about fifteen minutes, I mused on the possibility until we got home, and he made his tour of my modest one bedroom house. I think of myself, usually, as a pretty gracious guy. I may be much more spoiled than anyone's heard me admit, certainly lucky, but I'm aware of it; and I have, I like to think, reasonably good manners. I try to be a decent person, a polite guy, to pay attention to others' feelings. I'm not likely to go to someone's house, take a five-minute tour of the place and return to the living room, saying, "*c'est tout?*" with that nasal Parisian whine. "Is that all?"

Indeed, there may only be one bedroom, but the rooms are large and high ceilinged. There's a fireplace, a disorienting but richly verdant view of the canyon out half the windows, a view of LA out the back half, a redwood terrace running around the whole house, orange trees, lemon trees, one voluptuous palm. Not really a step down from the sights, the sort of place you see frequently on North Moore Street where his Mom lived, in front of an eight story concrete bunker once filled with Gouda cheese. At least here there was a citrus aroma whose subtlety was appealing when contrasted to Tribecca's distinct redolence of various *fromages,* though their absence in Laurel Canyon might be what our Francophonic tot found wanting.

"Yep, that's all, the whole joint," I told Jesse. I looked around for my sleeping bag, found it, and handed it to him. "When we need more space, there's the great outdoors…however you say it in French, I've forgotten."

"*La campagne?*" He wondered, the countryside. I shook my head.

"*Dehors?*" Outside? He screamed.

"Not quite," said I, though I found the thought not all that unappealing. But no, I wasn't going to put him in the yard. "Try the terrace."

"But I can't sleep out there," he screeched in French. "I won't have my light."

There's Gallic logic for you.

"But you'll have the stars," I said, a little meanly. So I have a sadistic streak (blame it on my dad, yes, that's it). I'm sorry, I was perspiring already, and the kid had just arrived.

"I can't sleep with them (the stars)," he declaimed. "They're too bright!"

"I'll get them turned off," I said.

He didn't think I was funny. He clutched his soccer ball so tightly it lost its shape in his little arms. He looked around the room like a trapped ferret. This wasn't my idea of a beautiful relationship. This was no kid from central casting (unfortunately—had he been, I could have sent the urchin back.) I, who hate TV's idiotic preciousness, its wise guy kids, would have settled for a cute kid, at least one who speaks English as a preferred tongue.

But what could I do? How couldn't I feel moved? I was the only person, west of Paris, that he could remotely count on, his only protector on the continent. Did it really matter if I liked him—did it really matter if he were mine? I'd volunteered, after all.

So I gave him the bedroom for the night, of course, large, "masterful" and overlooking the city's glamorous lights that distended, like phosphorescent plankton, toward the beach and the sea. There he could be snug if he wished, with the drapes pulled tightly shut and the splendid view obscured—comfy, just a kid who looked like a bloated beaver, his turquoise night-light, and his dreams of his glamorous, absent mom.

I took the tiny sleeping bag I'd recently acquired (for him), to the spot behind the screen, up against the huge picture window giving onto the terrace. Didn't sleep a wink either.

The stars were too bright.

So what *do* you do?

Sarah had been right. I was completely unprepared for this feral intrusion into my life. When you decide to have a child (i.e. when someone consults you about it, if you're a man), you have the 7,8,9 months to begin to adjust, to try to imagine what a third party might mean to your life. The gestation period is for you. It was, however, precisely because no one thought any amount of time would make me ready, mature enough for the exercise that I was deemed, from the gitgo, irrelevant, unable to enlarge myself enough to participate in the great parenting endeavor, even to be consulted on its occurrence. How was I going to do it more quickly now? This still didn't make much sense.

The morning after Jesse arrived, I was roused from my near total absence of sleep, from my fitful turning, by the light, peculiarly refracting off the morning smog—only to hear the alien sounds of this other entity, my little intruder. He was crying, holding onto himself, tightly and by the shoulders, as if the world would disappear if he weren't careful, from one day to the next.

"*Qu'est-ce que je fouts ici,*" he elegantly said--asking "what the fuck" was he doing in my place—when I went to the bedroom and glanced inside. When I didn't respond, soon or well enough, he suddenly ceased sobbing and looked past me, out at the haze.

He'd removed the green and red satin jacket, with Paris-St. Germain emblazoned on its back, the soccer ball on the left lapel, the number 7 on the right. He was now wearing the tee shirt he'd slept in on the plane, the only piece of American clothing he'd brought with him (his jeans were triple stone washed and rhinestone studded overalls and his shoes were French too). The tee was green, with black graphics. "Don Juan at the Public," it said. Between the "Don Juan" at the top of the shirt and the "At the Public" at the bottom, four characters' faces overlapped like playing cards in a hand, each a slightly different version of the one before. And each was the face, in profile, of Jesse's mom.

Standing and looking out at the waves of vegetation outside, all green fronds and yellow and red bougainvillea, he held himself by his biceps. His fingers grasping the sleeves of his tee, and his thumbs stuck back into his chest, he nervously and incessantly massaged the stenciled image of his mother's temples (just as she often did, trying to dissipate the force of the migraines she too often got). "*Qu'est-ce que je fais ici?*" He asked somewhat less vulgarly. He looked even more lost without his anger.

"What did your mom tell you?"

"That she didn't feel very good. She needed to be by herself so she could get better," he said, in French, of course, and with a sniffle. "Why'd she have to leave? I took care of her when she had the flu!"

He curled up away from me, toward the light, the terrace, Los Angeles and way out there, the sea.

So that's where I took him, as you take every tourist in for a visit, to the sea. He could have been more interested. He figured, paraphrasing Ronald Reagan, he'd seen one sea, one ocean many times (the Atlantic, "*cent fois, au moins*"), he'd seen them all. "What's so special about this one?"

"The sun for one," I told him, as we headed from the hills, down La Cienega until we passed the freeway, hit Venice, then followed it all the way to the beach. The sun wasn't as demure as it is in Normandy where every perfectly sunny day's like a lunar eclipse, memorable and marked. When I'd visited Sarah's family homestead on that Normandy beach, I'd spent the time watching cows lactate, camembert and cider ferment while rain came down so steadily and hard it appeared a permanent attachment, like icicles in winter, to the deep vegetation. She and I would bicker over bilingual Scrabble with her mom, when I'd catch the mom cheating, feeling her letters before dropping the undesirables back into the sack. Sarah, embarrassed, preferred I ignore her mom's peccadilloes. But, a bad loser, used to winning, I never quite managed to be gracious to this woman who never quite approved of me.

The Pacific was a dirty blue when Jesse and I first spotted it, frothy, yet still majestic enough to rivet both these urchins' attentions. It took us away from thoughts of the other continent, the other coastline, and swept us up in the bay's pungent odor, its cool rippling breeze. You forget about the sea out here if you live in the hills, as you forget about Central Park if you live downtown in New York. You live in a different city—but the sea is what this place is all about, what brought everyone here.

It tugged the two of us right up to its edge, moments after we hit the beach where Jesse, feet bare and gingerly moving toward the water, said, "the sand is so hot!" He couldn't believe it, nor this either. "The water is too, wow!" In Normandy, in mid-August even, people freeze to death out there, lose limbs to frostbite (thus the reason for, the utility of the male and female one-piece bathing suit, why the old films you see, at the beach, feature women in dresses, under umbrellas; they were trying to stay warm, away from the wind).

"Lukewarm," I said. "It's not hot, but it does feel good." I had his hand, and we were walking out in the surf. It came up to about my knees and his waist. Tiny little stick figure he was, he followed me farther and goaded me. "Let's see you swim."

"You first."

"No, it feels like a bath. You can't swim in a bath," he said, as if the water would roast him, not the sky.

The waves were small, breaking softly toward us. We were at the south end of Venice, near Marina del Rey, where a big pier jutted to our left. "Let's do it together, at the same time," I suggested. "You do know how to swim, don't you?"

"No, not in water like this. You'd boil!" said he, of course in French. "I don't want to…" His annoyingly nasal voice rose was momentarily quashed by a California wave, which crashed against his chest and splattered on his face. He spat out the salty spray and wiped his mouth.

"So how does it taste?" I asked and plunged into the water headfirst. When I came up, a yard or two away from Jesse, he was looking strangely at me. "How's California taste?"

"*Degoulasse*," he said, "disgusting." This was getting tiresome.

"Gets better the more you're here," I said. "The more you get used to it, the more you'll like it." And to prove the point I picked him up and raised him over my shoulder. "Try some more."

"Non, non *assez*, enough," he said, like an elegant older gentleman assailed by a gang of youthful offenders.

I lifted him higher, over my head, and threw him squealing, howling into the three or four feet of water—no more, Sarah, I swear. But instead of swimming, he continued shrieking, wailing as if his dignity were soiled, as if I'd offended him. I watched and giggled until I saw him flailing at the water, until his head dipped under the level of his hands, until his eyes looked up but didn't break the surface of the water. Then I leapt his way. I got my hands on him, and I lifted him out of the bay. He was coughing and spitting out the seawater, shaking his head like a dog in a bath.

"*Je peux pas nager*," he cried. « *Sale con.* » « I can't swim, you asshole. »

First day out with the kid, this boy who might have been mine, and I almost drowned him.

Our "swim" prematurely terminated, I tried to play soccer with him on the beach, but he wouldn't let me dribble long with the ball—he kept stealing it away from me. When he said, on those rare occasions when he failed to detach me from the ball (yes it's true, at 3 foot ten, age 5 almost six, with a head which came up to my waist and legs like Whiffle ball bats, he still moved way more deftly than me) was, "You don't understand a thing about the game. 'Ricans' never do."

"Ricans" is the stylish French slang word for us power mongers and world despoilers, the Americans. The French disdain and envy us, even after we've shown we can ruin an economy and massively nationalize industries with the most egregious of their own politicians; it's the scale we do it on which impresses and annoys them, almost equally.

So this "Rican" let Jesse spend the next few hours dribbling his soccer ball in circles around me, ever wider, while I worked on the script of "Luck for the Lovelorn." I tried to make it something similar to but less derivative of Heaven Can Wait, which is, of course, a straight steal itself. Hollywood "development people" are fond of saying there are only a very few stories out there to write—one can merely invent new variations on older plots. Though I've often thought this was a sleazy argument to diminish writers' stature and their salaries as well, here I was doing what they'd want me to do, trying to fit this plot, these characters into a Hollywood shoe, one of theirs. I was trying to reunite my two romantic heroes—the angelic woman we love and her devilish former boyfriend, currently deceased—without killing her off.

But was it possible, period? Can you get back together with someone, out here in real life, outside the screen or the monitor, this side of Cinerama? Or isn't it rather that, no matter what the half life of your particular love, however nostalgic you or the other may be, you can never go back? Sitting on the beach, sweat blurring my newly written pages, I thought of the obvious, of Sarah. She hung over me, as I watched her kid, maybe mine, move in circles away from me; and anxieties surged over me like sand flies. "Jimmie, oh Jimmie Mack," I heard her sing as she once did. "When are you coming back?"

Where was she? With what French rapper in his twenties? With which 55-year-old director, 40-year-old star, writer, businessman, industrialist, fashionable shrink? Why did it feel like my business; why did my thoughts feel tugged that way? Who was doing the pulling?

"What did your mom tell you last time you talked to her?" I asked the kid when he paused to dun me for some money to buy an ice from a passing Mexican vendor.

He gave me a wry look, much too knowing for a five year old (did that explain his coordination, how bad he made me look at soccer? Was he a teenager, really, a lycee student with a thyroid problem?) "She said," he said, "that she loved me; she'd be back soon. But she just had to be by herself awhile. She had things to take care of, so she had to *"foutre le camp"* (get the fuck out of Dodge).

I'd like to say that proximity to this kid changed me immediately and dramatically--that I continued to fit myself around Jesse, to let him have his way. But in fact, the first thing I did, that very evening, was take my room back. We had two Mama's boys here, and he may have been the more emotionally developed. There just wasn't any way, I told myself, that I could camp out on the floor, by the terrace, for the rest of his time in L.A. I was too large to fit on the sofa, too moody and settled in my habits and too literal to find any romance in evenings under the stars, with the bright lights below twinkling in my eyes like motes of sand. No, I needed my big king size bed, its familiar sag.

Here's what I did: I bought him a pup tent, which we pitched on the window-filled wall, by the terrace. When I'd been a kid, I'd tried hundreds of times to make my bed into something similar, hiding under the covers so I could read well past my bedtime, without my fastidious father being aware of this repeated transgression of the House Rules. He caught me one time in five, this a familiar theme of my youth. Here I provided Jesse, who could read though he wasn't impassioned about it yet, with two lights, both attached to my word processor's power strip—one a tensor lamp, the other the night-light, turquoise as his mother's eyes.

He brought the Watchman himself. It was Phillip's last gift to him, a left over from the man's errant youth, and Jesse cherished it. Perhaps he should have stayed with Phillip. Separation, I now saw, must have been hard on both of them. Phillip knew all about soccer; he's played it, I learned from Jesse, in prep school at Hotchkiss. You never would have thought it—large and gangly, Phil looked anything but athletic; yet apparently, his stringy arms, long and slightly freakish like a dying elm's, made him the perfect goalie; and cerebral, smart, he'd learned a lot about the game and communicated his enthusiasm to the kid here.

I wanted to be able to do the same. I'd watched soccer in Europe, fallen in love with the French team, was shocked or rather amused at the carnage in the English game but particularly appreciated their announcers. Yet none of this substituted for skill, for the body's familiarity with the ball, the emotions' automatic response to the collisions and evasions of a couple of semi-grown men, for the instinctive recognition and thrill at somebody else's accomplishment. I played soccer like I spoke French, leadenly.

I could have bought books, I guess. I did buy him a couple of video games that featured the sport. But ultimately I got the feeling that it wasn't the connection to the sport so much as my inability to appreciate its nuances, to participate in the dream of it that most disappointed him.

After the first few days, after numerous attempts, Jesse ceased asking me if I wanted to play and began dribbling his ball alone on the deck outside and practicing headers against the laundry room wall. Part of the time he was crying while he pounded the ball off his head, against the wall. He missed his mom, the man she used to live with, didn't trust me. Why had she sent him my way? What was, what wasn't I doing wrong?

"Find him some friends," Jeannie said immediately. "I can't believe you haven't done it already."

"I don't know any," I said. And that was the truth, more or less. I wasn't from L.A. Did kids exist here? Where was I to meet them? I lived in a tight little world. Balzac may have written huge books, Dickens too, because they experienced so much, interacted with so many. In France in Balzac's day, every apartment building was a microcosm of the country, shopkeepers on one floor, aristocrats on another, petit and grand bourgeois on still others. In L.A. or NYC, in my day, my neighborhood was more like a dorm. I met and loved and saw people who were more or less like me, single, in the arts, from 25, 30 to 40, 45, ghettoized. Some had been married, most were seeing someone, almost all childless except for a few, anxious and increasingly incapable of sharing their lives. Kids didn't fit in; they just weren't there unless they were holdovers from previous cohabitations. I rarely saw them when they were present at all, but Jeannie had a couple of ideas.

This surprised me, for I had assumed that once Jesse arrived, Jeannie would most likely disappear. Instead, his presence simplified our troubled conjunction. "Look, I like you, Jim," Jeannie said, when she found a baby-sitter and the two of us escaped his jaundiced eyes for a dinner five days after Jesse's arrival. We were at Minouchi's, an odd Italian restaurant right out of the sixties' idea of Italy, a place where older men took their mistresses more often than their wives, for the lights were so low one couldn't see across the table much less the room; no one could bust them. There was a stag on one wall, frescoes of peasant villages on another, everything a richly hued mahogany, funny to me, romantic and humorous to Jeannie. She'd always liked it there, may have had memories she neglected to share with me.

Yet she put her hand over my wine glass when I tried to fill it more than once. She looked at me across the white tablecloth, candlelight flickering on her face (which suddenly seemed exceedingly beautiful, more so as she spoke, you'll see why), and she said, "Careful. You're not just taking care of yourself now...you can't afford to get busted driving home. You're living for two now."

"Jeannie, I'm not pregnant. I'm not even sure I'm a dad."

"So what?" She had clear eyes, a smile as she spoke, grinning I suppose at the way I squirmed. "I think you're a good person, Jim, kind," my uneasiness at the compliment provoking this amendment, "a little immature for your age, maybe, but not nearly as disappointing a person as you think..."

I sat up and rubbed my chin. There was a buzzing on my nerves' ends.

"Not as sexy either," she continued. I smiled and sat back. "But I like you, Jim." I didn't know what to make of this confession. She did, however: "it's just our relationship is absurd. Let's call it quits and try to be friends. What do you think?"

Basically, I thought that she was brilliant. For fifteen minutes, I was flushed, disturbed and hurt, didn't quite know how to look at her again. I was used to her inquisitive, her dubious look, the pull and tug of our coupling, this competition to see who was going to be absent first, who was going to stretch farther away than the other. Yet, listening, I couldn't quite dispute the accuracy of her analysis. We were an absurd couple. I was flattered that she cared about my friendship, though some part of me still thought that no one—let alone someone as incisive and accomplished as she—would want to be with me without an amorous relation, romantic delusion playing its part and overwhelming her natural good sense.

Maybe that was true, but Jeannie didn't let me go, once she seemed to let go of the two of us. She decided to help me. She knew, for instance, so much more than I did about Jesse. She'd thought about kids when I was just beginning to think I might need to find a way out of my self. Because she had figured out quite a few things more quickly than I had, she turned her attention to orchestrating a life in California for Jesse.

A few days after she left me, head rubbernecking, watching her car drive off, she called and said she'd found a recreation center, a parks department near Laurel Canyon; and the three of us went together, looking for a soccer team for the kid, for something for him to do.

Unfortunately, they didn't have a team, not in the late spring and summer. The soccer leagues didn't start until the fall. In the summer, they had a sort of day camp for kids Jesse's age, something we would look into, but that was still almost a month and a half away. We were at the end of April, and what they had, already a week into its season, was t-ball, baseball, a game I thought I knew how to play. They said they'd make an exception for Jesse since a couple of teams had lost some kids. Their parents were taking them to sets elsewhere in the universe. I was thrilled.

Jesse said, *"On joue pas au beisbol en France"*—they don't play baseball in France.

"So what? You're an American citizen; we play baseball here."

He shook his head. "I'm French too," he said. "Like my mom. She's in Paris. We're going back there (to live)."

"Not a chance," I told him. I knew her better than that. "She's the one who brought the two of us, her and me, back to the States. She loves New York. She's making it here as an actress. She's staying, you watch."

"What's it to you?" He asked me, more or less, in French, with a charcuterie owner's snarl.

"You want this kid?" I asked Jeannie. "Maybe we can get him a part, something like the young Charlie in the Manson story."

We were at the West Wilshire Recreation Center and the superintendent, a nice guy by the name of Bert, was trying to hide behind his beard. I think he was embarrassed for us, the unlucky parents, hadn't understood the situation, and didn't need to know.

"T-ball," he said to Jesse, "is a great game. You get to meet other kids—kids you'll be friends with for life right here in L.A."

"OK, but I'm going to live in Paris. I'm leaving this place just as soon as I can," the kid said to a somewhat startled Bert, in English. I was proud of him.

"See?" I told Jeannie. "He's quite fluent in English."

"What a quick study you are!" She exclaimed. "He's been speaking English to me since the day we shook hands—wake up and smell the coffee, Jim."

"It's burnt and bitter, smells Turkish to me...but is that the truth?"

"His speaking English?" She asked with a grin and put her hand on my arm. "You're a bright guy, Jim, but sometimes, I think you're lucky you don't have to remember to breathe."

I think I'd heard that line before, a few times. I may even have authored it.

"Okay, Jesse, let's go," Bert said in his avuncular way. "It's game day. I'll show you what this is about. You don't have to make up your mind today. Just take a look, let me know what you think. Maybe you'll even like it."

Surprisingly, Jesse did what he was told. The two of them walked briskly out of Bert's cramped, sea green cinderblock office, Jesse hypnotically following this waddling Pied Piper through the smelly community gym where a couple of teams of thirty year olds battered each other in a basketball game, and out into the bright light and the thick, densely particulate Southern California air.

A stridently hazy sun beamed over a smattering of baseball fields, one up behind the rec center where some ten and eleven year olds were playing, another few sunk below, inside a vast plain where some city planner of the fifties had evidently imagined a huge man-made lake would grace West central L.A. It would have lasted a week or two before the mosquitoes would have taken over the entire Fairfax district, unleashing platoons of the ultra Orthodox onto city hall. So, wisely, it was converted mid-build into a park where this day twenty or thirty people were taking lessons on competition canine showing from a man with an electric megaphone.

"Very good, Biff," the instructor said as we passed an earnest, heavily mustachioed fellow who was seriously curbing the enthusiasm of his toy Chihuahua. "Stand tall. Stand proud."

Half the dogs were mongrels. Why not? This was an eclectic and unassuming neighborhood. Right behind two large ladies with miniature Schnauzers were a rash of parents and their uniformed scions, the five to seven year olds who formed the T-ball teams. The Yankees and the Royals, they'd taken their places on a well-groomed orange clay infield—the

Yankees out in the field, the Royals at Bat. The parents, most of them anyway, sat anxiously in the small stands. Assorted fidgeting dads patrolled the sidelines.

"Is one of these two the team for Jesse?" I asked Bert. I was kind of hoping it would be. I'd only been a Yankee fan for a little more than 3 decades, since I was old enough to hear about my dad's favorite, Mickey Mantle, who'd come from Commerce, Oklahoma, ninety miles away from the stadia of my charmed youth. I wasn't unhappy when Bert answered "yes," wasn't unanxious when I asked which team, was altogether absurdly pleased when Bert looked my way and said "the Yanks."

Then he amended that, adding "that is, of course, if Jesse wants to play."

Bert was obviously a mature human being. He had a well-developed sense of priorities. He'd seen his share of hyperactive, over-identifying adults racing frantically about the park, manically overseeing their uninterested progeny. He knew the dire results.

"Oh, I'm sure he'll want to play, right?" I looked Jeannie's way.

"I'm not," said Jeannie.

"God, he's got to...the chance to play for the Yankees, who'd pass it up? Look at the uniforms. They've even got real pinstripes."

Bert, Jeannie and Jesse looked at me as if I were a complete loon, not even age appropriate for the 11-year-old league up above us.

I didn't notice, though: "They're from New York, the Yankees, Jesse," I helpfully mentioned, in case the little guy didn't know. "Your hometown. What do you think?"

"Sais pas," said he, in his raunchiest Parisian accent--sounding and looking with his long hair and his spindly legs like an even smaller Piaf. "*Quel drole de jeu*"—what a funny game.

He sidled Jeannie's way, allowed her right hand to slip onto his shoulder. "I don't know about these California kids," he said to her. "They're supposed to be pretty weird."

"They are. It's something to think about," said Jeannie, nodding his way.

He nodded back. His body rocked back and forth against her side, his hands, his arms still wrapped around his soccer ball.

He didn't know, but I did. The kid was going to play T-ball. Either that or he could join Francois Truffaut's Wild Boy, say out in Topanga Canyon someplace where it's rumored that the pets of the sixties, ocelots and huskies, monkeys and a tiger or two run loose.

Just joking there, but this T-ball, as we watched it that day, was entrancing, hilarious. As you probably know, it's baseball without the pitching; the ball is placed on a yellow plastic tee, off which the kids hit. It's a preparatory league for kids five to seven, before they reach the little big leagues. Since everybody plays, the outfield is littered with little bodies; and a third, maybe a quarter of them on the Yankees were girls. Not five minutes after we started watching, a ball came floating toward the plumper of two Asian girls. She happened to be braiding her hair, or readjusting her red bow, something of that nature when the ball arrived; and she didn't let it disturb her. The ball dropped no more than three feet from her, just wafted in like a giant raindrop, took two little hops and settled in front of her.

Not only didn't she notice the ball, she didn't even bother to look in that direction, even as a couple of her more engaged teammates came running her way, screaming. She didn't pay them any attention. She continued, blithely, to work on her hair. One of the coaches sprinted out toward her—there are two or three of them on the field, interspersed among their miniscule charges—yelling, pleading, "Daphne, please. Please just pick the ball up." Her indifference overcame the coach's absorption in the game, and he started laughing. You figured this had happened before. I laughed with him.

Jeannie, on the other hand, was screaming, "Pick the ball up. Pick it up." She was a real competitor, I should have known. Finally the third baseman, who was about four foot five, a real giant among his compadres, arrived and grabbed the ball. Giving Daphne a dirty look, he hurled the ball back toward the infield; but in his haste, he forgot to release the ball itself and tossed himself about five feet forward. The human shot-put. The ball dribbled out of his hand on impact.

I was laughing, spitting out the water a mom had offered me. I noted how Jesse looked my way curiously, as if it were the first time he'd seen the deranged, the mentally unbalanced at such close range. But what can I tell you? I don't know how to play my cards anywhere near my vest—which may be why I'm not a great negotiator, why I never would have been the lawyer my father imagined.

The kid, Jesse, on the other hand, showed far more aptitude. "So what do you think?" I asked him once the game ended, after the teams had played their obligatory maximum, an hour on the field. The Yankees had lost by a run in a tight two-inning game, 23 to 22. We were walking back up the incline, toward the rec center, which looked something like a concrete butterfly, a miniature version of the old TWA terminal, Saarinen's building. Same premature decomposition around the edges.

"I like Paris Racing's uniforms better," he said to me, in his language of course. He got right to the heart of the matter.

"Really? I like the pinstripes on the Yankees—none of those little boy shorts like in soccer." I manfully asserted.

Jeannie laughed, howled at my "competitiveness," as she'd later deem it. "Right," she said, "those baseball 'knickers' really must look gentlemanly—to someone from Oklahoma."

Having put me in my place, she took Jesse by the shoulders and began to mediate. "Jim's trying to say, Jesse, he'd like it if you played on a team this summer…"

"The whole summer?" He asked her anxiously, in English. "I have to stay that long? I'm not going to be here for the whole summer, am I?"

"No chance," I began trying to reassure him. He looked so distraught. "*Je te le jure.*"

"Speak English," he said. "I can't understand you."

"Let's throw him in the pool," I urged Jeannie, and I picked him up. Over to our right indeed there was a pool. He started to cry, and Jeannie, after she threw me a ferocious look, ripped him away, and took him into her arms.

"He was being mean to me," I protested.

"You are ridiculous," she said, and it was hard to argue with her.

We reached the upper level, and I shook hands and thanked Burt, who said we would have to let him know by the next day if Jesse wanted to join; he was doing us a favor letting Jesse in after the season had begun.

I told him I understood, and Jesse went to take a couple of turns on a nearby swing. He kept going higher and higher.

"Control yourself, Jim," Jeanne advised, as I looked nervously Jesse's way. "Be calm. It works better. Don't be such an hysteric."

Who me? An hysteric?

Jesse came back looking determined--round as a beach ball, his cheeks pumped out, and his eyes little points. They were green by the way, his eyes a teal green—one of the children of the damned, for sure.

"You want me to play?" He inquired in French, no compromise there.

"I think you'd like it, I really do. You'll meet a lot of other guys, girls, might be fun."

He nodded, then a sly look came over him—as if he were cross-eyed, one eye a floater. "Okay," he continued, "but you know the tent?"

"Yeah?"

"I like the bedroom a lot better."

"What do you mean?"

"I'll play….if…if I can have the bedroom back."

"Not a chance."

Jeannie started laughing.

"Okay, then," said he dejectedly and glanced Jeannie's way for support. She eyed me as if I were Idi Amin Dada. These two were an ignoble conspiracy, attempting to deprive me of whatever sex life I might have dreamed I could still have. Had my dad faced this? Is this why he'd let me go my mom's way and holed out, seven days a week, eleven hours a day in his office--alone, sullen and pre-occupied, voluntarily or not? "Weekdays?"

"Two days a week," I finally said. "Every third day."

"Every other day," said he. He was born to this—he looked like Pere Goriot, like a French beet farmer, like the owner of a charcuterie. He'd picked up some color that afternoon, on his cheeks and his nose, though no veins had broken there yet to mar the handsome face with its memorable eyes. "One day in two," he repeated, in French.

What could I do? Did I have any choice?

Guilt conquers all. He knew how to work that, with all of us. When we came back to my place in the Canyon, Jeannie tried to leave us at the door. But Jesse wouldn't let her go. Jeannie drove a Saab convertible, an elegant silver; and when she bid the two of us goodbye (kissing him) and tried to back out of my drive, Jesse hung onto her door, his eyes drowning inside their sockets like two cows lost in a torrent. You'd think he'd never seen a woman before.

"I'll see you soon, Jess," Jeannie said. "I'll be back in the next couple of days."

"Jesse, come over here. Get away from there," I said, trying to play authority figure, the responsible adult. He didn't so much as glance my way. I was worried she'd speed from there with his tee shirt caught in her door. "Right now, Jesse!"

As my voice rose, hers dropped, lost its manic overdrive and her cleverness too. When she was moved, Jeannie spoke in an entirely different tone, deeper and huskier and half again sexier. It was the lure of this voice, which made me feel nostalgic. I strained to hear it, instinctively. But I didn't catch a word. That tone was now reserved for a five year old. And I was ridiculous enough that I confirmed her earlier observation, I was competing with him.

"We'll be back in a minute," she yelled up my way, in her normal, confidently abrasive voice. And Jesse, having paid no attention, one more time, to his putative parent, clicked open the Saab's elegant silver tone; and the two of them sped away from me, down the hill.

"Don't get the wrong idea," Jeannie said when they returned over an hour later. This meant, of course, that there was more than one idea to get. Solipsistic, it took me another couple of hours to discern this (I'd been doing nothing while she was gone except watch the trees grow, too rapidly). I finally began to conceive of this gathering in terms of the three of us, with only Sarah, perhaps, floating there as a fourth in the smoke of our barbeque.

"I just felt so sorry for the kid I said I'd stay for dinner," she explained, as she took a bag of Whole Foods groceries from her stylish car. The bottom was soggy, from the wet vegetables, freshly watered. "He said he'd never had barbecued ribs before."

It made sense==the rare Americans eating pork these days are frequently Jews, like Jeannie. They get off on the transgression. We goyim are wary of meat again—and the pig specifically. Satchel Paige told us so. Jesse had probably never even seen it. His mom was most likely on a diet of yams, something she'd picked up from a Bengali healer or a modish psychic.

But I made an exception in my personal dietary regime and enjoyed myself. Jeannie put some honey in the sauce—and that stickiness, coalescing with the meat's surface, made the skin crisp and my fingers aromatic well after the meal.

Off my terrace, we could see Jacarandas beginning to bloom. Their purple grey blossoms bursting over the canyon were the last colors to disappear into the night. This could have been the south of France. Houses sat behind verdant foliage (perhaps too much vegetation for the south of France), just a little bleached out by the pollution creeping into the canyon that night like fog.

I liked the sense of estrangement I felt, how this might have been Rio, Tuscany, anywhere.

Jesse was unusually quiet, following Jeannie doggedly wherever she went. He only sporadically glanced my way, and then as if he were pondering some major decision, this a day full of them. Jean Paul Sartre at 5. After dinner, Jeannie told him it was time to go to bed—so refreshing to hear someone else undertake this arduous chore. How many nights had I listened as he couldn't even cry himself to sleep?

He grabbed hold of her, more tightly.

"Look Jesse," she said. "You promised. That was our deal: I'd make you supper, and you'd go straight to sleep. You swore on it."

"I had to," he said to her.

"What do you mean 'had to'?" Jeannie was smiling, but small lines, like accountant's notations, marginal notes, pinched her eyes. She looked as if she regretted asking the question.

"I couldn't leave you with that guy," said the five-year-old gallant. "You're not going to sleep with him, are you?"

Somehow I had the feeling he was speaking of me. But no one asked my point of view. Jeannie's forehead flexed. She didn't look my way. "Just mind your own business, Jesse," she told her admirer humorously.

"But he doesn't like you like I do." Jesse was in love.

"How would he know?" I inquired.

"You, mind your own business too," she said to me this time, less kindly. I felt ever more jealous.

"Go to sleep, Jesse," I said, and I took him by the arm.

"*Laisse-moi,*" he said, pulling away like an outraged matron. "*Fout le camp.*" True to himself, always, the little shit-head was telling me to fuck off.

I picked him up. He screamed, cried and started to bite my arm.

This was ridiculous. "You wanted the bedroom," I said. "You get it." I walked in and flipped him onto the bed there, shut off the light and, when he screamed as I tried to tuck him in, I closed and locked the door behind me. I didn't know what I was doing, obviously.

"Don't be such a sadistic bastard," Jeannie said, when she of course opened the bedroom door and went inside to console the urchin for another half hour, maybe longer.

When she came out, I was outside on the fake redwood terrace looking up at the moon which, through the haze, looked three or four times larger than normal, like an invasion force ominously floating on waves our way.

"He's amazing," Jeannie said. "Better hope he's yours. He understands everything! I wonder how long that will last."

Sadly, I hadn't yet understood what he'd already gleaned. But I was getting there, right to the source of her frankness. "Did you have to break a date to stay?" I inquired.

"In a manner of speaking," she replied. "I don't know if he even remembered—it's always hard to tell with him." She looked suddenly discouraged; and her sweeter self and deeper voice emerged from her outer shell like a succulent little clam.

"Jerry?" I wondered. "Or Charles? I hate to see it happen to those guys." Perhaps, though it didn't of course stop me from feeling jealous— nor did our newly established "friendship." I'm a twisted guy.

I wanted to put my arm around her shoulders. They seemed smaller than they often were, invitingly so. When Jeannie wanted me—or liked what she felt, she often put her thumb in her mouth, unconsciously. Here she seemed to sigh, to move my way, leaning on me hopefully. Gently, then, I put my arm around her.

She looked up at me. "You're completely out of your mind," said she, separating herself.

But, for a change, I didn't think I was. "I was just trying to give you something to hang onto," I said. "Me, if you want."

She looked at me twice, her gaze sharpening between glances. "Maybe. I guess that's possible," she said, tentatively.

She took my arm in both her hands and kneaded it as we walked to her car. "You're getting there, Jim...I don't know if I would have believed it. I don't even know if I like it," she added with a sweet grin. "Your abandoned puppy act is a pretty good one. It works well enough on me, but who knows? Before long, you may find yourself doing a fair impression of an adult..."

Little did she know. I might have appeared as if I were moving out of adolescence finally, after a mere twenty five years there (puberty too came late for this boy), but I was moving into full scale infantile regression. Or close enough: what's baseball, after all, for an "adult" but an excuse for manic depression, an unalloyed slide back into the past?

Mine was checked only by my quasi-son's complete indifference to our national pastime. *"On s'en fout de beisbol en France,"* he so elegantly explained.

He wouldn't go to practice without his soccer ball, which he'd dribble along the foul ball lines to his harried coaches' dismay. While they tried to corral as many of the rest of his teammates as they could, Jesse would be practicing free kicks into the chain link fence that bordered the park.

Both his coaches were named Lewis, though they spelled the name differently, and both I liked. The first Lewis was a black lawyer on his second divorce; the other Louis, called Lou, was a white accountant, cheerful and disarmingly honest in a particularly appealing way. He once told me he was "born to be an accountant," and he loved the little leagues because he'd always been meant to be a coach, never a player. "I was born," said he, "an adult. The problem was I had to spend 18 years in a kid's body. I never knew what to do with it."

At the park to help his own son avoid similar embarrassment, he was the only coach in my long experience of these insanities who was totally unconcerned by his kid(s)' performance. He really meant what the other coach, who took every swing and every fielding play as seriously as I did, said to me one day: "this is when it's just for fun. Nothing matters here."

Louis, dubbed Lou, said instead: "when it get serious, if it ever gets serious for Clark (his son), I'll get worried. The Porchnoys weren't put on earth to win ball games. We were put here to shelter the take."

This was a fortunate attitude, for Clark may have been the least physically gifted athlete on the team. He resembled, as his dad must have at the same age, a CPA at 5. He was also Jesse's favorite teammate, similarly having a nanny from Guadalupe. Perhaps that was the link, a little patois inflected speech. His mom was a torts lawyer—and the sharpest person in this round family. She'd laugh at me, those few Saturdays she was at the game, as I tried to be cool when balls were hit Jesse's way, and he, more often than not, was otherwise engaged and wouldn't bother to pick them up.

An infielder in my errant youth, a shortstop, I cried when I'd boot a grounder, cried when I was moved to first base because the coach decided I was the only one who could consistently catch the ball. "How can a first baseman ever play shortstop for the New York Yankees?" I'd whined.

Jesse didn't share that particular concern. Lewis and Louis could put him anywhere they wished. He'd stand in the outer fields, his glove hanging over his knees like an old lady's shawl; and when he was lucky, when the two Lous weren't thinking—and hadn't separated him from his buddy Clark—he'd spend the time talking and kicking rocks. I usually found this funny, more or less (rather less unless a friend, say CJ, was around and wouldn't let me not laugh)—though it always made me reflect upon the improbability, after all, of this outfielder being my flesh and blood.

But there was real danger in the kid's indifference to the game. The second Saturday he played, Jesse was gesticulating expansively, like a boulevardier on his third Armagnac, when a line drive scooted past him to Clark who calmly fielded the ball, hesitated and then, throwing it toward second base, hit Jesse in the side of the head. I sprinted out of the stands, the only possible parent the kid had within 6000 miles, and reached him right after Louis and Clark did. He was on his back and uncharacteristically quiet, unmoving. I was afraid he'd lost consciousness.

When I turned him over, as gently as I could, he glared at me and began to bawl. "See, it's going to kill me—your stupid game," he shrieked in French, and tears blotched his florid face. "Mama!" He howled. "I want my Mama."

We all did. But where was she? In whose arms?

She did call regularly, if at irregular hours. Born in the States, educated here and in France, she'd spent her life shuttling between the two, but, apparently, she still hadn't fully understood the time difference--at least not as well as her five year old. When the phone would ring at, say, 5 a.m., he'd avidly leap to it. "*C'est toi, Mama*," I'd awaken to hear him shout.

Now Paris and L.A. are separated by nine time zones, nine hours except in those freakish cusps of the year when they switch their daylight savings time before we do. For the other 340 days of the year, there's a six-hour difference between New York and Paris, nine between Paris and L.A. Why did Sarah almost always reach us some time around six a.m.? Had she still been as poor as we'd been when we were together, not all that many years before, I might have understood that she was forced to sneak calls from the government offices of friends.

Maybe instead, I thought, the time was conveniently before her various rendezvous—perhaps that was it.

Of course, I would have been the last to know. She didn't confide in me, didn't converse with me much at all when she called. "How are you holding up?" She would ask ironically. Then she'd conclude by telling me to "hang in there," equally ironically. These were the two poles of a three, a five-minute conversation at the most.

She spent most of her time consoling her son (as well I suppose she should have—it's just that I was jealous, envious of the maternal concern in general and in particular). The two spoke English together mostly, but only of course if I wasn't within earshot. When I came around, Jesse would look like a cornered mongoose and would glare my way until I'd leave the room.

From what I gleaned from his Mama, the major summer action in Paris was climatic—a not unpredictable surfeit of rain. Then the Piccolo Theater, back in action, had set up at the Theatre de L'Odeon and was offering Sarah the lady in their version of Macbeth. She was ambivalent: apparently this was going to be the tale of some suburban street gangs' battle for control of various housing complexes. She didn't know, after Don Juan, if she could face another modern gloss on better work.

She mentioned to me, too, that she was listening to a lot of French rap, that French rock had really improved too. I'm not stupid. I took this as a hint about whom she was seeing, a confession of whom she was loving— probably an 18 year old with a couple of piercings, Chinese character tats, and a tongue stud (not sure about the facial hair).

At that week's practice, after his dramatic beaning in the outfield, Jesse spent more time looking at the fences behind him than at the two Lous in front of him, who were oh so diligently trying to explicate the nuances of the game. This may explain why he didn't catch a ball—not one ball during the practice. I am ashamed to say I was mortified. CJ was there at my side, laughing at my embarrassment. Yet I could hardly imagine how ineptitude could be taken to such an extreme (even Lee H., that kid in my junior high with the Coke bottle glasses, actually managed to catch a ball every now and then) or that its demonstration could bring my putative kid such apparent joy (he actually giggled as the adults around him wailed like penitents scourging one another).

After I spoke to him, once the sides changed, about how he had to pay attention to what he was doing, if only out of respect for his teammates, he took what looked to me like new determination up to the plate—and failed to hit the ball. This was no small feat: the ball was set waist high on the black batting tee, and the tee stand was placed in the center of the plate. Twice he hit the stand a foot below the ball, strikes one and two. "Take a big breath, Jesse," I urged him. And he swung and evaded the rare and ignominious t-ball third strike by about a quarter of an inch. The ball dribbled off the tee toward the third baseman, a big bully of a kid who stepped around the missile twice before hurling the ball into deep right field.

Always alert, Jesse held onto the first base bag, having fallen over it on his approach, and refused to let it go, as if it were the phone line when his mother called. He started screaming when Lewis pushed him toward second base after the third or fourth outfielder mishandled the ball. Throwing up his hands, Lewis gave up with a laugh, and this precipitated a slight change in my valiant putative scion. He took three or four or maybe even five hesitant steps toward second base—and stood there transfixed amid the commotion.

While Jesse peered confusedly around, the other team's fielders finally managed to retrieve the ball, and one of them began waddling his way toward Jesse, ball in hand. Then the ball was snatched from him by the team's shortstop, one of the few who had apparently some interest in and knowledge of the game. And this kid sped toward Jesse, who didn't care. Lewis had given up hope. Another parent, a guy named Roger, father of our team's clean-up hitter, did care, however. He raced from the stands and started pleading, "Please. Please don't just stand there, fellow. Do something!"

The man could barely keep himself in foul territory; he didn't realize that with Jesse, this French grain merchant, you have to bargain, to offer something in return. Failing that, the shortstop kept coming, getting closer and closer—the kid was a clear seven years old, a third, okay a quarter a lifetime older than our own little hero, a good third again as tall. When Jesse finally got a good look at this lout, he just began to run, on general principles—but not within the base paths, no, he ran toward the pitcher's mound and then veered toward the outfield. He was automatically out, of course, at this point, but that didn't stop his oafish opponent from making sure, as the kid later said when asked why he tagged Jesse out by smacking him right on the nose.

For the second Saturday in a row, Jesse collapsed onto the ground, crying, and this time, rather than emerging with a nasty bump on the head, he peered up at the gathering herd of concerned adults with a Vesuvian nosebleed.

Blood spurted onto his nifty uniform, then spread over onto me and onto Jeannie, who was trying to comfort the disaffected child. The blood stained her crisp cotton shirt and her rhinestone incrusted two hundred dollar jeans, while his whimpering waxed and waned with her attempts to comfort him (they were inversely related, of course). "Take him," she finally said, totally exasperated, just unwilling to absorb more masculine petulance. "What am I doing? He's not even mine."

She looked crushed, as we walked past Jesse's teammates in the dugout. Clark waved faintly our way.

"Apologize to Jeannie," I said to Jesse, which of course didn't affect him in the least. I led him toward my Riviera, where he immediately wiped his hands on its pristine, original seats—cost 400 dollars, and the and the pleather will never be the same.

"You're not dying," I added. "It's just a nose bleed." I knew about them; I'd had hundreds, which might have been more evidence of my paternity if not for the fact that I'd played through all of mine. But, when I told him, that didn't lessen his indifference. "I could care less," he let me know. "I hate this sport. It's boring, there's nothing to do and *ca va me tuer*." It's going to kill me.

It looked ominously if he might be onto something. His nose wouldn't stop bleeding. The blood wouldn't coagulate in spite of all our efforts, not for the half hour he spent lying down in the car with his head tilted up on Jeannie's knees, nor for the subsequent half hour we passed going up Fairfax, through Little Tel Aviv, down Melrose past Fred Segal's and up again into Laurel Canyon, where his Calvary finally ended.

Jeannie was in tears too after she helped Jesse out of the car and up the tortuous steps, through the citrus trees to our place. "Little boys can be so mean," she said after we'd arrived upstairs and put Jesse into my bed. The expression on her face seemed the sum of a lifetime of experience, more than a comment on this one kid.

"What did he say?"

"It doesn't matter," she said and sniffled.

I put my arm around her, as if that helped. I think it made her mad. "He told me," she said, imitating his supercilious accent, "'I don't have to listen to you—you're not as pretty as my mother.'"

"As if that has anything to do with it," said I, dutifully, "Anyway, it's not true. He's just scared. His nose has been bleeding for almost an hour."

"You're all in it together, aren't you?" She said, grinning grimly.

"Every last man of you, even the supposedly 'evolved' ones like you. You're all nasty and mean and misogynous."

Jesse left his room, and like a tiny but well-fed coyote was slinking around the wooden deck near the tent. Blood still trickled into the right side of his mouth, joined tears and saliva and slid down his chin. He looked awful and touching, a potent combo.

"*Qu'est-ce que tu regardes?*" He wondered, when he spotted my glance. "What are you looking at?"

"Some conspiracy we've got going," I said to Jeannie. "About as solid as Saddam Hussein's was."

"That's because you men are such freaks. You don't know your friends from your enemies."

Apparently left out of our conversation, the kid sniffled loudly, and I went over to him with a Kleenex. "Here, Jesse, take this," I said and held it out to him.

"Leave me alone, okay?" He screamed.

"But Jesse, I'm on your side," I said plaintively.

"See what I mean. Exactly," Jeannie said. "He just hasn't figured it out yet. Like I said, you're all so paranoid and mean you're never going to get it."

"Yeah," I said, "I guess that's what wars are for."

"Oh, shut up," said she.

I did discover something, though it required another fifteen minutes of close interrogation before I finally was bright enough to ask, "Do you want to call your mom?"

His sniffles abated immediately. And five minutes later, at the sound of his very disturbed mother's voice (was it because of her concern over her son's minor injury or because we were waking some Jean-Pierre next to her, who, I hope, never got back to sleep?) Jesse's bloody nose— you guessed it—dried up, the blood congealed from his nose down his cheeks and chin at his mother's first word, like the Italian miracle, the wooden relic in reverse.

This was our cue to "foutre le camp," as he would have said had we lingered much longer or even asked his wishes. Thus I left the room, though I didn't exactly respect his privacy. I went out of the house, down the steps past the side terrace, underneath and in front of the house, where I climbed the steps back upstairs to the terrace that abuts the room he was in. I wanted to listen in on his conversation. I wanted to know what he thought.

"You are a bigger child than he is," said Jeannie, exasperated, as she followed me.

"No argument there."

"Give him a break, a little space."

"No chance. I'm not yet that mature," I told her, and of course she knew that only too well. "People just don't change that much, that quickly."

I began to spy on the little guy, from behind the lemon tree's tentacular branches. I watched his lips move as he spoke English with his mom, something he never would have consented to had he known I was within earshot. But it seemed to revive him, to energize and animate him. He paced the room like a stand-up comic, waving the phone in his hand as if it were a mike, using it for emphasis. He worked his invisible audience, hesitating, waiting for her approbation, her apparent laughter invigorating him. Did he imagine he had to perform for her, that he had to amuse her, that the moment he failed she'd be off the phone and into somebody else's life? Or was that, rather, my own sickness?

Watching me watch my possible son, Jeannie looked around and down to the orange trees below, and she said, "this is nuts," to which, intent upon Jesse's lips, trying to decipher his mutterings, I didn't reply.

"You are loony, Jim, completely out of your gourd," said she. She looked crushed, but Jesse was more the object of her sympathy than me. He looked like Jean-Pierre Leaud, in The 400 Blows, hurt and anxious and about to try to flee. Both of us wanted to declare ourselves, to show ourselves on the terrace, and to go inside to take care of him. But, as if he knew, he turned his back and paced over to the other side of the bedroom, lowering his voice.

Jeannie extended her hand, with its fine wrist and long pianist's fingers, and tenderly took my arm. A minute or two later, her hand slipped off me.

I felt both her offer and her withdrawal. But it was just a moment of weakness—or rather, she had a weakness for my moments of weakness.

In front of us, inside the house, Jesse's act closed. He grasped the phone cord with both hands about a foot or two below the receiver—and let it dangle like a pendulum out of balance, from his right side to his left. He bit his lower lip, denying himself tears; then he withdrew to the tent he once loved, burrowing in.

When he looked out of it, he gazed directly at us, but his eyes didn't focus. He didn't acknowledge our presence.

By the time Jeannie and I came back into the house, a little later, Jesse had transferred his pain to the living room. We both went toward him, two middle-aged waifs imagining we could comfort this five-year-old adult. After my mooning eyes lingered on him a little too long, he said, without even returning my glance, "it's my turn in the bedroom." He strode somberly that way, taking his self-pity to a private spot, working conscientiously on it like a dog on his bone.

Here perhaps was the real conspiracy, the one between a man and the object of his affection: would Jesse ever learn what I clearly hadn't quite gleaned yet—to appreciate women themselves more than the melancholy they inspired? Would he forgive them their sporadic inattention (their interest in somebody, anything else)? Or would he always push them compulsively away once they were near, afraid they'd leave him? Could a real father be any help here?

On the day Jesse's nose burst, Jeannie stayed awhile after he put himself to bed (and commandeered my room with the better tube). She didn't exactly reach my way again, though I guess that's what I'd been hoping for. She kept her hands in her lap, pulled everything back in: the slack in her sequin encrusted jeans, her white cotton blouse, the large lips which seemed to embarrass her (I thought, Angelina-Jolie like, they might be perceived as her sexiest aspect. She thought they hinted at the presence of other ethnic groups in her gene pool, evidenced a violation of some great, great, great grandmother, a rapacious Mongol's appearance).

Diffidently, then for this cocky girl who would later surely head up a studio, self-denyingly perhaps, she said, "So--go ahead and go."

"Huh?" I eloquently responded, a little taken aback.

"You heard me," she said. "You did finally get those last stitches taken out, didn't you?"

"Yeah, but not because I was planning to make any pilgrimage soon."

She laughed. "Taking them out hasn't improved your comprehension all that much."

"What do you mean?"

"Take him to his mom. I think she's waiting for you."

"Really?"

"God, guys are dumb—or is it just you?" I smiled. She continued, "How did you men last this long on the planet?" I'd tried, unsuccessfully, to suggest a reason or two in my book, most having to do with female generosity; but obviously she hadn't paid much attention. "Why do you think she left him with you in the first place?"

There were a few thoughts which jostled, like dying bugs, on my personal windshield, but a small dust storm jammed my esophagus, my trachea, clogged my throat.

"You're just not going to figure out anything at all," she opined, not all that gently, "until you figure out that one."

"Which one is that?"

"Come on. What you feel about her. Until you decide, you're never going to have a real relationship with anyone else...go over there and see her, okay?"

So much intelligence excited me—I moved off the floor and onto the couch near her. Knowing me too well, she moved into an adjacent chair.

"But I don't even know if he's my kid yet." I slid back to my spot in front of the TV, ceding her the couch. I was fighting a holding action. My troops had long since been overrun.

"What does that have to do with anything?" She asked, then paused. "Does it matter whether he's your kid or not?"

Here was the point perhaps.

"I'm not sure," I said. "I wish I could say that for sure. But I can't. I'm a guy."

Her eyes seemed to harden. She didn't seem charmed. And the whirlwind inside me felt more like a swarm of locusts, moving from my right pectoral to my left, chewing both up. Moths maybe, ugly fat ones, monarch butterflies. And something inside me seemed to shift.

"Okay, maybe it doesn't matter," I heard myself say. "Maybe it doesn't matter much at all."

It must have mattered a bit: I called my mom. I haven't talked about her as much as that Philadelphia interviewer might have supposed ("Mama's boy! Mama's boy!"). That may be because I still have trouble framing her—as if she's just on the other side of me, all around me, like water enveloping a submerged limb. Every push is a useless thrust through it; no withdrawal, no retreat is possible. It's always there, taking up the place you leave, like amniotic fluid.

My mother and I talked, nonetheless, about twice a week and, even if her son still felt defensive about this 1800 mile extension of the maternal umbilical, she was still doing fine, brave as always. She had fifteen or twenty friends with whom she had spent most of the afternoons of her marriage; and they visited with increased frequency now, trolling for beers, whiskey and gossip, able to consume huge quantities of all three.

I suspect that, however much Mom may have missed her husband, she didn't regret having to wash at his entreaty, elaborately and carefully, every plate and glass, scraping away each miniscule food particle *before* inserting the dishes into the dishwasher. I rather doubt that she was still using old milk cartons, at her husband's insistence, to gather up the day's kitchen scraps before transferring them to the garbage bin. My father had been very Germanic in his obsessiveness, however much Welsh blood had crept into his jet-black hair and fair eyes. My mom, in her mid-sixties, was discovering the delights of take-out food while buying herself the largest American car she could find (we Oklahomans are a pathologically patriotic people even in our revolts, like this one), a Lincoln Town Car, the kind debonair Hispanics push on television, which gets fewer miles per gallon than an SUV.

Hers, she told me, was a dazzling red.

When I reached her this day, she said, immediately, "Are you all right? Do you need anything?"

A familiar question though I was no longer in college and, unusually, I did need something. "Can I ask you a question?" I wondered.

"I suppose so," she responded, warily.

"I was watching Jesse the other day"—she knew about this, that I was taking care of Sarah's child, though she was puzzled by it—"and when he got off the phone with his mom, he looked like he was underwater, like he'd been kicked in the head."

"Yes," she replied cheerfully.

"Well, I was just wondering…"

"If you were kicked in the head? There was that car accident going to Texas that time…"

Was she being serious or ironic? Maybe she'd just been drinking. I didn't know; perhaps that's why I still get them confused, can't separate being earnest, being committed from being foolish. Is it because we float culturally in the amniotic fluid of cheap and automatic irony?

My confusion wasn't acknowledged. She had more to say. "And then you were hit by two baseballs that one season, both by that Holmes boy…" She giddily continued to enumerate my accidents, my contusions, the fall from the tree, the fight with Mike Melcher, the constant sports afflicted nose bleeds.

I found myself exasperated by these memories, her presumption of my amnesia, her apparent addlepatedness; but she swiftly nullified the grounds for my concern. When I said, "no, Mom, I know all that, I remember. I was thinking about Jesse," she interrupted me, saying, "thanks for sending his picture. I liked the two of you. You would have loved sporting that uniform, now, wouldn't you have?"

"Yeah, but I was wondering about uh, about him and his mother."

"Well, he's hers," she said emphatically. "That's the way it is; they always are."

Why did this disturb me so?

"You mean because she doesn't know who the father actually is," I began to say.

"Oh yes, she does," my mother said. "Women always know, deep down,; just sometimes it doesn't matter that much..."

Outside, the kid himself was bouncing headers off the side of the house, off the terrace and the wall to my left; shaking the house, but who knows what he actually heard?

"And so, what do you..."

"He's her baby," Mom continued. "Just like you were mine."

The headers pounded the wall like a fighter's fists on a boxing bag. "What, uh, what should I do, Mom?" I asked, for want of anything better to say, with a voice that sounded like a small twig being crushed underfoot.

And she told me. "It doesn't much matter, now. You've already done it, done all you needed to...she's a good person; he'll be fine."

I received a second letter from my "friends" at the CHRIST LIVES! Network. Their first communication had been a card informing me that IMPORTANT NEWS was coming, and, presuming it was an eschatological warning, I had discarded it. "Dear Brother Adams," this second missive began, "your Witnessing will soon gladden millions of souls. Praise be! Enclosed you'll find the date and time. Just tear off the card, scan it and post it on line for family and friends. Then sign the other half and send it back to us. In His name," signed H.O. Hastings, Director of Communications. It also gave me their internet address ("Christ is on the Internet 24 hours a day at www.ChristLivesNetwork!") where I could "follow the good tidings."

Saturday at 7:30 --"Primetime!" it said in bold print--I was going to be on the air. I checked and double-checked the name there and on the outside of the envelope. Adams is a common surname.

Fortunately for me, I told Ruth Porchnoi about the letter at the Yankees practice Wednesday. Obviously, it was a slow day at the office, for she came without a brief. The two of us watched together as our boys looked for change, money, butterflies in the deep outfield. They didn't do much with the grounders or fly balls that came their way. "Look, this is getting embarrassing," Lou told his son Clark emphatically, in his whispery voice. "I'm the coach here. I don't expect you to catch the ball very often, but you could at least make an attempt every once in a while. Clark, pay attention!"

"Lou," Ruth said, "Stop shouting at him! Let him dream."

"Being yelled at is part of the experience, Ruthie. That's what sports are about to fat, uncoordinated kids with vision problems. He's got to get used to it."

"Not my boy," said Ruth, and she looked ferociously at her husband, explaining perhaps her more frequent appearance as of late at the games and practice. Maybe they weren't the perfect family after all. I looked over at her; she was rather attractive, with eyes hinting at a certain sexual awareness.

"Wait around a couple of years, Jim," Ruth said, as if she surmised the thoughts behind my look. "I kind of like you." I think she was kidding. "It must be those TV appearances; they do it for me..."

"I was kind of hoping they'd been forgotten."

"Nothing is. You know that. They'll be syndicated soon, prime time in the 200s or 300s, if not the nines or fives...there are many opportunities for you to be remembered. Warhol's 15 minutes have been blown past...we're talking hours now, re-runs; there's just such a demand for content."

"God, I hope not."

She smiled my way, which inspired me to tap into her apparently greater awareness of the cable universe. "Do you know by any chance whether this sort of thing ever gets on the Christian networks...do they review trade books?"

"I don't watch a lot of Christian TV," Ruth Porchnoi said. "Neilsens for the Christian networks aren't real high in your Jewish households. Christmas trees, bacon, yes, but not the Family Prayer Hour."

I laughed.

"But seriously, folks," the lawyer in her reappeared, "what are you getting at? Anything specific?"

"I mean I got a letter—two of them now actually—from this Christian network wanting me to sign a release."

"Don't sign it. Don't even get near it," she said, seeming a little excited for me. "What did it say?"

"Said my witnessing is going to be on prime time—exclamation point!"

"Do you go in for that sort of thing…'witnessing'?"

"Not since I was nine," I said. Then I looked Jesse's way and watched him miss the little round ball on the tee completely. "Don't worry, Jesse, you'll get it right now!"

And indeed he did. "That-a-boy," I screamed as he dinked a grounder off the tee and it trickled toward the shortstop. Rather than running, he looked my way irritably. The ball reached the first baseman, who fumbled it, then tagged the bag before Jesse was more than halfway up the baseline. Still, we were pleased. It was one of his longest drives of the season (hey, he was only five and refused to practice with his guardian— you wouldn't expect him to reach the fences, now would you? Even the infield track).

"Nine? You did that sort of thing at nine?"

"Hey, there were kids in my church who had been saved, born again, dedicated their lives to Christ and rededicated themselves by the age of nine," I helpfully advised her. "But, as I said, I'm a lapsed redneck. I'm not going up to the front of the church any more, not going to church at all."

She seemed to understand. So I continued, "It's a common name, Adams; perhaps the good folks at Christ Lives! have confused me with someone else, though who knows? I did sit in on a happy-talk hour in Tampa this winter with a former pastor of the same name. He was repenting of serial adultery, had a book out, "The Devil Made Me Do It"-- maybe they've got the two of us mixed up."

"It's unlikely. These guys have the best mailing lists in America. When is this thing going to be on? Did they say?"

"Saturday night right after our game."

"I'd record it if I were you," she said.

I listen to women, as we know. I do what they tell me to as frequently as I can. Sometimes this can take you out of your life, sometimes right around the world.

Jesse had a big Saturday that week after all. He got his second and third hits of the season...or so the T ball scorer called them. They were hit hard anyway or rather he made contact, even if the balls skipped directly at people; and he did get on base (hits are awarded generously in T ball) when the balls were fumbled. He made his usual base-running gaffes, of course, but he succeeded in scoring once. Flubbed a chance in the outfield, actually running away from a ball hit toward him that, unfortunately, let in the winning four runs. He might not have failed so egregiously had his buddy Clark backed him up. But Clark and his mom went off early that day, in the third inning, after Clark suffered a serious contusion when he swung and missed at a third strike and whacked himself in the right thigh with his Alex Rodriguez special silver bat.

My tight CJ was a sad witness to this debacle. Back from another failed pilot—this one about a middle aged Vietnam veteran turned veterinarian (Viet Vet it was called) --which had been cancelled before they finished shooting the pilot, after the second day's takes, he was pacing the right field line, feeling sorry for himself, when Ruth ran screaming onto the field, then took her damaged boy back to their Volvo station wagon. When

317

Lou tried to join her, she yelled, "Fuck off. You and your sports addiction. You're trying to kill my boy."

CJ thought this augured poorly for the Porchnoi clan's future, though he restrained himself from trying to comfort Ruth. Still he missed Jesse's second hit, a hard smash off the first baseman's glove, into right (okay, perhaps not a smash, maybe a deflection). When Jesse pulled into second, stopping there misguidedly on what should have been a triple to gaze longingly toward his departing friend and his friend's mom, I caught myself pleading with the kid like his coaches. Like them, I gave up in mid-exhortation. The exercise might have been pointless, but my heart pounded long and hard, nonetheless.

"Is that really your boy?" CJ indicated, heartlessly.

"Where have you been, deadbeat? I thought you were going to pay attention to his at-bats."

"I think I need a new lawyer. These failed series add up; they're damaging my career." He looked Ruth's way.

"Leave her alone, C," I said, catching on, not the dude's best friend for nothing. "I like Lou."

There he was, putting his arm around Jesse, whom he'd just wheedled into taking third on a ground ball hit no more than ten feet in front of the plate. The only coach in the league always in full uniform, he looked like Yogi Berra with a visible IQ. He smiled and encouraged the next batter, but he seemed lonely out there, sonless, lost on the third base line.

"I may miss him," I said, in a moment of melancholy, one of those waves of premature nostalgia that sweep over me at the mere idea of separation, any separation at all.

"His wife, maybe. I can see you missing her," said CJ. "But since when have you got another male friend?"

This was a sad truth—I didn't have that many, that's for sure, though CJ was certainly one; and he stuck with me all the way home. He was always there, somehow, when my image flickered on a television screen.

It took us awhile to get to that point, however. After Jesse made his crushing, game-losing error, I hustled up to him, consolingly, as the players were ambling off home. "Everybody makes mistakes. They're part of living, learning," I encouragingly said. "But your hits were great, kid..."

"Right," he mumbled.

He refused to look my way. I grabbed him and lifted up his chin. We were in foul territory, outside first base and past the bleachers. There were tears, red blotches around his eyes.

"What in the world are you crying about?" I asked.

CJ had joined us by now and looked pensively at Jesse before glancing at me, comparing the chins, I suppose. "Maybe he is, after all," CJ said.

"Depends on what 'is' is," I responded. Jesse looked confused.

"I think you know," CJ said. Then he turned his attention to the kid. "You know, Jesse, your old friend Jim here is one of the worst sports in L.A. Don't let him give you a hard time: he still cheats at tennis."

"So you lost the game," I said philosophically, putting it all in perspective after giving C a dirty look. "So what? The Yankees aren't Paris-St. Germain...what's a loss for them?"

"This from a guy who throws his racket when he misses an overhead," C said.

Jesse's head snapped away from my fingers.

"From a guy who quits when he's losing, Christ almost cries," C continued.

"*Je ne veux plus vivre ici,*" the kid yelled our way. "*J'en ai marre.*" I've had enough of this place, said he. And he stalked off toward the car.

"I don't know if he's yours or not," C said with a wan grin. "But he's fucking nasty enough...no doubt about it."

Accurate as the kid might have been about the hypocrisy of his older handlers, he was only partially correct about the States. This place can be pretty extraordinary, keeps putting the new back into New World as witness my "witnessing."

It took us awhile to return to our wooden palace, the tree house we lived in (and how many of these do they have in Paris?). Before we arrived there, we tried to propitiate our miniature ruler, to buy the little fucker off. We stopped at one of West Hollywood's 100 ice cream stands, a *gelateria* on Melrose, whose sumptuous and delectable ice cream, Jesse decided, wasn't quite as good as they have at Bertillon on the Isle St. Louis. He figured his mom was probably having one there now, wouldn't believe me when I told him it was 3 a.m. in Paris—his mother was probably doing things that neither one of us wanted to think much about. He left most of his cone on his Yankee uniform, a mango/blackberry smear which, however bright, would be difficult to expunge before the Twins ended our (his? Their? My?) regular season.

He also picked up a twenty year old beached blonde, her hair streaked blue-grey to match her eyes, who used Jesse's presumptive—and heretofore undiscovered—cuteness to hook into CJ. She remembered C, evidently, from an episode of CSI San Antonio he had done. I think he bombed a fertility clinic in that one. A bad mother—the hero, a former anchorwoman, Shirley Yu fed CJ to her pet carp in the end.

The girl fussed over Jesse's uniform, and C suavely let her come our way. "Max here's going to be on the tube tonight," C said when this Crystal sauntered over to us.

"Impossible," I said, to his dirty look. "It's another cracker, a namesake…Adams…there are millions of us."

"He's too modest," C said when the girl's loopy grin, her big eyes lifted toward him admiringly. Clearly, star that he was, he wasn't going to have to work on this admirer; she was enraptured by the voice alone. "Jim's the dude who wrote Venus Rising, you remember it?" She didn't.

"Luck for the Lovelorn, the book?" Didn't wake a single synapse. "He's getting his big TV primetime debut tonight."

She smiled at that, impressed, and even gave me a second perusals as if to verify her good judgment before settling her blue grey eyes on CJ. She knew he was her kind of guy. The next time she turned her eyes my way, they'd lost whatever lascivious gloss they'd projected, momentarily, before. Then too, CJ secured the deal by adding in there someplace, "So what if it's a Christian Network? It's TV." As with most Angelinas, that would prove a deal-killer, worse than a porn flick, which was the point.

"It's somebody else," I chimed in again. "Honestly," but no one was paying much attention any more—or even listening. Cindy preferring my taller, equally green-eyed friend, I was back alone with the five-year-old curmudgeon; and we know how much he enjoyed his Uncle Jimmy's companionship. He put his headphones on, like an NBA star, the moment we hit the car, just waved at C (or was it Crystal?) when my friend's black Porsche lapped our Riviera.

"Okay, let's get to it," C said after beating us home by what must have been a few minutes. Though I drive like a grandmother, he's the one who looked fatigued, already—had little purple lipstick traces underneath his ears and on his neck. Cindy, by contrast, looked refreshed, invigorated.

"Make yourself at home," C smiled at her when I opened the door for them—and Cindy did, once we were inside, taking over two-thirds of the couch. C eased in beside her, Jesse took the Barcolounger, and I sat up I sat up front, on the floor.

"Are you ready for this?" C asked and pushed the button, bringing up "Christ Lives." I'd recorded the program, just as Ruth had instructed. We all took a deep breath, as Brother Gene came flamboyantly but ever so solemnly on the air. I don't know why, but his hair at that moment, like a sponge efflorescing underwater, looked green as if to match his suit. A creamy satin shirt glistened from under his lapels, a foil for his toothy grin. "The Lord has blessed us with a marvelous treat today, praise be!" he said after welcoming one and all to the Praising Hour. "Yes he has, and if afterward you feel this way too, like I do, why don't you send Him something back? You know the place, you know our numbers"—an address, then an 800 telephone number flashed across the bottom of the screen, a real area code and another series of digits for Nebraska residents. "Let the Lord know your heart's been touched, won't you now? Make this Salvation Day today the resurrection we've all been talking about since Easter—when the Christian Word and the Holy Spirit are going to brighten so many lives. That's what we're going to witness today, all over this great land of ours.

"Today, just as we've been promising you in our promos, we're going to watch some of what Jesus has reaped this spring—a great Christian Harvest of the Reborn. Just like Jesus raised Lazarus from the dead—and we believe, we know he did!—so other blind men and women, dead souls, are going to rise up for Him tonight in renewed Christian Faith. They're going to rise up to Him, as he did pushing the stone off their hearts. And we're going to rejoice with them through all the marvelous witnessing you've been sending us, yes your home movies, your camcorders, your DVDs and tapes—all these remarkable products of man's invention testifying to the Lord's Higher Technology, yes, to the presence of the Lord, Father and Son, bringing this huge revival of the Holy Spirit all across this land.

"So here we go. I know I'm excited. I'm sure you are there too, the High Definition Resurrection! Roll them, Eddie"—Brother Gene sounding like a sportscaster on a particularly big NFL Sunday night. He moved back so we could see the big screen next to him. There was the murky image of a mid-American river. Two families stretched out on both sides of a polluted stream, fifteen to twenty kids, only two women. One was about thirty years old, the second about 60; they eyed each other suspiciously as a septuagenarian waded into the water.

"One of the biggest harvests of the Video Resurrection is right here, and what an amazing story it is! Clyde Leroy's families, by two different women, were united today after 20 years of ferocious quarreling, which has torn apart the beautiful town of Mountain Manor, Arkansas. But look at this, Praise the Lord." A guy wearing an Arkansas Razorback cutaway waded out into the brackish waters at the head of the two groups, and he motioned them to come toward him. "That's the Rev. Billy Jon Perkins, the former great Razorback safety who has brought these two fierce elevens into the even greater safety of the Lord's hands…"

"Next," CJ said, and he fast-forwarded to a grainy clip of half an entire football team, "the defensive starters of the Alabama Crimson Tide, who have scored the ultimate touchdown, together: they pledged, all of them, to give their lives for Christ…"

Dressed in white robes, with Roll Tide on the sleeves, they entered one after the next into the Alabama swimming team's pool; but before we could see the full baptismal service, CJ sped us past the Tide into the Florida State penitentiary where a 20 year old psychopath repented crimes we didn't want to hear about.

But we moved on. I was nodding off about here, only prodded into consciousness by CJ's incessant chuckling. A Catholic, C was a better receptacle for this kind of born again swill; nodding, he looked like a tall swig of milk, into which Cindy was slowly seeping. Her head on his shoulder now, she only roused herself for a peek at Kathy Marie Clifford and family echolaliaing in the clearest of the next set of videos.

Shortly thereafter, I snapped out of my troubled reverie to see the picture surface mottled, the colors turning darker as the camera bobbed in an unsure hand: "Hold it, C," I said. "Back up there some."

Once he did, we heard Eugene announce "Kathy Marie's not the only celebrity on the network. We have another today. The Lord welcomes them all, large and small. This one you might have seen on the Good Morning Caffeine show this winter, promoting a guide to adultery, among other things. The Devil's with us always, as we know; the Evil One's amongst us, but the Lord Jesus gives us a stern eye and lends us his mighty swift sword—and out there in Oklahoma City, Brother Will Barnes has been wielding that mighty swift sword. He's been doing wonderful, wonderful work with his Soldiers of Our Savior—SOS they like to call themselves. Just look at this witnessing he's sent us."

It was comforting somehow that Eugene got the city wrong. But only momentarily: Will's voice came on over the bleak and familiar image of the intensive care lounge at St. Francis Hospital, Tulsa, Oklahoma.

"Sometimes, most times," Will began, folksily, in a close shot, his glasses off, the brown eyes made blue (contacts; evidently vanity wasn't banished from the SOS), "We look in at our national television networks, and we see men and women floundering before us, lost and barely afloat. And we think there's nothing we can do. Somebody else is going to have to redeem that man up there, that woman. We say to ourselves 'I can't make a difference.' But we can! We can make that difference. We can be Soldiers for Our Savior.

"When I saw James Maxwell Adams—we used to call him Jimmie—on Good Morning Caffeine, the Lord spoke to me. He said, 'Will, you know this guy; he's lost and at sea. Bring him home to me'...and folks take look at him as we did when we went to see him. This is indeed a human soul in need."

"Will"—I knew him as Billy—Barnes' image faded, giving way to mine. Out I came, from the pink shrouded grey metal doors of St. Francis toward the hospital lounge.

"My buddy, my old partner, you poor fucker," CJ said. "You look like Lee Harvey Oswald."

"That's the hospital, the intensive care section," I explained. "This is the day before Dad died. Did he say anything about that?"

"No, but your soul is, as Will might say, in flux, in transit," C said. "That's part of losing a parent, I guess...nice long shot, huh Cindy?"

"Yeah, this is so moving," Cindy said.

My face floated on the screen like a dying jellyfish. Panic and puzzlement—and was that relief?—alternated over me as the Soldiers of

Our Savior, aka SOS, stood and welcomed me into their midst, or adjacent to it at any rate, temporarily posing as forgotten friends.

They had purpose galore, however. "We were people from his past, reminding him of who he was" was Will's way of putting it. "Of who he could be—and he came to us this day, like a sleepwalker returning to his bed, like a homing pigeon returning to its roost...Dare I say it? Like an animal retrieving its master..."

CJ was hooting behind me at these similes gone wild. I was transfixed. Jesse was hiding inside his tent, peeking out, catching the adult version of his own distress, as would be ever more clear.

"We hugged Jimmy; we embraced him, and we asked him to let us pray for him and his dad," Will continued, in his narration of the event. Arms linked around me, like squid's tentacles. There was an inky color, which transfused the HD, against which the white Bibles the troop now took out glowed disturbingly, neatly trimmed in gold.

Will continued on. "Like Saul at Ephesus, Jimmy was confused at first. His soul fought mightily against us. His life, his career, all had been predicated, like Saul's, on the illusion of the self. Yes, we can say that here was a man whose soul had disappeared into the air waves, literally, its particles no more solid than the hundreds of pixels which form a television image."

Will had a point there, though it was submerged under the bombast. Two, three cutaways of himself alternated with shots of my panic stricken face: here indeed was the slow-learner, the late-developer in all my transfiguring obtuseness.

"And then suddenly we told him," Will rhapsodized, "that we were with him. Our prayers for months, ever since we'd witnessed him on the television, they had been for him—lifebuoys for his soul. All he had to do was reach out. 'Come home to us,' we said, 'stretch our and take our hand, for we are here, as He is here. Stand up with us, stand up for Our Savior."

The camcorder focused again on me, my face resplendent with terror and dismay. Will didn't linger long on that image, but I was forced to do so. CJ froze the frame and did the commentating, "Max! What a guy! We are all so proud of him, right, Jesse?"

Jesse showed himself in the doorway, but refrained from responding. Did he see the resemblance there in the frozen frame--the pallor, the anxiety, the hint of self-satisfaction obscured by the fear of one's own rising anger? Indeed, I looked quite a lot like Jesse when he got off a phone call to his mom.

"Walk this way, Jimmie." Will aka Billy Barnes screamed in the background. "Come to Him, my friend. Come to Jesus!"

Effectively, I rose just as he asked. I was making my way, as quickly as possible toward the door of the room, as I recall; but this didn't quite happen on the tape.

There was a tremor in the image on the screen; and we cut to me, my back, my arms raising toward the sky, sort of. The figure there, while wearing a white shirt similar to mine, seemed to have hair about three or four inches shorter than mine, and his neck was about twice as thick--so we would be prepared to argue in court. They had substituted someone for me, were misusing my image, misrepresenting me.

But for the moment, the camera picked up Will again, surrounded by his flock, his apostles, one might say. His hands rose, as if in response to "my" hands rising: "Behold the Lord is with us," Will said. "Jesus truly Saves." And his hands folded around the back of the man in front of him, "me", as "I" collapsed face forward into Will's chest, into Faith.

The frame froze once again on the telecast, like the famed last image in "400 Blows"—only this time I was dazed and in Will's arms and his face looked rapturous. Immediately, the studio audience at Christ Lives! burst into applause, terrifying and fulminous acclamation.

"Wonderful, just glorious with a capitol G," the Reverend Eugene now said, as he came back in front of the screen, arms uplifted in front of the huge projected image of Will and "me." "We're going to have this man on next week, Brother Will Barnes. What amazing work! Praise be! Praise be!"

CJ froze the image too, on the Reverend Eugene before the video's last shot of Will and "me." "I think the man's completely out of his mind," CJ said, before he added, with his familiar droll grin, "either that or it's a Sign."

I looked at Jesse, who inched his way back into the room. As he stared at me up there on the TV, he looked terrified, like an aborigine seeing his first photograph. Looked as freaked, as pole-axed as I did on the screen.

"It's a sign," I said.

"Take him to Paris—I think that's a great idea," Ruth Porchnoi said. "I was wondering when you'd finally get it."

The women knew—they know; like salmon going upstream, they get the message simultaneously. "The kid's sweet, James," (sweet? I wondered: weird word choice there), "but he's dying for his mom." She paused just a beat. "What about you?"

"It's weird, but I'm happy to have him here."

"I wasn't talking about the kid—I was talking about his mom. Are you missing her too?" Ruth smiled knowingly my way.

"Can you ever go back?" I asked her. "I'm not sure you can. I mean she was smart enough to get rid of me once, don't think she's gotten a whole lot dumber." A bevy of geese flapped their wings in my chest as I contemplated her question.

She must have heard. "You don't believe that," said she. "I mean, it might be true, but you don't think so, not you."

"What makes you say that?"

"I've been watching you. You still think, for instance, that Jesse might turn into a baseball player. You're a romantic, James."

She was indeed the lawyer for me. Forget Jeannie's friend Jerry. Ruth had said she'd take my case against the Christ Lives Network—though she thought, in court, I might be better off represented by a goy, "someone who understands the nuances of your rites." She'd chuckled then, though.

"So you think I'd have a chance?" I asked—but not about the case. She knew that too.

"Don't you want to know—for Jesse's sake?"

"What do you mean, 'for Jesse's sake'?"

"Have I gotten someone wrong here? Or isn't he with you for a reason?"

"It's a long story."

"I don't think so," said she. "She sent him here. Think about him."

Maybe it was about time. He was all of—but only—five.

"Treat yourself," she continued. "Go first class. You may not be able to retire on this, but you're definitely going to get richer, thank the Lord, as they say there on the Christ Lives Network. And I don't mean to be sacrilegious."

"What do you think?" I asked Jesse that evening over dinner. I'd grilled halibut, but of course he wasn't eating it. He was eating his customary grilled (fried) ham and Gruyere cheese or Croque Monsieur as he and the French liked to call this malodorous meal. "Would you rather go to Paris now or…"

"*Quand* (when)? Now?" He snapped in Franglish.

"Tomorrow say, would you rather go tomorrow—or after the Yankees last game, next Saturday. Unless of course we win then, in which case we have the play-offs, really exciting time, we'll…"

I was looking at the neighboring Jacaranda tree which, with just a few of its purple blossoms left, looked like a spinster, an old widower among the robust citrus trees. So I didn't notice, for a second, that he was

staring at me one more time, as if my mental wattage couldn't keep his
night lite lit.

"Not the Yankees, huh?" I surmised correctly. "They'll probably
be better off without you anyway…"

He smiled for a change and nodded. "Yeah, I'd only lose them
another game," said he in his fluent French, flawless—and clearly without
pain at either the memory of his many errors in the field or the image of his
baseball-free future.

"You're not kidding me, are you?" He suddenly, nervously asked.
("Tu te moques pas de moi ?")

"Nope," said I, grinning. His joy pleased me. And I had no good
reason to be in California at that moment. I hadn't written a word on the
Luck for the Lovelorn project in two weeks, and it didn't look as if things
were going to rapidly improve in that department. I couldn't find its tone
any more inside myself. For the previous week, any time the phone had
rung, I'd asked Jesse to answer. I hadn't wanted to explain my difficulties to
Irv, even to Irv's Irv. "We're history here," I said to Jesse.

He laughed, smiling radiantly.

"Are you…did you lose a tooth lately?"

He nodded. "*Il y a deux semaines*," he said. Two weeks ago.

"Why didn't you tell me ? Jeez, we give money for that. "

He showed a little interest.

"Is this the first one you've lost ?"

He smiled ambiguously. "You can give it (the *fric,* the money) to
me now if you want."

"I don't give it out," I said. "The tooth fairy does…you ever hear of
the tooth fairy ?"

Politely he continued to grin, but as he shook his head 'no,' the edges of his mouth stiffened, like crude clay figurines hardening. I think he thought I was completely out of my gourd, but he was polite. He wasn't going to risk endangering his trip to France by contradicting me in any way. He was also a little more buoyant than usual. You might even say he was positively manic for so (frequently) depressive a kid. They could chain me up, dope me, electroshock me, lobotomize me, institutionalize me—*il s'en foutait*, he didn't care. He was going home to his mom.

Love, Again…

Part 4

Love, Again…

I understood because I had a mother too, whose presence engulfed me, whose absence used to empty me, rather like a canal floating my little boat along (what an image there). When I called to tell her I was heading east again, most probably to France, she said she understood. She said it was "probably better"—here her brave voice seemed to break—"especially for Jesse. A boy should never be away from his mom all that long."

I didn't disagree, though not many months earlier I might have made the effort. Then she said, "I'm sure he's ready, but are you?"

It wasn't real clear, even up at 35,000 feet, which we reached a couple of days later. There, I wasn't merely afflicted with my habitual fear of flying. I had a kind of near total loss of personal cabin pressure. My altimeter was jumping like dice over a craps table.

Three months before, I'd been an aging, increasingly solvent (to my surprise) bachelor, self-supporting but alone. Now in one of those miracles of modern technology, I was perhaps the only father in my larger family. Across from me, in another tourist seat on this Air France plane was a face looking very much like my mother's dropped into an impish integument, a child's body, maybe my child.

Peering his way, I looked this disturbed, I guess: when I asked Jesse how he was doing, he replied, with great patience (as I'd heard him talk to himself when he practiced alone with his soccer ball outside), "*Parle Francais.* You're going to need the practice."

Not necessarily: English seemed to work fine with his mom, whom I'd—we'd—awakened once again the day, so it sounded, this time at 7 p.m. her time. It must have been a cabinet minister she was seeing, so I thought, this the end of an arduous 5 a 7.

"Are you ready for us?" I asked her.

"Actually," she said, simply. "I am."

"Well, then, Jesse and I will be on a plane tomorrow," I said.

"It's about time," said she; and a laugh, deep and throaty, broke from her long slim neck and made mine, 6000 miles away, flush with joy.

"We're not going to bother you, are we?" I asked. "You've got space for us?"

"Hey, Jimmy, that problem's never been mine."

This was happening too quickly, too smoothly. It didn't feel bad, even for a preposterous "control" freak like myself (preposterous because so rarely in control), just bizarre, something like those long moments when a car is free floating, between your mistake and an accident, the fishtailing into a dish. Couples don't reunite successfully, with any frequency. I knew that. I wasn't even sure I liked the kid.

Still, his mother jumped out there on the other side of the protective glass, upon our exit at Roissy, Charles de Gaulle airport. Her eyes were brighter than the kid's nightlight, shimmering like the Caribbean underneath a subtle gold scarf she wore fashionably on her head, like a twenties movie star. And her smile was large enough for any number of klieg lights, not to mention the two of us men. When we'd been younger and together, she'd entertained tables of friends by putting her entire fist into her mouth, touching her nose with her tongue.

Here her hands went to Jesse and lifted him up with a sweep. His face, on the other hand, looked too scared as she cradled it to be moved—as though he feared if he blinked she might disappear.

We may have shared the same expression.

"You look at your wit's end," she said to me.

"It's a 12 hour flight," I commented.

"Sure, that must be it," said she, with a wink; and she took my arm—just reached out there as she had so often done before and led me away, back to my, our past. (How proud I'd always been when she'd gripped me thus, as if I were a/her man).

She didn't have a car, only took taxis as always, well past 30 now and a mother and still unable, unwilling to drive. At one time, when I'd liked her consequent dependence, when I'd lived for it, I found this cute and endearing.

Now, like everything occurring, I found it disturbing. I wasn't fully in the moment; I was a foot or two outside it, that far inside and outside myself, so it seemed, both a seer and a fool—maybe just a former acidhead suffering through another flashback. But I'd been dreaming of this for so long, riding into Paris with Sarah at my side, imagining the experience but never allowing myself to believe in it, any more than I was doing at that very moment. Jesse was the surprise, the joker, the added element that hadn't exactly appeared in my reveries.

Paris was greyer than it had been that day when Sarah and I had traveled out to the airport to catch the plane home. Beautiful, of course, once you got off the dingy *peripherique* and hit the Avenue du Maine, though it was a polluted dun color, as if suspended in its air were all the exhalations of its majority of smokers—one of whom was our faintly jaundiced lady taxi driver with the corn-colored cigarette hanging from her thick lips, Bogart style. She yelled as she drove, complaining constantly about the "cretins" trying to outfox her on the many traffic rotaries; but I was too dazed to care, on another wave length altogether, and it was surprisingly, amazingly picked up.

After I requested, in my accented French, that we go through the 14th arrondissement into town, Jesse repeated my directions in his snotty and impeccable French, without his usual condescension. Our driver said it wasn't logical to go that way, but she conceded after Jesse insisted; she did what he told her to do.

It was illogical, as so many of the rest of the world's actions are to the French, but logic was hardly the point here. We skirted the exquisite Parc Montsouris, then cruised past the Closerie des Lilas, which Sarah (and Hemingway) had loved and whose extremely well priced steak tartare and chips sustained me for most of my last year there and made me continuously fearful thereafter that I might be afflicted with mad cow disease. We passed the Jardin de l'Observatoire, where I'd once spied Beckett walking; the Pantheon where Voltaire was buried; the dilapidated hotel where our own insignificant and delusional scrivener had first stayed, where Sarah had refused to set foot ("I'm not squeamish," she had said when she looked at my room—she was very French then, "not fastidious like you Americans, but this just isn't possible.")

The best macaroons in town were nearby; Sarah had introduced me to them. We had sat out front of the café, looked at the rows of elms just across the way, and seen through the green spiked fence circumscribing the Jardin du Luxembourg; and I couldn't then believe how fortunate I felt—or how I would ever get back home.

"*C'est beau, après tout, Paris,*" Jesse said when we passed the Rue des Ecoles, the Sorbonne up the street. "But it's not sunny like L.A." His eyes shone, looking at his mom—and they didn't dim any, for a change, when he turned them onto me. "They could use some more trees—like that purple one we have."

We? He was speaking English, but I was so moved I didn't notice.

"It's huge, and it's got all these purple flowers, Mom," he continued, as if his voice had lost its tether. His hands, which had been attached to his side, so you'd have thought for the last month, weighed down by his oversized baseball glove, took off gesticulating, like unleashed spaniels. "They fell all over everything, but were our favorites, huh Jim?"

He looked at me for confirmation; and of course, what can I say? My eyes were welling—I'd changed but not that much. Yet this was different: I was grinning too, at my own ridiculous mawkishness, but also at the rare and unadulterated happiness I felt.

"You're a sweet guy, Jim," Sarah said. "Sometimes I forget."

"*Cingle*," Jess said, "*dingue*." Then he changed his mind and his language, whirled a finger around his ear. "Craaa-zy."

He was right, of course, but for more reasons than he could have imagined. These were an ecstatic's tears, flush on my face, as I smiled. My cheeks tingling against this wetness, I was happy even as I was trying to discern what I'd done to deserve this, even as I was trying to confirm that the hand there on my arm was the woman's I once knew. "There, there," Sarah said to both me and her son, in between the two of us, "I'm so happy to have you both here."

Jesse gave her a wild-eyed look, insinuating, declaring once more his doubts about my mental and emotional stability. "Hey, Jesse, be a little more respectful. You never know who you might be talking to," Sarah said.

She grinned shyly my way, and her smile lit up those turquoise eyes. Their light seemed to infuse the apartment we reached, minutes later, on the rue des St. Peres. The two of us had lived nearby our best and last year in Paris, at the end of a courtyard on the rue Garanciere, just off Saint Sulpice. That apartment could have fit into the dining ell of this one, but both had the bountiful branches of large maple trees filling up the bedroom windows. There were two bedrooms in this one, and Sarah took her son to the larger one; I took his. After traveling all night, 12 hours on the plane, I could barely differentiate between my dreams and this reality.

There was a working fireplace in the smaller bedroom, white molding and those large high French windows, which fold out from metallic center knobs. I opened them out toward the courtyard, while the blue grey light enfolded me and spirited me away. I shed 15 or 20 pounds, the semblance of a career, being blessed, all that; and I got my dad back, another generation listening in as Jesse's voice grew fainter talking to his mother in the room next door, lulling me finally to sleep.

I woke to find Jesse's mom next to me, though I didn't know her as such. I knew her by her long and elegant neck, which seemed lineless to me, tight, a vein throbbing, anything but maternal.

"What took you so long?" She asked, in reality as in my imagination.

"You," I said, "it took you this long to decide you wanted me here, to call me."

"It took me this long to be prepared for you."

Her hands took my head, both sides caressing my jaw, then my hair. Her eyes seemed more green than blue. She was wearing a Comme les Garcons dress, which, though layered, came off in my hands. Was I there, was this happening?

I eased my way toward her, feeling along, trying to believe what I felt, to find out where my imagination ended and she began. It must have been where her imagination commenced, for, hard to turn over for years, hard to release, she didn't bother to disrobe any more fully but pulled me deeply inside her. She began to come before I was even aware of my stretch, before she may even have been aware of me. Where was the friction we'd once pushed off against? I wondered, watching her, was astonished as she came back to me, taking her pleasure again, gently slapping against me like waves against a levy.

I didn't get there as rapidly; I was afraid. I was where I wanted to be, as I'd imagined I'd rather be when I'd been with no few others; yet I couldn't rise to this moment's surface. I couldn't release into her until she looked up, surprised and almost hurt, those iridescent eyes shining under that amber scarf; and she slid her hands behind me, keening, and pulled me deeper inside her.

"You're so much gentler than you used to be," said she, with a languorous smile, her head next to mine in Jesse's tiny, half bed. I was ready to sleep, but she got there first; and I found myself, charged with her energy, overwrought and unable to keep my eyes closed—like many a woman I've known.

Fifteen, twenty minutes later, my arms seemed numb. The rain began again, and I now saw the lines that had begun tracking her eyes and realized I'd always known they would only enhance Sarah's beauty. I saw the woman she was becoming as opposed to the one I remembered leaving me. And I got scared, there you go; everything dried up inside like the sweat on my chest. She breathed gracefully next to me, her exhalations just reaching my ears, blowing my hair gently as I moved my head from underneath her arm on the pillow, to her rib cage, her heart, her chest. I was itching and uncomfortable, on this tiny double bed, but buzzing from more than fatigue.

I got up and went through the late morning's dim, rain-filled light to the larger bedroom where Jesse was curled around a pillow, in the middle of his mom's king size bed, his right hand tucked, thumb-first into his mouth, his left reaching out, as if to someone. I crawled into bed with him, and I put my arm around him, trying not to wake him up.

He pulled his left hand back to his right and turned over, away from me, to the other side of the bed. He didn't feel different, only I did. The rain licked the cobblestones downstairs, turning my energy to melancholy, and Sarah evidently heard it, felt it too. Within minutes, she came, groggy and sleepy-eyed into the bedroom and slipped in between Jesse and me, into the large cool opening there in the middle of the bed. Immediately, of course Jesse turned back over and slid next to her, moving into the crook of her arm. She kissed him on the cheek without opening her eyes—then she draped her other arm around my shoulder and went to sleep.

I didn't get there though. I leaned further over, past Sarah, and, as she turned under me, I put my fingers, my ear up against Jesse. It sounded like a rainforest in there, bursting, growing, almost frightening in its din. I turned again toward Sarah, and I placed my ear against her this time, tightly, my fingertips touching her body. I was so addled I was taking my own advice "Listening (3)" to her; and I heard exactly nothing, not one thing.

Sarah turned in her sleep and Jesse followed her, his arm chasing his mother's shoulder; but not quite capturing it. I felt a new wave of sadness well in my eyes. When I looked up at the ceiling it moved like a pool of water shaken by rain. I felt what I took to be chest pains, breathed with difficulty. What, I asked myself, was I really doing here? They were perfect together, if slightly askew, what was this all about?

As if agitated by the same thought, Jesse moved again, his arm flailed and his hand tipped up against the scarf his mother still hadn't removed. The scarf slipped off the back of her head, and I saw that she'd lost her thick dark hair. She was virtually bald.

I felt like I'd licked my finger and stuck it into the wall socket, dropped an electric razor into my own water. I understood, suddenly, what I hadn't seen. She'd had to be alone, as she later told me, to deal with the lump they found in her breast and the treatment it entailed. She couldn't afford to be treated in the states; it was only her French passport, which was getting her through this round of chemotherapy. She hadn't told me because she hadn't wanted to scare her child, or me because she didn't want my fear and anxiety to infuse and overwhelm Jesse…or me either for that matter.

Just the sight of her did overwhelm me. I reacted, audibly I suppose, because she opened her eyes; when she looked at me, she didn't pretend anything at all. I reached my hand out toward her. I asked, "Are you all right? Are you going to be okay?"

She took my hand. "Thanks for taking care of my boy."

"But you, how are you?"

I could barely see; emotion flooded over me, my blood beating, pounding in my chest, and she started to cry; and then her lips formed a tender grin. She said, "I think I'm going to be fine; that's what they're telling me. I'm just a little tired, all the time."

Her hand dropped mine and moved to cradle her son. I rose and went to the window, looking at the light outside, which was mauve rather than slate grey though still filled with rain. The bedroom was on the courtyard side of the building; and down below there echoed across the cobblestones the sound of the concierge's kids playing. This at least was the Paris I remembered, though it all felt different suddenly.

I left the bedroom for the living room. Its 8-foot windows gave onto the Place St. Sulpice, where I'd first lived in Paris, up the corner around the Rue des Canettes. The place had seemed different, not the most handsome in Paris, but the most luminescent. The light here had appeared golden—and looking across the living room, it still seemed to be so. A palomino color surged through the tulle curtains, reassuring me, as if Paris' sameness might still the mutability of all of us in it.

Faint chance: I walked up to the curtains and parted them—and looked out into this "limestone light." It wasn't quite as natural as I supposed: suspended at the other edge of the place, amidst the rain and fog, was what could have been a UFO. Yellow and red, it was way too garish for this elegant area. I strained to see it clearly: the red colors were heart shapes, placed together like hamburger buns. Between them were plastic slabs simulating lettuce leaves, a tomato, and 2 meat patties. "Love Burger," a golden neon sign blinked on and off.

"Love Burger." I took my low-grade depression and deepening anxiety back to the bedroom where the light was purple and suffused both mother and child. They each had thumbs near their mouths. You could see that similarity. This one too: though Sarah was now quiet, she had often talked in her sleep when we'd lived together; some times she had even laughed—and here her child seemed to be smiling, at least until his mother turned on her side, away from him, toward the spot I'd left, spreading out over that side of the bed. Jesse, like a trope, then moved onto his stomach. Even in sleep his head still regarded his mother's back, as if to make sure she'd stay with him.

I felt for him, and I felt much like him. I walked over to the bed, kissing his mother on the neck, at which she gently smiled. Then I took my place next to Jesse, where there was room. After a few moments, Jesse's right hand moved, if not exactly toward me, at least my way. I reached over and took his wrist, which was all of two, maybe three inches in diameter, yet as fine and resonant as a flute. And I understood finally that this was what I had come so far to feel and understand. His pulse beat against my fingers like hail on a roof, gradually coming over the next few minutes into a complete and astonishing synchronicity with my own.

Love, Again…